Latch Key Kids

First Printing: 2020
ISBN-13: 978-1-942086-15-4
PL-127

Paragraph Line Books
Oakland, California

www.paragraphline.com
www.johnlsheppard.com

This novel is dedicated to my sister Nancy.

Thanks to Jon Konrath for all of his work on this book.

Latch Key Kids

a novel

by

John L. Sheppard

Paragraph Line Books 2020

Introduction

By Jon Konrath

When John told me he was writing a book about his childhood in Florida, a lot of specific images came to mind. Aside from reading his most excellent book *Small Town Punk*, which was also set in the Sarasota of the past, I have my own memories of Florida, which have morphed considerably over the last few decades.

In 2020, if you mention Florida to most people, the first image that pops in their head is "Florida Man," the common trope where every horrible news story about the Sunshine State is amalgamated into a single figure, a shirtless meth addict with face tattoos who rampages though a Walmart, sexually assaulting produce and appliances before tearing someone's face off in the parking lot and cannibalizing them. If you put "Florida Man" into a news search, one would think all twenty-some million people in the state were driving drunk and loaded on painkillers, killing innocent bystanders with samurai swords from their pick-up trucks. The 27th state has become synonymous with white-trash chaos and anarchy.

But when I was growing up in the Seventies in the flatlands of Indiana, Florida was a more mystical place, where lush, golden oranges grew everywhere, and the wealthy upper crust "wintered" and traveled to theme parks and ocean resorts. My classmates with rich parents jetted down to Orlando every holiday break to spend a week or three at Walt Disney World or in the waterfront timeshares of Fort Lauderdale. On the years they didn't go to Colorado or Vermont on ski vacations, my popular classmates returned to school in January with dark tans and tales of white-sand beaches, rides on Space Mountain, and endless trips through the buffet line at inclusive resorts. (I should say I heard these tales third-hand. These Izod-clad people weren't my friends. I was two or three castes below them, with the computer geeks, glue-huffers, and juvenile delinquents.)

In contrast, my family usually drove to inner-city Chicago for Christmas, where me and a dozen or two cousins sat in one room of my grandparents' three-bedroom apartment, playing whatever board game we happened to bring with us. We listened to my grandfather — my mom's father — tell the same six stories over and over, which were either racist rants about his neighborhood being taken over by Hispanics, or endless screeds about the last-place Cubs and how the god damned Wrigley family kept losing almost a hundred games every year. (To be fair, he was a fan back in 1945 when they went to the World Series. He named his dog after Mickey Livingston, and then had to endure fifty years of the worst baseball imaginable. No wonder he was so miserable.) In the next room, my aunts argued about who had the worst medical problem that year. We weren't allowed to leave the yard because we were told constantly how we would get robbed, shot, and/or abducted. And this was before cable TV. It wasn't much of a vacation, and the soot-covered snow of the windy city in the peak pollution years of the seventies was the exact opposite of Florida.

My other grandmother and my oldest uncle went to Florida every winter, doing the snowbird thing on the cheap, driving a pickup truck down south, renting a cheap place for a few months, cooking their own meals, and avoiding any amusement parks or resorts. My grandmother had a weak heart and wanted to avoid the brutal lake effect blizzards that slammed the Michiana area every year, so this was her escape. They would always return in spring with the same presents: crates of oranges, postcards from tiki restaurants and places with real mermaids swimming underwater in large tanks (with hidden oxygen hoses), and weird Florida candies: coconut patties, chocolate covered orange peels, saltwater taffy, and citrus jellies, always packed in a cardboard box with a clear plastic window on top, cut in the shape of the peninsula state. One year, they got to see a Space Shuttle launch. They actually launched people into space in Florida! Did I mention the no snow part? Christ, I was jealous. Florida sounded like a dream.

In 1983, my parents finally took us all on a big family trip to Florida. They were on the verge of a divorce, and some genius marriage counselor convinced them it would make everything better if they loaded five people in a compact station wagon, drove 1200 miles each way. We'd spend two weeks in expensive theme parks every day, and cram into a single hotel room every night. We planned to divide our time between Tampa (Busch Gardens) and Orlando (Walt Disney World, and the brand new EPCOT Center), with a lot of wandering around in between. I have no idea how they afforded to do this, but I imagine it was all a big point of contention. (Spoiler alert...)

Driving around places like Tarpon Springs and the seedier parts of Tampa revealed to me that Florida wasn't as glorious as I'd previously imagined. We spent a lot of vacation wandering through beaten old Florida stores that looked like they'd peaked back in 1964. They were filled with dusty old seashell art, outdated t-shirts, and expired Florida candy. Gulf Road wound past shack houses with faded and chipped paint, fishing shops with hand-painted signs, and bizarre off-brand chain restaurants I'd never seen before. We'd sometimes eat at sad, greasy diners that reminded me of the sitcom *Alice*, usually complete with a Flo-like waitress and a dining room that hadn't been cleaned since the Civil War. I started to see a Florida that wasn't better than my recession-era Indiana existence, just different. And every thing I saw was a sad attempt to cash in, and somehow grab a bit of the tourist dollar away from Walt's all-encompassing oligarchy.

The Disney trip itself was an incredible folly of errors worthy of a National Lampoon movie. A freak blizzard hit the country, and on Christmas day, we stomped around EPCOT in below-zero weather. Inside the magical new spectacle of the future era of human innovation, the buildings were running their heaters at 200% to thwart the once-in-a-century cold snap, and rolling blackouts plagued the exhibits. Every tourist had an identical blue and white EPCOT hat from the gift store, and bundled up in a half-dozen $40 Mickey t-shirts to avoid dying of exposure. We still had our Indiana garb, but even with moon boots, ski gloves, and a snowmobile mask, I was miserable. Despite being born in North Dakota, I am not a winter person.

One day, we waited in line for hours at the Mexico pavilion in EPCOT, trying to get into an indoor ride and have a few minutes of heat. I learned a new Spanish phrase that day: *El Rio del Tiempo*. The River of Time. The *River* of Time. It was a splashy boat ride, the mist of heavily chlorinated water keeping the ambient air even colder than it was outside. We also got stuck on other rides several times because of the power blackouts. On one exhibit, the Exxon Universe of Energy, we got stuck for twenty minutes in a people-mover that was inching past a diorama of fake life-size dinosaurs lolling around a tar pit. Sitting in the heat was great, but the diorama had smell-o-vision scent generators pumping out the intense odor of rotting dinosaur shit over our stranded train car. That summed up the entire Disney experience, that and my parents bitching about crowds, traffic, lines, and most of all, prices for food inside the parks.

My parents filed for divorce a few days after the long drive home. That was about two weeks before I turned thirteen. There are a lot of other events that delineate the end of childhood, like a growth spurt or a new school. But that brief Florida experience is pretty heavily entwined with the end of childhood, an end of innocence.

This isn't really a book about Florida. It's not a book about nostalgia of the Seventies, either. There's plenty of both; it's set in Sarasota back in the Nixon years, and there's lots of references to the shows and clothes and foods and toys of that era. But *Latch Key Kids* is more about childhood, the actual feeling of childhood, and how it quickly slips away. It's about how your early years have a certain purity where you don't think about if you're rich or poor, if your parents are good or bad, if you are popular or a geek. You're sheltered. You think about bikes and baseball and GI Joe and cartoons and old monster movies on the snowy low-power local UHF station.

And then at some delineating point in childhood, this all suddenly changes. You realize your parents aren't infallible. You see that they're struggling to make it day-to-day, and they're making mistakes you think you wouldn't make if you were in charge. You start to doubt them, and then you start to doubt everything in life. Maybe mom can't really cook, and there's real enjoyment in food that isn't burnt to a crisp. Maybe dad's poor business sense isn't the way to handle one's financial life. Maybe your pyromaniac cousins aren't normal.

During this rude awakening period is usually when the social pecking order in school starts to matter too much, especially because it's a gateway into future relations with your preferred romantic type. And maybe you're a football player and big for your grade and you immediately float to the top of that order, but if you're one of us reading books for fun, maybe you didn't. That struggle is real.

I think the thing that resonates most with me in *Latch Key Kids* is how John ties together these nostalgic memories of the past with how he developed as an adult. You can track the feelings, failures, and doubts of his present, seeing how they really started in his childhood. His various reactions, neuroses, and feelings of today are all based on how people in his childhood treated him, how they nurtured, indoctrinated, or broke him. Contextualizing the present with the thoughts of the past were some of the strongest feels in this book for me, and I hope they are for you too.

* * *

Decades after my first trip to Florida, I went back a few times as an adult. I lived in New York, and in some contrarian hipster doofus fit, decided to go down and spend a few weeks in cheap motels on the Gulf coast. I'd drive around aimlessly all day, observing the strange mix of big money resorts butted against abject poverty. This was the early 00s, and Florida Man was in full effect. Scientologists owned most of Clearwater. Gun stores were everywhere. Fast food chains had near-lethal burgers bigger than your head, weaponized with bacon and mayo and tater tots, served with five-thousand calorie milkshakes containing entire bags of candy. There were more Waffle House restaurants than schools. It was pure chaos. I loved it.

On the second trip, I met up with John. He'd returned to Sarasota, and was living in an area that was probably empty fields during this book, but had since been plowed up into subdivisions, identical houses sold off to people who couldn't afford them, with high-interest adjustable-rate mortgages that would collapse a few years later. I told John about the long drive I took to Polk City, the middle vacant Florida you really don't want to visit. (Coincidentally, my dad now lives near there every winter.) This scenescape reminded me of the very start of John's book *Small Town Punk*, four kids with a car stuck in a ditch in the flat nothingness of eastern Sarasota, with no houses and nothing but scrub palmetto and dead land for as far as the eye could see.

We drove around Sarasota before dinner, and he gave me the *Small Town Punk* reality tour, showing me the deranged house his dad built, the former location of the infamous Pizza Hut, and the theater of his childhood, which later because the porno theater where Pee Wee Herman was infamously caught in the act of entertaining himself. (It was bulldozed and a cheap family restaurant is in its place, probably with a great blue-plate special.) We wandered the core of town, which is filled with various buildings, museums, and monuments the Ringling Brothers built as part of their palatial estate. They fell into disrepair, were given to the state but largely ignored, then bought by the university and somewhat restored. That stuff's a nice tourist attraction, but I was more interested in seeing the actual places behind the images in my head from reading *STP*.

I loved reading *Small Town Punk* back when John and I first started talking online in the early 00s. Despite the name, it had little to do with Punk Rock™, the officially-sanctioned music and fashion trend you buy at your local Hot Topic store in the mall. It was more about "punks" as in "you punks get off my lawn and get a damn job!" *Latch Key Kids* is a prequel to *Small Town Punk*. Same kids, same town, same feelings and emotions, except *STP* is about the teen years, and Reagan's America. If you like this book, go on Amazon and hunt down a copy of *Small Town Punk*. (But make sure to find a used copy of the 2002 edition, with the sneakers on the cover. The 2007 re-release was completely butchered by the publishing company, and they inexplicably put a kid with a skateboard on the cover, even though the book has nothing to do with skateboarding. Punk rock!)

Enough blabbing. I really enjoyed working on this book, and I hope you like it too. He's hinting that there's a third book coming next year to make this a trilogy, so stay tuned at ParagraphLine.com for more news on that.

— Jon Konrath
Oakland, California

"The proverb says that Providence protects children and idiots. This is really true. I know because I have tested it."

— Mark Twain

Suncoast Digest

Years later, Sissy would say, "You remember. Of course you remember. How could you forget?"

"No," I'd insist. "I don't remember that at all."

The summer we moved to Sarasota, one of the local news anchors shot herself live on television with a gray, little pistol. Bang, went the report, sounding like someone clapping together a pair of wood blocks. That's the way Sissy told the story. I don't remember any of it.

Sissy and I were up early, she told me, eating Cocoa Puffs out of the box, dry. We paused and looked at each other, stopping mid-crunch. Sissy swallowed her mouthful of cereal and asked, "Did that just happen?"

"Did what just happen?" I asked.

That cereal. I remember that. My teeth were sugary rough. I sucked at my molars. But the dead woman. Was there a dead woman? And why did Sissy insist on watching this woman every morning on some public affairs show called *Suncoast Digest*?

Wait. I remember that part. It was because the anchor was clearly weird, for one thing. Like you knew that one day she'd do something odd on the air and if we missed it, Sissy would never forgive me.

For another, the anchor had a recognizable accent. She was from our part of Ohio. It was like hearing the voice of home listening to Christine. Christine! That was the anchor's name.

The picture on the color set wiggled. It made everything orange, or maybe that was the 1970's. Maybe the 1970's were particularly lurid. There was this dead woman slumped over in a field of wiggling orange. There was another person screaming. A man wearing a headset ran up. He waved at the camera and then some color bars glowed. They were primary colors. Soon enough, an episode of *Gentle Ben* came on to replace *Suncoast Digest*. A boy and his pet bear. Sissy turned the dial, clunking through the channels that we could get from the antenna on the roof. She found nothing satisfying and turned off the set.

"You have so much to learn about life, little brother," Sissy said.

"I'm your big brother," I said.

"Sure you are."

"But I am. I'm almost two years older."

"Do we have any orange juice?" Sissy smiled, showing off her dimpled cheeks. Adults liked to pinch them. "Do you think she's really dead?"

"Who?"

"My God, you're dumb. How'd you get so dumb?"

"I don't know. I think I got it from Dad."

"That makes sense." She stood up, so I stood up, too. She handed me the box of Cocoa Puffs. I rolled up the waxpaper bag inside and clicked the boxtop shut. "That weird anchor lady. You think she really shot herself?"

"I don't know. I don't know what you're talking about."

She made a little fist and rapped gently on the side of my head. "Knock-knock. Anybody home?"

"Stop making fun of me."

"You make it so easy, little brother." She went into the kitchen and I followed her.

Our parents weren't home. They were off at their jobs, which involved sales. Our father was a traveling paper salesman, going from one print shop to another selling boxes of paper. He spent three or four days a week away from home, which no one objected to, most of all our mother.

Our mother sold china at Maas Brothers department store in downtown Sarasota. When the new mall was finished, she was promised a job working there. The new mall was under construction about a mile away from us. In the meantime, she had a bit of a commute.

The kitchen was outfitted in harvest gold appliances. Everything was new. The house was new. Our father had been involved in a lawsuit a year before and had done well for himself, therefore the new house with the new appliances. We each had a bedroom. I used to share a bedroom with our brother Sparky, who was older than me by a couple of years. Sissy called him, "Mister Spock." When he was born, it was like he was already 40 years old. He carried himself with such gravity that adults often deferred to him. If he'd bothered to put on a suit and tie, he could have walked into any office in America at the age of 12, informed them that he'd just come from corporate headquarters and that he was now in charge, and no one would have batted an eye. They would have said, "Yes, Mister Pepper. The corner office is right over there."

I was the middle child. I never had that neglected, middle-child syndrome that was popularized by Jan on *The Brady Bunch*. I had huge chocolate eyes, long eyelashes and dirty blonde hair. When Mom took me with her on trips to the grocery store, adult women would accost her in the aisles and ask to hug me. I hated it. Mom would allow it and then tell me on the car ride home how much it tickled her to watch me squirm as strange women odored with strong perfume grasped me their arms and cooed that they'd like to steal me. In the car, Mom would reach over and stroke my hair and tell me that I was her favorite, and not to tell the other two.

Where was Sparky while Sissy and I hung around the house? I don't remember. He was probably in his room. Or he was at a library diligently doing math problems that he'd assigned himself even though it was summer. I don't know. So much of childhood is shrouded in fog. And so much of it is blown up into something much bigger than it was at the time.

The two of us were still in our pajamas. They were lighter weight than any other clothes that we wore. Sissy wore an oversized yellow t-shirt with a gigantic smiling orange on it. The orange stated that it was in favor of Florida sunshine. I wore a thin polyester top and bottom that advertised the Miami Dolphins, Florida's only professional team at the time. I hated the pajamas because I was an ardent Cleveland Browns fan, even though the Browns were far away and they were pretty lousy. Mom bought both of the pajamas on sale at Maas Brothers and then used her employee discount. Neither one of us wore slippers.

I helped Sissy climb up onto the kitchen counter and she walked along it opening up cabinets and peeking into the top shelves. Sometimes Sissy found squirreled away money up there, hidden in old coffee cans, and then we'd ride our bicycles to the old mall, Gulf Gate Mall, where there was a Walgreen's with a lunch counter. We'd each get a shake (mine chocolate and Sissy's vanilla) and then spend the change on gooey, fruit-flavored Now-and-Laters. If there was enough money, Sissy and I would go over to the used bookstore and buy Ace paperbacks—science fiction for me and gothic horror for her. If Mom or Dad asked Sissy about the missing money from the top shelf of the cabinet, she'd ask them with a straight face, "How'm I supposed to reach way up there?" If they turned to me, I'd look nervously around, shake my head and jam my hands into my pockets. Sissy and I were the same height, even though I was older. Our parents assumed, correctly, that Sissy was in charge, so why would they question me?

This morning, we came up empty.

I put away the cereal.

The two of us retired to our respective rooms to get dressed, talking through the thin wall separating the two rooms.

"That gun looked real. It wasn't like watching *The Mod Squad*," Sissy said.

"Uh-huh," I went.

"I didn't see a lot of blood or anything."

"Okay."

"How could you miss it?"

3

"I don't know. Are you nervous about going to Catholic school?" It was a bad attempt to change the subject.

"I don't know. Why should I be nervous? Maybe those nuns should be nervous about me. I don't know why I have to go and you get to go to a public school."

"Because you're a girl. Girls have to be protected."

"That's stupid!"

She'd get no argument out of me. "At least you don't have to go to Pine View, like Sparky." Our brother had been accepted to attend Pine View School for the Gifted, which was a public school for smart kids. There was a whole interview process involved after you took an IQ test. There were only so many spots available there. If you told someone in Sarasota that you went to Pine View, they'd respond, "Oh. You're one of *them.*"

I was going to go to plain old elementary school. I was going to try to blend in. That was my plan. Sometimes when I couldn't sleep at night, which was already becoming a problem, I practiced making ordinary conversation in the bathroom mirror. "Hi. I'm Buzz. What's your name? I sure do enjoy all the stuff you enjoy. Yes sirree, Bob." I'd practice smiling in a way that I thought wasn't off-putting—a normal smile well-executed by a normal boy. "How about this weather? It's a scorcher. Wouldn't be so bad if it wasn't so humid." I'd made a study of the way normal people talked. I didn't want the first comment about me in my new school to be, "You're weird."

We'd moved around a lot. I'd been to four different schools in four different places, but the reaction was always the same. This time, I swore, would be different. This time I wouldn't eat lunch alone. This time I wouldn't get beat up on the first day of class during the first recess. "I am just like you. I am an ordinary person with ordinary thoughts." And... smile. Also, I swore that I wouldn't spend all my time in class drawing. Instead, I'd attempt to pay attention and perhaps learn something. So far I hadn't learned anything useful in school save that other children were mostly monsters, just like my father.

Any useful knowledge came out of the science fiction books I read and the out-of-date encyclopedia set that Mom bought on sale one volume at a time before I was born at a grocery store back in Ohio. We also owned an unabridged dictionary that was bought in the same way. First we bought the binder, and then we bought one letter at a time, the pages in shrink wrap that we'd pull off and then we'd place the pages in the binder. Once complete, the dictionary could be lugged from room to room. It mostly stayed with me. My science fiction books had new, complicated words in them and there was the joy of looking up these new, complicated words. The complicated concepts were handled, sometimes poorly, by the Kennedy-era encyclopedia set.

The bathroom we three kids shared was next to Sparky's room. Eventually, during my mirror soliloquies, he'd rap on the bathroom door and tell me to shut up and go back to bed.

Our parents' room was on the other side of the house. They had their own bathroom over there. There was a den, a kitchen and the dining room to traverse if they wanted to come over to our side of the house.

There was a Florida room on the front of the house filled with good furniture that no one ever used.

We had a screened porch on the back of the house called a "lanai," because people apparently confused Florida with Hawaii. There was some aluminum folding furniture back there and a glass-topped table in case anyone got the idea in their head that they could eat outside in 95-degree boiling heat while exotic insects buzzed around and the occasional pigmy rattler found its way in. A sliding glass door separated the house from the lanai.

Sissy and I finished dressing and slipped into another of our routines, which was sitting on opposite ends of the couch from each other and discussing whatever happened to be on our minds. For Sissy, it was the woman we saw kill herself. Why did she do it? Did she have a soul? Would she go to hell because she was a suicide? The answer to the last question, according to Sissy's Catholic indoctrination, was a definite yes. Sissy thought that was unfair. "I don't know why God has to be so judgmental," Sissy said.

"Isn't that his job?"

"God wouldn't be so judgmental if He wasn't a man."

"I'm a man. Sort of. I will be a man if I don't get run over by a car or something."

"You know what I mean." Our understanding of men came mostly from our father, who was temperamental, held complete power over us, was ethically suspect and not particularly smart, sort of like the God from the Old Testament.

"Yeah," I said.

The door to the garage swung open and we both froze. It was Mom, so we relaxed a moment and then she said, "What are you two weirdos doing?"

"Nothing," we both chimed together.

"Nothing, huh?" she said suspiciously. She was home early from work. We soon found out the reason. "Your father is coming home from the road today. We have to clean this dump up. I have to make him supper." She looked expectantly at us. Her hair looked like it recently had been worked on. She had some lady in the Maas Brothers salon who put her hair through a process called "frosting" that made Mom's hair look blonde on top. I could smell the chemicals from where I sat. "Come on! Chop! Chop! Look alive!"

We sprang to our feet and ran to the kitchen. We fought over the can of lemon Pledge hidden in the cabinet under the sink and Sissy won. We each grabbed an old t-shirt and got to work.

Mom turned on the hi-fi and put on the *Mary Poppins* soundtrack. By the time we got to "Spoonful of Sugar," most of the furniture was dusted and Mom appeared, changed out of her work pantsuit and into a plain blouse, blue capri pants and Keds. She dragged out our loud vacuum cleaner, plugged it in and immediately shoved it around aggressively, attacking our feet if we happened to be in the way. We leapt up onto the couch to avoid getting run over.

By the time she was done with that, the first side of the record was finished. Mom put away the vacuum, turned off the hi-fi and started in on lunch. For herself and Sissy she cut up radishes, celery and carrot sticks and poured herself a glass of V8 juice along with a generous splash of vodka. She poured a plain V8 for Sissy.

"You still in your PB&J mode?" she asked me. I generally ate the same lunch for months and sometimes years. At that time, I ate nothing but peanut butter and jelly sandwiches on gooey white bread, cut diagonally. She poured a glass of milk for me into a former jelly jar that featured the Archies. "Don't bite through the glass. We're not going to the emergency room again." I had a habit of breaking drinking glasses with my teeth and cutting up my lips in the process. I was getting past that phase and resented Mom for a moment for bringing it up.

I turned on the TV and clicked around until the noon news came up. They were talking about the dead anchor.

Mom slipped off her shoes and sat with her legs in front of her on the couch. We sat on the floor in front of the set. "What are they saying? What is all this? Some woman shot herself on the air?"

"It's nothing," I said.

Sissy got up on her knees and turned to face Mom. She made her hand into a pistol and stuck it behind her own ear and then said, "In keeping with Channel 40's policy of bringing you the latest in 'blood and guts' and in living color, you are going to see another first — attempted suicide." Then she pulled the trigger and stuck out her tongue and collapsed face first on the carpet.

"You were watching? Both of you?"

"Yes," Sissy said.

"No," I said.

"Which is it?" Mom demanded.

"I wasn't watching," I said.

"Come here," Mom said to both of us. She waved us over. We cautiously walked over to her. "I'm sorry you saw that. But this is the type of world we live in. It's not great." She crunched down a radish after swirling it in a patch of salt on her plate. She took a long gulp of her doctored V8 and set the glass down. "I don't know what else to say.

Don't tell your father. You'll get him angry. No one wants that. Don't you two want to play outside?"

"It's too hot," Sissy said.

"If you wait for it to cool off, you'll never go outside. Finish your lunch and go try to be normal kids for once. Don't you go getting Buzz into trouble, Miss Tishenbaum." That was Mom's nickname for Sissy, sometimes shortened to "Miss Tish." I never figured out what it meant.

"It's not my fault," Sissy said.

"It's never your fault," Mom said. "Isn't Phil Donahue on or something? Change the channel. I don't want to hear about this dead person. There has to be something else on." She sighed. "I have to make your father his dinner. And you have to eat it! Yes, Buzz. *You* have to eat it. And you have to not make faces while you eat it." Mom wasn't exactly the best cook in the world. "I promise I won't make Brussels' sprouts tonight." She rolled her eyes. "Do your best. You know how angry your father gets when you don't eat." A week prior, he'd picked me up by the upper arm, yanked me out of my dining room chair and tossed me across the carpet. Mom had to restrain him from kicking me across the dining room. He reserved his violent rage for my mother and me. Mom waved me closer and she ran her fingers through my hair. "Don't look so sad. Don't hang your head. Everything will be okay."

Sissy changed the channel over to Phil Donahue. Carl Sagan was on. "You're telling me that you don't think there's a God?" Phil asked him.

"Occam's razor," Dr. Sagan replied.

The audience booed.

We finished our lunch, took our plates and glasses into the kitchen and put them in the sink. We went into the bathroom we shared and brushed our teeth. We looked at ourselves in the mirror and then at each other in the mirror.

"Hello, Mirror Universe Sissy," I said.

"Hello, Mirror Universe Buzz," she said. "How are things over there?"

"They are all in reverse, thank you very much."

"As they should be. I hope it isn't as hot there as it is here." She turned to the real me. "You ready?"

"As I'll ever be."

We crept out the front door and the blast of boiling air rolled over the top of us. We squinted into the blazing sunshine. We decided to go on foot to the model homes at the end of the street. If the salespeople on site weren't too attentive, we could sneak into one of the homes and cool off in the air conditioning.

Most of the houses weren't built in our neighborhood yet. There were concrete slabs with copper pipes jutting out. Some of them had wooden frames erected. We got to the end of the block and there was a house that was just about finished. There weren't any workmen around, so we pushed inside and walked around a bit. Almost everything was in place except for the wall-to-wall carpeting. Wood shavings littered the floor. Empty Gatorade bottles were left on the kitchen counter. The tile floors were mostly glued down, but powdered in white dust. The house was a duplicate of our own house, but not lived in yet. Soon, strangers would be in it. We went to our respective bedrooms. In Sissy's bedroom, there was an outlet for a phone installed. "Fancy," Sissy said, squatting down to take a look at the little plug. In my room, there was a raccoon eating a sticky roll. It turned and glared at us evilly. We screamed and ran out of the house.

We walked down to the model homes at the entrance to the neighborhood. "Let's try this one," Sissy said. We opened the door and crept inside. It was, again, the same floor plan as the one we were living in. The walls were covered over in beige stucco. A large mirror hung over the couch in the Florida room and over the bed in the parents' room. "Why so many mirrors?" Sissy asked.

"Maybe people like to look at themselves," I offered.

We looked in the kitchen drawers and found Bic pens and a gold-embossed business card for Clyde Carrion, Head of Sales.

Once our clothes had dried of sweat, we left through the sliding glass door and went back out into the torturous heat. This version of the house had a swimming pool. It was a little kidney shaped affair, just big enough for a couple of people to splash around in. "I'm sorry I didn't wear my trunks," I said. I knelt down on the non-skid surface and ran my hand through the cool blue water, my nose filling with the scent of bleach.

That's when Sissy snuck up behind me and pushed me in.

I swallowed a mouthful of chlorinated water and then rose to the surface, shaking. The water felt almost icy.

Sissy laughed, doubling over with the giggles.

"I hate you so much!" I shouted at her, climbing out of the pool via an aluminum ladder.

"Hey you kids!" a salesman said, exiting out of the back of a model home two doors down. "Get the hell out of that pool! Get out of here!" He was only a door down when we sprinted out of the backyard and back onto our street.

My clothes slapped wetly against my body. My tennis shoes squished as I scampered alongside Sissy. "I'll get even!"

She started laughing again and had to stop for a moment. The salesman ended his pursuit and went back inside.

We walked down the sidewalk together, back toward our house. I was already beginning to dry. "What do we do now?" I asked her.

"You need to dry out completely, otherwise Mom will freak out and accuse me of brainwashing you into something."

"You pushed me in."

"Yes. Yes, I did."

"You seem awfully proud of yourself."

"I am, actually. You got the better end of the deal. You got to cool off."

"And you got to laugh at me."

"Don't be so sensitive. You'll look back at this moment and think, 'I wish Sissy would have pushed me into more pools.'"

"I don't think I'll do that."

"Whatever, little brother. Oh, lookie!" Sissy pointed at the under-construction house.

There was a family parking a flashy car outside. A tall, gangly teenager with shoulder-length blonde hair got out of the back seat. A girl with the darkest hair I'd ever seen got out of the other side of the station wagon. A mother and father emerged. They walked up to the house.

"Wait til they meet their new roommate," Sissy said.

"You're gross, Steve!" the girl shouted at her brother.

"Shut up, Brandy!" Steve yelled at his sister.

I slowed down. I was looking at the girl, staring at her. She was wearing a black dress with little red polka dots all over it. She wore a pair of black mary janes. Her shiny black hair cascaded down her shoulders to the middle of her back. There was something about the way she carried herself. I felt weird inside my chest. Sissy grabbed my forearm and tried to pull me along. I could tell that Sissy wanted to meet them, make their acquaintance, and then tell them about the raccoon. She liked doing things like that.

The father was examining the garage door skeptically. The mother opened up her handbag, extracted an amber bottle, unscrewed the lid and popped a tiny pill into her mouth.

Steve poked Brandy and Brandy poked him back. I couldn't take my eyes off of her. I think my mouth was open a bit. I was having trouble breathing. I stopped mid-stride and wouldn't move.

"C'mon," Sissy said. "Let's catch them before they go inside."

"You go ahead," I said. "I'll stay here."

"What's the matter with you?"

"Why do people constantly ask me that?" I snapped. "I'm fine. There's nothing wrong with me. Nothing."

The black-haired girl waved at us happily and bounced a little on her toes.

"Fine. You stand here like a goof. I'll go talk to them." Sissy jogged away from me.

I momentarily forgot how to swallow and coughed a bit. I shivered as the pool water evaporated off me.

The mother and father disappeared inside the house. The brother leaned against the shaded side of the house, pulled out a pack of Marlboros, tapped out a smoke and lit it with a metal lighter. He blew a smoke ring up at the sky. He noticed me standing there and glared. "Hey kid! Yeah you! Get over here!"

I finally found myself able to move. I walked toward him. He had to have been well over six feet tall. When I made it to him, he grinned. "Ain't much to you, is there?"

"I guess not."

"What are you doing standing around? How'd you get wet?"

I told him about the pool.

"So you were doing a little breaking and entering, huh? Nice. You want a puff?" He handed me the cigarette. I didn't know how to hold it. I took a small drag and couldn't stop coughing. I nearly dropped the smoke. He patted me on the back and plucked it out of my fingers. "I'd offer you another puff, but I wouldn't want you to die or nothing. I'm Steve." He stuck the cigarette back in his mouth and offered me his right hand.

I shook it. "I'm Buzz." I coughed some more.

"We're moving here from Louisiana. First chance I get, I'm going back. Got me a girl there. Figure I can work on the oil rigs and make a lotta money. Buy a sweet car. There any teenagers in this neighbor, or only little squirts like you?"

"We just moved in, so I don't really know."

"All right. I got some advice for you." He took a knee, the cigarette bobbing in his pink lips as he spoke. He was working on a blonde mustache. "First day of school, this is what you do." He poked me in the chest, knocking me back a little. "You walk up to the toughest kid and punch him right in the guts. That'll let everyone know not to screw with you."

"Thanks." I didn't think I'd do that. Generally, I was the one getting punched. I was a head shorter than every boy in my grade in the last few schools.

"Don't mention it. Oh, and if you get any ideas about my sister, I'll chain you to a cinderblock and toss you right back into the pool you just clumb out of. Got it, little man?"

"Got it." I backed away from him and walked around the corner of the nearly finished house, right into my sister and her new best friend having a chat.

"And here he is now, my little brother," Sissy said.

"Mmm-hmm. How'd he get wet?" Brandy had green eyes sparkling with intelligence and mischief. Her skin was alabaster white.

"He, very clumsily, fell into a pool," Sissy said. "I have to watch out for him all the time. It's embarrassing."

"For one thing, I'm not her little brother. I'm older by almost two years. And for another, she pushed me in because she thinks that kind of thing is funny."

"Maybe it *is* funny. Are those your real eyelashes?" Brandy was already wearing makeup. The red dots on her dress were pictures of cherries. Her voice had the same effect on me as music.

"What? Um. Yes." I blushed uncontrollably.

"He's kinda cute," Brandy said.

Just then, her father emerged from the house holding a dead raccoon by the tail. He tossed it into a half-filled construction dumpster in the yard. "Vermin," he stated, wiping his hands on his sansabelt slacks.

"I told your father not to kill that thing," her mother said in a thick Irish brogue, walking past us toward the car. "I'm getting in the car. We'll be leaving now. Children! Pay attention! We're leaving!"

Brandy ran over to her father and hugged him around the waist. "Daddy!" she shouted. He patted her on the head.

Steve flicked his cigarette out toward the dumpster and missed it.

"What have I told you about smoking?" her father asked. "Get in the car! We'll discuss this at the hotel." They all got into the car. The engine roared to life.

Sissy and I were merely children. Easily ignored.

Brandy cranked down her window. "Bye, Sissy! Bye, Buzz! See you later!"

We watched them drive away. "Well, well, well," Sissy said, crossing her thin arms across her chest. She arched her eyebrows at me.

"What?"

"Well, well, well." She laughed. "The good news is you're almost dry."

Hope Hospital

My chlorine-scented clothes and squishing tennis shoes gave me away to our quick-on-the-draw mother, who was on her third vodka-and-V8. We tried to sneak past her, but she wasn't having it.

"Look at you." Mom stood up and polished off her drink. "You look like a drowned rat. What have you two weirdos been up to?" Before either of us could make up a lie, she said, "Never mind. I don't want to hear it. Was there property damage involved?" Before Sissy could lie about the second question, Mom said, "I don't want to hear that either. Go change your clothes, Buzz. Put your tennis shoes next to the fridge to dry off. Dinner's in the oven. Wake me up at four, or before that if your father suddenly decides to show up." She took a knee and smoothed my hair away from my face. "Such a little weirdo. I can't believe I made you. Have I told you lately about that pregnancy? Ugh. It was the worst." I could smell the booze on her breath.

Mom had told me time and again how much she suffered while she was pregnant with me. She had a tipped uterus. She had to stay in bed for months. "No," I lied.

"I'm not telling the story again. Not today anyway. You can forget about it. You can enjoy stories about your mother's suffering some other time." She turned to Sissy. "My pregnancy with you was a walk in the park, but you've been a pain in the rear ever since."

Sissy said, "I have no idea what you're talking about."

"Of course you don't. But someday you'll be a mother and, if there's any justice in the world, your kids will force you to understand." She regained her feet. "I have a headache. You've given me a headache. I hope you're proud of yourselves."

"I can't speak for Buzz—"

"Why not? You do it all the time," Mom snapped.

"But I'm *awfully* proud of myself," Sissy said without missing a beat.

"Yes you are, aren't you? Try to keep it down to a low roar out here while I'm taking my nap. And remember to wake me up at four. Earlier if your father makes his grand entrance. And no doing what you two usually do when I'm not around. I don't know what that is, and I don't want to know, but I'm sure I wouldn't like it. If his lordship, your brother, manages to show up at some point, tell him to set the table. We're eating in the dining room tonight like real people, not a bunch of savages staring at the TV set."

"I don't know if I can remember all that," Sissy said.

"And you said that with a straight face, too. You lie so well, Miss Tish. You'll make a great wife some day."

"Thanks, Mom!"

"It wasn't a compliment. But you knew that already, didn't you? Of course you did. I have a headache. Four o'clock. Remember. Four o'clock."

Mom tromped off through the kitchen and then dining room. We heard her bedroom door shut with a definitive clunk.

A moment later, Sparky cautiously entered. He was dressed in a pale blue mock turtleneck, khakis and a pair of athletic shoes. Sweat dripped off his curly blonde hair, which framed his dour, pale face. Under his arm was a copy of Kurt Gödel's *Collected Works: Volume 1*. "What are you two up to?" Sparky asked us.

"Nothing," I said.

"Then why do you smell like a YMCA?"

"I fell into a pool."

"Does Mom know?" He gritted his teeth. "Never mind." My stupidity was a bottomless pit of irritation to him, along with my subservience to Sissy. He looked at the TV tray, which had Mom's empty V8 glass on it. "How many of them did she have?"

"Three, I think," I said.

"Maybe more," Sissy added.

"Then Buster is coming home." Sparky rarely called our father "Dad." He treated Buster with barely concealed contempt. And the shocking thing was that Buster took it for the most part.

"Mom says that you have to set the table," Sissy said.

"Does she?" His expression didn't change. It rarely did. Our brother had the greatest poker face. Combined with his mathematical skill, he could have made a fortune in Las Vegas if he didn't also have a rigid set of ethics. That is to say that if he'd had our father's sense of right and wrong, he would have been rich by the time he was 30. "I can't be sure, but I think I smell chicken. That's never good news."

We three looked at each other knowingly. A chicken had sacrificed its life for us toward no good end.

"Can't wait to watch Buzz gag on it," Sissy said.

"Yes, another entertaining evening in this miserable place. I'll be in my room," Sparky said.

"You have to set the table," Sissy said.

13

"I believe that in the hierarchy of this family, I hold a position above yours."

"You can believe what you want, Mister Spock." Sissy placed her hands on her hips and cocked her head at Sparky.

Sparky snorted. "I could spank you if I wanted. But I'm not going to. And the table will get set at some point. I'll delegate that to the two of you, which means Buzz will end up doing it."

"Are you gonna let him get away with talking to you like that?" Sissy asked me.

"Like what?" I went.

"That's the spirit." Sparky slipped past us to his room and his door shut with a similar clunk to Mom's.

"I guess I better change clothes," I said.

"Narrate your life, why don't you?" Sissy was always upset when I didn't take her side against Sparky.

I went into my bedroom and shut the door. I'd ended up with the maple chest of drawers that Sparky and I had once shared. Most of my clothes were folded up inside it. I peeled off my moist clothes and still-damp underwear and placed them in the little wicker hamper next to the chest of drawers. I put on a new set of clothes and my only other everyday shoes, a pair of worn-out tennis shoes with frayed laces and holes near the heels. I preferred these shoes to the newer ones.

"You're missing it!" Sissy shouted. It was her soap opera, *Hope Hospital*, which may have had something to do with a hospital in the distant past, but was now mainly concerned with a mad scientist, a weather machine, an Australian secret agent and a blonde couple with alliterating names who somehow went from being ordinary people working in a hospital to being involved with weather machines and Australian secret agents. Soap operas were girl stuff and I wasn't supposed to like it, but Sissy insisted that I needed to watch if only to allow her to have someone else to discuss its finer plot points with. I had to admit, if only to Sissy, that *Hope Hospital*'s insane view of adult life was at the very least interesting.

I rushed out, placed my wet tennis shoes next to the vent at the bottom of the fridge, and sat down on the carpet next to Sissy. But the ABC News logo popped up instead and the glowering face of the President soon appeared. Transcripts of what the President had said to his advisors, some of which were marked EXPLETIVE DELETED, had appeared in the paper recently. I didn't completely understand it, but I knew that the President was doing wrong things. He had a mean face that scared me, too.

The press had taken to yelling things at him. Some of the things they yelled were questions. Others started off with, "Isn't it true…?"

"We might as well change the channel," I told Sissy. "He never shuts up. The press doesn't either."

"Depressing." Sissy got up and turned down the sound with the little ON/OFF knob. "I wanted to watch *Hope* today." She made a little dissatisfied noise in the back of her throat. "I can't get her out of my mind. I wish I could forget things like you do."

"Who? The anchor lady from this morning?"

"Yes, the anchor lady from this morning. Don't pretend like you didn't see it. It was horrible. I told Brandy about it and she couldn't believe it."

"Your new best friend," I said.

"Your little crushypoo." Sissy closed her eyes and made kissing sounds. "Mwah-mwah-mwah!"

"Shut up!"

"Make me!"

We ended up fighting Florida Championship Wrestling style. I was somehow winning. Then she tickled me under the ribs, tackled me and I couldn't stop laughing. "Stop it! Stop it! Mercy! Uncle!"

Muffled from the far bedroom, we heard Mom shout, "Pipe down out there!"

Sissy stood up and raised her fists above her head. "I am the American dream! The woman of the hour, the woman with the power!" She paraded around like that, kissed each of her thin biceps, and then we both sat back down in front of the set while the President sweatily defended himself from behind a podium. "Why's he still around?"

"The President?" I asked, out of breath. My ribs were sore from all the laughing.

"Yeah. Shouldn't he be in chains in some sort of island prison right about now, surrounded by the Army? And picking maggots out of his gruel?" Sissy read a lot of books with chapters like that in them.

"I don't know."

"You almost won that wresting match, Buzz. You've got to get better at defending yourself. I won't be around to help you this year. I'll be stuck at Incarnation School, telling off nuns."

"I know, I know."

New town, new school again this year. I was filled with apprehension.

The President was off the air and Merv Griffin was on. We watched him for a while.

"Have you seen that stupid uniform I have to wear? I might as well wear a big sign saying, 'I'm an idiot.'" Sissy made her own macramé vests after our grandmother taught her how to knit.

"You showed it to me already. I'll see enough of it when you have to wear it next month."

"It's so depressing that we have to go back to school already. We didn't even get to go to Cleveland this year."

Because of the move, we'd skipped our annual pilgrimage back to the place of our birth, where we'd stay with our maternal grandparents.

15

Usually, I'd get to go see the Cleveland Indians lose in their empty, broken-down ballpark with our grandfather. Sissy would hang out with our grandmother and attempt to learn how to cook Czech food.

I peered out the sliding glass door at our backyard, which was just beginning to grow in. Buster had been too cheap to spring for sod, so the yard was seeded. At some point we'd be able to play out there. There were also vague promises that we'd finally get a dog. Only Sparky had had the pleasure of dog ownership. Family legend had it that our uncle Ralph, Mom's little brother, had let Sparky's German Shepherd outside and she had been hit by a city bus. Since then, no dog. We had to be content with our own company.

I gazed up and saw the sky blackening. There are two seasons in Florida: the rainy season and the dry season. The darkening sky meant that it was past four o'clock, past time to wake up Mom. I leapt to my feet and ran to set the table.

Sissy followed me into the dining room and harangued me about bending to Sparky's will. "You won't get in trouble if Sparky doesn't set the table! You give in too easily."

What she didn't get was that I liked things to be settled as much as possible in the house. If things were unsettled, I was the one who got it in the chops, not her. Buster doted on Sissy. She could say anything she wanted to him. If I looked at him sideways—wham! Mom described it as treating *your father* as if he'd escaped from a lunatic asylum. She also said that she knew that if anything ever happened to her, he'd stick by her no matter what. "If I lost a leg, your father would take care of me. He'd do anything for me. You have to take the good with the bad. That's life."

I finished setting the table and then brought out the plastic salt and pepper shakers and a stick of margarine on a tea saucer.

We heard his car pulling up just as the thunder started. I froze and stared at the front door from the vantage point of the dining room. I tried to manage my fear. If he saw my fear, it would enrage him. We never knew what kind of a mood he'd be in. We never knew what might set him off into a different mood. Sometimes, he could be nice. He'd bring presents if he made some sales on his route. I got a Nerf football one time. Those were the good days.

Sissy rapped on the parents' bedroom door. She cracked it open. "He's here," she whisper-hissed.

"I'm up! I'm up!" Mom said, her voice a bit slurry from sleep and alcohol.

The front door swung open and Dad stood there in his garish polyester suit, dripping a bit from the sudden downpour. "What a gulleywasher!" He beamed good-naturedly, and I unfroze. I didn't know whether to walk over to him or not. Sometimes the good mood only lasted moments and I didn't want to walk into a fist. Sometimes it lasted all night, even after he argued with Walter Cronkite during the evening news. He considered Cronkite to be a communist. So I stood rocking back and forth, unable to propel myself toward my father, or run away from him. "What're you doing over there?" The question was directed at me. We regarded each other across the Florida room, filled with our unused good furniture.

"Nothing. Setting the table," I said.

"*Nothing. Setting the table*," he repeated in an effeminate voice. "Don't stand there like a dummy staring at me. Go do something. Christ almighty."

I turned around and looked at the table. Was anything missing? Maybe I needed to put out some white bread? Action was required. Movement.

Sissy ran past me over to our father. He knelt down and gave her a hug. "How's my girl today? Making all the boys cry?"

She pushed away and playfully slapped his chest. "I'm too young for that."

I slipped into the kitchen and pretended to check on the roasted chicken. I turned on the oven light and peered in. All I saw was the dutch oven, nickel-plated with black handles, with the lid on. There was no food to see.

Mom came up behind me and shooed me away. She was wearing her floral housecoat and slippers. "Go ask your brother if he needs an engraved invitation to dinner."

I walked through the den, quickly peeking over toward the front door from that vantage point. Dad was still engaged with Sissy. Or maybe she was keeping him busy so he wouldn't remember how much he despised me.

I knocked on Sparky's door. "What?" he barked.

"Mom wants to know if you need an engraved invitation to dinner," I yelled through the door.

"Fine. I'll be right out."

I went down to my room, closed the door and sat on my bed. I tried to calm myself. It wasn't easy. Buster wasn't terribly bright, but he had a way of sensing fear. The door opened and my breath left my body. But it was Sparky. "It's okay. It's just me. Come on."

"Okay." I got up. I realized I was shaking. I took a deep breath and gained some composure.

The dutch oven was on a metal rack in the middle of the dining room table. The lid was off, exposing the culinary crime lurking within. The sloppy remains of an overcooked chicken was in there, the skin and meat melted off the bones. Semi-peeled carrots had been jammed into its cavity, along with whole stalks of celery. Mom had sprinkled some seasoning on it from tins that dated back to the 1950's. "It's still good," she'd say when we asked about the ancient seasonings. Reconstituted mashed potatoes minus dairy products filled a ceramic bowl. The chicken grease at the bottom of the dutch oven was meant to be the gravy substitute. A can of corn had also been heated up.

The various containers were passed around. Our father sat at one end of the table. Our mother at the other end. Sparky and I sat on one side, with me nearest to our father. Sissy sat across from Sparky and me. I loaded up on the corn. I tried to take as little of everything else as I could.

Our father took everything that we didn't eat. He wasn't satisfied with what I took, so he added some extra to my plate. The only serving implement in the dutch oven was a large spoon, so the large spoon clacked down repeatedly onto my plate.

This wasn't as bad as when our father went hunting for rabbits back in Ohio and we had to eat the dead bunnies that were littered with bird shot, but it was pretty close.

Sissy ate very little, and no one took any notice.

Buster's eyes were on me, on my face, to make sure that I looked like I was enjoying the bounty that his hard work had made possible. My fright made my throat constrict. I kept my eyes down on the inhuman mess on my plate. Buster dragged the dutch oven over to himself, stuck his fork inside, twirled it, and extracted most of the chicken's skin on the tines of his fork. He stuck the mass of skin and fat into his mouth and masticated loudly. "Eat," his muffled voice demanded.

I silently shoveled it in. I gagged once, but managed to hide it. I ate as much as I could get down, which wasn't a lot.

Buster had miraculously moved on to other subjects. "Made a big sale down in Punta Gorda today." Buster sat back in his chair. For dinner, he'd stripped down to his v-neck undershirt and boxer shorts. Dribbles of chicken grease decorated the center of his chest under the V. His bare belly stuck out from under the v-neck like a lower lip. "Big sale. Might win that color TV set after all."

"That's wonderful," Mom said.

"We can put that old color set in our room. And then the kids can have the black and white Magnavox. Would you like that?" he asked me.

"Yes," I said cautiously.

"If you finish that whole plate, you have dibs."

I took a deep breath. Concentrated. I didn't really care about the TV set. I wanted to get off the old man's list. I told myself, "You can do this." I closed my eyes and prayed for a moment. Jesus needed to get off the bench and help me out here.

"Look at that. See? All he needed was a little motivation," our father said.

"You need to ease up on him," our mother said.

"Always taking his side. You're making him into a little queer."

"He has a girlfriend," Sissy interjected.

"Him?" our father said contemptuously. "You gotta be kidding me."

"I'm not kidding," Sissy said. "They're super cute together."

"I'll be damned," our father said. He slapped me on the back and I nearly vomited up the dinner. "I gotta go watch the news. See what those jerks are doing to our President today." He got up and farted heartily. He picked up his half-finished can of Red, White and Blue beer. "Girlfriend huh? No kidding. Jesus, I swear I thought this kid was gonna turn out queer with all the art crap and reading those fruity books."

I glared over at Sissy and she mouthed out, "You're welcome."

I watched Buster amble away. His v-neck in the back was sticking up, revealing the scar from his unnecessary back surgery that had won him his settlement. We heard the TV clunk on and the theme song for the evening news pipe up.

Yes, that surgery won him his lawsuit and got us the new house. We all looked back at the time of his surgery as one of the best in our house. He was stuck in bed for weeks on end and pumped full of painkillers. We got money from the government, which was often better than what he got from his sales commissions. Mom had bought the black and white Magnavox so he could watch the Watergate hearings from bed and shout, "Traitor!" at John Dean. Buster's job back then was selling mobile homes. Or maybe it was selling aluminum siding. I'm unclear on which. Maybe both.

So now we were in Sarasota. It was a new start. Maybe things were looking up.

My stomach rumbled. I looked over at Mom. She took me by the hand into the master bedroom and through to the master bathroom and stroked my hair while I threw up into the avocado-colored toilet. "Quietly," she whispered. "We can't upset your father. He's in a good mood." I finished and I washed my mouth out with Listerine. The chemical taste cleansed away the grease. I spat into the avocado-colored sink. Mom wiped down the toilet. "Hurry up and go back out there before your father notices."

Sparky was in the kitchen scrubbing the dishes and then placing them into the dishwasher. Sissy was sitting with Buster in the other room while he railed against the national media. There was an entire list of reporters that our father considered commie symps. If their hair was a smidge too long, they were hippies, too.

"Can I help?" I asked Sparky.

"You feel better?" he asked.

"Yeah."

"Go get the stepstool and you can scrub out the dutch oven."

I fetched the stepstool and grabbed the steel wool. I scrubbed the dutch oven hard. Eventually, all the burnt patches of chicken skin popped free. Sparky finished cleaning it and I dried it off and put it away.

Sparky and I walked through the den past Buster. "Where are you two going? Can't keep your old man company?"

"We're going to go read," Sparky said deliberately, enunciating every syllable like Buster was a moron, speaking for us both.

He sat glowering at us and then gave up. "Go on. Go read."

We split up in the hallway and each went into our respective rooms. My stomach still hurt from throwing up. I picked up Ray Bradbury's *Martian Chronicles* and rolled onto my side. My ribs hurt. At some point, I fell asleep.

Mom must have come into my room and undressed me and put on my pajamas, and tucked me into bed. I should have been bigger by that time, but I wasn't. I was still small enough that she could do that.

I awoke at some point. It was dark. I saw a silhouette of a large man in the doorway. The lights were all off. He was standing there. I could hear him breathing, his nose whistling. I knew who it was. Eventually, he tossed my tennis shoes onto the carpet next to my bed and shut the door.

Many years later, when I was a PFC in the Army, I shared a barracks room with a soldier named PFC Dan Tweety from Owosso, Michigan. I didn't hold his Michigan affiliation against him. I had the bottom bunk and he had the top. He shook me awake one night. "Hey, Pepper. You okay?" he asked.

"Yeah, Tweety. Why'd you wake me up?"

"You were moaning in your sleep. You said some stuff."

"Stuff? Like what?"

"You kept saying, 'Don't hit me, Dad. Please don't hit me.'"

"I'm sorry," I said. "Sorry I woke you up."

"It's okay," Tweety said. "We've all been there."

Weeds

We were standing in our front yard, such as it was, inspecting the vegetation. There wasn't much growing there, but it appeared to be grass to Sissy and me. Mom and Sparky crouched down to inspect.

"No doubt about it," Sparky said.

"Crabgrass," Mom said. "Figures that your father would pay for a lawn and we end up with mud covered over in weeds. Mister Big Shot. Mister Wheeler Dealer."

Sissy and I were already backing away. We knew what was coming, and we meant to make our escape before we got sucked into one of Mom's gardening projects. In our last house, she decided to prune the rose bushes. By the time she was done, nothing was left but rose bush stumps and we'd gotten our fingers and arms punctured by thorns from carrying away the hacked-down remains of the plants. The only fun part was pelting each other with rose petals. "Slowly," Sissy whispered to me, pulling me along with her as she backed away. "Quietly."

"Where do you two weirdos think you're going?" Mom demanded, turning on us.

Sissy let go of my forearm and we both froze.

Sparky crossed his arms and squinted at us through the blazing sunshine. "Appears they're making their getaway."

"I'm splitting you two up!" Mom said. "You!" She pointed at me. "Help your brother clean the garage. Your father made a mess in there. And you!" She pointed at Sissy. "You'll help me yank these weeds up."

"Do I have to have Buzz's help?" Sparky asked. "I'm fine on my own. And Buzz is… untidy."

"Then teach him to be tidy. Is that so hard?" Mom was on her knees already, yanking at the long cords of grass. They went pop-pop-pop as the roots dislodged from the soggy ground. "Go get that tin bucket from the garage, Miss Tish."

Sissy, Sparky and I walked into the garage. Tools were strewn all over the concrete floor, along with concrete dust and mud from Buster's shoes. Sparky looked like he was about to have a stroke. A vein popped from his forehead. He stood surveying the wreckage. "How can Buster do this much in just fifteen minutes? I timed it. Fifteen minutes! Do you know how long it took me to organize this garage? To put all the tools in their proper places? To hang that pegboard over there?" The pegboard was partially dislodged from the wall. He ran his hands through his curly blonde hair. The whites around his pale blue eyes turned red. Sweat beaded up on his upper lip and dripped down his roman nose.

"A very long time?" Sissy offered with a giggle.

"Yes! A very long time! I'm glad you find that hilarious!"

"And yet, sadly, I do," Sissy said, tilting her head and grinning, showing off her bright white teeth. "Oh, the cross you've borne throughout life. It's a big one. A heavy one. With sharp edges."

"Get out! Get the bucket and get out!"

"He's all yours, Buzz. Remember your Red Cross training from last summer. Save him if he needs saving."

"I thought that was for drowning."

"It *was* for drowning!" Sparky roared. "Out of the garage! Go!" He flapped his arms around a bit.

Sissy snatched up the galvanized tin bucket and headed out to yank up the yard.

"I have formulated a plan," Sparky announced. "Step one: Remove everything from the garage and place it in the driveway. Step two: Clean all the tools thoroughly. Step three: Sweep the garage from the back to the front. Methodology is important here. If we break the garage into four quadrants, we can efficiently—"

"Quadrants?"

"Yes, little brother. Quadrants. Now pay attention. You don't appear to be paying attention. What are you looking at?"

"Have you seen these little lizards? They're pretty cool."

"Yes, I've seen the lizards. Actually, they're called 'brown anoles.' They're not native to the state of Florida. That's called an 'invasive species.' Now, as I was saying—"

"Look at this one here right here," I said, crouching down. "Check out how he's bobbing head like he's saying, 'Hey, man. How's it going?' Check it out! He has a little beard." I tried to pick him (or her) up, but the little inch-and-a-half long critter was quick and skittered away. I stood up. "I want a dog. Don't you want a dog?"

"Of course I want a dog. I want another German Shepherd." Sparky looked at me as if I'd dropped out of the sky in a space egg. "Just do what I tell you to do and we'll get the garage cleaned."

"We could put the tools back where they're supposed to be and sweep up. Done in ten minutes."

"Or we could do the job that we've been tasked with properly."

"I prefer my plan."

"Then it's a good thing that I'm in charge."

Sparky supervised as I toted each tool out to the driveway and I arranged them in some sort of ascending order based on size and utility. We had a brand-new gas lawn mower that was painted English racing green. I dusted it. My dusting didn't meet Sparky's stringent standards so I had to observe as he showed me how to properly clean it from front to back without leaving behind streaks on the paint job.

"It's a lawn mower," I complained.

"Having standards is its own reward," Sparky said.

Sissy hauled over a bucket of weeds that looked an awful lot like grass. "How's it going?"

"Is there some reason you're over here?" Sparky asked her.

"Oh dear. I see some dust on that lawn mower."

"Where?" Sparky demanded.

She pulled out a string of grass and shook it over the top of the mower. Dirt and mud sprinkled down. "Right about there."

"Get out of here," Sparky said, pointing away.

"Don't let him do the Vulcan mind meld on you," she stage-whispered to me.

"Go." Sparky crouched down and recleaned the mower.

At some point, everything was out of the garage and step three was emergent. Brooms. I saw those in Sparky's hands. He was moving toward me brandishing brooms. One was meant for me. It would come with a lesson in proper broom-handling techniques. That's when I saw the moving van at the end of the block, out in front of Brandy's and Steve's house. I noticed also that my bicycle was parked near the sidewalk and pointed out toward the street. And it was so very clean, my bicycle, after Sparky demonstrated his bicycle-maintenance prowess on it. The chains were lubed and the tires were at the appropriate PSI. These tasks were all part of owning any kind of wheeled vehicle, Sparky assured me.

"Any questions?" Sparky asked shortly before he departed in search of brooms.

"If Captain Kirk got into a fight with the Six Million Dollar Man do you think he'd have a chance? I say 'yes' because Captain Kirk always has a fighting chance."

"Any questions about cleaning, organizing and maintenance?"

"None."

"I'll be back with the brooms in a minute. Don't touch anything."

And now, here he was, brooms in hand.

The choice was clear. I made my break and hopped on my bicycle.

Sparky didn't make much of an effort to chase me down. I'd mostly been impeding progress.

I turned my head as I sped away and watched him put down one of the brooms and go back into the garage with the other, grateful that his idiotic little brother had finally gone on the lam. Possibly, it had been his plan all along to drive me away with his special brand of tedium.

When we were adults, and Sissy had children of her own, if her kids didn't behave, she'd ask them, "Do you want me to invite Uncle Sparky over to explain math to you?"

"No, Mommy!" the kids would shout. "Please! We'll be good!"

Within moments after I made my break, Sissy was riding her freshly maintained bicycle alongside mine. Her fingernails and knees were dirty from all the yard work. "Free!" she shouted. "They won't take us alive! You hear me, coppers? Top of the world, Ma!" She shook her fist at our mother, who was standing in the middle of bales of pulled up crabgrass shaking her head. Sissy turned to me and said, "One more minute of that and I would've gone nuts. Good job, little brother."

"Thanks."

We pulled up in front of the freshly minted house, only the third real house on the block, if you didn't count the model homes near Beneva Road. Steve was out front. His mustache had grown in somewhat. His blonde hair had grown out to nearly shoulder-length. He may have grown an extra inch. He was wearing a pair of cut-offs and a western shirt with pearl buttons. He'd cut the sleeves off the shirt, possibly with a dull knife by the look of it. He wore a pair of bedraggled Adidas jogging shoes and white sweatsocks with blue stripes at the top. "Little man!" he said, shaking his head affirmatively. "And his unruly sister. You the welcoming committee for this sad-ass town?"

"Close enough." Sissy put down her kickstand and dismounted. I did likewise. "Brandy around?"

"She's inside," Steve said, jerking his thumb toward the door. "Getting her room organized."

Sissy bolted inside.

"What about you?" I asked.

"What about me, little man?" His lips curled into a sleepy smile. "I travel light. And when I buy my car, I'll travel fast." He reached into his shirt pocket and produced his pack of Marlboros and the metal lighter. He flipped the cigarette into his lips and quickly lit it, blowing out a perfect smoke ring a moment later. "I'll show you how to do that one of these days, little man. You ready to start school? You ready to kick some ass?"

"I'm ready," I told him, and I meant it. I'd been practicing by throwing haymakers at a pillow in the shape of Charlie Brown in my room with the door closed so Sissy wouldn't make fun of me. She heard me through the wall and made fun of me anyway.

He knelt down and raised his hands, placing the cigarette in the corner of his mouth. "Show me what you got."

I swung my arms in huge arcs, mostly missing his hands. I quickly got tired and bent over to gasp for breath, hands on knobby knees. "Gimme a sec."

"C'mon, man. You're not gonna win a lot of fights wailing around like that. Let me show you what my old man showed me." Steve turned his body in a Ali-like stance. He bounced on the balls of his feet, brought his fists up and jabbed at the air. All of his punches were straight. "Straight like an arrow," Steve said. "Pop-pop-pop. Now you do it." He took another knee. I imitated him the best I could, my small fists slapping against his palms. "That's better. But now go full force." I hit harder, as hard as I thought I could. "Take all that fear and turn it into power. Imagine all of your fear coming out of your body and being shoved into that other kid's body." I looked him in the eye. "Do it." I reached inside and found it. I let loose three punches, the last of which made a loud pop in Steve's hand. "Whoa! Stop, stop. You got it. Make sure you get close to that kid, because he'll swing his arms like you were doing a minute ago. He can't hurt you if you're standing close. He'll only hit you with his arms. Big deal, right? Last thing. Find a wall to back up against so no one can get behind you. You don't want that kid's compadres sneaking up. Find a wall and hit him like you just hit my hand." He shook his hand and showed it to me. It was quickly turning from red to black. "You bruised the shit out of my hand, little man. Good job."

"Thanks, Steve."

"Anytime. Gimme some skin!"

I jumped, but he held the hand too high for me. He put an arm around my shoulders. "Let's go see what the ladies are up to."

We walked inside the house. Steve first and then I followed. It was like our house, except someone had turned it into a mansion. The furniture was made of real wood. The wall-to-wall carpet was plush. There wasn't any linoleum, just ceramic tile. The light fixture glowed and glittered like diamonds. A bulldog trotted up to me and licked my hand. "A dog!" I shouted a little too loudly. I crouched and petted it and the dog rhythmically gasped and slobbered. "What's his name?"

"Bruce Lee," Steve said.

"Hi, Bruce Lee," I went, talking to the dog. I sat down in their foyer, on their elegant tile, and petted Bruce Lee who cozied up into my lap, enjoying the attention. "Do you know karate, Bruce Lee?"

Bruce Lee made some satisfied grunts.

"Who's that?" It was their mother, the Irishwoman. I got up and went into the den, peering into the kitchen. Bruce Lee followed me in and then plopped down onto the cool tile kitchen floor with a grunt. They'd gotten real wood cabinets instead of the particle board cabinets we had. I saw an Amana Radar Range above the stove. And this Irishwoman looked so elegant, too. She was thin and pretty in a way that suggested that she'd gone to great lengths to be thin and pretty. Her makeup made her look like a movie star, or at least a guest star on *Columbo*. Her hair was perfectly coiffed. She had a glass of red wine in one of her precisely manicured hands. She took a delicate sip and then placed it on the countertop. "Who is this? You must belong to Sissy. I can see the resemblance. Come here, lad."

I walked over to her and she did what adult women always did with me. She gave me a hug. But this time it didn't bother me. Her perfume reminded me of the rose petal fight I'd had with Sissy. This stylish woman smoothed my hair out of my face with flawless hands that seemingly had never seen a day of work. "How did you get such soft hair? You're like a chinchilla! Oh, and those big brown eyes and rosy cheeks. You're an adorable little thing. You must come over as often as you like."

"Yes, ma'am."

"None of that. Call me Missus Bondurant. In a few years, you can call me Fiona. We'll figure that out whenever we get there. I'm sure it'll be soon. You're a growing lad. Look at you! One more hug, for the road." And she hugged me again. "Now run along. Go find your sister."

I looked around and Steve was gone. Bruce Lee had also made his escape.

Mrs. Bondurant picked up her wine glass and polished off the contents. She found a compact in her purse and checked her lipstick before pouring herself another glass.

I walked among their expensive possessions. It reminded me of going to my great uncle Tom's house in Akron. He was an executive with Goodyear Tire and Rubber. Uncle Tom's house was larger, but his stuff wasn't quite as nice as all this. I would have been afraid to sit on the Bondurants' couch or touch their Zenith TV set, or place a record on their Bang & Olufsen stereo that was encased in a brushed metal and glass cabinet. It made our all-in-one Emerson hi fi purchased with S&H Green Stamps sitting on top of a pine cabinet that we'd gotten at a yard sale look a bit sad in comparison. I knew a bit about the finer things in life having seen them on TV.

I walked down to what would have been my room and there was a weight set in there along with a poster of Linda Carter thumbtacked to the wall. The floor had a thick black mat covering it. I took a left into what would have been Sissy's room and found Brandy in there instead, but no Sissy.

"Um, hi," I went, trying act casual. Like I wandered through other people's houses all the time.

"Hi yourself. Buzz, right?" Brandy was wearing a black t-shirt and tight black jeans. She wore black Converse All Stars. She had bright red fingernail polish lacquered on. Her black hair was cut into a shag and framed her face. Her hair was so black that it seemed to have a blue sheen to it. She had glittery eyeliner and bright red lipstick on her full lips. Her skin was arsenic white. It was a thoroughly unusual look for the time.

"Neat," I said, looking around at her room. A half-dozen professionally framed posters lined the walls. One poster with a psychedelic eye in the middle of it said, "13th Floor Elevators." Another had a white man with an afro and a few other guys and said, "MC5." Another poster on the wall simply said, "STOOGES."

"Stooges," I said.

"A band," Brandy said. "You never heard of them?"

"No," I admitted. "Never heard of them." If a band didn't play on AM radio, they were beyond my reach.

"When I get to travel with my daddy, he takes me to record shops. Not the corporate ones. Have you ever been to Paris? London? Frankfurt? Music makes me feel better."

"Um." I was suddenly intimidated. I had no business being in this house with these cosmopolitan people. I wanted to escape, to get the hell out of there as quickly as possible. I felt shabby. Ashamed. When I eventually went to Paris, London and Frankfurt, it was as a soldier stationed in Europe. At ten, the only places I'd been to were of the generic American variety—Ohio, Missouri and Nebraska. Now Florida. We went where our father went. He chased dreams of easy money. Our father was enraged that a million dollars hadn't dropped out of the clear blue sky and into his lap. Someone had promised him that this would happen. That promise had been broken. "Where's Sissy?"

"She had to go use the facilities. Wash up. her hands were covered with dirt and I don't like that. Her knees looked awful, too." Brandy sounded like someone from California. Like she should be catching a wave. Everyone in her family had a different, lilting accent. Her father, when I'd heard him speak before, sounded like he was from Brooklyn.

"What are you doing here in Sarasota?" I asked defensively.

"Daddy wanted a change. He wanted to get away from Louisiana. Sarasota is close to Tampa and Daddy can fly out of there for his job. He's a traveling engineer. He solves problems."

How were we living in a neighborhood that had a traveling engineer in it? In the months ahead, we'd have a college dean move in next door to us on one side and a retired auto executive on the other side. He didn't have to work. Our backyard neighbor was a General Electric executive who also traveled. These people all dug swimming pools and had ornate furniture and shiny cars with chrome accents and automatic windows. One of the eventual neighbors had a replica horseless carriage that he'd drive around the neighborhood, offering kids rides in his pricy toy. So how were we living there? I eventually discovered, through listening to my parents argue bitterly, that Buster had us mortgaged to the hilt, even after getting his settlement. I'd get to listen to my parents argue loudly about money in the den at night while I laid in bed with my hands clapped over my ears, hearing it all. Eventually, we'd move to a more appropriate neighborhood. But that was years away.

Sissy crept up behind me and gave me a poke. I was relieved to see her. I was afraid that I'd say something stupid to this worldly person and give myself away as a joke. Sissy was never intimidated by anyone. If the President of the United States suddenly appeared in the room, she would shake his hand and then ask him why he wasn't in prison yet.

"Are you ready for your magical mystery tour?" Sissy asked her.

"Yes," Brandy said. She'd brightened upon seeing Sissy, too.

"Step right this way," Sissy said. I followed Sissy through the house. Brandy was behind me. As we passed by Mrs. Bondurant, who was enjoying another glass of wine, Sissy said, "How's it going, Fiona?"

"Fine, love," Mrs. Bondurant replied.

"How come you get to call her Fiona?" I asked when we were outside.

"She told me I could," Sissy said.

Brandy had peeled off from us to go into the garage. The garage door rumbled open—it had an automatic opener—and Brandy emerged on a bicycle that probably cost as much as our family car. It was black with white tires and had both a front rack and a back rack. She rang a little brass bell attached to the handlebars.

We mounted our Schwinns. Sissy took the lead.

Brandy's family lived in the corner house. We rode our bicycles down to the end of the road, where there was a pond.

"There's an alligator in here, so don't go swimming. You have a pool, so you shouldn't be tempted anyway," Sissy said.

"It's gross," Brandy said, squinting at it. She produced a pair of sunglasses, huge round ones with black lenses, and put them on. "So much sunshine. People must go mad down here."

"I'm planning on it," Sissy said. "Maybe halfway through high school. Especially if my parents decide to keep sending me to Catholic school."

"Religion," Brandy said. "Ick."

"Not a fan?" Sissy asked.

"No way. My parents were brought up Catholic, and they hate the church. They think subjecting kids to church is like child abuse."

"It is." Then Sissy said in her news reporter's voice, "Their theology discussion at an end, the trio moved along toward their next destination. That destination involved air conditioning and books."

"Yes, please," Brandy said.

We pedaled alongside the pond, which narrowed into a channel. At the end of the channel, we rode across a short bridge and came into the part of the neighborhood that had already been built. We traveled past houses with brightly colored stucco walls and curvy ceramic roof tiles. We came to the end of the road and took a left onto a street with grassy medians and short palm trees, and on past a golf course. There was little traffic. A Lincoln Continental Mark III honked at us and we pulled up onto the sidewalk from the edge of the road.

"Road hog!" Sissy shouted in mock rage.

A little further along, we stopped and watched a small alligator, a four-footer, its mouth open, chase a little old man across the fairway. He got into his golf cart and drove away. We continued on.

Eventually, we pulled into the library's parking lot and placed our bicycles alongside each other on metal bike rack. Brandy took a chain that was coiled up under her seat and used it to lock up her bicycle. "You're not locking yours up?"

"Who'd steal them?" Sissy replied.

We went inside and the supercooled air wrapped us in its embrace.

The librarian, a fusty elderly woman in a pink pantsuit with a wide collar, her bouffant colored a minty blue, peered at me over her glasses and said, "There you are!"

"Here I am," I said glumly.

"Go get your hug," Sissy teased.

I walked over and the old lady hugged me so hard I felt my back crack. "So sweaty," she said, smoothing my hair off my forehead. She went back behind the counter and produced three books for me. They were Hardy Boys adventures. "I'm sure you'll love these," she said. "They're new and I already checked them out for you."

"Thank you," I said. "But I haven't brought back the other books yet."

"We can live a few more days without Ray Bradbury's books. These are more appropriate for a boy of your age anyway."

When we got to a large wooden table, Sissy disappeared and came back with a hardcover titled *Dark Moon, Lost Lady.*

"Where's Brandy?" I asked her.

"She went to the bathroom to fix her makeup. Some of it streaked in the heat. Makeup! She's so lucky. Her mom's so cool."

"Fiona."

"Yes, Fiona."

"What am I supposed to do with these kids' books?" I waved the Hardy Boys books at her.

"As long as you stay on library lady's good side, I get to keep checking out these halfway decent novels. So you take them home and then bring them back in a week. I don't care. Keep letting her hug you, too."

"She smells like a dust mop."

"So what?"

"Missus Bondurant smells like roses."

"Did Fiona hug you?"

"Yes."

"Didn't take her for the type."

"Well, she is."

"Lucky you."

"Lucky me," I said morosely. "How long should we stay out? Mom's going to be mad at us."

"She can't stay mad at you, which is good for me. Same crime, same time. That's called being fair." She waved the book at me. "I could do with some home detention anyway. This book isn't going to read itself."

Brandy walked up to the table and sat down across from us. She had a library copy of *Popular Science*, encased in a heavy, clear plastic cover.

I turned in my chair and opened up one of the Hardy Boys books and pretended to read it while watching her in my peripheral vision. She looked up from her magazine and stuck her tongue out at me and I laughed.

When we were cooled down, we gathered up our books at went to the counter. The library lady took a look at Sissy's book and made a face. "I really shouldn't let you check that out. Your mother might get mad at me."

"You can put it on her account," Sissy said, producing Mom's library card from her daisy appliquéd wallet. "She wanted it."

"Oh, I guess that's okay," the library lady said skeptically. She pulled out the card and wrote my mother's name on it, LOLA PEPPER, and then date stamped it. "Tell your mother she needs to bring back *Ancient Evil* before Monday."

"I'm… I mean, she's finished with it already. Easy peasy," Sissy said.

"Aren't you pretty? Are you new here?"

"Yes," Brandy said.

"Because most little girls your age around here don't wear makeup. And those black clothes must get mighty hot out in the sunshine. Your parents shouldn't let you go around looking like that. Some boys might get the wrong idea about you."

Brandy crossed her arms and blushed angrily.

"C'mon," Sissy said, hustling her out the door and back into the blast furnace that is Florida in August.

"I don't *like* her," Brandy said deliberately in her surfer girl voice.

"I don't blame you," Sissy said.

"I'm going to go explore for a while," she said, unlocking her bicycle. "I'll see you around." She rode off in a huff.

Sissy turned on me after Brandy rode away. "Why didn't you defend her?"

"Me?"

"Yeah, you. Why didn't you defend her?"

"What was I supposed to say?"

"Something! You were supposed to say something!"

"Like what?"

"Like: You're a stupid cow, you stupid cow library lady!"

"Why didn't *you* say it?"

"Because that's *your* job. How did you get to be so stupid? Did all those hugs from strange ladies cut off the air to your brain?"

"Maybe."

"Maybe, huh? I can't be around all the time to make sure you don't screw up. So quit screwing up."

"Okay. Jeez." I took off my belt and used it to tie all our books together and then strapped them to my handlebars.

We rode home in silence.

When we got there, the garage was immaculate, save for the permanent hole in the garage wall in the shape of the nose of our Ford family truckster, which wouldn't fit entirely in the garage with the door shut without the hole. We couldn't close the garage door until the nose of the car was firmly in that hole. The outside of our house was not ornate. It was stucco'd on the exterior with a white ceramic tile roof up top. It was painted in an uncheerful green, somewhere between a moss and a mold.

Sparky was standing outside covered in sweat. "I've been waiting for you. I'm going to show you where to park your bikes."

"Where's Mom?" Sissy asked.

"One of the new neighbors came by. Some Irish lady. She told Mom that she was pulling up the grass. That crabgrass is called 'Saint Augustine' grass down here and it's the real grass. Mom told her she thought that was the most idiotic thing she ever heard in her life. The two of them are inside. I assume that they're drinking the wine that the Irish lady brought. She also brought her own glass."

"Uh huh," Sissy went.

"She told me to call her 'Fiona.'"

I threw up my hands. I put down the kickstand, hopped off my bike, unstrapped the books and tossed Sissy hers after she rolled her bike over to Sparky and told him to put it wherever it was supposed to go, that she wouldn't be participating in his stupid game. Sissy took my belt out of my hand and chucked it into the garage. "Oh no! Something's out of place!" Sissy stomped through the garage and into the house.

I heard Mom shout at her, "You're in trouble, Miss Tish!"

"Yeah, what else is new?" Sissy shouted back.

Sparky shook his head at me. So much useless emotion. I watched his eyes following someone in the street and turned around. It was Brandy riding past, not acknowledging either of us, her head held high, like a queen on horseback.

"What's that all about?" Sparky asked me.

I ran over and kicked my bicycle, which sent a shock of pain though my foot. I dropped the Hardy Boys books.

Sparky picked them up and said, "Aren't you a little old to be reading these?"

I hopped over on one foot and snatched them away from him. "I guess not. I guess I'm just a little kid!" I hobbled through the garage and into the house, where I found Mom and Missus Bondurant in the den polishing off the wine and having a great time.

Mom was half-snockered. "Go to your room and don't come out until I say you can come out."

"This one's a little darling," Missus Bondurant said. "Look at that wee face."

"Yeah? You can take him home with you if you want. Free of charge. You only have to promise to keep him." Mom looked at the books in my hands. "Hardy Boys? You get nostalgic or something? And where's your belt? You better not have lost your belt."

"I hate everyone!" I shouted dramatically. I threw the books on the floor and then kicked them with my bad foot. "Everyone!" I went to my room and slammed the door.

Nixon's Last Day

I heard the TV, but sometimes that was a hallucination. My brain sometimes interpreted white noise as a constant laugh track. I looked at my Big Ben clock, ticking loudly on the nightstand next to my bed. The radium hands told me that it was 1 a.m. We weren't running the air conditioner this week—it was like a challenge Mom told us—so my window was cranked open a bit allowing in the steamy Florida heat and the noise from the water pump coming from our future backdoor neighbor's place. They, like everyone else in the neighborhood but us, were installing a swimming pool. If you dig a hole in Florida, it will immediately fill with water and then wildlife, thus the constant droning of the water pump sucking malarial water out of the hole that had been dug for the pool. The builders would have to hurry and put the concrete in, otherwise no amount of sucking would stop Florida from taking the hole back. After the concrete went in, they'd have to fill it with water, otherwise the empty concrete pool might pop out of the ground like a cork, forced out by the constant pressure of sopping wet ground. Or crack like an egg for the same reason.

The neighborhood pond didn't exist until the developers dug the hole. They needed the dirt to create pads for the houses. There are no basements in Florida. If you built a house over the top of a basement, the basement would eventually collapse, or the house would pop up out of the ground like a capsizing ship.

I opened my door and crept out of my room and into the den. I found Mom sitting on our long couch, her bony feet crossed out in front of her, watching a black and white sitcom, the laugh track braying. She was dressed in her oldest housecoat, her chemically treated hair in rollers. She was eating radishes, swirling them in a puddle of salt on a tea saucer, crunching them. She noticed me standing there in my thin pajamas, my hair damp with sweat.

"It's okay," she said, smiling. "Come here. Come to your mother." I noticed the drink next to the tea saucer, a Manhattan by the look of it, with three maraschino cherries at the bottom of the amber glass and some slivers of ice floating at the top. She waved me closer.

I walked over to her and stood next to the TV tray. She patted the spot next to her on the couch and I sat down. She took me into her arms and ran her fingers through my hair.

No one touches me like that anymore. No one. The simple act of someone who loves you stroking your hair cannot be measured, quantified. Here in my bachelor apartment, many years in the future, the air conditioner kicking on and off, I draw my mother's face from memory and the tears spill down my face and onto the paper. In this age of irony, we're not supposed to own up to these feelings, and maybe, in this too-private moment, I'm not. I miss my mother, who died so long ago. I miss being loved by someone who knew me for who I am.

When I was married, I would have been embarrassed to ask my wife to hold me like that, even though I craved it more than the sex we shared. We had spectacular sex. My wife was an expert at it, making up for my shallow pool of pre-marital experience. But we were never close. I'd learned over the years to be a closed-off person, not allowing anyone to know me. That included my wife. And because of that we ended up divorcing. She sent me a note after our divorce saying, "I never really knew you." True enough! I'm unknowable, by force of habit.

"How did you get the nice hair in the family?" Mom asked. "What I wouldn't give to have your hair."

"I don't know."

"Well, no one expected you to know." She kissed me on top of the head. "Are you nervous about starting school again?"

"A little."

"Don't get into a fight."

"It's not my fault that kids want to beat me up." I'd been to four different schools in four years. The first day was always a trial. The year before, I'd seen *Cool Hand Luke* on TV, and knew what I had to do. I let the other kid beat me until all the girls cried. "Don't get up!" When I came home, my mother was scandalized by my bloody shirt, bruises, swollen-shut eyes and busted lips. She insisted on showing up at the school the next day to dress down the teacher, a woman who was barely out of school herself. Miss Sedlachek was nice enough, but she was kind of a dope. At least that's what Mom concluded after speaking with her.

"Go get a spoon. Hurry up." I went into the kitchen and opened one of the drawers, pulling out a teaspoon. I quickly brought it back. Mom dug one of the cherries out of the bottom of the Manhattan along with a generous amount of booze. "Open up."

I opened my mouth and she placed the cherry and booze in there like it was medicine. I chewed and swallowed, coughing a bit.

"You can sit with me for a while longer," Mom said. "I don't mind."

So I sat down with her again. I remember resting my head against her, closing my eyes. I woke up in bed the next morning. Or maybe it was afternoon. The windows were closed and the air conditioner was blowing. I walked through the house. It was empty. I was rarely completely alone back then. It was liberating and scary.

I spend most of my life alone now. It is still liberating and scary.

I went into the bathroom that I shared with Sissy and Sparky. I drew a bath. I took off my pajamas. I saw myself in the huge bathroom mirror, along with the floral wallpaper that blanketed most of the rest of the bathroom. In the mirror, I saw an undersized child with protruding ribs, a mop of blondish-brown hair atop his head, long eyelashes and thin eyebrows, but otherwise hairless. I looked into my eyes in the mirror and saw the beginnings of a lifelong sadness beginning to take root. I didn't see what was so huggable about me. The bathtub filled, I turned off the taps and got in. I held my breath and submerged into the slightly too-hot water, my arms crossed against my chest like Dracula in his coffin. I pretended that I was dead. I came up for air and lounged in the tub until my fingers and toes pruned and the water turned tepid. At some point I rubbed a bar of soap around my body in a rudimentary attempt to become clean. That was a losing battle in Florida. All you had to do was walk outside for a few minutes and you'd be bathed in sweat.

Washing in Florida is mostly removing one layer of sweat so that it can be replaced by another.

I got out of the tub, watched the water gurgle down the drain, and stood under the air conditioning vent letting the cold air dry me as the a/c struggled to keep out the heat.

I walked down to my room naked. I laid down on my bed under the air conditioning. I wound my Big Ben clock. I put on my tightie-whities and then a pair of shorts done up in red, white and blue stripes, and a sunshine yellow t-shirt. I put on my worn-out tennis shoes, the ones with the frayed laces, no socks. I rarely combed my hair back then. It mostly did whatever it wanted to do despite any efforts I made to tame it.

I strolled into the kitchen, lord of the manor, and climbed up onto the counter and found my bottles of prescription cough syrup stashed up high in a cabinet. There were two of them. One was caution tape-colored, the other traffic cone orange. I preferred the orange. It had a sticky texture on my tongue, and filled the top of my skull to the center of my chest with a feeling like having a glass of ice water poured into me. The yellow one was okay, too, but far less potent. It had a more medicinal taste to it. I compared the two bottles, holding one in each hand. The yellow one had more liquid in it, so I decided to go ahead and take a swig of that, for fairness' sake. "Here's mud in your eye," I said, unscrewing the child-proof cap. I peeled the crust of dried medicine from around the bottle's mouth and ate it. Then I took a quick chug. I put them

35

both away, climbed down, and immediately felt a familiar wave of tranquility wash over me. "Holy Mary, mother of God," I whispered. "Pray for our sinners."

I found a Robert Ludlum novel on the end table next to the lamp. I picked it up and flipped it open. I was about an English professor investigating a vast international conspiracy that was taking place, for some reason, at a sleepy New England college. It was breezily written and fun. I could see why my mother had picked this one up. I was three or four chapters in when the door from the garage burst open and my sister came in toting a paper bag filled with groceries.

"Look who's up," Sissy said. "Get your beauty sleep in?"

"Maybe," I said, dog-earing my page and placing the book back where I found it.

"How far did you get in that one? Did you get to the S-E-X part yet?" Sissy set the groceries down on the kitchen floor. She slapped her hands together and then showed them to me. "Look at my hands."

"What about them?"

"Why aren't you carrying in the groceries?"

Mom walked in with two bags, one in each arm. "Look who's up! Get your beauty sleep in?"

"I already said that," Sissy said.

"I don't see you carrying groceries. I only see you standing around yammering like there aren't groceries in the car. I suppose you think they'll carry themselves in." She set the groceries on the kitchen counter. "Well?" She was looking at me.

I got up and went outside. The roiling heat washed over me and I began to sweat anew. It was nice being clean for an hour or so, but Florida wasn't having it. I grabbed a doubled-up bag, which was full of canned vegetables, and lugged it indoors.

"Where's your brother?" Mom shouted at me. "Where's he hiding?"

"I don't know," I said. "How'm I supposed to keep track of him? He's like some sort of secret agent." I thought about the college professor in the book, who was also a secret agent.

Mom was half-psychic. "Have you been reading my book?"

"What? No!"

"You *have* been reading my book. You have your own books. All that weird science fiction. My books are for adults."

"Because they're full of S-E-X," Sissy said, bringing in the final bag of groceries. "I brought in more groceries than you did, Buzz. You barely did a thing!"

"How am I in trouble?" I asked helplessly.

"Look at him standing there, like he's innocent," Mom said, putting away the groceries. "But he's been reading my book. I can tell just by looking at him, all squirmy, that he's been reading my book. I guess I can't leave anything out without you going through it. Your poor old mother has so very few joys in life, and you have to make me feel bad about one of them. I guess that's my cross to bear. Along with hoping and praying for a daughter and ending up with this one."

"I knew it would come back to me!" Sissy said, hands on hips. "It always comes back to me."

"Now she's shouting at me!" Mom said. "I'm cursed! You kids finish putting away the groceries. I have a headache. I have to lie down." She walked out of the kitchen, through the dining room and into her bedroom, shutting the door.

"You should put the groceries away because I had to go to the store with her. She got into an argument with the cashier about a can of peeled tomatoes. It was humiliating. Then she was directing traffic in the aisles again like a cop." Sissy walked over to me and stared into my eyes. "You got into your cough syrup again."

"So? It's *my* cough syrup."

"You're only supposed to take it when you have a cough."

"I'm heading off the cough at the pass, John Wayne-style."

"Sure you are. You know I don't like it when you get all dopey on your cough syrup. You're no fun when you're all dopey."

"You can go hang out with Sparky."

"Who knows where he is? I sure don't."

I managed to get the groceries stowed in the cupboard and fridge. I came around a corner and Sissy was standing there with a bottle of Windex. "Hold up there, pilgrim," she drawled out. "I'm going to need you to drop your gun and raise those hands."

I pretended to undo a pistol belt and slowly raised my hands. "B-but wuh-what did I do?" I yammered out, in an approximation of Jimmy Stewart.

"Get those hands up higher, or I'll blast yuh!"

I sprinted into the kitchen, flung open the cabinet below the sink and found a bottle of Fantastik. As Sissy ran into the kitchen, I leapt onto the kitchen counter belly first and slid over it and back into the den, nearly landing on my head. She fired and missed and I returned fire.

It developed into an epic, hour-long gun battle, with me securing a roll of toilet paper and a bucket of water, wetting the toilet paper and flinging it at her, and Sissy wetting down paper towels in the kitchen sink and chucking them at me.

The battle was fully raging when Sparky walked in on us, aghast at the disorder. Pieces of paper towels and wads of toilet paper were stuck to walls and furniture. Our bottles of cleaner were nearly gone, and ammonia permeated the air.

"Have you two completely lost your minds?" Sparky asked indignantly.

We each stood up slowly and looked around the room at the wreckage. "Um," I went.

"That's what I thought," he said. "Where's Mom?"

"In bed," Sissy said.

"Then we'd better clean all this up quietly, right?"

When he made sense, we both followed his directions. So we let him be the boss. He supervised all the cleaning up, and there was a lot of it. When we were done, he sat us down on the couch and gave us the obligatory lecture about cleanliness, order and the many satisfactions involved in cleanliness and order. "Speaking of which, I'm going to have to insist that you comb your hair," he said to me.

"Comb my hair?"

"It's a very simple process, one that even you can comprehend. Now, go get your comb."

"I don't know where it is."

"Then go find it."

I went into the bathroom and searched through the cabinet under the sink and in a drawer that was supposed to be dedicated to me, but that Sissy had taken over. I found the comb in the back of the drawer. It was one of those black plastic numbers that cost 25 cents at the checkout counter.

"I think this is it," I said, returning with the grooming implement in hand.

"That better not be mine," Sparky said.

"For crying out loud," Sissy said. "Here's what you do, Buzz. Punch him right in the mouth. Don't let him tell you what to do."

"You can be quiet, madam. I'm speaking with our little brother. He needs instruction."

"If he needs instruction, I'll be the one to give it to him, Mister Spock."

"I'm in charge here. You'll both listen to me."

"Slug him, Buzz. Right in his stupid, know-it-all face."

I looked back and forth from one to the other. It was all so confusing. I held up the comb. "Ready."

"Ugh!" Sissy went. "I can't sit here and watch this! I'm going to my room."

Sparky had me comb my hair over the opposite way that it usually fell, and then comb it all the way back, and then all the way forward. Finally, he had me comb it the way it usually fell. "Much better. Go take a look in the mirror."

I went into the bathroom and looked in the mirror. I didn't look any different than usual, but I didn't have the heart to tell Sparky. I tossed the comb back into the drawer. I walked back out into the living room and said, "Yes. Much better."

We heard the bedroom door open and Mom came walking out in her housecoat and slippers, her hair in curlers. "What time is it?" she asked groggily. She sniffed the air. "Did you kids clean up? Without being told?"

"Yes," Sparky said, his eyes darting nervously. "It's a surprise."

"What a nice surprise! Did this one help?"

"Yes," Sparky said. "So did Sissy. She's so tired that she had to go to her room."

"This is unexpected. What would you like for dinner tonight?"

Sparky and I looked at each other. It would have to be something pre-packaged. Something that wouldn't have Mom's culinary touch. Something marginally edible.

"Banquet frozen dinner?" Sparky offered. "I can put it in the oven for you. No problem at all. I'll even make the mashed potatoes to go along with it." Sparky was getting good at mashed potatoes.

"Can of corn?" I offered. I could put that into a pot and let it heat.

"Sounds nice. You're such nice kids. Even the other one. Can't believe she helped out."

"She was in charge of the Windex," Sparky said. "Buzz here even cleaned the walls." Our eyes searched the room for a moment and we both settled on a tiny scrap of toilet paper stuck to the wood paneling, which we quickly looked away from.

Mom plopped down on the couch. "One of you kids want to pour me a glass of wine?"

"I'll do it," I said.

"Let's have your brother do it, honey. Remember how you broke the wineglass last time? And where's Miss Tish? She should be out here. Your father's not coming home until tomorrow, so we're going to have a nice relaxing evening. Hang out like we're a family or something. It'll be relaxing."

"Okay, Mom," Sparky said, returning with a glass of red wine.

"You're okay heating up dinner?"

Sparky nodded his head. He liked being in charge.

I turned on the TV and it was full of newsmen. They were abuzz over rumors that the president would be resigning. They were all grave, older white men and every word out of their mouths sounded important. On the half-hour, one of them would recap the day's news, which was that the president would come on TV during the night and resign. And then some boring guy that no one had voted for would take over as president and things would be normal again, whatever that was.

Sparky finished up dinner and all of us made a plate in the kitchen and took it out to the den. Sissy and I sat on the carpet together. The food tasted approximately like food. Sparky was willing himself into a becoming a home chef by watching Julia Child's show on the PBS TV station. "Butter!" she'd shout, and Sparky would take note. Sparky did all the cooking when we were college roommates. The first time I ever gained substantial weight was in college.

Walter Cronkite said that the president would be going to San Clemente after he resigned. "Is that an island prison?" Sissy asked.

"It's where he's from," Sparky said.

"Is where he's from an island prison?" Sissy asked. "With French guards? Who have rifles with bayonets?"

"No," Sparky said. "This whole thing has been insane."

"I voted for Kennedy," Mom said. "Back when they were running against each other. Nixon's always been a sweaty little man. And that mousey wife of Nixon's is creepy. 'Republican cloth coat.' What does that have to do with anything? Kennedy had great hair. And Jackie is pure class. All of the Kennedys had great hair, come to think of it. Your hair looks just like Bobby's did, Buzz." Mom was getting a little tight. I think she was on her third or fourth glass of wine. "President Kennedy was very handsome. And of course he was Catholic. He was funny, too." Her face darkened. "Don't tell your father that I voted for Kennedy. He's a Nixon man. He's going to be very upset that he's resigned."

"Nixon will try to build a rubber life raft out of old raincoats to get away, but the guards will catch him and bring him back. He'll eat the maggots out of the rotten mush they give him because maggots are full of protein," Sissy said knowledgeably.

"I'm trying to digest the dinner your brother slaved over, Miss Tish," Mom said. "I don't want to hear about that sweaty little man eating maggots."

"Also, he's not under arrest," Sparky said irritably.

"You two should get ready for bed."

"But I want to watch the guards haul Nixon away," Sissy said.

"Guards aren't going to be hauling Nixon away," Sparky snapped. "He's not under arrest. He's merely quitting his job and going home."

"They'll drag him away, kicking and screaming," Sissy insisted. "For the Republic!"

"Get ready for bed and you can come back out and watch the rest of this. It's the only thing on now anyway," Mom said. "Sparky, go get your mother another sip of wine." She waved the empty glass at him.

We rushed into our respective bedrooms and changed into our pajamas.

Eventually, after another boring hour of important old men gravely intoning their dismay about the state of the nation, we finally got to the part where Nixon resigned. First there was the Seal of the President of the United States on the screen, and then there he was with his hooded eyes and sinister face. He talked about all of his accomplishments. He talked about how he was a peacemaker. He talked about how Congress was too busy with him to do the nation's business. He talked about himself for what seemed like hours. Somewhere in there, he resigned.

"That's it?" Sissy roared. "Where are the guards? Where are the heavy iron chains? We've been cheated!"

"Go to bed," Mom said. "It's over. Your father will be upset."

"This whole thing went on forever!" Sissy shouted. "The people demand justice!"

"So what's the new guy's name again?" I asked.

"Ford," Sparky said. "His name is Ford. He's from Michigan."

"How did someone from Michigan end up as president? Is that legal?" I asked.

"Michigan is part of the United States, despite what Buster has to say about it," Sparky said. Buster was a big Ohio State fan. Every time he saw Michigan head coach Bo Schembechler on TV he'd shout, "Traitor!" Before he was the head coach of Michigan, he was assistant to Coach Woody Hayes at Ohio State. Buster put Woody Hayes ahead of Jesus Christ as the greatest human being ever to live.

Eventually, we'd find out that this Ford guy, our pretend president, in addition to being from Michigan, had also played football at Michigan. It was too much to take.

Sissy and I wandered off to bed. We talked through the thin wall separating our rooms. "I heard you two telling Mom that we cleaned the house."

"It's kind of true," I said.

"I bet she didn't really believe it."

"She seemed like she believed it."

"It was a nice lie. Sparky did a good job selling it."

"He's not as bad as you say."

"I know. I have to give him grief. That's my job. I have to keep him on his toes. You, too. You're both so dumb in your own stupid ways that I feel that it's my duty as your only sister to help you along in life. I don't know where either one of you would be without my constant guidance."

"I can hear you talking through the walls, you weirdos!" Mom shouted. "Shut up and go to sleep!"

"Love you, Mom!" Sissy sang out.

"Oh be quiet!"

We shut up. The air conditioner clunked on and cool air blew in over my head. The pool pump behind the house made its clamor. In all that white noise, I drifted off and dreamt of Richard Nixon being dragged away by Robespierre and the Jacobins through the streets of 18th century Paris to the guillotine, shouting, "I'm not a crook!"

The Mystery of Faith

Because Sissy was going to Catholic school, we all had to suffer by going to mass at some point on Saturday or Sunday and giving the church a few dollar bills stuffed in a special envelope with our name on it that let them know that we were going to church. Otherwise, we would have had to pay full price for Sissy's schooling. Suffering was part of our faith. The other part of being Catholic was experiencing guilt any time we felt even the slightest hint of pleasure.

Eventually, I would end up in Catholic school, too. But that was years away.

We went whenever Mom wasn't working on either Saturday or Sunday. Her work schedule varied at Maas Brothers. All that china wasn't going to sell itself. We learned terms like "Fiestaware," "Corelle," "Royal Vienna" and "Wedgwood Blue" from listening to Mom complain about her customers, who were either a mass of uncultured nitwits with no taste, or snobs who knew too much about fine china. "No one should care that much about plates."

One of her customers looked at her name tag and informed her, in a snooty British accent, that "Pepper" was a poor person's name where she came from.

"Is that right?" Mom said. "Welcome to America, honey."

Rarely did our father attend church with us. He was raised as a Methodist, but converted over to the Catholic Church for Mom's sake. Mom married him because he drove a convertible Chevy, rolled his jeans over his engineer boots, and slicked his dark curly hair back with some sort of grease. Plus, she said, he looked like her heartthrob—Harry Belafonte. Dad came over to our grandparents' house one time when the two of them were dating and set his wallet on the counter on his way to using the facilities. Mom and Uncle Ralph lunged for the wallet, dug through it for his driver's license and were disappointed to find out that he was officially Caucasian. I found this story hilarious because my father is a virulent racist. He used the "N" word in casual conversation and once said that Martin Luther King Jr. "got what was coming to him."

My mother forgave him his racism because, she said, she was in love with him and you forgave people for all sorts of things when you were in love with them.

In my teenage years, I would daydream of the Black Panthers showing up to drag him away and put him on trial for all his hate crimes. It never happened, of course. The last I heard, my father was living in a trailer park near Lakeland, Florida with his third or fourth wife.

I asked my mother what happened to the convertible Chevy. She said Dad sold it and bought a Renault, which was a lemon. After the Renault, he settled on Fords because his late father worked in the Ford assembly plant in Lorain, Ohio. Both his parents were dead before I was born.

Dad's mother, who my mother described as saintly and quite possibly Black, died of a brain tumor that was the size of a grapefruit. Brain tumors, in my experience, are all the size of a piece of citrus. It was the 1950's and no one could do anything about it but give her morphine and sit and watch her die, which Dad did. Dad's devotion to his mother was part of the reason that my mother fell for him. I think it was the entire reason. She was willing to ignore everything wrong with him because he'd done one thing right. He'd shown a loving devotion to his mother during her illness that touched my mother's heart irrevocably.

Dad's father died after driving his car into Lake Erie off a cliff. He was probably drunk, which is a problem on the Pepper side of the family. Most Peppers I've met are devoted drinkers. Most of them are sociopaths, too.

Mom found Dad's latent Methodism suspicious, so she never pushed him to accompany us to church. He mostly stayed home and watched TV, which he considered a better use of his time.

"Have you ever been to a Methodist service?" Mom asked me one time during a car ride to the grocery store. "It's not like a real church. It's phony. You can tell that they're just pretending to worship God." The only churches I'd been to were the ones that my mother forced me to attend, all Catholic. She assured me that I'd be scandalized by what goes on in a Protestant church and to avoid them at all cost.

"Consider it done," I told her.

The only Catholic activity that my father participated in was a co-ed Catholic bowling league. Beer was involved, which my father approved of, and there were trophies to be won as well. Mom was an excellent bowler and so was Dad. They were raised in Ohio, where it is considered a national pastime. So with the promise of beer and trophies, my father found his faith at Sarasota Lanes.

I am a lousy bowler. To be completely clear, I am a lousy athlete. There is no American sport that I have not graced with my athletic incompetence. In high school, at Sarasota Central Catholic, I came closest to a sport that I was almost good at. I ran track. I ran the 400, the 800 and the mile. I was somewhat fast, but never quite quick enough to win. I ran so hard that I would vomit at the end of each race. If I didn't eat beforehand, I would dry-heave, which is worse than vomiting in my estimation. So out gushed my mother's hideous version of spaghetti, with its watery unseasoned sauce and noodles overcooked into mush.

My mother considered dried parsley the ultimate seasoning and used it in just about everything. The other seasonings were used so sparingly that we had the same little tins all the way through my childhood. I came home on leave from the Army once, and spun the lazy susan in our cupboard, admiring the classic designs on the vintage seasoning tins from the 1950's. I was a trained illustrator by then, having gotten a BFA at the University of Florida. My MOS in the Army was 81E, which is illustrator.

On this Sunday, the last one before school started that Monday, we were sitting in a hard wooden pew looking toward the front of the church at the corpse of our Savior tacked to a couple of wooden boards. He wasn't in great shape. Above His head was a sign that read: *INRI*. Sissy helpfully interpreted it as meaning, "I'm Nailed Right In." "And He is, too. Those Romans don't fool around," Sissy whispered to me.

"What are you two weirdos talking about?" Mom hissed at us.

"We're praying," Sissy said.

"I'm praying that I don't get beat to death at school tomorrow," I said.

"I'm praying that the priest today isn't Father John," Sissy said.

"Amen to that," Mom said. "Boring old jerk. And Buzz... stop being so dramatic."

We'd only been coming to this church for the few months that we'd been living in Sarasota, but Father John was already one of the lowlights. He dragged out mass until the next mass was ready to start. He did all the longest prayers in the hymnal. His homilies were the definition of tedium. His monotone voice was full of scorn. He was worse than Father Vito who none of us could understand. "What's he saying?" Mom would ask through the whole Italian priest's mass. Father John was worse than Father Gerry who talked about how much he suffered back in Ireland, which was a lot to hear him tell it. "The Irish think they have the misery market cornered," Mom would mutter irritably. "Big deal. I grew up in Cleveland. You don't hear *me* complaining."

Yes, Father John was the worst, and he was as American as Eisenhower. Kind of looked like Ike, too.

The only one of us who was actually praying was Sparky, who was still down on the kneeler. His eyes were closed. Finally, he crossed himself and sat back in the pew.

"That took a while," Mom carped. "Whatever it was you prayed for, it had better be worth it."

"I prayed for patience," Sparky said.

"Good luck with that," Mom said, nodding toward the back of the church. The processional had started, along with the droning organ music.

We all stood up and there he was, slowly ambulating down the center aisle along with a couple of long-haired altar boys. It was Father John and his bitter, pinched face and his coke-bottle glasses.

"Clearly, prayer doesn't work. I should have lit a candle or two," Sissy said.

"Quiet," Mom snapped. But you could tell by her expression that she was in no mood for Father John either.

We were, all of us, duded up in our finest polyester and rayon. The church was air conditioned, so we at least had that working in our favor. I could feel myself weakening, like I wanted to make a break for it and sprint out the door and down Bee Ridge Road as quickly as my feet could take me. I imagined myself running down the road right up until I tripped over an errant hubcap or threw up. Or both.

"Doom," Sissy whispered dramatically in the voice of the local horror show host, Doctor Paul Bearer. "Doo-oo-oom."

Mom squinted angrily at her. "Mmm-hmm," she went. "I have my eye on you. Both of you." She could threaten to tell our father about us. That was usually a last resort. It was a crap shoot whether he'd care at all about our behavior at church. At this point in his day, he'd be eating Eggo waffles with extra margarine and syrup, which had a soothing effect on him. Maybe golf would be on the tube, or a Sunday morning war movie featuring Lee Marvin slaughtering a bunch of Nazis. At 11 a.m., he'd crack his first beer of the day, saying, "It's noon somewhere."

"This is taking forever," Sissy said.

"Let us proclaim the mystery of faith," I said.

"Please shut up," Sissy said.

"I'm hoping for God to strike me dead at some point," I said.

"Quiet," Mom said. "And no blasphemy in church. You can save it for the parking lot if we ever get out of here."

Eventually, Father John made it all the way to the altar, but not without a stumble or two. The altar boys looked ready to catch him if he clattered to the floor, but it wasn't necessary. The service began and Father John took his sweet time reading and reading the same stuff we had to hear every Sunday. We'd memorized most of it. There were three prayers: the medium one, which was the usual one; the short one, which only young priests used; and the long one, which only Father John read. Somewhere in that long prayer, Father John could be heard praying for the pope and every Saint in existence, each syllable enunciated in sharp reproach to everyone who was squirming in their seats, which was nearly every parishioner. During the homily, I leaned against Mom and she allowed it. She patted me solicitously and said, "Don't worry, it'll be over soon."

45

"Don't lie to him," Sissy said. "Liars go to hell."

"I'll deal with *you* when we get in the car," Mom said.

Sparky's eyes had glazed over. I think he was working out a math problem on an imaginary blackboard, his happy place.

At some point, we were all getting up to go to communion. Christ Himself was inside each flavorless wafer that was placed on our tongues. We watched a family futilely attempt to escape after they took communion, but Father John was quicker than he looked and blocked their path, shaming them back to their places in the pews.

Then came Father John's admonishment at the end of mass, about how the Catholic faith was not like the works bar at Burger Chef. "You are not allowed to pick and choose the ingredients of your faith. And what are you doing, young lady?"

He was looking at Sissy, whose tongue tip was sticking precisely out of her mouth, her nose squinched up like a pig's nose.

"Oh, I can't believe it!" Mom said loudly enough that it echoed throughout the church. Everyone was looking at us now. "That's it! We're going to have a discussion when we get home!"

The tongue retracted and Sissy's mouth transformed into a sly, satisfied smile, her nose returning to its usual button shape. "What?" she went.

"And *you* stop laughing!" Mom shouted at me.

Sparky audibly groaned. His cross to bear was having a chaotic family. Disorder upset him. Sparky had a collection of immaculately maintained Matchbox cars that he kept in precise order on top of his bureau. Sissy liked to sneak into his room and slightly move one of the cars, just enough that he'd notice it. An hour or two later, we'd hear: "Who's been moving my cars? Stay out of my room!" And Sissy would grab my forearm with both hands and giggle uncontrollably.

My Matchbox cars were always destroyed. I made little ramps and sent them flying, crashing them into walls and each other. I'd make screaming sounds as the imagined drivers, knowing that they were flying to their respective dooms, gasped out their rage at the dying of their individual light. I left the cars on top of the water heater so their tires would be flat, just like with my Army men, who I'd leave on top of light bulbs until they melted. I stole Sparky's wood burning kit so I could bore tiny bullet holes in the sides of the Matchbox cars. Sorry, Bonny and Clyde, but justice has caught up with you in the form of an FBI hit squad. Blam, blam! Sparky would find these ruined cars and ask me how I could do such a thing. "I dunno," I'd unhelpfully explain with a shrug. My G.I. Joe suffered a similar fate, tied up with dental floss and interrogated by the Viet Cong atop a charcoal grill. "Talk, American capitalist pig! John Wayne won't save you now!" I'd imagine G.I. Joe spitting in my face. I'd cooly wipe the spit away, puff on a candy cigarette, and inform him that my masters in Hanoi and Moscow had already signed his death warrant. "Ah, hah-hah-hah!" There was no saving G.I. Joe. My father caught me doing this and asked, "What are you doing? Playing with dollies?" He snickered at me. My face burned red with humiliation. That's when my heavily scarred G.I. Joe went permanently into a box in the back of the closet. I hid my Matchbox cars, too, because if Mom found them, I'd get the lecture about how I destroy everything and break her heart in the process and how it was too bad I wasn't a normal child with normal interests and that my destructive tendencies were probably Sissy's fault in some way that Mom hadn't yet figured out. Then she'd look at whatever I happened to be drawing and ask, "What's that supposed to be? Something weird?" Usually, it was something she'd consider weird—big-headed aliens abducting Johnny Cash for instance. "Come with us, Man in Black. Mars needs music." And Johnny Cash retorts, "My name is Sue! How do you do?" Or I was practicing drawing Jim Brown, the greatest athlete in human history. One or the other. By the time I was ten, I could have wallpapered my room with portraits of Jim Brown. I went through a lot of orange and brown crayons.

Shortly after I got out of the Army, I went to see *Mars Attacks!* at the AMC 6 theater in Sarasota Square Mall with Sparky. When Jim Brown strode onto the screen, Sparky noted drily, "Now I know why we're here."

"Jim Brown!" I went, pumping a fist.

Somehow, we made it to the Ford family truckster without running into the priest. We slowly navigated out of the parking lot and toward Bee Ridge Road, where a Sarasota County sheriff's deputy was standing in the street, stopping traffic to allow the Catholics to escape from their purgatory on earth. Mom was fuming. The truckster jerked forward and backward as she stomped on the gas and brakes, sometimes simultaneously. Our mother's driving made it possible to get car sickness after ten minutes riding with her. Sparky sat up front in an impossibly erect manor, the only member of the family who'd bothered to belt himself in. Sissy and I slid around in the backseat, like passengers on a ship traversing a troubled sea. We occasionally both ended up on the same side of the vehicle, sliding across the vinyl bench seat, slamming into one door or the other.

"I've never been so humiliated in my entire life!" Mom shouted over the top of WKXY, which was blasting out of a tinny speaker embedded in the dusty dashboard. "You're havin' muh babe-uh!" Paul Anka sang. "I can't even tell you how much trouble you're both in. But not you, Sparky. As usual, Sparky is the only one who can manage to behave. I don't even know what I did to deserve this. The only saving grace is that you'll all be in school tomorrow. You'd better shape up! That's all I have to say." It wasn't all she had to say. She continued her tirade the rest of the car ride home.

Sparky got out and opened the garage door and Mom slowly navigated the truckster in until its nose fit snuggly in the hole in the garage wall that had been created the first time Mom parked the car in there. Sparky shut the garage door, making sure he was on the driver's side before closing it. There was only an inch separating the back of the truckster from the garage door when it was shut. No one had ever commented on this ad hoc parking arrangement.

"Go change out of your church clothes," Mom told us. "And don't mention the *incident* to your father. I don't want him flying off the handle just because you two can't be bothered to behave yourselves."

So our punishment ended up being our mother's tirade in the truckster. That was something we could both live with.

We pushed through the door and into the den, where our father was laid out on the floor like some snoozing beast in a zoo, a half-dozen empties arrayed around his bulky body. He was wearing a v-neck t-shirt and a pair of cut-offs, shoeless and sockless. The TV was blaring out a random Western. The Indians were losing, just like back in Cleveland. He woke up and observed us walking in. "You have a good time in church?" he asked Sissy.

"I did," she said beaming. "I don't know about the rest of them."

"What about you?" he asked me.

"It picked up near the end," I said.

"All right. Good enough. What's up with your mother? She in one of her moods?" Buster eyed Mom warily as she huffed her way through the den, into the kitchen and through the dining room so she could go into their bedroom and change.

"You know how she is," Sissy said conspiratorially. She leapt over Buster and went to her room.

Sparky came in and glared at Buster contemptuously. Buster said, "You ever change the oil in a car? I ever show you how?"

"I can figure it out," Sparky said.

"Because someone needs to change the oil in your mother's car."

"Okay," Sparky said. "I assume that means me."

"This isn't a free ride," Buster said.

"I didn't assume it was," Sparky said.

"I bought the oil filter and the oil. They're on the workbench."

"Thank you for that bit of information."

"I'd show you how it's done," Buster said, sitting up. "But you know. My back."

"I'm aware of your condition."

"I wish you wouldn't give me so much lip."

"I wasn't aware that I was giving you lip. I will adjust my behavior in the future."

"See that you do." Buster turned and glared at me. "What are you looking at?"

"Can I help?" I genuinely wanted to be helpful. It wasn't a ploy.

Sparky said, "Your help isn't required."

"Let him watch," Buster said. "He's got to learn at some point."

"He can watch," Sparky said. "But no touching."

Buster managed to pull himself to his feet with great effort. "God damn back," he grumbled. His legs spasmed.

"Go get changed," Sparky told me. "I'll meet you out there."

I put on my worst clothes in anticipation of having them splattered with oil. I imagined myself tugging on wrenches and jacking up the car. I imagined all that work pumping up my muscles. I imagined myself wiping well-earned sweat off my forehead. It was glorious and manly. Then Brandy would like me, because I was all sweaty and manly and smelled like motor oil. By the time I got out there, the garage door was open again and Buster had backed the car away from its customary position of being embedded in the wall. I was ready to fetch cans of oil. I was ready to jack the car up. I was ready for any way I could be helpful. I was practically hopping up and down in joyful anticipation of being a useful human being who was worthy of a pretty girl's love.

The car engine was ticking as it cooled. Sparky placed a cinderblock behind the back tire and inserted the jack in the slot in the bumper. He jacked the car up. He'd taken the car's manual out of the glove box and knew where the little nut was underneath. "Observe, little brother." He unscrewed the lid up top where the fresh oil would go in. "Do you know why we do that?"

Buster said, "Let's not take all day." He kicked a metal pan under the car. "Get a move-on."

"Right," Sparky said, giving me a little apologetic shrug. He slid under the car, on the dusty garage floor, with a socket wrench in his hand. A minute later, I watched black motor oil glug out of the bottom of the car and into the metal pan.

"Go dig a couple of milk jugs out of the trash," Buster said.

Can do! I thought. I pushed through the side door out to where our metal trash cans were located, on the same pad with our air conditioning unit, which was straining as usual. I found the packaging for the oil filter there and tossed it aside. I found a couple of empty plastic milk jugs and brought them inside the garage.

Sparky was under the car again. "This oil filter doesn't fit."

"Do I have to do it myself?" Buster shouted. "Fine! I'll do it myself." He pulled Sparky out from under the vehicle by his ankles, got down and slid under the car himself. We heard him grunting for several minutes. "Doesn't fit? Bullshit!" He crawled out from under the car and, with showy effort, struggled to his feet. "I have to do everything around here myself. I put the nut back on, too." He shoved the spout onto the first oil

49

can and emptied it into the hole up top. "You two pour the used oil into the milk jugs and then bury the jugs in the trash."

We poured the thick, used oil into the milk jugs. I wiped the pan down with one of my old shirts, which had been converted into a rag.

Sparky and I carried the warm jugs of used oil out to the trash. That's where he spotted the oil filter box. He picked it up and did something that Buster hadn't bothered to do. He read what was on the side. "This is for a Chevy!" Sparky said. "Stop!" Sparky ran back into the garage with the box.

But it was too late. Buster had let the car off its jack and was starting the engine. Brand new oil spurted all over the place. Buster shut down the engine and attempted to accuse Sparky of wrongdoing, but it wasn't going to happen. He stood before Sparky's rage, a contained and yet frightening thing because of its focus.

Sparky held out the box and said through gritted teeth, "You bought the wrong filter." It was a statement. It was an accusation. It was a judgment. Guilty!

Buster backed up a step. "How was I supposed to know?"

Sparky held out his hand. "Money."

Buster pulled his bloated wallet out of the back pocket of his cutoffs. He gave Sparky a few bills. Sparky neatly folded the money and stuffed it in his front pocket. "I'll be back." He walked over to his bicycle and mounted it. He rode off toward Gulf Gate Mall, where there was an auto store. It was a few miles away. That would give Sparky time to finish seething.

Buster turned to me and said, "How was I supposed to know?"

"It's a mystery," I said. "Like God's grace."

"Stop saying weird stuff," Buster said, and he went inside, slamming the door behind him.

Fight!

I walked down to the bus stop on my own. Sissy's Catholic bus would come later. Sparky's Pine View School for the Gifted bus already came. I made my way down to the corner of Captiva Drive and Beneva Road to wait for the bus to Gulf Gate Elementary School. I could have ridden my bike to school, but it was the first day of school and I needed to save up my energy for getting beat-up. Nothing takes it out of you like someone you just met beating the tar out of you. Bike rides are nearly impossible with bruised ribs.

I was in my new school clothes. I had on a paisley shirt with a huge collar and a gold zipper. If I pulled down the gold zipper, my sunken chest would be revealed. I was no Tom Jones, so I kept it zipped to the top. Body shame is part of being Catholic. I wore a pair of blue hip-huggers with flared legs. I had on a pair of brown earth shoes, which were driving me nuts because the toes were higher than the heels. There was some reason for that. On the sole was an etched picture of the bottom of a foot. If I stepped in sand or mud, it would stamp a cartoon image of a bare foot there. Underneath, I wore a pair of too-tight briefs and knee-high sweat socks. I hated these clothes. They were all picked out by my mother at Maas Brothers, where she got an employee discount.

I was standing by the side of the road, awaiting the bus, when I heard footsteps clicking on the melty asphalt behind me. I turned around and Brandy was there, dressed less weirdly than usual.

"Buzz, right?" she asked.

"Right," I said. "And you are…?"

She laughed musically. "You know who I am."

"I guess I do."

"You look a little nervous."

"It's the fifth annual, 'Beat Buzz Up Day.' This isn't a day of celebration for me. Quite the opposite, in fact."

"Girls can be mean, too." Brandy's makeup was slightly toned down. She wore a blue-striped nautically themed top and white bellbottoms. She had on the same black shoes from before—mary janes.

We both carried empty bookbags. By the end of the day, they'd be full.

"I thought you'd be going to Pine View with my brother," I said.

"I'm sick of going to schools like that. I wanted to go to regular school for a while. See what that's like." She smiled winningly. She had a look in her eye that I recognized. I saw it in my own eyes when I looked in the mirror. It was a sadness that was beginning to seep in through the cracks in my foundation. "You can hang out with me, if you like. I have a mean right hook."

"It's okay. Your brother put me through a course of instruction." I attempted to smile at her. I'm not sure how it came out. Badly, judging by her reaction. "Fighting may not be necessary. These Florida kids may be different. Less prone to violence."

"I wouldn't bet on it," she said. "Anyway, the offer stands."

"I'm sure you'll find some girls to hang out with."

"Suit yourself." She turned slightly away from me and peered off into the middle distance, indicating the end of the conversation.

So I'd screwed that up nicely. In the years to come, I'd outdo that performance over and over. But let's not get ahead of ourselves.

We watched silently as a yellow Blue Bird bus trundled slowly our way, stopping at nearly every corner on Beneva Road, clogging up morning traffic, such as it was. Sarasota was a sleepy small town at the time, most famous for once being the winter home of the Ringling Brothers circus. Across the street from us was a cow pasture. In a few years, it would transform into a PGA golf course and gated community. For now, we got to watch hybrid Brangus cattle mill about chewing on tufts of crabgrass, occasionally peering up at us with their stupid moo-cow eyes, their ears flapping around as bugs circled their heads.

The bus made it to us, huffed to a stop, and the door squealed open revealing a driver with stringy hair wearing a trucker's hat, a red tube top, cut-offs and a pair of dirty flip-flops. She did not look at either one of us. Her mien informed me that I was beneath her contempt. I climbed on board the bus and saw one bench seat that was unoccupied near the rear of the bus. I made a beeline for it and sat down. The seat was hard green vinyl and slightly tacky, like someone had scraped chewing gum off it recently. That was probably the case, judging by the number of kids chewing gum on that bus.

Brandy sat next to another girl further up. Neither of them acknowledged the other.

The bus door squealed shut and, with a pop and a hiss, the bus began to roll forward.

A pair of hands slapped down on my shoulders, and an enormous face loomed into view on my right. "You're new," the moon face said. It was framed by brown hair. A premature mustache was making an appearance on its upper lip.

"That was quick," I said aloud. "A new record."

"A new what?" the moon face asked.

"A new record. This is the fastest time ever. Are you going to beat me up on the bus, or are we waiting til we get to school?"

"You misunderstand me, friend. I'm being friendly." He squeezed my shoulders hard. "We're friends now. You and me."

"Okay," I said.

"You have a name, new guy?"

"Buzz."

He laughed. "That's a name?"

"It's what I go by, so sure."

"You didn't ask my name."

"What's your name?"

"Billy."

"Hello, Billy."

"You must be rich coming out of that new neighborhood."

"Not me."

"What about the girl you got on with? She rich?"

"I don't know. Probably."

"I will have to meet her then. Rich people are different than you and me. Know how?"

"How?"

"They got more money!" He laughed at the joke for a while, and then I joined in to be polite. I'm not sure if he knew he'd borrowed the joke from Hemingway, but I did. In addition to Ray Bradbury that summer, I'd been reading Hemingway and Steinbeck. Adult concerns—my father's concept of manliness, for example—were mysterious to me and the books, especially Hemingway, seemed to shine a light on what formed them. "Moving up." Billy got out of his seat and sat down next to me. He was a massive sample of human being, nearly adult-sized. We soon figured out that we were in the same grade and in the same class. "Mind if I cheat off you?" he asked.

"Do you mind getting B's?"

"Not at all!" Billy laughed again. It was contagious. I laughed along with him. Part of the laughter was relief that Billy wasn't going to beat the tar out of me. Part of the laughter was that Billy was laughing genuinely, that he was that kind of kid. He was big enough that nothing bothered him. He offered me a raspberry Now-and-Later and I gratefully accepted. That morning's breakfast of Cap'n Crunch had curdled in my stomach during the walk to the bus stop. The roof of my mouth was ravaged by the sharp ends of the cereal. I hadn't let it marinate in the

53

milk long enough to become mush. "Me, I'm always hungry," Billy said. "Just about all the time." I told him about my mother's cooking and he whistled appreciatively. "Dang!"

I thought, Hey! Maybe I won't have to fight after all. Maybe hanging around with Billy will discourage the inevitable beatdown. We pulled up in front of Gulf Gate Elementary in a traffic circle with about a half-dozen other buses. Billy decided that he wanted to meet Brandy, so pushed forward and got off with her.

I got off the bus nearly last, wasn't paying attention and bumped into a large kid who immediately took umbrage. "Who you think you are?" the kid asked. He was a massive Black kid with strapping arms, wearing an orange and brown tank top, jeans that had seen better days and basketball shoes. He had a pick stuck in his afro, which glittered like it had jewels in it.

"I'm sorry," I said sheepishly, backing up a step.

"Naw. That ain't gonna do it," the kid said. "That won't do at all."

The bus he'd gotten off of was full of other Black kids. They'd been bused in from Newtown, the Black community on the far north side of Sarasota. It was a long, court-mandated ride to come to a school full of middle-class whites. The other Black kids crowded around. This was the closest I'd ever been to a Black person and I was starstruck. I thought of Jim Brown. I thought of Henry Aaron, Reggie Jackson and Muhammad Ali. He was insulted by the look I was giving him, my mouth agape.

"You and me, little white kid. We gonna have a fight," he said, grabbing a handful of my silly shirt. "And you will know my name afterward. I'm Reginald Hightower, and I'm going to knock your ass out. First recess. Better see you there." He pulled me closer. "Don't worry about finding me. I'll find *you*." He let go of my shirt with a little shove and walked away through a whorl of children with a strut in his stride.

Where the heck was Billy? I wondered. How could this happen?

I got lost trying to find my classroom, even though Mom, Dad and I had visited the school the week before during orientation and the principal herself, Miss May, had shown us where the classroom was. Miss May asked my parents if we were related to Congressman Claude Pepper, who represented St. Petersburg, a city north of us, and was known as "the angel of the elderly" for his fight to keep Social Security flowing.

"No, ma'am. No relation," I told Miss May. "He's successful."

My mother cackled over this. My father fumed.

Bells were ringing. I was late. I managed to find the classroom and entered under the watchful eye of Mr. Morgan, our bedraggled teacher. He was wearing frayed clothes that were about ten years out of date, a skinny black tie with food stains on it, scuffed penny loafers and horn-rimmed glasses. He coughed for a moment and then pointed out a chair/

desk combo that was empty. Billy sat in the chair in front of me, blocking out the teacher, the blackboard and casting a shadow on my little desk.

I peered around the parts of the room that I could see. There were only a few Black kids in there. Unfortunately, one of them was Reginald Hightower. He stared over at me and mouthed out, "Soon." I turned my head away and all I saw was the back of Billy's shirt bulging over the top of his too-small-for-him desk.

We went through all the first day of class gyrations, including passing out textbooks and lectures about proper school behavior that seemed to be pointed at the few Black kids. They crossed their arms and leaned back in their chairs, staring down the worn-out teacher. Mr. Morgan coughed a lot. He took a ten-minute break on the hour, returning smelling like my grandparents' house in Cleveland. They were the only smokers in the family. During those ten minutes, when we were left on our own recognizance, Reginald Hightower would shamble over to me, crouch down next to my desk and say, "Soon." Then he'd go back to his seat and would sit there, not talking to anyone. Not even the other Black kids.

At some point during all of this, all the "new" kids, the ones that had come from other schools and out of state like myself, had to get up and introduce ourselves. It was like an interview on a talk show and I treated it accordingly, putting on my TV voice. "First of all, I want to thank you for that question! No, I'm not originally from Florida, but it's part of America, which is the greatest country on earth, I think all of us would agree!" This was always my downfall. I tried too hard to please the audience, who looked at me as if I was a space alien. I got no laughs for all this effort.

"Yes, but where are you originally from?" Mr. Morgan pressed.

"Um. I'm from... Cleveland." And finally, I'd gotten my laugh. Cleveland was a national joke at the time. The kids, without fully knowing why, all laughed until they were red-faced at the mere mention of my beleaguered hometown. A few years before, the river running through the middle of town had caught fire. During a press conference, our mayor's toupee had caught fire. The baseball team was awful. They'd held a promotion, Ten-Cent Beer Night, that summer that had made national news for the drunken riot that ensued. The football team wasn't much better than the baseball team, its championship years receding into the past. We had a hockey team for about five minutes, and they left. Clevelanders, including my own family, were leaving in droves.

Billy got up and talked about how his family used to live in Tampa, and now they lived in Sarasota. He said he was going to keep an open mind about Sarasota, though at this point, he preferred Tampa.

Reginald Hightower got up and said that he was at our school under protest, that he would have preferred to stay in Newtown, and that he considered most white people to be crazy now that he'd met a few of us.

A few of the other Black kids, when called upon to introduce themselves, said that they agreed with Reginald Hightower.

Mr. Morgan said that busing would make all Americans equal and he was all for it, even if it was expensive and that meant that he wouldn't get a raise this year and would have to work extra shifts at the car wash to make ends meet. Then he checked the clock and said that it was time for a break.

Billy turned around and told me about meeting Brandy and how he'd invited himself over to her place, "to check out how rich people lived." He made it sound like an anthropological expedition. He'd bring his Polaroid camera, he told me. He'd document. I imagined him wearing a pith helmet, khakis, desert boots and knee socks, and maybe a Sam Browne belt. He could grease up his nascent mustache with some sort of wax. Wear a pair of binoculars around his considerable neck.

"Did you bring along a sack lunch?" he asked me. "I'm hungry."

"I'm on some sort of lunch program," I said.

"Me, too."

"I was wondering."

"Yes?"

"You wouldn't mind helping me out with this Reginald Hightower situation, would you?"

"I believe in letting my friends fight their own fights. But if any of his buddies try to sneak up on you, I'll take care of it."

"Fair enough. Thanks."

"Don't mention it."

I could feel the fear welling up inside me. I looked up at the clock. We were closing in on recess time. A bell would ring soon, tolling out my doom.

It rang.

I staggered out the door, my legs wobbly, my heart hammering in my skinny, hollow chest. I walked over to an area near a classroom that looked like a doublewide. It was a temporary classroom placed there in anticipation of Gulf Gate Woods students and the newly bused-in Black students overwhelming the little elementary school. I stood in the shade of the doublewide awaiting Reginald Hightower, who did not disappoint.

He came strutting up cracking his knuckles in anticipation of turning me into rice pudding.

Billy came walking up behind me.

Several Black kids walked up behind Reginald Hightower. "Kick his ass, Reginald," a girl said. She was wearing a macramé vest that looked like the ones my sister made. Her afro was similar to Reginald's, with the glitter and everything.

Reginald wanted to bump chests for a while, as the other kids formed the familiar circle around us, egging us on. Billy held a lot of them back from crowding us. We were standing awfully close to each other when

Reginald threw the first blow, swinging his arm in a wide arc and hitting me with his forearm and not his fist.

That's when I remembered my training from Steve.

I went into an Ali-like stance, bouncing on my toes, my arms up, fists clenched in front of my face. I channeled all the fear I felt, not only at that moment, but the fear I felt when I was asleep during the times when my father was home, not knowing if he'd decide sometime during the night to pull me out of bed and beat me for some imagined slight. I took that fear and I focused it into four or five straightforward punches in quick secession, rat-a-tat-tat, and then a quick uppercut into Reginald Hightower's stunned face, a loud crack. I watched him fall down. "Fly like a butterfly!" I shouted. "Sting like a bee!"

Reginald Hightower sat on the ground stunned, but the Ali quote made him smile.

And then I realized what I'd done. I'd intentionally hurt someone. I felt awful. I didn't know what to say, so I offered him a hand up and he took it.

At that moment, the withered and nicotine-stained hands of Mr. Morgan clapped on our shoulders. "Are you finished, gentlemen?"

"We're finished," Reginald said.

"Yes," I said. I was fairly certain that I'd broken a bone in my right hand. I shook the hurt out.

"Come with me," Mr. Morgan said.

His hands did not leave our shoulders all the way to the principal's office, where we sat in adjacent orange and chrome chairs facing a magazine rack filled with *Highlights For Children.*

Reginald broke the silence first. "Where did you learn to do that?"

"A teenager in my neighborhood showed me. Plus, I've watched every Muhammad Ali fight on TV."

"The Greatest."

I turned to him and said solemnly, "He *is* the greatest fighter. But the greatest athlete in human history is Jim Brown. His greatness cannot be denied."

"Jim Brown? Jim Brown you say?" Reginald Hightower grinned cooly at me. "You and me, we're gonna be friends. What you say your name was?"

"I'm Buzz Pepper."

He taught me a handshake that was right out of a movie or a TV show and I swooned.

"Anybody messes with you, Buzz Pepper, he's messing with me. You gonna teach me how to box like Ali?"

"Yes I am."

We did our special handshake again and I decided then and there that that was one of the greatest moments of my life.

We were called into Miss May's office and she lectured Reginald mostly, saying that she wouldn't put up with thugs in her school. She said she'd call our parents and let them decide what our punishment should be. She dismissed Reginald, who looked relieved that he didn't have to listen to her anymore. "Close the door behind you, Reginald," she said.

She came around the desk and did what middle-aged women always did with me. She gave me a hug. "Look at that little face," she said after the hug, taking me by the chin with her smooth fingers, lacquered nails shining. Her blonde hair was primped and sprayed up into the approximate shape of an oversized football helmet. She had the scent of chemicals and a floral bouquet. She wore a white blouse with a pink vest and matching pink slacks, and white, high-heeled boots with zippers up the sides. "He didn't hurt you, did he?"

"Um. No," I went.

"Because I could expel him if he hurt you. Easy."

"He didn't hurt me. I won the fight."

"Aw. Sure you did." She smoothed my hair off my forehead and patted my shoulder. "You have such soft hair. I wish I had hair like that."

"No. Seriously. I won the fight."

"You're such a cute little thing. It's adorable little boys like you that got me into teaching, and now administration work. You can come to me anytime you want." She patted me on the head, and then got up and walked behind her desk. "If that boy does that again, he'll get the paddle." She pulled a paddle up from under her desk. It had a taped handle at one end and a flat paddle at the other. A few holes had been drilled neatly through the paddle end, presumably for the sake of aerodynamics. It appeared to have several layers of shellac on it. It was a lovingly crafted corporal punishment device.

I eyeballed the paddle warily and backed up. "May I go back to class now?"

She hefted the paddle by the handle and gave her opposite hand a couple of slaps with the business end. "Yes, you may go. I'll still be calling your parents."

For some reason, I said, "Thank you."

"Oh, not at all. Scoot!" She smiled at me through pink lipstick. She had pink eyeshadow on and pink rouge. There wasn't much about her that wasn't pink or white.

I went out the door and closed it behind me.

The obliviousness of adults always puzzled me. They were supposed to know things. They were supposed to know what they were doing. It was clear, at times, that they had no idea at all what was going on. I walked back to class in a somewhat daze, blinking my eyes rapidly, talking a bit to myself. Mainly, I asked, "What just happened back there?" And my answer was, "I have no idea."

58

I found Brandy walking the halls with a large, wooden object in her hand. Someone had used a wood burner to scorch onto it: HALL PASS. "Hi," I said to her. She ignored me.

I watched her walk away and felt a new pain in my chest. I had no name for this pain.

I caught up with Reginald and we walked together. "That white lady give you grief?"

"I have no idea. I don't even know what she was talking about."

"Yeah, that's white folks for you." He put an arm around my shoulder. "We'll sit together at lunch." It was a declaration, not an ask.

We walked into the classroom together as Mr. Morgan was coming back from another smoke break. "Well, if it isn't Sugar Ray Robinson and Rocky Graziano, back from 12 rounds at Madison Square Garden. Good to have you back, boys. You bury the hatchet?"

"Yes, sir," Reginald said.

"That's good. We can't have you kids fighting all the time. It's the first day of school, for crying out loud. Lots of school year left, if you know what I mean. Not a lot of tread left on my tires, if you know what I mean."

We didn't know what he meant. I had no idea who Sugar Ray Robinson and Rocky Graziano were.

At some point, we broke for lunch. We lined up outside the cafeteria. Billy, Reginald and I were put into the school lunch program line, while the rest of the kids went into the normal line. We were each handed a tray and made our way to a long white table with attached bench seating. Reginald and Billy shook hands. The rest of the black kids eventually sat down with us as did the poor whites. Reginald announced that the two of us were friends, and if that didn't sit well with them, they'd have to fight him. Everyone seemed to think that Reginald had won the fight, which worked out well enough for me. Now I had the two biggest kids in school as my friends. This day was brightening more and more. So why did I feel this weird anxiety in my chest?

I glanced across the room and saw Brandy sitting on her own, away from all the other boys and girls. She picked at the food on her tray.

I looked down at my tray and was puzzled by one item there. "What's this blob thing?" I asked. I peeled this white blob off my tray and held it up like a piece of bologna. I wiggled it.

"That's grits," Bobby said, taking it from my hand. He tilted his head back and lowered it into his open mouth.

"Grits, plural? As in more than one grit? Because it seemed pretty singular."

"My mama makes them at home with butter," Bobby said, having swallowed the grit object like a duck. "They're usually not in one piece like that. You eat them with a spoon out of a big old bowl."

There was a hot dog on my plate with a packet of ketchup. The ketchup packet had a drawing of a tomato on it. There was a slice of stale white bread. Several crinkle-cut fries had been placed there, too. I picked up one of the fries and it fell apart. I wasn't sure what to do with a hot dog that was all on its lonesome. No bun. I used a metal fork I'd been issued to poke at it.

I looked across the cafeteria at Brandy. I wanted to get up and go over to her. I wanted to apologize, even though I wasn't sure what I'd done. Mostly, I wanted her to feel better. Sissy would know what to do if she was here, but she was probably already in trouble with the nuns at the Catholic school. Mom would be getting calls from our respective schools that afternoon. Mom would be there to take the calls because she'd taken the day off from work in celebration of our not being in the house.

"What's the matter, Buzz?" Billy asked.

"Brandy looks kind of sad, don't you think?"

He looked over at her while picking up the piece of white bread from my tray. "Yes," he said while thoughtfully chewing a bite out of it. "I should go over and cheer her up." He used the remaining bread to wipe down his empty tray and stuffed the bread into his mouth, poking at bits of bread stuck in his incisors with his index finger afterward. He stood up with the tray, took it over to the hole in the wall where the trays went, and I watched him sit across from Brandy, making goofy faces at her. She laughed musically, and I felt both better and much, much worse.

That afternoon, I skipped getting on the bus and walked home instead. It would be a very long walk, I knew, especially lugging all my new books, but I couldn't bring myself to watch Billy and Brandy sitting together on the bus, having a good time. Billy waved out the window to me as I walked along the sidewalk. I waved back. Brandy was visible, too, not looking at me. Looking forward. I felt like I did when I was in trouble, except worse.

After all the buses passed by, including Reginald's. I heard a car honk and turned around. A purple El Camino pulled up to the curb. I looked through the rolled-down passenger side window and none other than Steve Bondurant was sitting in there. "You got your car!" I nearly shouted.

"Pretty sweet, ain't it little man?"

"It's cool," I said. He'd put a thick coat of wax on it and polished the car to perfection. The pick-up truck part of the car had some sort of black cover over the top of it. It had chrome wheels and huge fat tires and the engine was purring like a kitten.

"Wanna ride? I was going to offer one to my little sis, but she got on that danged bus too quick." He reached over and popped open the door. I got in, slid into the bucket seat and shut the door, dropping my bookbag on the floor. The interior was just as cherry as the rest of the car. He had a chrome shifter that looked like a pirate's sword. The accelerator was in the shape of a chrome bare foot. He'd padded the dash with thick, black, precisely cut carpet. All of the instrument gauges were chromed and new. The steering wheel was crafted out of a solid chrome chain and a Chevy logo gleamed in the middle of the wheel.

"Wow," I went appreciatively. "This is the coolest car ever!"

"Thanks, little man. I knew you had excellent taste." He clicked on the stereo and popped in an eight-track of *Houses of the Holy*. "The Song Remains the Same" came blasting out of speakers from the doors and directly behind our heads. It was an amazing amount of sound. The car and my teeth vibrated as we rolled through old Gulf Gate and into Gulf Gate Woods, a very short trip the way Steve drove, leaving black marks through the neighborhood as he skidded and accelerated around turns.

He lit a cigarette with the car's lighter and took a long drag, blowing the smoke out of his rolled-down window, his long blonde hair fluttering in the breeze. He had on a pair of mirrored aviator's glasses, tight jeans, cowboy boots and a Black Sabbath concert t-shirt. Steve gunned the engine a bit, its throaty roar competing with Led Zeppelin.

He pulled into my driveway and turned down the tunes. "You kick some ass today, little man?"

"I did what you told me to do. We got called to the principal's office. I'm friends with the guy now. He's bad ass, like Shaft. The principal's going to call my mom. Maybe she called her already."

"Shit yeah, little man. Give me five." He held out his hand and I slapped him five, and then I turned over my hand and he slapped me five.

This was clearly a banner day, except for one thing. "Can you tell Brandy that I'm sorry?"

"What do you have to be sorry about?" he asked me seriously.

"I don't know. I said something this morning, and now she doesn't like me anymore."

"What did you say?"

"I don't even know. But whatever it was, it was wrong."

Steve smirked knowingly. "Women, man." He took a long drag off his cigarette and then flicked it onto our meager lawn. "It'll be fine. Don't you worry. She'll forget about it in a day or two. Or three."

"Okay," I said, not believing him.

He reached across me and opened the door. "Go on. Go inside and take your medicine from your old lady. She'll be pissed at you, too. They don't like it when we fight." He grinned widely, revealing nicotine-stained teeth. "We all have to take our medicine sometimes, even if we don't understand why." I got out of the car and shut the door. I watched Steve back up into the street. He clunked the El Camino into gear and turned the stereo all the way up. "Sayonara, little man!" he said, peeling out for ten yards and fishtailing as the engine roared.

"Legend," I whispered aloud.

Pizza Night

The only record I owned as a ten-year-old was a forty-five of the theme to *Blazing Saddles*, which I played over and over on the portable record player that Sissy and I shared. The portable record player was a gift from our grandparents and looked like a sad, beige suitcase. Opened up, the lid contained a speaker. Where the clothes would have gone, there was a turntable. I sang along with Frankie Laine over the whipcracks. Sissy burst into my room one day with her hands over her ears, shouting, "Enough!"

The record was a souvenir of one of the adult movies that my father took me to. Over the years, he'd promise to our mother, on a Saturday afternoon, that he would be taking me to see *Million Dollar Duck*, or whatever the latest Disney offering was. In his Gran Torino on the way to the theater, he'd change his mind. He didn't like sitting in a movie theater full of screaming children. It was the screaming that got to him. Also, he felt embarrassed to be in a movie theater full of children. There was something unmanly about sitting amongst kids. My father was concerned about manliness nearly all the time. "You don't want to see that kid's movie, do you?"

"No?" I'd say hesitantly.

"We'll go see another movie. It'll be great. Don't tell your mother." He'd slap a big meathook on my tiny, bony shoulder in grateful bonhomie.

My brother opted out of these outings fairly early on. I recall Sparky saying, during a showing of *Easy Rider*, that he hardly thought this was appropriate fare for a child. Sparky was referring to me and not himself, even though we were both aged in the single digits at the time.

The only thing I remember my father saying in that darkened theater —was it in Missouri? Ohio? Nebraska?—was that he didn't know that this showing of *Easy Rider* was in smell-o-vision. Someone had lit a joint. I don't know whether Dad was kidding or not. He isn't the brightest bulb on the Christmas tree.

Together, we'd seen what I'll call here the Charleton Heston Doom Trilogy: *Planet of the Apes, Omega Man* and *Soylent Green.* After *Soylent Green,* I had nightmares for weeks about going into a suicide parlor and being processed into bite-sized snacks.

With *Blazing Saddles* that year, Dad had hit a home run. It was the best movie he ever took me to. On the way home from the theater, both of us exhausted from laughing, he cautioned me not to say the N-word in front of our mother. "She doesn't like it," he said, even though he used the vile word unsparingly himself. Because he wasn't terribly bright, the message he took out of the movie was that that Black people shouldn't be given positions of authority over the white race.

I'd taken a completely different lesson out of the movie, and that was that most white people were idiots. I'd seen plenty of evidence of that in real life. At school, hanging out with Reginald Hightower, I'd also come to the conclusion that most white people were crazy. Reginald pointed out their craziness to me all the time, including my own craziness. "You crazy," Reginald would inform me after I'd make a random observation in class, usually eliciting a groan from Mr. Morgan and unintended laughter from the rest of the kids. I liked getting a laugh, even if it was unintentional.

I turned to Dad in the car, after he said that Black people were not supposed be in charge of whites, using the N-word, and said, "Gol darn it, Dad, you use your tongue prettier than a twenty-dollar whore."

His hand quickly left the steering wheel and smashed into my face, his massive knuckles cracking into my nose. I'd taught myself not to cry out, or cry at all, during these situations. It would only serve to enrage him further.

He glared over at me and I stared at him like he was a coiled rattlesnake, my hands up to my nose. "Drop your hands. Let me see," he said. I put my hands down. "Ah, crap," he said irritatedly. "Why'd you say that? You know stuff like that makes me angry."

Slim Pickens had said it. It was a joke from the movie. We both thought it was funny at the time. "I don't know," I said.

"This is your own fault, but your mother is going to blame me."

"I'm sorry." I was always apologizing to him after he hit me.

"We'll have to stop somewhere and get some ice." He squinted at me. "You think it's broken?"

I'd already broken my nose twice before. I would break my nose a couple more times while living under the same roof as him. I poked at it and felt the bone moving. "Possibly," I said. My eyes were beginning to swell shut and thick blood was oozing out of my left nostril.

"Why does this always happen to me?" Dad moaned.

"I shouldn't have said that," I said.

"You're damn right," he said. "How would you like a popsicle? Maybe two?"

I was in no mood for a popsicle, but I knew the correct answer. "Yes!" I said it with the appropriate amount of enthusiasm.

"How did you break your nose?" he asked me.

"I fell on the way out of the movie theater," I said.

"Always tripping over your own feet."

"I'm clumsy."

"How did I end up with such a clumsy kid? You know I was captain of my high school football team. The quarterback. I could have gone to college on a scholarship. The whole nine yards."

"But your mother was sick and you needed to get a job, because your father was irresponsible."

"That's right. You remember."

"And you were the captain of the basketball team, too."

"I could have been All-Ohio."

"You were cheated."

"I'm always being cheated," he said darkly. "Even now. Right now. We just saw a great movie, and now I'm sitting here with you and your broken nose. Always tripping over your own feet."

I stopped talking and stared forward at the glove compartment. It was white, like most of the interior of the car, and had my father's dark fingerprints all over it.

He pulled in to a Lil General convenience store. The glowing sign featured a picture of a feisty general in a red uniform waving a magic wand with one hand and pointing at the ground with the other. He wore a blue sash and bright yellow knickers. The store had a barn roof and the exterior was composed of faux red bricks.

"Stay here," my father said, and he got out of the car. He returned several minutes later with a double popsicle wrapped in waxpaper, CHERRY printed across the paper. "Eat it before it melts," he said. He took the waxpaper from me, balled it up and chucked it out his rolled down window.

I ate the two-in-one popsicle quickly and was ready to throw the sticks out when my father took them from me. He opened up the glove compartment and pulled out some gauze and white adhesive tape. He wrapped the gauze around the end of each popsicle stick, had me tilt my head back, and then shoved the popsicle sticks in. He taped them in place. "There, that oughta work. I'll be back with some ice." He left and came back a few minutes later with a ten-pound bag of ice. He pulled the handkerchief out of his pocket, wrapped some cubes in it and tied it up with a couple of rubber bands. "Hold it in place. Let's get home before the ice melts."

He drove quickly home, parking in his customary spot on the curb. Mom's Ford family truckster got the place of honor in the garage.

We came in through the front door, me being led by hand since my eyes had swollen completely shut. He took me into the den, where Sissy and Mom were watching *Doctor Paul Bearer's Creature Feature* on Channel 44. Doctor Paul Bearer was lamenting that he had to show us "this horrible old movie" in his gravelly, tar-etched voice. I could see him in my head chain-smoking his way through another broadcast. "I'm awfully thirsty," Doctor Paul Bearer said. "That's why I drink Ghoul-ade." He chuckled in a way that let us know that he was in on the joke... that the funny part of the joke was that it was painfully unfunny. My sister and I both loved him for that, that he told unfunny jokes and reveled in their awfulness. He was a horror show host who was fearless.

"Oh my God!" Mom shouted. "What happened to him now? Can't he even go to a movie without getting hurt?"

"He tripped over his own feet, Lola," Buster said.

"Typical," Mom said in a way that indicated she wasn't buying it, but was going to go along with the lie for comity's sake.

"Help me put him on the couch, or in his bed," Buster said.

"Let's just put him here on the couch," Mom said. I could hear her rearranging things as I stood in the middle of the den on uncertain legs.

"Tripped, huh?" Sissy went.

"Don't start," Mom warned her. "Don't you start. You wanna watch this show, or listen to it through the wall? I'd think about my answer if I was you."

"What's up his nose?" Sissy asked.

"Ask your father."

"Well?" Sissy went.

"When I played football—" Buster started.

"Here we go," Sissy went. "Another boring football story."

"If you shut up for a second, and let me tell it—"

"Fine," Sissy snapped.

"As I was saying, when I played football, face masks hadn't been invented yet." Buster maneuvered me over to the couch and I quickly reclined amongst a thatch of pillows. "So one time, we were playing Sandusky High—"

"Archrivals," Sissy said with a bit of a yawn.

"Sorry this is so boring for you," Buster said. "I'll try to get to the point."

"I have a headache," Mom announced. I heard her walking away, her house shoes clapping against the linoleum floor in the kitchen, receding. I heard the bedroom door shut.

"So I dropped back to pass," Buster said.

"A classic three-step drop," Sissy said in the voice of Howard Cosell.

"Anyway, this big linebacker socks me right in the nose as I'm about to let the football go, and he jumps on the ball."

"The agony of defeat," Sissy said.

"So I go to the sideline and the coach is ready for me. He wrapped a couple of popsicle sticks in gauze, shoved'm in my nostrils, taped them in place and I went right back out there and played the rest of the game."

"Did you win?" Sissy asked pointedly.

"That's not the point of the story. The point is, you asked about the popsicle sticks. I just told you."

"So you lost."

"Yes, Sissy. We lost. Weren't you watching the movie? How about doing that and leaving your old man alone for a second and not jumping down my throat and making fun of me."

"Fine," Sissy said. "Move your feet, Buzz."

I sat up some more and moved my feet. She took my shoes off and I listened to them plop on the carpet.

I heard the fridge door open and the pop of a can being opened. I listened to Buster slurp and then emit a little belch. "Don't have kids," he said, probably to Sissy. "They're a pain in the ass."

"Can I have some more ice?" I asked. "This one's melted." I took the wet handkerchief off my forehead.

"God damn it," Buster shouted. I listened as he slammed out the front door. He'd forgotten the ice back in the car. He came back in with another slam and said that it had all melted and he wondered why I didn't remind him about it earlier. I listened to him chug the rest of his beer and let loose with a loud belch.

I kept my mouth shut.

"You know what I'm gonna do? Hey? You know what I'm gonna do? I'm gonna go get some pizza from that place on the North Trail. The one you all like. Demetrio's. How's that?"

"Can I go with you?" Sissy asked.

"You keep your brother occupied," he said. "I'll be back in a couple of hours."

"Couple of hours?" Sissy asked skeptically.

"Sure. They gotta cook the pizza, don't they?"

"And you'll just sit there, waiting for the pizza. Patiently."

"I don't know what you're trying to say," Buster said defiantly. "But the sooner I get outta here, the sooner you can enjoy some pizza." He stomped off. The front door slammed again.

"My pink butt he's going after pizza," Sissy said. "What really happened?"

"What do you think?" My eyes were beginning to open again. I got sick of breathing out of my mouth, so I gingerly removed the tape and pulled out the bloody popsicle sticks and all their sticky gauze.

"I think you mouthed off at him, probably by accident, and he slugged you."

"Congratulations, contestant number one. Got it on your first try. Don't tell Mom or Sparky. Especially don't tell Sparky. Mom will pretend not to believe you and Sparky will just get mad for no reason."

"I know how this works, little brother. You want some pop? Mom bought some store brand ginger ale as a mixer."

"What else we got?"

"There's Tab. Or Fresca. We've got those Planter's Cheese Balls in the can."

"I'll take a Fresca and the cheese balls."

Sissy got up and went into the kitchen. "Don't get used to this deluxe treatment. I'm only waiting on you hand and foot because you're stupid and got hurt."

"Fine," I said.

"You know full well that talking back to Dad is like baiting a bear."

"You talk back to him all the time."

"I'm a girl. He's not allowed to hit me."

"He hits Mom. She's a girl."

"She's a woman. She should be able to handle herself."

We made all sorts of excuses for our father's behavior for him. He didn't even have to participate in the excuses anymore. We were all ready to accommodate him.

Sparky came in from the garage. My eyes had opened some more. He stood staring at me. He was sweating through his clothes, his textbook in one hand—*Differential Equations*. "What happened this time?" he asked.

"I tripped," I said.

He sighed. "Did you?"

"I tripped."

"How was the movie?"

"The movie was great."

"Did you 'trip' before or after the movie?"

"After."

"And what did you say before you tripped?"

"'Look out below!'"

"Uh-huh. I suppose you think that's funny." He wasn't laughing. He rarely did.

"It's hilarious, clearly," Sissy said. "Leave him alone. Can't you see he's in pain?"

"Cheese balls," Sparky said. He took one and crunched it down.

On TV, Doctor Paul Bearer was having a conversation with Spinjamin Bock, his spider sidekick. Spinjamin was rattling off awful one-liners while Doctor Paul Bearer chuckled in his knowing way, glancing out at us, the appreciative viewers, the ones who also knew how hilarious bad jokes really were. It's not the bad joke that's funny. It's the cringe.

"Don't spoil your appetite," Sissy said. "Dad is out getting pizza. He'll be back in an hour or two."

"Of course he is. Getting pizza, that is. What else would he be doing for several hours? Certainly not cheating on Mom. No, that would be wrong. And we all know that Buster can do no wrong. Clearly. Buzz's nose is ample evidence of his innocence." Sparky said this through grinding teeth. He didn't like to show emotion, because if he did, it would soon blaze into a wildfire of all-consuming rage. So he shoved that rage inside and found his outlet in mathematics, the only thing he could bring inside the house that made perfect sense.

When we were adults, Sparky would find another outlet in bottles of freezer-chilled vodka. I think of my brother's suffering back then, of his inability to make everything mathematically right in our household, and it breaks my heart. I had no appreciation for his suffering at the time.

He called me up the other night from his empty, precisely ordered home and we talked for a while, just a couple of bachelors shooting the shit. I gave him these little gems of advice: "You should check yourself in somewhere. You should scream as loud and as long as you can stand it. You should stop drinking."

He was slurring his words, drunk. "How did my silly little brother get so wise?" he asked. "How did that happen?"

It was my job as a child to play the fool, to be the idiot, to be everyone's comic relief. I played the part too well. I'd convinced myself that I was a fool and an idiot. I convinced myself that my only value in life was making people laugh. I remain convinced to this day.

"You're swelling up again," Sissy said. "Let me go get you more ice." She went into the kitchen.

Sparky stood in front of me, his face passive and his eyes filled with anger. He finally gave up and went into his room, shutting the door and locking it.

The second feature for that day's double bill of horror started. Christopher Lee appeared on screen, his mouth open, fangs bared and dripping with blood the color of a cherry popsicle. He whipped around his cape and stalked off.

"Where's Peter Cushing?" Sissy asked, placing a dishtowel filled with ice on my face, covering my eyes. "Oh. There he is."

The doorbell rang and Sissy sprang up to go answer it.

"Answer the doorbell!" Mom shouted through her bedroom door. I could see her in my mind's eye splayed out on her bed like she was dying, her eyes covered with a moist washcloth, in her housecoat, her bony feet bare and still.

I took off the dishtowel and looked over toward the opening to the den. Sissy came through first, and then Brandy followed, dressed in her peculiar way, like she was ready to go to a very hip funeral.

"Hi, Buzz," she said. The tone was friendly. Then, as her eyes adjusted to the light, she said, "Oh my God, what happened to him?"

"He'll be okay. He's always falling down."

"Are you all right? Your face is all swollen."

"I'm fine." I could have been on fire, my body being consumed with flames, and I would have said the same thing. I took a sip of my Fresca to demonstrate that I was fine. "Cheese ball?" I shook the can in her direction.

"Ew. No."

"More for me, I guess." I crunched one down.

"You've had enough." Sissy took the can into the kitchen and resealed the plastic lid on top.

I licked cheese dust off my fingers and placed the melty dishtowel back on my face.

"Van Helsing!" Christopher Lee shouted at Peter Cushing.

"Oh, I like this one," Brandy said. "*Horror of Dracula*, right?"

"You are correct," Sissy said in her emcee's voice. "And now we go to our rapid fire round. 'In how many movies did Christopher Lee play Dracula?'"

"I don't know."

"Oooh. Sorry! The correct answer is one million, seven hundred thousand and... *two*." Sissy turned to me. "Johnny Olson, tell our plucky contestant what she's won."

I sat up and said in my Johnny Olson voice: "Please accept this consolation gift of a mink stole from Dicker and Dicker of Beverly Hills. Now let's have a nice round of applause for Brandy. Isn't she wonderful everyone? C'mon, let's give it up for her."

Sissy and I both applauded and whistled. The whistling made my nose hurt and I went back to reclining again. I tasted blood and snot in the back of my throat.

Brandy sat on our carpet next to Sissy. She turned and started flipping through my mother's collection of jazz records in the cheap pine cabinet that also housed the Emerson all-in-one stereo. "Someone has fantastic taste," Brandy said. "These jazz records are all classics." She pulled out a copy of Keely Smith's *Swing, You Lovers*. "Can I borrow this? Please?" She hugged the record to her chest.

"Sure you don't want to borrow Sissy's copy of 'Seasons in the Sun' instead?"

"'Seasons in the Sun'?" Brandy asked, making a face.

"Don't listen to that idiot. I would never, in a million years, own a copy of that awful song!" Sissy went into a familiar, to me, rant about how much she hated the song and the whiny voice of Terry Jacks, and after a lot of ranting, she got to the last part of her rant where she said that if Terry Jacks wanted to kill himself, as the song implied, he should

70

get right to it so that she, Sissy, would never have to hear that stupid song again.

"I'm not sure how you feel about 'Seasons in the Sun,'" I said, rubbing my chin thoughtfully. "Maybe we should tune into WKXY. They're still playing it on the hour, right after 'Helen Wheels.'"

"Someone wants his nose rebroken," Sissy said, smacking a fist into a palm. "I'm just about in a mood to accommodate him."

"You'd beat on a poor, sad cripple like myself just to satisfy your bloodlust. Typical of you, my sweet sister."

"If you weren't so miserable looking, I'd do my best Dusty Rhodes impression on you, little brother." She stood up and kissed her skinny biceps. "I am the American Dream!" She went into Dusty Rhodes' stuttering, lisping voice, "Y-you aw gonna find out what the Uh-Uh-American dream really is, uh-huh. You gonna know the pow-uh!"

"So you're not afraid of Terry Funk, Junior?" I asked in Gordon Solie's voice.

"Ter-uh Funk? He be afwaid uh muh pow-uh! He be knowin' the pow-uh of da American dream!"

"Do you two do this all the time?" Brandy asked. At least she was smiling. It was a confused smile. I guessed, correctly, that she wasn't a fan of *Florida Championship Wrestling*. It had become one of our summer obsessions, along with *Suncoast Digest*.

"Pretty much constantly," I admitted.

"We take time off to play boardgames," Sissy said.

"The boardgames have their own rules that neither of us fully understand," I added.

"Sometimes, the rules make themselves up as you play them. It's beyond human understanding." Sissy sat down again.

"Only Leonard Nimoy could comprehend it fully. And he's not available."

"Which is, let's face it, sad. Every household should have a Leonard Nimoy available to it. Our older brother is a somewhat reasonable substitute, but he spends his time in his room communing with his personal god, mathematics."

"I like math," Brandy said brightly.

"Then the two of you would get along," Sissy said. "Hey, our father is out getting pizza. You wanna stick around for dinner?" She was doing this for me. She knew I liked Brandy. And she knew that our father would be on better behavior with a guest at the table.

"Pizza? What's going to be on it?" Brandy asked.

"Meat," I said. "Lots of meat."

"No. But thank you for asking." She was still hugging the record.

"You can take that home with you, if you want," I said.

"Are you sure? Are you positive that your mother won't miss it?"

"It'll be fine. I take her records without asking all the time and play them in my room. You want to see my room?" Sissy asked her.

"Yes," Brandy said in her crisp voice.

I watched the two of them get up and walk out of the room, leaving me with Christopher Lee and Peter Cushing hamming it up on the TV. I slipped into sleep. I awoke with my father shaking me awake. He saw the fear and panic in my eyes.

"Relax," he said. "There's pizza."

I got up gingerly and walked into the kitchen. There were the picked-over remains of two pizzas in greasy cardboard boxes. I peeled up a slice of what looked like a sausage pizza from the box, taking a little cardboard with it. I put it on a paper plate.

I looked into the dining room and saw all the used paper plates in there. I counted the place settings. There were four. Brandy hadn't stayed. I saw Mom's used, empty wineglass, a drip of red in the bottom of it.

"Where is everybody?" I asked, and then looked around. Nobody was in the room, not even Buster. Where had they all gone?

I peered past the kitchen sink out the kitchen window and saw them all outside, greeting our new backyard neighbors. There was a boy and a girl. There was a perfect-looking white woman, a Barbie come to life. There was a husband in a short-sleeved shirt wearing a tie as fat as a lobster bib, patterned like a red lava lamp. He had a carefully orchestrated combover in lieu of a proper rug and long, bushy sideburns. He smoked a pipe. The boy and the girl chased each other around in circles while Sissy and Sparky observed them off to the side.

I wasn't invited. I could not go out there until my face had returned to something close to normal. I took my pizza into the dining room and sat by myself in Buster's chair, looking at the new neighbors through the dining room sliding glass doors. I watched them frolic. I took a few bites, chewed and swallowed, and then pushed it away.

I picked up all the paper plates, including mine, and threw them in the trash.

Thermonuclear Risk

The yuletide season rolled around with another Mel Brooks classic movie—*Young Frankenstein*. I'd been such a keen watcher of *Doctor Paul Bearer's Creature Feature* that I anticipated all the jokes and began laughing seconds before they started. My father was freakishly pleased with my laughter. "It's funny how you got all the jokes before they happened," he said with a chuckle as we exited the theater.

We drove home from the theater in good spirits. But I kept my mouth shut just in case. Dad didn't seem to notice. He talked good-naturedly about his paper sales, which were picking up lately, but not enough that we'd caught up with all the bills. We were behind the eight ball, my father said. We were running hard, but the bills were running harder. "God damn inflation! That know-nothing Ford is responsible," Dad said. He wore a bright red WIN button that he kind of poked at. "This button is as useless as that Michigan man!" WIN stood for Whip Inflation Now. I wasn't sure how wearing WIN buttons was supposed to stop inflation from happening. It was another aspect of adult life that I found puzzling.

In class, Mr. Morgan showed us a movie that featured Weimar Republic Germans pushing wheelbarrows of cash to the corner market so they could buy a loaf of bread. He showed us the movie so we could understand inflation. "Then the Nazis took over," Mr. Morgan said. "Any questions? Good. Time for my break."

My mother had been working double-shifts in the china department of Maas Brothers department store. She was anticipating the day when her commute would be much shorter. Sarasota Square Mall, which was being constructed on a former cattle field on the corner of Beneva Road and the Tamiami Trail, was getting closer to being fully built, and when it was, Mom was going to transfer from the downtown store to the new one—a five-minute commute. Workmen could be seen erecting all the stores. When we rode past it on our way south toward Nokomis and Osprey, we tried to guess at what stores would be going in. They were listed on a sign, but the print was too small to make out as we zipped past in the Ford family truckster. We knew one of those stores would be Maas

Brothers. Visiting Mom would give us an excuse to go to the mall, to bask in its air-conditioned luxury.

But they wouldn't get the mall finished in time for Christmas shopping and it was a shame, said Mom. She guessed it had to do with the general laziness of people who lived all their lives down south. They lacked the industriousness of people from the north. "That's why they lost the Civil War," Mom said. "Laziness. They couldn't exactly make their slaves do all the fighting for them like they made them do all the other work. They never got used to doing their own work down here. It's sad, especially for Black people who are expected to pick up all the slack while the whites treat them like they're a bunch of jerks. Plus, all these southerners are full of hook worms. Can you imagine? Don't walk around outside barefoot, kids. You'll end up as lazy as these people. And don't drink out of the hose! You don't know what could be in there. Malaria or hepatitis or something."

Mom liked to hate-watch *The Waltons* and *The Andy Griffith Show* and do a continual commentary. For *The Waltons*, she said, "Look at them sitting around! No wonder the Great Depression lasted ten years. Everyone up north had to carry their dead weight through the whole Depression. Then World War Two happened and they had no choice but to go to work." And for *The Andy Griffith Show*, she'd say, "You ever wonder where all the Black people are on this show? I'll tell you where they are. They're doing all the work while these lazy jerks are hanging around Floyd's barber shop or the sheriff's office like a bunch of bums." She'd make these declarations from the comfort of the couch, eating raw scallions swirled in puddles of salt and drinking Carlo Rossi wine, her hair in curlers, her feet up, wearing her thin floral-patterned housecoat.

To this day, I love turning on either of those shows so I can hear my mother's voice again, reeling off her litany of complaints.

She held a special contempt for those who populated 18th century costume dramas. "Can you imagine the smell? These dukes and ladies look nice, but they didn't believe in bathing. They were all full of fleas and their body odor had to be overwhelming, even after they slapped on their version of perfume, which I'm sure wasn't all that fragrant. They were a bunch of primitives, after all."

She would only get starry-eyed when movies came on from the 1940's or 1950's. They reminded her of her childhood. "That was back when everyone got dressed up to go anywhere. A man wouldn't think of leaving the house without a tie on. Your grandfather put on a suit to go to work. He'd change into his uniform there, and then go out and deliver the mail. Then he'd change back into his suit before coming home. Your grandmother scrubbed the floors of rich people's houses. She'd get dressed up to do that. Sometimes she'd let me and your uncle Ralph go with her just to get a look at how those people lived. Boy, did I get an eyeful! It wasn't pretty what your grandmother had to clean up. She came when they weren't home and left before they came home. Ralph and I had to sit in the kitchen and be quiet. When your grandmother was done, we'd get on the Rapid Transit and go home. What was I talking about? Oh, yeah. Everything was nicer back in the 1950's. Except it wasn't great for Black people. It isn't that great for them now, come to think of it. And we had polio back then, too. So maybe it wasn't wonderful, but look at those clothes and the cars. And listen to the music, too. By the way, did either of you find out what happened to my Keely Smith record?"

We had to admit that we had no idea what happened to her Keely Smith record.

"This one probably knows," she said, pointing at Sissy. "And that means you probably know," she said, pointing at me. "I don't care how it finds its way back into this house, but it had better, or heads will roll." She smiled, glancing over at the TV. "Look at that dress on Rita Hayworth. Classy."

My birthday was shortly after Christmas, so Mom asked me what I'd like in the way of presents, "keeping in mind our current financial situation."

"I'd like a black pocket t-shirt, pegged jeans and boxer shorts instead of tightie-whities."

"Are you sure about that?" Mom asked. "I'm not sure about that. Why black? Are you getting morbid on me, Buzz? I don't like the idea of you wearing black."

"Johnny Cash wears black."

"You're not Johnny Cash. I don't like it at all. And why pegged jeans?"

"I don't like the way bellbottoms slap against each other. I don't like the sound. Dad wore pegged jeans when you met him."

"It was the fifties when I met your father."

"You said you like the fifties."

"No. I don't want you wearing pegged jeans. You should wear bellbottoms like everyone else. And you're too young to be wearing boxers. You'll get briefs." She took a sip of wine. "That's it? That's all you wanted?"

"I guess."

"Don't pout. I don't like it when you pout."

"I'm not pouting."

"You are pouting, and you need to stop. Smile every once in a while. It won't kill you. Show him how it's done, Sissy."

Sissy put on a big, cheesy smile. "*Don't cry out loud,*" she sang. "*Just keep it inside and learn how to hide your feelings.*"

I stood up. "You've both been very helpful."

"The movie isn't over. You're not staying for the end of the movie?"

"I have homework. I think. I'm pretty sure I have homework."

"No one has homework over Christmas vacation," Mom said irritably. "What kind of sadist is that Morgan character? Do I need to give him a call?"

"Okay. Maybe I just want to read? Can I please go to my room?"

"Most kids consider it a punishment to go to their rooms. Meanwhile, your brother spends his whole life in his room and now *you're* asking to go to your room. What the hell's the matter with you kids?"

"I'm fine," I snapped.

"Fine then. Go to your room. Be a hermit like your brother. Oh, to catch a glimpse of your brother. He's like the rare white buffalo. Indians should worship him on the high plains." I took a single step toward my room. "And another thing, you didn't eat enough tonight. Don't think I didn't notice you taking about half a portion. That's why your growth is stunted. You're doing this just to punish me, I know. I have no idea why you want to punish your mother, but you do." I took another step. "It's fine though. Go hide out in your room. Don't expect me to cry a river over you. Not after you've continually broken my heart."

"Just go," Sissy said, laughing.

I walked away.

"What are you laughing at, Miss Tish? You're worse than the other two combined! It's been one long string of misery since you showed up." It went on and on.

The war between my mother and sister didn't end until Sissy's first child was born—a tiny screaming premie. A girl. Mom saw her granddaughter for the first time and her heart melted. A few months later, I was on active duty in the Army. When I came home on leave the first time, Mom and Sissy were freakishly close. Sissy was pregnant again. They were best friends at last. I remember the two of them sitting together at Sissy's kitchen table, comparing notes on raising children. Sissy said to Mom, "I finally understand you. You weren't being mean. Most of the time, you were kidding around."

Mom reached over and squeezed her hand.

Thinking of the two of them, sitting there like that, brings to mind a song I learned in Army basic training while marching around Fort McClellan, Alabama:

Around her neck
She wore a yellow ribbon
She wore it in the springtime
In the merry month of May
And if you asked her
Why the hell she wore it
She wore it for her soldier
Who was far, far away.

I didn't understand the song at the time, but I understand it now. It's not so much about the Army, as it is longing to see someone one last time. In this case, I'm the one wearing the yellow ribbon and Mom and Sissy are the soldiers.

They're both gone. Both Mom and Sissy. I think back and I wish that I hadn't left the room that evening, that I'd spent that little extra time with them. But I didn't. I went to my room and picked up my library copy of *Tinker, Tailor, Soldier, Spy* and immersed myself in the world of British spycraft.

Sparky came into my room the following morning and told me that I needed to come out to the garage and help him pull the Christmas junk out of the attic. It was a two-man job. We were going to set up the tree weeks after everyone else in the rapidly filling up neighborhood had already done so. Our Christmas junk was all contained in a series of soggy, corrugated cardboard boxes labeled with appropriately festive red and green magic marker. I recognized my handwriting.

The Ford family truckster was missing, so Mom was back at the daily grind that morning, dealing with snowbirds buying Christmas presents at low, low holiday prices. She probably wouldn't reappear until late that evening, after my bedtime, having worked another double shift, her bony feet sore from all the standing.

Sparky pulled the cord for the attic and down came a pine ladder that unfolded and clacked onto the oil-spattered garage floor. Another cord hung in the garage that held, at its end, a neon-green tennis ball. Sparky had set that up for Mom so that she'd know when the Ford family truckster had nestled its nose into the permanent hole in the garage wall. The tennis ball would plunk onto the windshield next to the rearview mirror when the parking process was complete. So Mom didn't need a ground-guide anymore.

Sparky climbed the ladder. Even in the middle of winter, I could feel the heat pouring down from the attic, where it was permanently 120 degrees, dark and full of musty odors.

The first item to come down was a box filled with faded and dusty ornaments that had been purchased in the 1950's. The box was not heavy at all. Easy day.

The next box to come down was filled with burned out Christmas lights. It was a mixture of old style bulb lights the size of an adult man's thumb and newer strings of lights that were as tiny as teardrops. The new lights would go on the tree. The old lights would go on the house.

In our last house, our father had strung the old lights inside the two front bedroom windows. He pulled the shades and the lights burned black holes in them, with an accompanying stench like Akron, Ohio.

I opened the box and saw those old lights and remembered my father taking us on a drive through Parma, Ohio during the Christmas season.

Everyone in Parma tried to outdo each other with their lights. I remembered the Christmas music playing on the radio and the dazzling displays that dripped off people's homes and made their way into their yards. Glowing baby Jesuses in glowing mangers. Cheery hollow Santas. I also remembered what happened after that trip. On our way home to Cleveland, we stopped at a little mom and pop grocery store. Mom and Dad were arguing in the front seat. Dad shouted, "You're pushing my buttons, Lola!" Sissy was still a baby. They had her in a car seat. I took my customary place sitting on the hump. Dad screeched the car to a halt in front of the store and Sissy's head jerked forward and hit the window. She cried and Dad went from being angry to being concerned in a blink. He opened the door and saw Sissy's head. In a few moments, she'd developed a massive goose egg on her head and Dad freaked out.

"It's fine," Mom said. "She'll be fine."

"I'm sorry," Dad said to the baby. I remember this because it's the only time I can remember him taking responsibility for something he'd done.

"Go get some ice," Mom said. "And don't forget the milk."

He walked away from the car with a look of panic on his face.

"His mother, your grandmother, died of a brain tumor," Mom explained to Sparky and me, matter-of-factly. "Your father was very close to her." Sissy cried and cried. "You'll be fine," Mom assured the baby. "It's just a little bump on the head."

"A little bump on the head," I said aloud.

"What's that?" Sparky asked, looking down at me from atop the ladder.

"Nothing," I said.

"Get ready. This is the big one."

Sparky pulled the Christmas tree along with him as he stepped down the ladder. It was encased in its cardboard coffin. We'd bought the tree a year or two before during a post-Christmas sale. It was a plastic replica of an evergreen broken down into components. I grabbed one end of it and Sparky grabbed the other. We toted it inside to the Florida room, where we kept our un-sat-upon furniture and untrod-upon carpeting.

We dropped the tree with a thud approximately where it would soon be erected. Sparky and I pulled off the lid and a banana spider came crawling out. Sparky stomped on it.

While he assembled the trunk of the Christmas tree, I went into the garage and brought in all the boxes one-by-one, handling them cautiously. I came back and watched Sparky screw one part of the trunk into another and then slide the four feet into plastic slots at the bottom. He stood that up in a corner of the room. Then came the branches, each labeled A, B, C, D, E depending on their position on the trunk. It was only a couple of years old, but the tree was already shedding plastic needles like a real tree.

I walked into the kitchen to get a glass of water. I found my plastic glass—I still was rarely allowed to use a glass made of glass since my days of biting through glass glasses—and filled it from the sink. I looked out the window and saw Michael Jorgenson, our backyard neighbor's kid, in our backyard on his balance beam. His parents gained my parents' permission to place a balance beam and a pitch back machine—a springy net with a red box woven into the center—in our yard since their yard was entirely occupied by their pool. I was allowed to use either device if I felt like it as long as I got along with Michael. Michael needed both of the devices to develop his coordination, which was far worse than mine. He made me look like an Olympic athlete in comparison. Sissy stood beside me and the two of us watched Michael fall off the balance beam and tumble into our patchy lawn over and over.

"It's a little sad," Sissy said.

"No kidding," I said.

"So what's Mister Spock doing in the next room?"

"Assembling the Christmas tree."

"Pour me a bowl of cereal. And, hey, pour one for yourself while you're at it. I have to go supervise."

"Product 19 or Cocoa Puffs?"

"What do you think?"

"Product 19 it is then."

"Don't court death, little brother."

"Cocoa Puffs it is then."

"Attaboy." She slapped me on the back and went into the next room. As I poured two bowls of cereal and slopped some milk in each bowl, I listened to my brother and sister go through their usual routine.

"Need some help there, Sparky?"

"No."

"Let me help you out."

"I don't need help."

"I think this branch was put in the wrong spot. Let's just switch these two."

"No, no, no. Please leave the room."

"Did someone ask you to put this up, or did you make up this job on your own?"

"Mom asked me. It's for you two kids."

"It's good to have a responsible adult around the house."

"Are you making fun of me?"

"Would I do that?"

"Yes."

"Okay. You caught me. Let me swap out these two branches."

"Get out!"

"Fine. See if I ever help you again."

I turned on the TV and we sat in front of it, watching *Tennessee Tuxedo* and slurping down our cereal. When we were done, we took our bowls over to the sink and watched Michael throwing the ball at the pitch back machine and missing it over and over, chasing it out of our line of sight.

Sissy said, "I can't help but think that we're witnessing the story of his life."

Michael finally got upset and threw the ball as hard as he could at the webbing and it caromed back and smacked him in the forehead. He tumbled backward, crying out in pain.

"Maybe we should assist?" I asked.

"Mrs. Jorgenson will be along shortly," Sissy predicted. "Action Barbie."

Sure enough, we watched her emerge from the sliding glass doors and out of the pool cage, daintily jogging over to Michael. She was dressed impeccably in a bright red midi skirt and a sleeveless white blouse. She wore pearls and a pair of shiny shoes that matched her skirt. She didn't have a hair out of place. She assisted Michael to his feet and traced the bruise on his forehead with a perfectly manicured hand. The two of them went back inside the pool cage and then through the sliding glass door into her house.

"What's it like inside there?" I asked Sissy. She'd invited herself over to the Jorgenson's out of curiosity once.

"Not a speck of dust," Sissy said. "Their Christmas tree is real. All of the ornaments are blue and the lights are all white. Kind of elegant." She nudged me in the ribs. "Ready for some fun?"

"We're not going to help Sparky hang the ornaments, are we?"

"That's exactly what we're going to do."

"I'm not sure I like your idea of fun."

"You do. You just don't want to admit it." She had that right.

We walked into the next room to find Sparky opening up a box filled with our sad collection of ornaments from Christmas Past. Some of the items were handmade paper ornaments, yellowing and curling, the glued-on glitter flaking off. Most of them were original to our parents' marriage, bought at a time before children, when Birdland was still a place for hepcats to go and swing, baby, swing. "Just in time," Sparky deadpanned. "Here's how this is going to go: I'll unwrap each ornament." Each of them were wrapped in individual sheets off a papertowel roll. "I'll tell you whether it is high, low or in-between. All ornaments will be placed in precise intervals from each other. Some of these ornaments will have to go in the back because they're not looking great. Others, clearly, belong in the front. Shall we begin?"

"Can't wait," Sissy said.

"I'm not sure I like the way you said that," Sparky said.

"And yet, here we stand," Sissy said.

80

In less than fifteen minutes, we were ushered out of the room and told to do anything other than help Sparky place ornaments on the tree.

That left us free for a game of Thermonuclear Risk. After an hour, Kamchatka was a radioactive wasteland, as were the Western United States and Great Britain. "The British probably deserved that," Sissy said, placing a red game piece from Sorry! on Great Britain, designating it as uninhabitable. "I'm bored. How about you?"

"I'm bored, too."

"Let's have some fun."

"This fun doesn't involve moving around the ornaments on the tree, does it?"

"It's like you read my mind, little brother." We walked over to the Florida room and found the tree perfectly symmetrically decorated. Even the tinsel was uniformly placed. "This will not do." Sissy rearranged the tree in such a way that it didn't look that much different, but it certainly wasn't perfect anymore. "Much better, don't you think?"

"Sparky's gonna freak."

"Like I said: Much better."

Dad came walking in through the front door, wearing his plaid suit and carrying a book of paper samples under his arm. "Since you like to draw, I thought you'd like this paper," he said.

I walked over and he handed it to me. "Thank you. This is great!" It wasn't that great, but Dad required constant and lavish praise.

"Did you kids decorate the tree?" he asked. "It looks good."

"Thank you. Sparky did most of the work," Sissy said. "I merely added some final touches."

"Your mother isn't going to be home tonight, so I gotta make dinner."

We looked at each other and then him. "You sure about that?" Sissy asked him.

"Yeah. Your mother isn't gonna be home."

"No. The second part."

"I can make dinner."

"Have you ever made dinner?" Sissy asked. "I'm not being insulting here."

"How hard could it be?"

Sissy was practically vibrating with anticipation of how hard it could be. "That's the spirit, Dad."

"Anyone can make dinner."

"I agree," Sissy said, smiling ear-to-ear. She giggled and hopped up and down. She grabbed my arm and I dropped the paper and quickly picked it up.

"I'm gonna make a casserole."

"And I'm gonna watch!"

"I'm not sure I appreciate your tone," Dad said. But it was Sissy, so all was forgiven.

She followed me back to my room as I put the paper away. "Fire and explosions!" she practically shouted. "Where do the parents keep the Instamatic?"

"I'm glad *you're* excited," I said.

"Don't worry. We'll be eating at Pizza Hut tonight. Guaranteed. What are you going to get at the salad bar? I want some of that macaroni salad. Let's get an order of garlic bread!"

"He's going to be angry."

"It'll be fine."

"Fine for you."

"Fine for us all. Don't worry. I have it covered." Sissy rubbed her eyes for a moment. "Oh, the crocodile tears. I feel them coming on. Such sadness that dinner exploded. Boo-hoo-hoo."

"It's not convincing when you're laughing at the same time."

"I'm like Brando. I have to be in the moment, Fredo." We'd been allowed to stay up and watch *The Godfather: A novel for television* on NBC.

"How am I Fredo?"

"I don't know. The sad sack thing, I guess. Hurry up! We're gonna miss the whole show."

We walked out in time to see Dad emerge from the bedroom in his v-neck t-shirt and boxer shorts. "Where does your mother keep the, uh, pots and stuff?" he asked. He didn't wait for a reply. He dug around and found the Corning Ware ceramic casserole dish and the accompanying glass lid. He placed the dish on the stove top.

Sissy and I sat down on the kitchen countertop to watch, swinging our feet beneath us. When Dad opened up a can of condensed mushroom soup and upended it into the dish, she grabbed my forearm. He dumped a box of frozen carrots in there and a can of tuna fish. He sprinkled some uncooked egg noodles in and mixed it around with a serving spoon.

I whispered to Sissy, "What if we have to eat this?"

"What's that?" Dad asked.

"Looks delicious," I said.

Then Dad turned on the stove burner to high.

"Fear not," Sissy said.

We didn't have to wait long for the ceramic casserole dish to explode, cracking into five or six separate pieces. The casserole mess caught fire on the burner, flames shooting upward to the kitchen ceiling, leaving a circle of char.

Sissy squeezed my arm so hard that I cried out. "Ow!"

"Yee-hee-hee!" she went.

"No reason to be scared," Dad said, turning off the burner and dumping a glass of water on the flames. He stood there for a moment, studying the wreckage. "I don't understand what went wrong." That's when Sissy began to cry. It was an emotive performance, crocodile tears, red face and all. The red face was probably from suppressed laughter. Dad came over and hugged her. "There, there," he went.

"Now we're not gonna have any dinner!" Sissy complained dramatically. "Oh, and Mom is going to be so, so angry when she sees this!"

"Sparky!" Dad yelled. "Get out here and help!"

Sparky emerged from his room. He stood in the den sniffing the air quizzically and then entered the kitchen. "What the—?"

"Don't say a word. Not one word. Help me clean this up. And see if you can find that leftover can of paint out in the garage."

"Did you try to make dinner?" Sparky asked.

"Your mother wasn't going to be home tonight."

Sparky looked over at Sissy and knew. He shook his head at her. She sat upright and wiped away her tears. "I guess Pizza Hut is out of the question," she said.

"Is that what you want, honey? Pizza Hut?"

"We can't afford it," Sissy said sadly.

"We *can* afford it," Dad said.

"No, we can't," Sparky said. "You told Mom that Christmas was cancelled because we're broke."

"We can afford a meal," Dad said. "I have some room on my MasterCharge."

Sparky shook his head. He sighed. He gave up. "I'll go get the paint." He turned to me. "I suggest that you figure out a way to get all of that into the trash." He gestured to the steaming pile of rubble on the stove.

It took about an hour, but we made the stove and ceiling look pretty much like they had before Dad decided that he could cook.

In those days, Pizza Hut was a middle-brow dining experience, complete with a salad bar, pricey pizzas, little rounds of garlic bread and paper placemats with Pizza Hut Pete dancing merrily on them. Each table had a red checkerboard tablecloth and a glowing red candle. There were waitresses to bring pitchers of Pepsi to the table, to be poured into red plastic cups filled with ice.

Eventually, as teenagers, Sissy and I would both work at that same Pizza Hut.

Sissy would die in a Pizza Hut, shortly after midnight on our mother's birthday, shot in the back of the head during what was initially thought of as a robbery.

But on this night, Pizza Hut was the lap of luxury.

We were happy, all of us. Even our father. Even Sparky.

But Sissy was the happiest of us all.

She, more than any of the rest of us, understood life. She understood that it was made up of moments that were both sad and hilarious, and she chose to embrace life's hilarity. I remember her laughter that evening, It was contagious. It was filled with joy. Her father had exploded dinner. It was a scream.

Enter the Schnauzer

"I wanted a dog for my birthday," Sparky said. "Not a rat." He left the den and we listened to his door close.

"That went well," Sissy said.

"I got socks for my birthday," I said. "And a thawed-out Pepperidge Farm cake."

"Tough! That's life!" Mom shouted. "No one gets what they want!"

"Spoken like the voice of experience," Sissy said.

"Watch it, Miss Tishenbaum!" Mom said. "You're on thin ice."

We stood in a semicircle around the tiny, gray puppy, who appeared to be slipping in and out of consciousness. Someone had chopped the puppy's tail into a nub and snipped her formerly floppy ears in half so they were Vulcan pointy. She had a white beard and sea-spent eyes, like a wee ancient mariner.

"Who's naming the puppy?" I asked.

"Her name is Gretchen," Mom said. "That's the dog's name. Anyone who has a problem with that can take it up with a court of law and you'll lose."

"Shouldn't Sparky name the dog?" Sissy asked.

"Oh, you'd like that, wouldn't you? Forcing your brother to name a dog that he clearly doesn't like." Mom crossed her arms. She was still dressed for work in her pastel pantsuit and hard shoes. "Who's going to take the dog outside? Someone better." Mom crouched down and shouted in the puppy's face, "No one's taking you outside! What a welcome, huh?"

The puppy winced at Mom and let loose a little croak out of the back of her throat.

Anything that Mom took care of didn't last long. The houseplants were evidence of that, crinkly brown in their pots arrayed around the lanai. Sissy and I would have to take charge of the little pooch.

"She's full of life," Sissy said, still wearing her green-plaid Catholic schoolgirl jumper, her golden hair woven into braids. "I wonder who picked her out?"

"She was the last one in the litter. Besides, the breeder said we can make a lot of money if we get her pregnant with another purebred Miniature Schnauzer."

"Teenage pregnancy," Sissy said, tsk-tsking. "The scourge of our times."

"Everything's a joke to you," Mom carped.

"When everything stops being a joke, I'll let you know," Sissy said. "In the meantime, I'm going to continue laughing."

"Well laugh while you take your new dog on a walk. There's a leash around here somewhere. And pick up after her! We're not savages."

Sparky's Pepperidge Farm cake was thawing in a Rubbermaid plastic cake carrier on the kitchen table. He hadn't requested the cake or the puppy, and he'd walked away from both.

"Buzz, see if you can find some candles in the junk drawer."

"I thought I was taking the dog on a walk."

"Fine! I'll find the candles. Your brother had better grace us with his presence for his birthday, or he's in trouble."

Sissy sang the birthday song while putting the puppy's leash on. She gave it a slight yank and the puppy didn't react. Gretchen sat in the same spot, stunned. Maybe all of Mom's shouting put her into a trance. Maybe it was being in an unfamiliar environment. Maybe, by becoming a member of our family, she'd figured out that she was screwed and had already given up.

"I would have named her 'Mandy,'" Sissy said.

"That's a stupid song," I snapped.

"Shut up. Barry Manilow is sweet," Sissy said.

"That dog's name is Gretchen, end of story. Period! Full stop!" Mom shouted. "Now take your new dog outside! All you kids did was complain that you wanted a dog forever and we finally get you one and this is my thanks! Fine!"

I picked the puppy up and she was shaking. "It's okay. Everything will be great. You'll see."

"Liar," Sissy said.

We went out the front door. I set the puppy down on the thick carpet of St. Augustine grass and various subtropical weeds that composed our lawn. We weren't going to win any yard of the month awards. The puppy stared off into the middle distance, not knowing what to make of her situation. Sissy handed me the leash and crouched down. "All I know is that someone is going to get dressed up in my old baby clothes. That ought to cheer you up, Gretchen." She scratched the puppy's chin and she made a little sound halfway between a snarl and a cry. "You're gonna fit right in."

Brandy was riding past on her elaborate French bicycle and came quickly to a halt. She pulled up to the sidewalk in front of our house and parked the bike. "Is that a puppy?"

"That's the ongoing theory," Sissy said.

"She's, uh, not all there," I said.

"Of course she's 'all there,'" Brandy admonished me. "She's just scared. Everything's so new, including you." She was dressed in a pair of black jeans and a black t-shirt that said, NEW YORK DOLLS in bright red, a cartoon tube of lipstick underneath. She sat down on the grass and cooed at the puppy. The puppy's eyes lit up and she ran over to Brandy, yanking the leash out of my hand. "She's a sweetheart." The puppy licked Brandy's chin and then ran in circles around her, yapping happily. I felt a warm sensation whirling around my heart. "You better grab her leash before she runs out into the street."

"What?" I went, and then snapped out of my reverie and quickly caught up with Gretchen, scooping her up. She licked my face.

"How old is she?" Brandy asked.

"No idea," Sissy said.

"Someone butchered her ears and tail." Brandy tsked a bit.

"A breeder," Sissy said. "Before we got her."

"Fascists!" Brandy said.

My heart leapt.

"Where were you going in such a hurry?" Sissy asked.

"I finished that book you told me about!" Brandy said excitedly. "You were right. Stephen King is a genius. I was taking it back to the library."

"She made you read *Carrie*, too, huh?" I said. "Hey! Aren't you the one who says that you don't like fiction? That you don't need someone else to interpret life for you?"

"But your sister has such great taste," Brandy said in her California voice. "I trust her."

Sissy smirked and shook her head in the affirmative. "Did you hear that, Buzz? Don't be such a naysayer. In Sissy We Trust."

"I have good taste," I said lamely.

"You were dancing and singing along to Leo Sayer in your room the other day."

I blushed and got angry. "I wasn't… How would you know if I was dancing?"

"I can tell when you're dancing. I can always tell." Sissy turned to Brandy confidentially and said, "It's sad, really." To me, she said, "AM radio will be your downfall."

"I'm allowed to have private moments." My face was burning.

"Let me go get my bicycle and we can go to the library together," Sissy said. "I'll be right back." Sissy ran into the house, leaving me alone with Brandy and the dog for a moment.

Brandy walked over and petted the dog. I swallowed hard. She was so close to me. These were such new feelings. I had no idea what to do with them. "I think it's cute that you dance to Leo Sayer."

I blushed and swallowed again. "Um. Thanks."

The garage door opened and Sissy emerged on her bicycle. She navigated her way out into the street and skillfully rolled around doing figure eights. "Say goodbye to each other and let's go!"

Brandy said, "Goodbye, I guess."

"Everyone does what she tells them to do eventually," I said.

"That's because I'm always right!" Sissy shouted from the street.

"You didn't say 'goodbye,'" Brandy said.

"I don't always have to do what she tells me to do," I said. Then I shrugged and said, "Goodbye."

Brandy got on her French bicycle and rolled away, accompanied by Sissy.

I sat on the lawn playing with the puppy, holding onto the leash so she wouldn't run into the street. She quickly exhausted herself and stood in front of me panting. Then she peed and pooped in quick succession. I hadn't brought anything with me to pick up the poop. I scooped up the dog into the crook of my left arm. I walked into the garage and found a garden trowel hanging on a hook, came back out and scooped up the poop, and took it to the garbage can on the side of the house on the same pad as the air conditioner. The garden hose was next to all that, neatly coiled by Sparky during one of his organization jags. I washed off the trowel with the hose, still holding the puppy in one arm. She seemed to enjoy the whole experience of watching me work.

The neighbor on that side of the house was Mr. Gray. Our houses were barely ten feet apart and I could hear him in his house singing along with Doris Day:

I love you a bushel and a peck
A bushel and a peck and a hug around the neck
A hug around the neck and a barrel and a heap
A barrel and a heap and I'm talkin' in my sleep

"See," I told the puppy. "Even adults sing along with the radio. Perfectly normal. Bet he's dancing, too."

Mr. Gray heard me and came over to the open window. "Yes, Young Mister Pepper, I both dance and sing."

It startled me a bit and the puppy, too, who yapped and growled out her disapproval. She struggled to get out of my grasp, so I set her down, while hanging onto the leash.

"Hello, sir," I said.

"Hello, yourself," he said, grinning through the window screen at me. "New dog?"

"Yes, sir."

"Bring her out front and let me introduce myself to her so she won't bite me in the future."

Mr. Gray was a recently retired executive. My father said that he had a soft grip when they shook hands. Buster called it a "wet noodle."

We met in Mr. Gray's front lawn, which had no weeds in it and was perfectly green and uniform. He was wearing a Hawaiian shirt and big, baggy shorts along with a pair of long black socks and shiny black oxfords. His white hair was clipped short and greased back with Vitalis. I recognized the scent. He had a neatly trimmed mustache. The whites of his eyes had a bluish tint, like certain metals when they corrode. He wore black, horn-rimmed glasses. He crouched down, somewhat painfully, and petted the puppy, who, after some hesitation, decided that she would tolerate him. After a minute or two of this, he stood up, painfully again, and said, "You both look like you could use a drink. I know I could."

I followed him inside his house. It was a smaller version of our house. The furniture was white and appeared to be made of straw and bamboo, like he was a British soldier stationed in a far-off land that they'd subjugated. I peered around the room, mostly at all the old-timey black and white photos. In one, Mr. Gray was posing with a bubble-shaped car and a pair of girls in one-piece swimsuits, sashes across their chests that said *1952*. In another, Mr. Gray and several other gentlemen were standing on a dais looking off into the distance, like they could see the prosperity of our great nation continuing on into eternity. In another, I saw Mr. Gray and Mrs. Gray getting married. A discharge certificate from the United States Marine Corps for Lance Corporal William Spaulding Gray hung among all this.

"You were a Marine?" I asked, pointing at the certificate.

"Yes, indeed," he said, handing me a tiny bottle of Schwepp's Bitter Lemon. "I was at Guadalcanal." In his other hand was a drink I recognized. It was a whiskey sour.

I was starstruck. None of the executive stuff made an impression on me, but I had a vision of Mr. Gray as a swaggering young Marine, standing in the jungle with a rifle held at port arms, a cigarette dangling from his mouth, covered in grit, no shave, his steel pot helmet at a rakish angle, talking about how he'd get those Japanese after what they did to his best buddy Clyde, and who would tell Clyde's poor ma back in Brooklyn that Clyde had got it right in the guts? Clyde, who was only days away from rotating to the rear! He just showed me a picture of his gal! She was a blonde with gams that went on for a mile, I tell you! She was exactly who we're fighting this war for! America! And the General Motors Corporation! Why, I tell you, I'll work for GM after the war because that's what America's all about! Opportunity!

What I ended up saying was, "Wow!"

"To be honest, I wasn't there that long. I got this strange mold in my ear from sleeping on the ground and it threw off my balance, so I ended up getting evacuated before the real fighting started."

"Oh," I went.

"But Australia was awfully nice. You haven't tried your drink. It's a mixer."

I took a sip and winced. It lived up to its name. "Thanks."

He took the bottle from me. "It's not for everyone, I suppose. We're not set up for children around here. Never had any of our own."

I checked out his bookshelf. It was filled with Reader's Digest Condensed Books. I pulled one out. It had *Airport, Nicholas and Alexandra, The Kitchen Madonna* and *Vanished* all in the same volume. I put it back.

"You like books? The missus gets those through some subscription scheme. Bunch of guff, if you ask me."

I shrugged.

"Listen, I have a business proposition for you. I've seen you cutting your lawn and I think you do a fine job of it."

I didn't do a fine job of it. I was barely competent and it generally took me five or six yanks of the ripcord to get the mower started. By the end, I was completely covered in dirt, bugs and bits of grass, and the grass was unevenly mowed. Thanks to all the weeds, no one could tell how poor a job I'd done. "Thanks."

"How about I pay you to cut my front and side lawn the next time you cut your lawn?"

"How much?"

"Ah! The smart businessman. How about seven dollars?"

Seven dollars! I'd never seen that much cash. I had to keep cool, or the jig would be up. "Why, seven dollars sounds acceptable to me."

"Excellent. I'm glad we could come to an arrangement." He reached out and we shook hands. Dad was right. It was a soft handshake. "Wet noodle" covered it nicely. "Oh, and another thing. If your sister and her young friend, and you, of course, would like to come over and swim in our pool, you'd be more than welcome to."

"Thanks. Is that part of the lawn deal?"

"No, that's anytime. Completely different. You could have said 'no' to the lawn arrangement and all of you would be welcome to come over for a dip."

"I guess that's fine then."

The puppy was yapping at a cockatiel flapping around in a cage in the kitchen. I quickly snatched her up and carried her to the foyer, where Mr. Gray was waiting. "Once you finish the lawn, just knock on the door and I'll have your money waiting for you."

"Roger dodger," I said.

"And don't forget to tell your sister and her friend about the pool."

"Sure thing."

I made my way back home quickly. Seven dollars! A fortune! And pool privileges, too. I thought it was a pretty sweet deal because I've never been very bright.

Mom was in the den, drinking a Manhattan, her feet up. She'd changed over to her housecoat and slippers. "Dinner's in the oven," she said drowsily. "It's a pot roast."

"Sounds good," I said, setting the puppy down and taking her leash off. She sniffed at our carpet and licked.

"Where's your sister?"

"She went on a bike ride with Brandy."

"The girl who stole my Keely Smith record? That one?"

"We lent it to her. She forgot to bring it back."

"Sounds like stealing to me. At least she has good taste, unlike you. Everyone heard you singing along to Leo Sayer the other day. And dancing around in your room like it was a discotheque."

"Great," I went, throwing my hands in the air. I changed the subject. "So I got a job from Mr. Gray. He's gonna let me cut his lawn for seven bucks."

"Let you, huh?"

"He asked if I wanted to do it."

"He's an old weirdo, if you ask me. But seven bucks is seven bucks. Don't tell your father. He'll just take the money. You go spend it on whatever you want, honey. Buy all the Leo Sayer records you want."

"I'm not buying any Leo Sayer records."

"Whatever you say." She shook her empty glass at me. "How about a refill? You remember how to make a Manhattan?"

"Don't spare the bitters," I said. "Three cherries." As I made her drink, I told her about Mr. Gray's offer to have Sissy and Brandy go over to swim in Mr. Gray's pool.

"Only if you're along," Mom said. "Don't let him try anything weird."

"Weird? Like what?" I handed her the drink.

She took a sip. "Not bad." She set it down on the TV tray. "Look, men are full of weird impulses. Your sister and her little friend are very attractive. Though that friend could use a tan. She looks like a ghost."

"I like her pale skin," I said.

"I bet you do, you little weirdo." Mom sat up a bit. "Hah! That's why you wanted the black t-shirt for Christmas! Because that girl wears black all the time! Oh, it's becoming clear to me now." Mom laughed mockingly. "You have a crush on her! Oh, honey. I think you're boxing above your weight class there." Mom laughed a bit more, and then pushed it inside. "I shouldn't be laughing, because it's sweet that you have a crush on a girl. Even if that girl will be dating the captain of the football team in a couple of years."

"I didn't say that I had a crush on her!"

"Like you could ever hide anything from me. I'm your mother! You think I don't know you? You take a little getting used to, if you know what I mean. You're an acquired taste. That girl will have her pick of all the boys, just like your sister, and you're never the first one picked for anything. Let's face it. I'm just being honest here, honey. You shouldn't get your hopes up."

"May I go stick my head in a bucket of water and drown myself now?"

"No. You may certainly not. You're too good a bartender to drown." She took another sip of her drink. "Where's the dog?" She peered around. "Hey! Gretchen! Get out here! Yo, ho!"

I got on my hands and knees. The puppy had crawled underneath the couch, driven there, no doubt, by the battering ram of my mother's voice.

The front door slammed open, and the puppy backed further under the couch, beyond my reach.

Buster came stomping into the room, dressed in his powder blue leisure suit. "Who left the garage door open? Something could get stolen!"

"No one's stealing our crap," Mom said. "Who's gonna steal the crap of the poorest people in the neighborhood? No one, that's who."

For some reason, that actually made sense to Buster. He nodded his head in agreement. "Did you get the dog?"

"Buzz is trying to coax her out from under the couch."

"Any idea when we can breed her? I heard that you can make five hundred per puppy."

"We only paid two-fifty for this one," Mom said.

"But that's because she was the runt. And the breeder wanted dibs on providing the sire." Buster had that gleam in his eye. Money, money, money.

I made little kissing sounds to the puppy. I could only see her eyes now, blinking.

"Oh, you're never going to get her out like that." Mom went in the kitchen, lifted the cake lid, and pinched a piece off of Sparky's thawed birthday cake. It was decorated with a half-dozen half-burnt candles. Mom pushed me out of the way and waved the cake at the puppy. Gretchen dutifully crawled out and nearly removed the tip of Mom's finger snapping at the cake. Mom picked the puppy up and plopped down with her on the couch. "Just us girls! Having a relaxing day!"

Buster lost interest and went to the bedroom to change for the evening.

Merv Griffin was talking with Elke Sommer about whatever her latest project was on the TV set. "Oooh," Merv purred at the sultry German actress.

"Should I check on dinner?" I asked.

"Go get your brother. It's *his* birthday dinner, so *he* should check on it. Where is he? Why isn't he out here? Is he in the witness protection program? Tell him the mob hit is off!"

I walked around the corner and tapped on Sparky's door. "Uh, Sparky…"

"Yeah, I heard everything," he grumbled through the door. "I'll be out in a second."

I went back into the den. Sissy came walking in from the garage. Brandy was right behind her.

"It's Miss Tish and the record thief," Mom said. "Right on time. Your older brother will shortly grace us with his presence. Who'd want to miss that?"

"I'm sorry about the record, Mrs. Pepper," Brandy said. "I didn't mean to keep it for so long."

"Did you love it though?" Mom asked her.

"I loved it," Brandy admitted.

"That's fine then." Mom talked to the dog. "What a polite young lady. Maybe she'll have some sort of influence on Sissy." She leaned down as if the dog was talking to her. "What's that? Sissy has a head made of stone? Why, what an observant dog you are! You'll get more cake later on."

"Yeah. Keep taking advice from a creature who eats her own poop," Sissy said. "I'm sure you'll get some sterling advice from her."

Brandy was standing next to me. She whispered, "Do you always talk this way to your mother?"

"Sissy does." I grinned at Brandy. "Sissy does whatever she wants. She always has and she always will."

"You admire her."

"Of course I do."

I felt Brandy's hand grasp mine, just for a moment, and give it a squeeze. "I have to go," Brandy said upon seeing my underwear-clad father stomp into the room. "I'll see you later, Sissy! Buzz!" She exited through the garage in a near-panic. Our family could be a bit overwhelming for the casual visitor.

"She's not staying for dinner? Cake?" Mom asked. She turned to the dog and shouted into her face, "I guess someone doesn't like fine dining!"

Sparky pulled the dutch oven out of the oven and set it on a trivet on the kitchen counter. He pulled off the lid and a cloud of black smoke escaped, billowing volcanically toward the ceiling before dissipating somewhat. "I'll try to scrape something out of the bottom," Sparky said without a bit of hope in his voice.

"It'll be fine," Mom said. She turned and shouted into the dog's face, "Isn't that right, Gretchen? It'll be just fine! I bet you'd love to eat that dinner! You're not a picky eater like *some* children I could name." She didn't have to say my name. It hung in the air, just like the charred remains of the pot roast.

The dog sat in Mom's lap, trembling, looking for a way to escape. There'd be no escape for her. None whatsoever.

The Perfect Cookie

My father insisted that I needed to participate in sports because I was lacking a certain manliness. "You don't have the killer instinct," he said, sadly. "You need that to survive in this world. You'll be eaten alive."

I didn't like the sound of that, so I tried to take sports seriously.

During the hour that Sissy was watching *Hope Hospital*—which now featured a bionic Bigfoot remote-controlled by the same madman who had the weather machine on the island—I took the opportunity to go into the backyard and make use of the Jorgenson's pitch back machine. In summers past, my grandfather had taught me all sorts of pitches, all with different grips. I threw screwballs, knucklers and a high lob that was meant to drop through the strike zone in such a way that it was unhittable. He also taught me how to place vaseline on the bill of my cap or down the seam of my trousers so I could throw a spitball. If I'd been even a marginal athlete, all of my grandfather's training might have done me a bit of good. But I had trouble getting the ball inside the red box on the springy net in front of me, and it was an adventure fielding the ball afterward. I often found myself saying hello to Mr. Gray as I ran past his backyard pool. He stood there shirtless, wearing large bathing trunks and scrubbing the pool with a brush attached to a long aluminum handle. "Practice makes perfect," he said. "Keep at it!" And: "That's the spirit!" And: "Remember, the pool is available! Bring your sister and her friend over anytime!"

I was grateful that he hadn't pointed out what a terrible job I'd done on his lawn. I'd squirreled the money he'd paid me away in a savings account opened for me by my father. The bank was in a trailer next to the future Sarasota Square Mall, which was now five months behind schedule due to, Mom assured us, the inherent laziness of hookworm-infected southerners.

My grandfather added that if there were union laborers down south, that mall would already be finished.

The day before, I'd ridden my bike down to the future mall, and parked in front of the bank trailer, which was in front of the under-construction bank. I brought along my passbook. The teller took my money and cranked the passbook into a typewriter and clacked in my new total. Along with a check from my grandparents for my combined birthday and Christmas, I was nearing the ungodly total of $50 in my savings account. I looked around the bank skeptically. It was in a trailer. What if someone decided to hook up a truck to the joint and tow it away? Then I'd be out fifty smackeroos! I said this to the teller and she told me they were insured by the FDIC, the federal government itself, so that I shouldn't worry. "But," I countered, "the federal government is currently being run by some doofus from Michigan. Michigan! He clearly doesn't know what he's doing with the inflation and the Mayaguez thing and all." The teller rolled her eyes and handed me my passbook. I looked at the shaky old guy who was supposed to be guarding the place, wearing a sad imitation cop uniform, sitting on a stool in the corner, and had even less confidence. No wonder old people stuffed money into mattresses, I thought.

I finally managed to hit the little box in the center of the pitch back machine, the ball rolled up to me, an easy grounder, and I reached down and nabbed it. This would be the closest I'd get to success, I decided, so I took the glove off and placed it next to the pitch back machine along with the ball. I looked over and saw Mrs. Jorgenson standing on the pool apron, a glass of Kool Aid in one hand and a cookie in the other. "Hello?" she called out. I looked around and realized that she was speaking to me. "After all that work, I thought you might like a bit of refreshment."

I walked around her pool cage and found the door on the side. I was being beaconed to Mrs. Jorgenson's perfect house. I let myself in. Mrs. Jorgenson was tall and elegant. She had on a white tennis outfit and unscuffed white tennis shoes. She was spotless, her blonde hair perfectly coiffed, her tasteful makeup evenly applied. She handed me a perfectly round and perfectly flat chocolate chip cookie and a cold glass of cherry Kool Aid. "Come in and sit down, please. I could use the company."

I followed her into her house.

She had made a place for me at the kitchen table, a glass-topped metal-framed round table with four metal chairs. I sat down at the place she'd set for me. I placed the cookie on a Fiestaware plate and set the drink down on a coaster that advertised Borden condensed milk. She sat across from me and smiled in way that nearly broke my heart. "Go on," she said. "Eat your cookie. Please."

I took a bite and it was like nothing I'd ever experienced in my short life. Later on, of course, I'd figure out why. Mrs. Jorgenson had made the cookie using butter and not margarine. She'd used real vanilla extract. The chocolate chips were brand-name, not the cheap kind. And, most importantly, Mrs. Jorgenson actually knew how to create edible food using an oven.

I took a sip of the Kool Aid. It had a nearly narcotic effect on me. Mrs. Jorgenson had measured out the correct amount of sugar for the Kool Aid. Mom never did. She shorted it by half a cup, and if we complained, she said no one could tell. "But we can tell, Mom!"

"I'm not buying it," Mom would retort.

"This is the greatest cookie ever made," I told Mrs. Jorgenson. "I'm not kidding."

Her smile brightened considerably. "Thank you," she said.

"No, ma'am. Thank *you*," I said, savoring another bite. I closed my eyes while chewing the heavenly cookie. This is what a cookie was supposed to taste like! No wonder other kids talked about cookies like they were something you were supposed to look forward to! "May I ask a favor? I'd like to take one home to my sister."

"Oh, of course! You can take a couple of them home with you. I'll wrap them up in a napkin for when you're ready to leave." She got up and opened up a fancy ceramic cookie jar on her spotless kitchen counter. She pulled out a fancy paper napkin and wrapped two cookies in it, tying them up with a thin red ribbon pulled off a spool that she kept in a drawer. She placed this in front of me. It looked like a birthday present. I was nearly moved to tears by her kindness.

I finished the cookie and gasped with pleasure as I swallowed the last little bit. I polished off the Kool Aid.

"It's so nice having you here, especially now that Michael and Susan are away. Michael is at a special camp for special boys. Susan is at pre-cheer camp." Mrs. Jorgenson wiped the table as she spoke.

"What's pre-cheer camp?"

"It's for little girls who want to be cheerleaders. The camp builds up their confidence."

"It's good to have confidence."

"Yes, it is. I wish there had been something like that for me when I was a girl. I never felt like I was one of the in-crowd. Do you know what I mean?"

"I do."

"I've always felt like I needed to do better. To be better. I never felt like I quite made the grade." She sat down across from me again. "My husband is always out of town. He travels for his work. It's important work, I understand that, but it can get lonely here. There's only so much time I can spend at the tennis club, or cleaning this house."

"Life requires purpose." I don't know why I said it. It came out.

"That's right. I hope you get to live a purposeful life. I've had two children. And can I tell you a secret? I've had two tummy tucks. Do you know what a tummy tuck is? It's plastic surgery. I've also had a nose job." She turned her head to the side so I could see her profile. "See how straight my nose is?"

It was straight as a ruler. "Yes," I said.

She showed me her teeth, too, telling me that they'd all been capped. "I work out all the time and never get to eat all these cookies that I bake because I'm afraid I'll gain weight."

"What happens if you gain weight?"

"Buzz, I don't know. I'm afraid to gain weight. I'm afraid all of the time of losing what I have here, but I don't know why I need to have all this. Come with me."

I stood up and she took my hand. We walked through her house together, looking into the two kids' rooms and their mountains of toys. We looked at her perfect dining room, with two sets of perfect china. "I bought the second set from your mother. She's an excellent saleslady." The china cabinet came from Denmark. Its wood was unblemished by fingerprints and unmarred by scarring. The dining room table and chairs had come from Sweden. We walked into her Florida room. The white leather sofa had come from Italy. The coffee table was from France. We went into her bedroom and she opened her closet for me. She pulled out dresses and named the men who designed each one. They looked like the same dresses from the Academy Awards shows. Her husband's side of the closet featured a half dozen suits that looked approximately the same and a tuxedo. She let me touch the cuff. It was like silk.

We went back to her kitchen. She handed me the daintily wrapped cookies. "You're a good listener."

"Thank you."

"Anytime you want to come visit, please come over. Just you. It's not that I don't care for your sister or your brother. There's something about you." She bent over and gave me a hug. For once, I didn't feel like it was an imposition. She smiled brightly at me and caressed my face with her impeccably maintained hand. If she had callouses from her tennis racket, I certainly didn't feel them. I looked into her eyes and saw a familiar look in there.

When I got married, I saw the same look in my wife's eyes. I thought that if I could make her happy, it would somehow make me happy. I remember standing with her in the Manatee County Courthouse, the two of us frightened of an uncertain future, frightened that we were going to each give up our autonomy for someone who was so familiarly sad. My wife was beautiful that day. I remember her wearing a simple dress, standing in front of me in a little side room in the courthouse, the two of us being married by a clerk of the court. Afterward, the clerk took my wife's camera from her and shot a picture of the two of us, nervous smiles and all.

I never told her how beautiful she was that day. I suppose I never will, now that the two of us have permanently parted ways. I'll probably never see her again. She moved out of state, to get away from me and the horrible memories we generated together, two sad people making each other more miserable.

Mrs. Jorgenson escorted me out through the sliding glass door, across her pool deck and out of the pool cage through the door. I walked back into our weedy lawn, which now featured dead spots thanks to the puppy's urine. I turned around and waved to her with my free hand. She gave me a perfect wave back and then retreated into her perfect house.

The last time I ever saw Mrs. Jorgenson was at my sister's wake. This unfamiliar woman came up to me and gave me a hug and talked to me like we were old friends. She was clearly drunk, wearing an old sweater with tissues tucked into the rolled up cuffs. "Don't you recognize me?" she asked.

"I'm sorry."

She said her name. She was talking to me like we were old friends because we were. She'd told me all her secrets over the course of four years, until we left Gulf Gate Woods, sitting with me in her kitchen. She told me everything at my sister's wake, standing next to a Publix cheese platter. Her husband had left her, and then he died. The two kids got married and moved away. They were distant. "Oh, but I do miss our little chats," she said. "Do you remember them?"

I said I did. I was still numb at that point, so I didn't understand that this sad woman wanted someone to talk to, someone who would listen to her. I was numb and I'd stay numb until I got married, and even then I remained trapped inside an unbreakable shell. I remain in that shell today. But that's no excuse for my behavior. I should have offered to go over to Mrs. Jorgenson's house, even if the fare was bourbon, judging by her breath, and not perfect cookies and sugary Kool Aid. I should have listened to her. I wasn't listening, and she drifted off to hit the open bar on the lanai. I reached over and picked up a cracker-sized slice of Monterey Jack, stood there with it in my hand, and then wondered why a piece of cheese was in my hand a few minutes later.

Sissy was waiting for me at our sliding glass door. "What do we have here?"

"The greatest cookies in the human experience."

"I see. You were in there for an hour. What the hell?"

"She's lonely. Her two kids are gone and the husband is gone. I'm a reasonable substitute for human companionship, I guess."

"Likely story," Sissy said, squinting skeptically at me. "Let's see the cookies." We went into the kitchen. I opened up the napkin and revealed them to her there on the same kitchen counter where we'd seen so many massacred dinners. Suddenly, Gretchen was sitting expectantly at our feet. "Well, well, well. Look who decided to make an appearance."

Gretchen grumbled and sat down, showing off all the work we'd been putting into her obedience training.

Sissy took a bite of the cookie. Her eyes closed. She set the remainder of the cookie on the kitchen counter and savored what she had in her mouth. After she swallowed it, she said, "My God. Is that what a cookie is supposed to taste like?"

"Yes," I said.

"You could have warned me that I was about to have a life-altering experience."

"I tried."

"You're not getting any!" she shouted at the puppy, who backed up several steps.

I broke off a small piece of mine and handed it down to Gretchen, who nearly took off the tip off of my index finger and thumb snapping at it. "Good girl," I told her.

"She's not *that* good," Sissy said. "No one's that good. I'm certainly not that good. I feel inadequate after one bite. If the host at church tasted this good, I'd have a better feeling that God was hiding in there. I'd pray to a God that tasted like this."

"You pray at church."

"I pray that mass ends as quickly as possible and God lets me down every time." Sissy picked up the cookie and sniffed it from end to end like a cigar connoisseur, her eyes closed. She took another bite, chewed it, and eventually swallowed. She opened her eyes. "So Mrs. Jorgenson, huh? You get the grand tour?"

"Yes."

"I didn't get the grand tour! I had to sneak around and look at everything for myself." Sissy grabbed my forearm. "Did you see inside her closet? Those clothes!"

"I shouldn't talk about it."

"Why not? Do you think you're gonna keep secrets from me?" Sissy squeezed my arm hard. "Because you're *not*."

"She showed me around the house. That's all."

"Uh huh. Did you get the hug at the end? Because women can't resist your sad, widdle eyes, can they?" Sissy made a sad face with a bulging lower lip. "Oh, sweet, sad Buzz! Gimme a hug, you poor sad creature." Sissy threw open her arms like she was going to give me a hug. "Boo-hoo-hoo."

I backed away, my hands up defensively. "Okay. That's enough."

"Oh, sad, sad Buzz. Let me give you a hug and take away all your sadness." She dropped her arms and glared bitterly. "Adults are stupid. You know that, right?" She picked up the cookie and finished it, chewing it down. "But at least some of them can bake."

The doorbell rang, so Sissy strode past me to go answer it. She was still dressed in her school uniform, her house key hanging from a chain around her neck, her hair woven into a pair of pigtails, pink ribbons binding the ends. She flung open the door, revealing a pair of men in their mid-20's, hair neatly combed and parted in the middle, wearing short-sleeved white dress shirts, dark ties and dark slacks. One of them had a Bible in his hands. Their eyes lit up looking at Sissy. I came up behind her.

"Hello," the one on the left said.

"What are you two selling?" Sissy asked coquettishly.

"We aren't selling anything," the one on the left said.

"Unless you consider the Lord something you could sell, which we don't," the one on the right said.

"I see by your uniform that you're a Papist," the one on the left said.

"Wrong," Sissy said. "I'm a Papist Idolator. Get it right, swifty." She slammed the door shut in their faces and locked it. She turned to me and said, "That was fun."

The doorbell rang again. This time insistently and repeatedly.

The puppy ran in circles yipping.

Sissy opened the door again. "Yes?"

"That was rude," the one on the left said.

"You're right," Sissy said, and slammed the door shut again. She turned to me and said, "This is getting better and better."

The doorbell went off again. The puppy, screwing up her courage, sprinted toward the door just as Sissy opened it and the puppy was outside, unexpectedly, and slammed on the brakes. The two men leapt backward. The puppy ran back inside and Sissy closed the door again, this time more gingerly because she was afraid of hurting Gretchen. Sissy locked the door and picked up the puppy, who licked her face nervously, making little angry growling noises interspersed with sad yowls.

I walked over to the front window and peeked through a crack in the permanently shut drapes. The two men were standing out front having some sort of argument. Finally, they walked out to a Bluebird school bus, painted blue and white. On the side, it said, FAITH BAPTIST CHURCH. The two men got in the bus, the doors closed and as the bus pulled away, I saw MARK written on the back. Three other identical buses eventually pulled past. They were labeled MATTHEW, LUKE and JOHN.

"Are they gone?" Sissy asked, standing next to me, still holding our nervous puppy.

"Yes," I said.

"What the hell was that all about?"

"They're Baptists."

"They're Baptists who couldn't take their eyes off my legs. Can't wait to have tits. That'll give them something else to look at."

"Where'd you learn that word?"

"Tits? I learned it by reading wholesome American literature, just like you." She set down the puppy, who immediately peed on the carpet. "I'll clean it up. You cleaned it up last time."

"No, I'll get it," I said.

"Stop being such a pushover," Sissy said. "I'm not always going to be around to save you from yourself."

"I guess," I said.

"You guess," she said, with an exaggerated eye roll and a "puh" of disgust.

We both cleaned up after the dog. I sprayed the spot with Fantastik and Sissy balled up a massive wad of toilet paper and dabbed at the yellow spot on the light green carpet.

We took the puppy into the backyard and tossed a ball that was too big for her to hold in her mouth. She pounced on the ball again and again.

"I guess Mrs. Jorgenson isn't going to invite us both in," Sissy said. "I really wanted another one of those cookies."

"You can have mine," I said.

"We'll split it in half," Sissy said. "That's fair. Then we'll each have had a cookie and a half."

Mr. Gray called over to us. He stood behind his pool cage, his toes on the dividing line between our properties. He'd put on another of his Hawaiian shirts and a floppy golf hat. We walked over to him with the dog on a leash. Gretchen forgot that she'd met him and growled and snapped when he crouched down to say hello.

"Friendly, isn't she?" he deadpanned.

"What's up?" Sissy asked him, pulling the puppy back with the leash.

"I wanted to renew my offer to have you over for swimming," Mr. Gray said. "I wasn't sure if your brother had told you of my offer."

"He told me," Sissy said. "We'll think about it."

"And your little friend, too. What's her name?"

"Brandy," Sissy said. "We'll let her know. Where's your wife?"

"The missus is out at a ladies auxiliary event for my VFW post. Spent the morning baking brownies."

"Brownies, you say?" Sissy said thoughtfully. "Hmm. I've recently developed a taste for baked goods."

"Oh, well… we can have brownies here when you girls come over. And you, too, young Mister Pepper. I've meant to compliment you on the excellent job you've been doing on the lawn. Top notch."

"All in a day's work, sir," I said.

Sissy leaned over to me and muttered, "He must be blind."

"What's that?" Mr. Gray asked, turning on his businessman's smile.

"I said we'll definitely consider your kind offer," Sissy said. "Nice seeing you."

102

"Later then," Mr. Gray concluded, and retreated into his pool cage while the two of us and the dog headed back into our house. Sissy let the dog off her leash and she trotted inside, squealing happily at the sight of our mother.

Mom was in the kitchen in her work pantsuit, preparing a casserole. For her birthday, she'd received a brand-new casserole dish that was identical to the one that Dad had exploded. She was indifferently chopping up a stalk of celery, hacking at it with one of our dull-bladed knives on the stained wooden chopping block. "What's this?" she asked, pointing the tip of the knife at the remaining cookie.

"That is what people outside of our family call 'a cookie,'" Sissy said. "Surely, you've seen them on TV."

"I know what a cookie is, madam! What's this doing in our house? Where'd you get it? What have you two weirdos been up to? That's what I'd like to know!" She scowled at the dog. "And don't think you fooled me by having the dog outside. I know she peed on the carpet again. I'm not blind!"

"Don't even know where to begin," Sissy said. "The only reason the dog peed on the carpet was because she was viciously attacked by roving bands of Baptists. She was traumatized. As was I. How about you, Buzz?"

"The Baptists wouldn't stop ringing the doorbell, no matter how many times we begged them to stop. 'Papist Idolators!' they shouted. I may have spotted a torch or two."

"This sounds like something you two made up," Mom said, hacking away at an onion now. She scooped it into the dish along with the celery. A jar of mayonnaise was open, as was a can of tuna. A bag of egg noodles was next to a steaming pot on the stove. We were never quite sure if Mom's food was safe, but she pointed out repeatedly to us that we were still alive, therefore we should shut up about how scary her cooking was. "So the Baptists brought over the cookies? Is that what you two were implying? And then what? After you accepted the cookies they tried to break in?"

"Mrs. Jorgenson gave me the cookie," I said. "I brought it in here to share with Sissy."

"You want me to believe she handed *you* a cookie?" Mom said, now slicing at an orange slab of cheese that had grown some sort of white fur that she wasn't bothering to scrape off. "What? Out of the goodness of her heart, or something? Is it stale? That's it, isn't it? It's a stale cookie that she wanted out of her house, so you accepted it because your mother is such a lousy cook."

"Nailed it, Mom," Sissy said. "First try."

"I *like* my cooking," Mom said.

"That makes one of you," Sissy said.

Mom picked up the cookie and took a massive bite out of it. She chewed and swallowed. "It isn't stale." She sucked on her teeth. "I've had better." She shoved the rest of the cookie in her mouth and chewed it down loudly. The puppy emitted a sad and angry growl from the back of her throat. Mom leaned down to Gretchen and shouted in her face, "Some people don't appreciate my cooking around here. Tough! They'll eat my casserole tonight, won't they? Or they'll starve." She dumped the noodles into the boiling water and set the timer for ten minutes. Then she changed her mind and set it for fifteen. To Mom, there was no such thing as an overcooked noodle.

"I'm opting for starvation," Sissy said.

"Like hell you are!" Mom shouted, waving around the knife. "And where's your brother? Did he take a three-hour tour with Gilligan and get stranded on a desert isle? Does he think he's the professor? Is he somewhere making a radio out of a coconut? Buzz, go knock on his door and find out if he's there. If not, we'll have to send out a search party."

I knocked on Sparky's door and, for once, he actually emerged. "I saw that cookie," Sparky said. "I didn't know where it came from, but it smelled so good that I was honestly afraid of it. Can you get more?" He grabbed me by the shirt front, which was something he never did. "I need to eat that cookie."

"Mom ate it," I said.

Sparky shook his head, all the hope draining from his face. He let go of my shirt. "I'll be in my room. I have homework to do." He shut the door behind him.

I felt guilty. I'd never even thought of offering Sparky the cookie, or asking for one for him. I vowed I would think of him more often, even if he did spend most of his life avoiding us.

After my divorce, I was broke and couldn't afford a vehicle. I rode my bicycle to work from my shabby bachelor apartment near downtown Sarasota.

Sparky called me up and asked, "Did you forget something?"

"Forget what?"

"It's my birthday," he said matter-of-factly. "You usually call."

"I'm sorry." I cried on the phone talking to my brother. I'd been so wrapped up in my own misery that sometimes I forgot that he, too, had lost both his sister and his mother.

"You don't have to get me a present. I know you're broke. Instead, I have something to give to you. I'll be there tomorrow."

The next day, he drove over from his place on the east coast of Florida. He knocked on my apartment door. We shook hands. He gave me the key to his car. "Here," he said, grim-faced as usual. "You can have it. I was going to trade it in, but you need it."

"You don't have to do this."

"Yes I do," he said. "Um. I'm going to need a ride back home. You mind giving me a lift?" He spent the night on my ratty, secondhand couch, and the next morning I drove him back to Delray Beach, getting used to my new car.

I spent the night in his orderly house that was filled with expensive gadgets and gourmet food. He had a custom-built kitchen. His dog followed me around for a while. She was his second dog after the first one from college died. This dog was getting old now, I realized. Dogs love us unconditionally and then remind us of the brevity of life.

I woke up the next morning and padded out to his kitchen, drawn there by the scent of coffee brewed in a stainless steel Italian espresso machine. He opened up a cookie jar and slid it across the counter to me. "Remember Mrs. Jorgenson? It took me a long time, but I think I recreated it."

I reached into the jar and pulled out a perfect chocolate chip cookie. I bit into the cookie and it tasted like pure joy.

My Athletic Career

Somewhere in there, I was a two-sport athlete. In the fall, I was a football player. In the spring, I played baseball. Buster signed Sparky up for both leagues, too, and he turned out to be the far superior athlete.

But Buster lavished his attention on me. He could imagine me as the quarterback for my high school football team, as he was for his. He'd captained both his high school football team and the basketball team and he'd get nostalgic talking about it, until Mom pointed out that under his guidance neither team won much and that the football scholarship he bragged about was to a school in rural Ohio that drew crowds smaller than his high school's. "You're pushing my buttons, Lola!" he'd shout, and then he took me outside for my quarterbacking lessons.

The first lesson was getting a grip on the ball. I couldn't because my hands were too small, so he taught me how to balance the ball in my grip with two hands and then fling it in a tight spiral, all while performing a three-step drop. "ONE TWO THREE PLANT YOUR FOOT RELEASE," Buster shouted. "AGAIN."

And again.

And again.

These football drills were wearying and endless, with Buster wearing his Ohio State gear, including a pair of threadbare scarlet and gray socks that he'd kept since the 1950's, back when he dreamt of going to Ohio State himself and captaining that team against hated Michigan, throwing tight spirals after three-step drops to receivers downfield who could actually catch his immaculate passes and run them in for touchdowns, unlike the kids he went to high school with, whom he wasted his best years on, his passes bouncing off their chests and going through their outstretched arms. "Worthless!" Buster complained. "All of them!"

I told Buster that I was too short to be a quarterback. Also, that I was uncoordinated.

"A field general has to have heart," Buster told me. "That's all he needs. That, and a good, three-step drop. ONE TWO THREE PLANT YOUR FOOT RELEASE. AGAIN." Sparky would have been the better candidate for all this attention, but Buster couldn't tell Sparky to do much of anything. "I don't understand why that kid has no respect for me." Also, Sparky wasn't afraid of him like I was, which Buster mistook for a lack of respect.

The football league that Buster signed us up for was called the Ringling Redskins, and all the teams in the league were named after Indian tribes. I played for the Chippewa and Sparky played for the Arapahoe. My team was in the junior league and Sparky's was in the senior league.

We practiced on adjacent fields near Pine View School for the Gifted. We wore uniforms that were donated by the Benevolent Society of Sarasota, a club for rich people. The only thing we had to buy was a cup, which came in handy for Little League, too. With all my football gear on, I could barely move. Plus, I was a head shorter than everyone else, which is a distinct disadvantage on the gridiron. Naturally, the coach decided that I should be a lineman. Buster was outraged and demanded that the coach see my three-step drop.

"Yes," the coach said. "Let's see it." He and the rest of his staff had a good chuckle. They had everyone line up and I stood in for the actual quarterback.

Miraculously, I managed to take the snap. I dropped three steps back and was plowed into the ground by a large kid, who blocked out the sun standing over me, my ears ringing like I'd been through a bomb blast. Little streaks of light danced in front of my eyes.

When I was in Army basic training at Fort McClellan, Alabama, I saw a similar light display at the night fire range, with tracers zinging all over a darkened range. I was awaiting my turn to go out to the range, standing on a ridge with other nervous private soldiers, our weapons held at port arms, range plugs inserted in the breach so the drill sergeants would know that the rifles weren't currently loaded. Earlier that summer, a private soldier had accidentally shot his drill sergeant with a weapon that no one knew was loaded. "Hey, Pep," this other private soldier said to me. "Ain't this pretty?"

"Yes. It reminds me of getting sacked during football practice."

"You were a quarterback?" the private soldier asked skeptically.

"Sure. For one play."

We both laughed and then the drill sergeant told us to at ease our shit or he would fucking PT us until we both fucking died. "At ease" is Army for "Shut the fuck up." "PT" means exercise, usually push-ups. So we shut the fuck up.

At some point after my sacking, someone waved some smelling salts under my nose and I returned to something resembling awake. By that time in my life, I'd been concussed multiple times per year, either

107

through accident or via Buster's fists, so I was able to fake my way through the rest of practice as a guard or a tackle.

On defense, I played safety, running as hard and as fast as I could at whoever ended up with the ball and then hanging onto him as dead weight until a competent teammate could run up and properly tackle him.

I was purely second squad material and spent a lot of my time standing on the sidelines, happy that I wasn't in the game. Though I was a veteran of concussions, I didn't enjoy them much. There was the nausea and vomiting for one thing. And the all-day headache, too. Sometimes, I couldn't remember things afterward and Sissy would have to remind me.

"Thought you were a goner this time," Sissy said, sitting next to me on the couch. Her ironic smile was missing. Her eyes were red.

"Goner?"

"You don't remember? That kid really laid a smackdown on you. Dad had to stop me from going on the field to kill him. I was crying. You don't remember me crying?"

"We played a game today. That much I remember."

"I was crying. Why's he making you do this?" She teared up again.

It was obvious why. I looked around at the interior of our home and couldn't recall how I'd gotten there. Also, I was holding an ice bag on top of my head for some reason. I set the ice bag down. "I feel dizzy," I said.

Buster came in the room. He'd reverted to his evening wear, a v-neck t-shirt and boxer shorts. He lumbered over and occupied the center of the room. "You have no killer instinct," he said. "You don't have to play football anymore if you don't want to. Your mother was very upset today and your sister cried." He said all of this with a mixture of disgust and contempt. "What the hell's the matter with you? Are you going to be a pansy all your life?" His voice was making my concussion headache worse. I made a face. "Are you listening to me?" he shouted. "God damn it, I'm trying to make you into a man!"

He was making me sorry that I had woken up. "I should hit the showers," I said, attempting to sound manly.

"You already took a shower, dummy. Would it have killed you to try harder? To try at all?"

My brother made the Ringling Redskins traveling team as an all-star center. As the center, he also ran the offense, calling the plays in the huddle. He'd make audible adjustments at the line if he didn't like what he saw. Buster had nothing much to say about Sparky's achievements because he wasn't a quarterback, but we went to all the games.

I sat where I belonged—in the stands next to Sissy. I had no business being on a football field. We'd drink hot cocoa out of my Peanuts thermos even though it was barely below 70 degrees. Room temperature was what passed for cold most of the time in Florida.

We drove across the state, following the team bus to Merritt Island, where the Ringling Redskins, a mixture of working class whites and Blacks, played a team composed of the children of NASA scientists and technicians. It was 72 to nothing at halftime. The coach on the opposite side of the field chucked a white towel toward the center, which was picked up by the wind and blown back into his face. Like the Apollo program, they were finished.

"No marshmallows this time," Sissy said, swirling the dregs of her cocoa in the red plastic cup that unscrewed from the top of the thermos. "Did we win?"

"It was an unparalleled act of complete destruction. Also, we're going home early because they quit on us. And they were so close to getting a first down last time they were on the field. Only eight more yards and they would have had it."

We sat in the backseat of the Ford family truckster as Mom navigated the battle wagon across the unpretty center of the state. We saw slash pines and palmettos, dead snakes in the middle of the road, fields filled with bug-covered Brangus cattle and tiny calfs trapped in tiny pens, ready to become veal. We saw turkey buzzards soaring overhead and heard the strange cries of strange hidden beasts. We didn't see many people. We didn't see many cars either. The bus was nowhere to be seen. Mom had veered dangerously off course. Bugs spattered against the windshield. I'd seen *Deliverance* at the theater with Buster years ago instead of *Snoopy, Come Home*, so I knew what could happen. I silently prayed to Saint Christopher to spare us from too much misery if the car ran out of gas or we blew a tire. "Just kill us outright," I prayed, my eyes closed. "Don't let them take us. Amen."

"Don't let who take us?" Sissy asked.

"What are you two plotting back there?" Mom asked, tapping both the brake and accelerator. We grabbed onto the arm rests like passengers in a crashing Cessna.

"Watch out!" Buster shouted. "God damn it, Lola! You want me to drive? Because if I drive we'll get there faster."

"We can't afford another speeding ticket!"

"I had one speeding ticket. One! But you'll never let me forget it, will you?"

"It cost seventy-two dollars. We don't have seventy-two dollars, Buster. How are we supposed to get by when you're speeding around and getting tickets? That's what I'd like to know!"

"It was one ticket! One! We paid it and it's done, okay. Turn the page. You're pushing my buttons, Lola!"

"The hillbillies," I said, turning to Sissy. "The ones with the banjos. If we get a flat tire, they'll take us to their hillbilly shacks and turn us into jerky. Squeal. Squeal like a pig."

"What's that about hillbillies?" Mom shouted. "There aren't any hillbillies in Florida. You have to have hills to have hillbillies."

"There are hillbillies in Pennsylvania," Buster said. "Lots of them. That state is full of hillbillies."

Mom added, "So if we ever go to Pennsylvania, you can complain about hillbillies. But not here."

"They're called crackers here," Sissy said.

"What are they talking about now?" Mom shouted. "Why are we discussing crackers? What's going on? I'm turning on the radio so I don't have to listen to all this talk about crackers. It's making me hungry."

"I'm hungry, too," Buster said. "Let's stop somewhere and get hamburgers."

Mom clicked on the radio and "Kung Fu Fighting" came pouring out of the tinny car speaker in the dash along with waves of static. We were close to Sarasota, the radio was permanently set to WKXY, but not so close that the station came in clearly.

The sun went down and I stared out the window at all the blackness. Up ahead of us, we saw the distant glow of civilization.

I closed my eyes and prayed harder, but under my breath so it wouldn't get Mom riled up. If she got upset, she'd lose sight of the road and crash the Ford family truckster into a drainage ditch, dooming us all.

Sissy grabbed my arm and whispered, "The crackers won't take us. Not enough meat on our bones. They'll take Dad because he's well-marbled." I opened my eyes and could make her out in the dim light coming from the dashboard. She was laughing at me.

"It's not funny," I said. "It could really happen. If you saw *Deliverance*, you'd know it, too."

"When did you see *Deliverance*?" Mom roared. "That's an adult movie! Who took you to see an adult movie?"

"He has to learn about these things at some point," Buster said lamely. He turned his head and glared at me.

"He had to have been eight when that movie came out! Who takes an eight-year-old to a movie like that? Are you deranged? No wonder he has trouble sleeping at night and can't keep on weight! You've traumatized him!"

"I swear to God, Lola. One more word."

"One more word and what? You'll use me as a punching bag? Go ahead, it's better than beating on Buzz! You think I don't know about that? I do! So go ahead, Buster. Take your best shot. I just hope you have the strength to pull this car out of the ditch!"

Buster went freakishly silent. We could hear him breathing in and out, getting himself worked up, as the radio came in clearer, playing Helen

Reddy's "Angie Baby." Even when the accusation was fair, our father took it as another slight against him. It was unfair that I'd accidentally leaked our secret. It was unfair that Mom was angry at him for taking me to adult movies. It was unfair that she called him out for beating on me, and on herself. All of it was unfair and there was only one way to settle all that unfairness, and that was with his fists. For the moment, he wasn't going to do anything, but when we got home, all bets were off. We all focused on his breathing, even over the sound of the radio, which was blaring out all the current hits along with commercials for Walt's Fish Market that went, "Three little fishies in an itty bitty pool…"

After a few miles of not talking, his breathing slowed and we all relaxed a bit.

We pulled into Lake Worth and found a Burger Queen. The carhop was dressed as a bee wearing a crown. She brought burgers and fries to the Ford family truckster and we ate in silence, all of us keeping an eye on Buster, who could have a meltdown at any minute, and then all of us were in trouble.

We finished our meal and the carhop took our trash away.

Sissy leaned over the top of the seat and hugged Buster around the neck. "Thanks for dinner, Dad."

"No problem," he said, his voice softening. "Anything for you."

Mom drove us the rest of the way home and pulled into the driveway. "I'll go get Sparky," she said dully, staring forward. "You two get ready for bed. It's been a long day."

"Did you want me to come along?" Buster asked.

"It's been a long day," Mom said.

"Okay, I'll make sure these two get into bed."

"Thank you."

We got out of the car and watched Mom drive away. We went in through the front door and the puppy lost her mind. She'd been stuck at home all day in a tall cardboard box lined with newspaper. We turned on the lights. Sissy picked her up out of the box. Her dog food was spread all over the place, she was out of water and tiny poops were amassed in the corner.

"Better take her out," Buster said. I put on her leash. "Let your sister do it."

Sissy opened up the back door, the dog happily circling around her. Sissy looked back at us with apprehension. Then she went out back with the puppy and shut the door.

"Where do you want to do this?" Buster asked me.

"My room," I said.

"Let's go then. Let's get this over with."

We walked back to my room calmly. I clicked on my bedside lamp. I turned around and faced him. "I'm ready."

Buster cocked his arm a little and punched me in the gut. I felt the air explode out of my lungs. To his credit, he pulled the punch a bit. I straightened up and looked him in the eye. I'd seen that look before. He'd enjoyed himself. "Get ready for bed."

I nodded. I didn't cry. I went cold inside. "Okay."

He left and I closed the door behind him. I put on my pajamas and said to myself, "At least it wasn't a head shot." I had that going for me.

In the spring, Buster signed Sparky and me up for baseball. Initially, we were on the same team, wearing purple t-shirts, purple ball caps, white pants and purple stirrups for Village Inn Pancake House. My brother was the everyday catcher for the squad. I was sent out to right field for three innings a game with instructions never to take the bat off my shoulder when I was at the plate. I walked a lot. The coaches were required to put all dues-paying players into the game for a minimum of three innings.

My ability to get on base due to my limited stature made me less of a liability than other incompetents on our team, so the coach decided, for reasons beyond my comprehension, to make me a first baseman. I stood at first base taking hard-tossed balls to the chest, arms, knees. As long as I got in front of the ball and let it hit me, I could pick it up most of the time and the runner would be out. There weren't too many sprinters in our Little League. Most of them looked a bit exhausted after making it halfway down the baseline. The coach took me aside and drilled me on how to bunt in case the time ever came for me to attempt to hit.

"Corner infield," Buster said over meatloaf dinner after I'd been promoted to a regular player. "Those are the power hitters. He must think you have potential."

Sissy laughed and then looked around the table. "Oh. You weren't kidding. Never mind."

Sparky had been called up to the older kids league by then even though he wasn't the right age yet. This was done after a petition was passed around amongst the Little League parents complaining that it was unfair that Village Inn had a kid who was clearly ready to play high school baseball on a Little League team. So my brother took his .450 batting average, 20 home runs and rocket throwing arm to Babe Ruth league, where he dominated for a while until the coach's son decided that he wanted to play catcher, having watched Sparky wow people with his prowess behind the plate. Sparky was benched for being "too young" and sat observing as an incompetent catcher blew his team's season. It probably bothered him more than he let on. He sat stoically as far away from the coach as he could get, his back impossibly erect, his expression unmoved by his team's lack of success.

After my game was over, my skinny body covered in welts, with three or four walks to my credit, I would make my way over to the regulation diamond and watch my brother sit on the bench. I sat in between my mother and sister, glove at the ready in case of a foul ball.

"Like you've ever caught a live ball in your life," Sissy said.

"I caught one. Remember that pop fly last week?"

"You looked as surprised as every one else when that ended up in your glove."

"These first basemen's mitts are pretty big," I said, waving the thing around.

"Will you two be quiet? I'm concentrating on the game." Mom was wearing capri pants and a big yellow shirt. She had on a pair of massive black sunglasses that she was sure made her look like Jackie O.

Sparky was pinch-hitting for the pitcher. He stepped up to the plate and took his stance, the same one that he'd borrowed from Johnny Bench. The pitcher threw one up high and tight.

"A little chin music," Sissy said.

"Hey, watch it!" Mom yelled at the pitcher. She grumbled, "Throw an inside heater on my son. Better watch it."

The next two pitches were low and outside.

"He'll come inside again," I said. "And Sparky will put the ball over the Toro lawn mower sign in left field."

And then he did. The loud ping of the aluminum bat left no question that Sparky's line drive would keep on going.

We all stood up.

"That's my son!" Mom shouted. "And that fat bum who coaches the team won't let him play!"

"Hey!" the coach shouted back at her. But the look on his face said, "Fair enough."

"Ow!" Mom shouted. "Ow! What the hell—?" She reached into her chemically treated hair and extracted a wriggling wasp covered in bird shit. She flung the wasp away and quickly left the stands, making her way over to the ladies room near the concession stand.

Sparky rounded third and looked into the bleachers. He saw only Sissy and me clapping wildly. Mom was nowhere to be found. We saw the look of exhilaration melt from his face and morph back into grim stoicism. He stepped on the plate and turned to go back to the dugout, where he would sit out the rest of the game as far away from the coach as he could get.

A week or two later, my exit from the playing field arrived. I was at practice with the team, being beaten mercilessly with baseballs by the throwing arms of my fellow infielders. I missed one ball after another and they pelted me like I was Saint Stephen.

Then the coach decided to have them bounce the balls off the clay infield right in front of me. "They get there faster that way," he said. The first ball bounced and went directly into my nose. I heard a familiar crack and felt a familiar sensation. I dropped my oversized glove and sat down on the base behind me.

The kid playing second said, "I heard that one. Man, your nose is broke but good."

The coach helped me to my feet and took me behind the back stop. "Geez oh man. Sit here the rest of the practice. Your dad's coming for you, right?"

My eyes began to swell shut. "You have any ice?"

"I'll see what I can scare up. Golly gee, you sure it's broken?"

"Yeah. It's broken."

"Dang."

Eventually, Buster showed up. My eyes were nearly swollen shut. I could see him through tiny slits, like looking through venetian blinds. He apologized to the coach for any inconvenience and led me to the car.

"You forgot your glove," the coach said, trying to hand it to me.

"Keep it!" I shouted at him. "I'm not going to be using it anymore."

"Okay. I understand you're upset," the coach said.

"Am I upset? Sorry! Golly, gosh, I'm danged sorry! Gee whiz!"

Buster took a step back. So did the coach.

And then I had a meltdown. I told the coach in no uncertain terms what I thought of his intellect and his coaching skills. I told him that any sane person wouldn't have put me at first base, and that he was clearly crazy. I told him that I hoped he'd get hit by a bus and burn in hell.

Buster hustled me into the car and drove me away. "You shouldn't talk to adults like that."

"As for you," I shouted, my voice generating its own strange power, "I don't care if you hit me for saying this: I don't want to play baseball. I don't want to play football. Your idea of manhood doesn't interest me. I'm going to draw pictures and I'm going read books and I don't care! Go ahead and hit me! Go ahead!" I shouted so loudly that my voice cracked.

"I didn't realize you felt so strongly about it," Buster said defensively. "You don't have to play baseball. It's fine. Really. You can draw all you want and read all you want. And what's all that about me hitting you? Are you serious? It's like you think you're an abused child or something."

I crossed my arms sitting in the white vinyl bucket seat of his Gran Torino, shaking with absolute rage. I growled like a trapped animal.

The funny thing is: I love football and baseball. If it wasn't for those two sports, I don't know what I would watch on weekends. Probably nothing. I'd probably get a whole lot more reading and drawing done.

A Dent in the Ultimate El

I found Sissy in the kitchen holding the back of a bag of Fritos next to the back of a bag of dog food. "What're you doing?" I asked her.

"Confirming a theory. I don't know who should be more worried, us or the dog."

I took the bag of Fritos from her and crunched one down. "Definitely the dog," I said, shoving more into my mouth. "Wish I had a can of chili and some Velveeta right about now."

"You're gross, little brother."

I rolled up the bag and put the wooden clothespin back on the top. "I know. You don't have to point it out to me." I leaned down and scratched the dog behind her truncated ears. "Is she grown up yet? I can't tell."

"She puts the 'miniature' into Miniature Schnauzer," Sissy said. "Mom says that whenever she has her first period, she's all finished. Just like us ladies."

"Ew!" I went.

"Ew, yourself," Sissy said, making a face. "Have you smelled yourself lately? You're pretty ripe. I told Mom she needs to buy you some Right Guard."

I sniffed my pits and was taken aback. "Jeez. How long has this been going on?"

"A while. I didn't want to upset you. I know how easily you get upset. And then comes the dramatic meltdown." She dropped to her knees, her arms outstretched. "I hate all of you! And all of humanity! It's unfair! Everything's unfair!"

"I'm not like that."

"You're exactly like that," she said, getting up. "Boo hoo hoo. Poor Buzz and his artistic temperament."

"Artistic temperament?"

"Just like his grandmother, Mom says."

"When did you start listening to Mom?"

"About half-past never. But she occasionally makes a good point, especially when it comes to her favorite child. How did the middle child become the favorite? I thought you were supposed to be ignored. And I'm the cutest, despite your sad Bambi eyes."

We heard Steve Bondurant roaring up and down the street in the Ultimate El, which is what he'd named his El Camino. He worked on the car in their driveway, continually tuning it up. I'd recently taken up skateboarding. It was my excuse for going down to the Bondurant's to hang outside with Steve and receive his teenaged wisdom, and maybe catch a glimpse of Brandy coming in or out. While I was there, Steve would put me to work rubbing Turtle Wax on and off the car, or detailing the tires with a toothbrush.

"Someone should throw a rock at his car," Sissy said.

"No one should throw a rock at his car," I said.

"You only say that because you're chicken. Bock-bock."

"I'm not throwing a rock at his car."

"Chump, chump, chicken!"

"I need to take a shower and wash my pits."

"You most certainly do. And then you'll 'ride' your skateboard down to the Bondurant's to worship at Steve's feet and hope that Brandy comes outside." She made a bunch of smooching sounds. "But by the time you get all the way down the street, you'll be pitted out again. No one wuvs stinky Buzz. It's so sad." Sissy made a sad face with a bulging lower lip. "All the tears I've cried thinking about how sad you are."

"Shut up."

"Never." She sniffed at me and crinkled up her nose. "You smell worse than some old hobo. Maybe you should ride the rails."

"Fine," I said in a snit. "I'll go take a shower."

I went into my room and found my little transistor radio. It was the same size as a walkie-talkie and only got AM radio on it, which was fine by me. Sometimes, I would listen to Herb Score call Indians games on the skip, or listen to the bowdlerized radio cuts of popular songs on WLS in Chicago at night. There was a station for over-the-road truckers that played sad country music that may have been broadcast out of Mexico. But mostly I kept the radio tuned to WKXY, which played the same ten songs over and over until they swapped out a song that was fading off the air with the latest hit. "Philadelphia Freedom" by Elton John had just replaced "Thank God I'm a Country Boy" by John Denver.

I locked myself in the bathroom and turned on the radio. "School's Out" by Alice Cooper was halfway through. It was that time of the year. In a couple of weeks, we'd be making our pilgrimage to Cleveland to sponge off of friends and relatives, crashing in strange beds, eating edible food created by competent maternal types.

At school, I'd said my goodbyes to Reginald Hightower and Billy.

Reginald may as well have lived on Mars or Venus. There was no way I'd see him until school returned in the fall. I'd invited him over anyway, saying that he could get a ride from his mother or father and stay the night. "Cool," Reginald said, but neither one of us thought it was possible. I may as well have asked Reginald to strap on a rocket and shoot himself into outer space.

Billy said that he'd be seeing me that summer. He lived over in old Gulf Gate and was only a bicycle ride away. Of course, he wouldn't really be visiting me when he came over to our ritzy neighborhood. He'd be visiting Brandy, who'd gone beyond being fascinating only because she was rich. "She's all girl," Billy said wistfully. "And she's been to France and she knows stuff."

During our final day, after we'd turned in our books and the classroom was stripped bare of all decoration, Mr. Morgan killed some time by pulling out a pair of clear plastic fake lungs with a mouth attached to it. "This was donated by the Cancer Society. It's supposed to discourage you from smoking." He placed a filterless cigarette from a white generic pack in the lips, lit it and invited Reginald to come to the front of the class and work the lungs like bellows. Soon enough, the lungs were covered in tar and the cigarette was half-smoked down. We weren't watching the lungs, though. We were watching Mr. Morgan's face as he became more and more frustrated. Finally, he plucked the cigarette out of the fake lips and placed it in his real lips, smoking it down to almost nothing in a few drags. "Waste not, want not, kids," Mr. Morgan said, spitting little bits of tobacco into a nearby wastepaper basket. "Was it Benjamin Franklin who said that?" He stubbed out the remains on the bottom of his scuffed shoe and tossed it in the wastepaper basket. "Does anyone know?"

None of us knew. "Who said it?" Reginald asked finally.

"Let it be a mystery for the ages," Mr. Morgan said, and then hacked and hacked. "That was some harsh tobacco kids." He recommended that if we took up smoking, that we try Kent with the Micronite filter. The bell rang. "Class dismissed."

I let the shower heat up before I got in. I was showering, yes indeed, like a grown man who has grown up body odor. I scrubbed my pits with the beige bar of Dial that Sissy and I shared, and then shampooed with a green blob of Prell. Still no hair under the arms, or much hair anywhere else than the unwieldy mop that sprouted from my head. The mop was turning more toward brown recently, but was still mostly blonde.

I sang along with the radio:
Will you meet me in the middle?
Will you meet me in the air?
Will you love me just a little?
Just enough to show you care?

I turned off the shower and whipped the bath towel around me like I was a bullfighter before wiping myself down. I went into the forbidden cabinet of Sparky, where he kept the hygiene products that I was not allowed to corrupt with my germ-riddled fingers. I found his can of Right Guard and spritzed my pits. Then I thought better of it and coated them.

I put his Right Guard back, hoping that I'd positioned the can correctly or else Sparky would know and give me a long lecture about not touching his things. I turned off the radio just as Sissy's new favorite song came blasting out of it—The Captain and Tennille's "Love Will Keep Us Together." She'd made pouty faces at Buster and he'd run out and bought her a copy of the album, so now I had to hear it all the time when it was her turn to have the portable record player in her room.

I plugged in Sissy's hair dryer and gave myself a Beach Boys poofy 'do, hanging my head down so it would be extra big.

"The wet look is dead!" I said, turning off the dryer. I dug around and found my hair brush and gave the mop a few strokes. I peered into the mirror at myself. Did I look like Robert Urich in *SWAT*? No, I did not. Was there a possibility that someday I'd look like Robert Urich in *SWAT*? No, that didn't seem like a possibility either. "No killer instinct," I said aloud. Robert Urich had that illusive killer instinct, and I clearly did not. I'd have to coast on the whole cuteness thing until that wore off in a few years, right in time for me to start dating. "It's all coming together," I said to my reflection. Me and the reflection laughed at each other. If only Sparky had some Hai Karate. I'd definitely slap some of that on.

I wore my towel back to my room and put on my best Hang Ten striped t-shirt, my long board shorts that went down to my knees and my new pair of Converse tennis shoes with the blue stars on the side, no socks. Mom said the shoes had to last me through the summer and fall. They were currently a half-size too big.

I pulled my plywood skateboard out of the closet, tucked it under my arm and walked out of my room.

"You're almost convincing," Sissy said. Her hair was cut into a shag that summer. She wore a red t-shirt, white shorts and a pair of Birkenstocks.

"Quit hasseling me, man."

"That was good, too. Authentic. The only problem is with the whole coordination thing." Sissy grinned evilly and clasped her hands together. "I'm ready to roll when you are."

"Stop following me down the street."

"Someone has to keep an eye on you so you don't die." She placed her hand over her heart. "I feel that it's my obligation to *be* that someone."

"You like laughing at me when I fall off."

"Certainly, there is that tiny bit of pleasure. But what is that next to the pleasure of saving a life?"

"I'm not gonna die."

"You don't know that. How can you know that with certainty?" She followed me out to the garage and mounted her bicycle.

I took a deep breath, stood atop my skateboard and rolled down the slight embankment of our driveway, hitting a stone and tumbling head first onto the hot pavement.

Sissy got off her bike, dropped it to the ground and ran over to me. "Oh my God, Buzz! Please give up. You're not coordinated enough to ride a skateboard. You probably shouldn't be allowed to walk by yourself."

I sniffed under each of my arms and declared, "I am not pitted out yet."

"Congratulations. Stop being so stupid." She touched my face. "No blood. Okay. So what's the plan? Ride all the way down to the Bondurant's ten doors away? Will you at least ride on the sidewalk?"

"I go where the skateboard takes me."

"So face first onto the pavement."

"Or grass. You don't know."

"Fine, but I'm keeping an eye on you."

Mr. Gray was standing out front, watering his lawn with a green garden hose. This, despite the fact that it rained buckets every afternoon at precisely 4 p.m. "Young Mister Pepper! Looking good! And Miss Pepper, keeping a watchful eye on her brother."

"And Mister Gray!" Sissy shouted. "Narrating the action! I feel an offer of pool use is about to be made!"

"Hah, ha!" Mr. Gray said. "Very good. Yes! The offer still stands."

"And what about my friend? Can *she* still come over?"

"Of course, of course!"

He spritzed me with the hose and I nearly tumbled off my skateboard. But this time, I was certain I would ride all the way to the end of the street without falling off. This would be my triumph! Sissy remained skeptical.

"Ten feet!" she shouted. "Fifteen feet! Is there no limit to the amount of time he can stay upright? Oh, the humanity!" She pedaled her bicycle along the curb on the street keeping a watchful eye, pointing out hazards. We were two doors away from the Bondurants. Then one door away. "Will he make it? Is this a new world's record? Should we call the people from Guinness?"

I looked up and saw Steve standing next to the Ultimate El, nodding his head in the affirmative. The Bondurant's front door opened, and Brandy walked out. She was dressed in her customary all-black outfit, her black hair shining in the Florida sun. I stood up straighter on the board. Surely, she'd see me navigating so artfully in her direction! She looked at her brother and saw him watching me, and then aimed her gaze at me. Our eyes met, I hit a crack in the sidewalk and tumbled ass over tea kettle into their next door neighbor's yard. My skateboard righted itself and kept on going. Brandy expertly stepped on the end of it, flipped it up and caught it. I stood up, my face quickly turning red. Sissy was no help at all. She'd stopped her bike, her foot on the curb. She was laughing so hard she nearly keeled over.

I walked over sheepishly and Brandy handed me the skateboard without a word.

"Who's impressed here?" Sissy asked. "Let's have a show of hands."

"Hey, hey," Steve said. "Be nice to your little brother. He's trying."

Little brother? Trying? Trying?! We were supposed to be buds, and he was treating me like I was a little kid. I felt a meltdown coming on, but I somehow mastered it, dropped my skateboard on the sidewalk facing the opposite direction and speedily zipped away in a mostly straight line.

"Sorry," I heard Sissy say. "Gotta keep an eye on him." She followed me home and into the garage.

"What exactly did you say about throwing a rock at Steve Bondurant's car?" I asked her.

"I was kidding."

"You were *not* kidding. You made chicken noises. Bock-bock, I believe you said. We'll see who's chicken, won't we?"

"You're really gonna do it?" Sissy asked. A devious smile curled up on her lips. "You'll take that blowhard down a notch?"

"I'll lie in wait like the mighty puma," I said. "I will chuck a rock and maybe even make a dent in his precious car."

"Well then. Let's pick out a rock, shall we? And a place to lie in wait. But first, we'll change clothes and leave these out on our beds. After the deed is done, we'll switch back into these clothes and act all innocent. You still have the mask from last year's Halloween costume?"

"You've been planning this for a while, haven't you?"

"Oh my, yes. Your hero is just another big mouth. I want a dent in his car while he's driving it. If I had a better arm, I'd do it myself. As luck would have it, I happen to have access to someone who spent his spring throwing a ball in the backyard. You were getting pretty good until you got your nose broken. I'm putting that pitching arm to good use." We went into the house via the garage.

The Ford family truckster was gone, so Mom had to be at work. Buster was on the road that week, trying to get as many sales as he could before the sojourn in Ohio. Sparky was wherever he was. We listened at his door. It didn't sound like he was in there, but he could be pretty quiet sometimes. We knew he wouldn't approve of the plan, which Sissy informed me was not to be questioned. "The plan is ready to go. The plan has sharp edges!"

She went into my room with me and dug through my dresser, finding my darkest clothes. "I'm gonna sweat to death in this thing."

"You'll barely have it on for an hour. Less than that if we're lucky. He drives around the block about once every forty-five minutes. I've been keeping track. Where's your knit cap? The black one?"

"I don't know. I never use it."

"Your hair is a dead giveaway. Your hair must not be seen during this mission. Our orders come directly from Division Seven. As always, should you or any of your IM force be caught or killed, the Secretary will disavow any knowledge of your actions!"

I found my werewolf mask from the previous Halloween in the bottom of the closet. "How's this?"

"Perfecto! I'll be right back." Sissy sprinted out of the room.

I put on a pair of dark trousers that were somewhere between Navy blue and black that were slightly too small. I slipped on a dark green t-shirt. I put on my dress shoes, which no longer fit and were scuffed and worn at the heel. I put on the mask. I looked down and saw the knit cap peeking out from behind the cardboard box with my discarded childhood toys in it. I pulled it out and slipped it over the top of the rubber mask. Sissy came back with a couple of Mom's old turtleneck sweaters from the 1960's. I took off the knit cap and mask, put on the turtleneck, and then replaced the mask and cap. "How's this?" I asked through a sweaty layer of rubber.

"We may just get away with this." Sissy left the room and came back wearing Mom's old clothes, the capri pants rolled up to fit and cinched with a skinny belt and the turtleneck rolled up at the sleeves. She put on a creepy mask that was supposed to look like a beautiful woman's face, but was cratered and distorted. "Suddenly, my life has taken on meaning," her muffled voice told me. She put on her own knit cap.

We crept out through the sliding glass doors, the puppy nearly sneaking out with us to the lanai. We shoved her back indoors and she made a dissatisfied little growl and yip.

"She wants to come along," I said.

"You'd only slow us down! We're doing this for you and all the other dogs in the neighborhood who bark at Steve Bondurant and his silly noisy car." Sissy turned to me solemnly and said through her unintentionally scary mask, "We're doing this for all humanity. Now hurry up and follow me!"

We crept past the Jorgenson house. Sissy knelt down and picked up one of the rocks that surrounded their bushes. She hefted it in her hand. "Not heavy enough to do real damage. Man, it's hot in this stuff! Let's hurry up." I followed her across the street and between two more houses.

Sissy found the rock she was looking for in the shrubbery next to Captain Slidell's widow's house. The captain had been fatally shot down over Vietnam, and the widow, twenty years his junior, had bought the home with his G.I. insurance money and maintained it with whatever pension the government had provided. She hosted loud parties during the night and nursed her hangovers during the day alongside her pool. We attempted to creep past, but she spotted us, a tropical drink in her hand, looking elegant in her red, white and blue swimsuit, oversized sunglasses perched on her tiny nose, her hair bleached by the sun and pool chemicals into a blondish minty green.

"Hey, Mrs. Slidell," Sissy said.

"Hey yourself, Sissy Pepper," the widow said. "What are you two up to?"

"Buzz here is going to throw a rock at Steve Bondurant's car."

"You don't say." She took a dainty sip of her drink through a straw. "Are you sure that your little brother will be able to heave that big old rock?"

"He'll manage. You don't mind our borrowing it?"

"Borrow away. If you're around tomorrow, come by and I'll teach you more about cribbage."

"And the art of seduction," Sissy said.

"Shhh. Don't give away a lady's secrets." She pulled a chunk of pineapple out of her drink with a tiny plastic sword and inserted it into her mouth. She chewed and swallowed, flinging the tiny sword into her pool. "I think I hear that teenaged delinquent heading this way now. Have fun."

We snuck up next to Captain Slidell's widow's air conditioning unit and crouched down. Sissy slapped the rock in my hand. It was smooth and pale, the size of a baked russet potato, heated up by the endless sun. I adjusted my mask so I could see. My breath had wet the inside of the mask until it was nearly dripping. Rivulets of sweat drizzled down my back. *Am I really going to do this?*

"Bock, bock," Sissy went, and gave me a poke in the ribs.

I heard the car peeling out as it rolled around the block. I heard the roar of the engine as it headed toward Captain Slidell's widow's house. Steve would have to slow down, since the widow's house was on the corner and this was his turn, so I'd have a pretty good shot.

The El Camino appeared quickly. I stood up from my car-hunting blind and chucked the stone. I'd thrown it at the front of the car, so it made contact with the rear, thudding loudly into the spot between the back tire and the bumper, leaving a fist-sized dent.

"Yes!" Sissy shouted, pumping a fist.

Steve slammed on the brakes, but the El Camino's massive tires hit a patch of oily tarmac and couldn't find purchase. And then he was downshifting and hitting the accelerator, too, in an attempt to get the car under control. It didn't work. He continued down the road, sliding, the tires spinning and white smoke obscuring whatever the hell else was going on.

Sissy and I stood watching for a moment, until we heard Steve's voice shout out, "You're dead! I will hunt you down! Dead!"

We ran.

We ran through backyards, side yards and front yards, skittering and shrieking as we ran. And laughing, too. We bumped into each other, tripped over various prickly bushes, got caught in a sprinkler, and then found ourselves in our own backyard.

We stumbled inside and Sissy and I ran around the house locking the doors and pulling the blinds and drapes. We stripped out of our clothes and ran into our respective rooms in our underwear, shrieking and laughing. We pulled on the clothes from the morning. We took our caper clothes and stuffed them into the bottoms of our hampers. We took the masks into the bathroom and attempted to flush them down the toilet. We were unsuccessful in that last part. The wet masks went into my box of neglected childhood toys right next to the scarred remains of G.I. Joe. I knew G.I. Joe's fear now, I felt. I knew what it was like to be pursued by a relentless enemy.

Was Steve Bondurant the enemy now? Not if he didn't know it was me.

Sissy, on the other hand, was triumphant. "Humiliate my little brother, will you? Treat him like your slave! Treat him like some sort of errand boy! Not on my watch!"

"Is that what that was all about?" I asked her.

A fist was beating on the front door. "Come on, out you little pussy!" Steve Bondurant shouted. "Come get some! I'll beat your little ass!"

The puppy hid behind the couch. We sat together on the floor being very quiet. Sissy whispered, "Did you lock the sliding glass door?"

I whispered back, "I thought *you* did."

We crept up to the drapes hiding the sliding glass door. Sissy gingerly pulled them aside. Steve had already sprinted around back and we could see him peering in through the kitchen window, which had no drapes or shades. Sissy clicked the little lever and the door was locked. But that drew the attention of Steve, who stomped over and glared in at us.

Sissy stood up. I stood up. Sissy pulled the drapes.

Steve straightened up a bit. He was looking behind us. We turned around and saw Sparky standing there giving him the imperious glare, the one that had stared down teachers and adults for as long as we could remember. Sparky gently pushed us aside, opened the sliding glass door and strode outside. He didn't shut the door behind him. "You need some help? You get lost or something?"

Steve was a full head taller than Sparky, but Sparky had broad shoulders and the voice of a man. Steve, despite the car and the facial hair, was still half boy. "No. Don't need no help. I thought that maybe…" and his voice trailed off.

"Maybe what?" Sparky asked in his man's voice. It was the same voice that my battalion commander would use in West Germany when he spoke to us in formation. *Matter of fact. Grave. Factual. Pay attention, I won't be repeating myself.*

"Nothing," Steve said. All the fight had gone out of him. He left sheepishly, walking around the side of our house. We heard his car start up and drive away. No squealing tires. No revving engine.

Sparky turned around and faced us. "What did I get you out of this time?"

"Buzz threw a rock at his car," Sissy said.

"I'm sure it was all his idea," Sparky said.

"Anyway, he didn't miss. That's the important part," Sissy said.

"Uh-huh," Sparky said. "I'll be in my room if anything else comes up. Oh, and Buzz? Stay out of my bathroom cabinet."

"Sure thing," I said.

He walked away from us and we listened as his door shut.

I closed the sliding glass door and clicked the lock. I tried out the door. Locked.

"I have to admit that he has his uses sometimes." Sissy looked at her nails, which she had recently started painting with strawberry-colored nail polish. "You hungry? Peanut butter and jelly?"

"I could eat." My hands were shaking. I clicked on the TV set and sat down in front of it. *Doctor Paul Bearer's Creature Feature* would be coming on in a few minutes.

Buckeyes on Tour

We piled into the Ford family truckster at 2 a.m. This was necessary, Buster said, to beat the traffic. Buster would pilot the Ford family truckster for approximately 75 percent of the trip. Say what you wanted about the man, he was a smooth driver. Mom was a herky-jerky driver. Much near-vomiting happened with her at the wheel.

I took my place on the hump. It was my responsibility as a proud middle child to man the hump. Tradition meant something in those days.

"We got a mighty convoy, rocking through the night!" I sang as we plowed north on U.S. 41 in the dead of night. "We got a mighty convoy, ain't she a beautiful sight?"

"Why can't the boy sleep? The other two are asleep," Buster asked Mom. They were passed out next to me, my two siblings, leaning up against their respective doors.

"I don't know. How am I supposed to know?" Mom complained.

"Build I-75 now!" I shouted, as we passed a billboard. "Get U.S. out of the United Nations! John Birch Society!"

"Would you like some of your cough syrup, honey?" Mom dug frantically through her oversized purse.

"World's Largest Rexall Drug Store and lunch counter, nine miles ahead!" I replied. "Ninety-nine seats!" The open road was exciting. At some point, there would be enough light to read one of the books I'd packed or draw my pictures on the sample paper that Buster brought home for me. Until dawn, reading the roadsigns would have to do. "Gibsonton, ten miles!"

Buster had installed a CB radio for the trip. We'd get there faster by avoiding Smokey the Bear and his speed traps. He listened to it through a beige earpiece.

Gretchen—she was officially a dog now—was loose behind my head, pacing and panting nervously. She'd never been on an extended car ride until now. Sissy and I had given her a bath in the big sink next to the washer/dryer combo. Fleas vomited blood as they drowned. We scrubbed her beard with an extra blob of Prell, but it remained brown, unlike the rest of her, which was gray and white. Her tongue was mostly gray.

Mom found the bottle of the orange cough syrup, my favorite, and handed it back to me. "Take a big old swiggeroo," she advised. "A chug. Maybe a chug and a half."

I did as ordered, and immediately felt that wave of relief wash from the crown of my head, now moist with panting dog breath, down through my torso and eventually spreading to my fingers and toes. I screwed the lid back on and and handed it forward. "Feeling fine," I said to no one in particular.

I woke up leaning up against Sissy, who shrugged me off. "Stop drooling on me," she demanded.

I blinked awake and saw that we were entering the Peach State. I slid forward and rested my arms on the front seat back. I rested my chin atop my laced fingers. Buster was still driving. The gas tank was near empty. "See Rock City," I read off a road sign.

"Look who's awake," Buster said.

"Wha-?" Mom went, startled from going road blind. She paused for a moment, in an attempt to stop herself from dredging up an old grudge, and then she couldn't stop herself. "When we were driving down to Miami for our honeymoon—"

"Not this again," Buster grumbled.

"When we were driving down to Miami from Cleveland for our honeymoon," Mom insisted. "I asked him to stop at Rock City."

"We were making good time," Buster said.

"It wouldn't have taken that long," Mom said. "What's the matter with taking a little detour for an attraction that could afford to paint its name on every barn in America?"

"And the Crystal Caves," I said.

"Exactly! But I guess I'll never see Rock City, not as long as your father has anything to say about it."

"Jesus Christ, Lola. We'll go there on the way back."

"I'll believe it when I see it," Mom said.

But we didn't go to Rock City on the way back either. Buster never took us there.

Many years later, when I was in the delayed entry program waiting to go to Army basic training, I went to live with my mother. She was alone in the last home that she and Buster had shared. Buster had left her two years prior. I moved in with my lonely mother, bringing along my rescue dog, a mass of fur named Bear. He and my mother hit it off. My uncle Ralph came to visit, bringing along his post-divorce girlfriend, a pretty redheaded woman who was closer to my age than she was to his. The two of them insisted on dragging Mom on a road trip to Nashville and told me that I should tag along. One of Mom's friends looked after Bear during our trip.

Mom and Ralph had their own comedy routine, which involved Mom calling Ralph a dummy constantly, asking him why he was so dumb, and Ralph telling Mom that she was the world's worst cook and housekeeper and that she was lucky any of her children survived. By that time, Sissy had moved out and Sparky had a job as a statistician on the east coast of Florida. They were alive and well. I was the worst of the bunch, as it turned out, skinny, weird and conveniently available in the car as a reference in case Ralph needed someone to confirm that my mother couldn't cook. We drove north enjoying their comedy routine, heading toward the country music capital.

Somewhere in Georgia, we saw the familiar signs for Rock City and Mom immediately began to complain how her now-ex-husband, whom she called, "Buzz's father," as if I was somehow to blame for him, had never taken her to this magical place.

"You wanna 'See Rock City'?" Ralph asked her. Without waiting for a reply, he said, "Let's go."

So we saw Rock City.

Now Mom had something new to complain about. "This is it?" she asked repeatedly, as we tromped around the cheesy tourist trap.

"This is Rock City," Ralph said. "It's clearly marked as such."

"Ralph, you dummy! Why did you insist on coming here?" Mom shouted at him. "I'd expect you to have more sense than this." And she went on and on, pointing out that the place was clearly a tourist trap and insisting that she'd only been kidding during all the years of riding my father about never getting to go.

"We're not going to Rock City today. We have hotel reservations," Buster said through gritted teeth. "We have to be there before five o'clock."

"Sure," Mom said. "Fine."

"You're pushing my buttons, Lola."

"Mm-hm. Sure. Fine," Mom said, tersely. "You want more cough syrup, Buzz? Or are you going to not read every sign on I-75?"

"I'll draw for a while."

"Draw quietly," Buster said. "Don't make all your stupid sound effects while you're drawing. I need to concentrate."

"I make sound effects?"

"Whoosh," Sissy said, blinking awake. "Kaboom. Blam-blam."

"Yeah," Buster said. "Like that." He reached over and turned on the radio. He spun the dial around and found the local equivalent of WKXY. "Do the hustle!" the radio insisted. In the 1970's, we hustled, danced and boogied. A lot of boogieing went on in the 1970's. Everyone wanted to boogie, even Buster. No exceptions. My father boogied as he drove, the car swaying from side to side, ruining my art project.

I gave up and put it away, back to share space with the dog in the massive cargo department of the Ford family truckster. I pulled up a book and tried to read, but started to feel carsick and put that away.

"Can I please lean up against the door for a while?" I asked Sissy. "I'll give you your spot back in an hour."

"I can't take the risk that you won't give it back," Sissy said.

"How long has this been going on?" the radio wondered out loud.

I turned to Sparky, but before I could say a word, he said, "The answer is no."

So I climbed over the seat and displaced the dog, upending her dishes of kibble and water. The dog yipped out her displeasure and leapt down to take my place.

"Grab the dog!" Buster shouted.

"Are you trying to kill us all?" Mom shouted.

The car sputtered as it ran out of gas. "Goddamnit!" Buster shouted. "You were supposed to remind me to gas up!"

"You're the one looking at the dashboard! I can't see it from here!" Mom shouted, equally aggrieved.

Buster shifted into neutral as we rolled along. "It's the boy's fault! He distracted me!"

"It's everyone's fault but yours," Mom said cooly.

"I've had it. I'm done!" Buster shouted. "Good thing I got this CB radio. Breaker One-Nine!" He keyed the mic as we rolled to a stop. A trucker, who'd apparently amplified his CB radio, keyed over the top of Buster and screamed. Buster yanked the earpiece out and said, "That just about busted my eardrum." The big rig blasted past us, aerials whipping around. The logo on the side of the trailer said EGO. Buster put the car in park, immediately pushed open his door and got out. I sat up and watched him stomping away from us in a huff.

"How does this thing work?" Mom asked no one. She yanked the earpiece out of the CB, picked up the mic, pushed the button on the side and said, "I don't know if I'm doing this right, but I'm a mother with three children stranded on the side of the road. My husband didn't think to gas up our car, but that's just typical of him if you ask me. Only one of my children is perfectly behaved, and all he does is hide out in his room all day ignoring me. The girl has a smart mouth. And there's something wrong with the middle one that no one can put a finger on. He's weird. Is anyone listening?"

Sparky said, "You have to take your thumb off the button."

Mom let go of the button.

"I see you, ma'am. Ford Galaxie Country Squire station wagon, blue with wood paneling? Over."

Mom keyed the mic: "That's us. The husband is the one walking down the road. We're all sick of him at this point, so it's fine if you don't pick him up. It's a hot day…" I watched a tow truck pull up in front of us. "…and I'm worried about the kids. The middle one because he's sensitive." Mom always made "sensitive" sound like a criminal offense. "The oldest one is sensitive, too, but he won't admit it. As for the youngest, the girl, she's not sensitive. Anything but. The mouth on her."

Sparky said, "You have to take your thumb off the button."

Mom let go of the button.

"Breaker, breaker. This is Tuna Fish," a deeply southern man's voice said. "If any of y'all ain't gonna help this lady, I'd be pleased to. Over."

"Breaker. This is Bingo. I'm already here, good buddy. Got it covered. Over."

We watched Bingo back his tow truck up to us. He got out and waved to Mom and hooked the Ford family truckster to the back end. He was a beardy guy with a trucker's hat on that advertised CAT DIESEL POWER. He wore a flannel shirt even though it was close to 100 degrees, stained jeans, and a pair of tan workman's boots. He winked at Mom, who gave him a slight wave.

"Who wants to ride with the tow truck driver?" Mom asked. "Any volunteers?"

It was an annual tradition riding with the tow truck driver. Usually, we'd blow up a water pump, or a belt would break, and then there would be steam coming out of the engine compartment, and my father would get out of the car and kick the side of it, always in the same spot so we wouldn't have extra dents in the car. We'd just have the one dent—the frustration dent. "Piece of crap!" Buster would rant. "Goddamn piece of crap! I'll never buy another Ford again. Found On Road Dead! That's what 'Ford' stands for." And then we'd buy another Ford, and another one, and another one. Mainly the new cars were Buster's sales cars, the ones he drove on his route. There was a Ford Fairlane, a Ford Maverick and, the latest, a Ford Gran Torino with white leatherette interior and bucket seats. The Ford family truckster wasn't swapped out as often and, thus, the exploding engine during our trips back to Cleveland.

The radio, which continued prattling while all this was going on, commented that, "our love is like a ship on the ocean. We are sailing with a cargo full of love and devotion."

Mom clicked off the radio and poked at the CB radio, trying to figure out how to turn that off, too. She turned off the air conditioner. "Roll down your windows. Sparky, go ride with the tow truck driver. Someone with sense should be with him. We all know how your father gets in these situations."

Sparky shrugged and got out of the car, shutting his door and Buster's, too. I watched him soberly shake hands with Bingo.

Buster had made his way back and began to argue with Bingo. Sparky then explained something to Buster, who finally gave up. The three of them ended up cramming into the tow truck together and we were off.

I sat up and faced the rear of the vehicle, watching the gray, uneven pavement as it sped underneath the car. I imagined that I was sitting next to my namesake, Buzz Aldrin, and the two of us were heading down to the Moon together. This time, someone named Buzz would be the first to step on the Moon. "Retro, go! Capcom, go! Telcom, go! Surgeon, go! You are go for landing," I heard in my head. "Houston, Tranquility Base here. The Eagle has landed."

Gretchen yipped and groaned. The whole trip was an annoyance to her.

We pulled off the highway about five minutes later. Bingo deposited us next to a gas pump, and Buster pulled some money out of his wallet and grudgingly paid for the tow.

We listened to the gas pump clang over and over as the empty tank was refilled by the attendant, who wiped down the windows with a greasy rag, swirling them with filth. More money came out of Buster's wallet. The attendant pointed up the road and Buster nodded at him and gave him a quarter, slapping it into the boy's hand. He looked at the quarter in his palm as if it was a turd that had been shat there, maybe by a passing seagull, and he swore a bit then shoved it in his front pocket.

We pulled through a McDonald's drivethrough and everyone got the same order—burger, small order of fries, and a Coke—except for Buster, who got a Big Mac. We ate in the parking lot, the engine off and ticking furiously, windows down allowing in flies from a nearby dumpster and an ungodly amount of heat. The only sound inside the car was Buster's mastication and occasional belches. We collected the bags and Sparky took them to the dumpster and tossed them in. Somewhere out on an interstate in America, we hadn't caused Iron Eyes Cody to weep a single perfect tear.

We managed to get back on the highway. I manned the hump again. We were on our best behavior.

Buster farted loudly. "Thunder," he noted. "Gonna rain."

Sissy and I giggled on cue. Sparky rolled his eyes. Mom's shoulders relaxed. Everything was going to be fine. We were going to be fine.

We made it to the Ramada Inn in time. It was on top of a hill in Cleveland, Tennessee. My father insisted that he did not pick out Cleveland, Tennessee just because of the name. "We all know where the real Cleveland is," he said. "This place just happened to be halfway." I walked in with my father and watched him check in, handing the lady behind the counter his Bank Americard. My father was proud of his collection of credit cards. He had about a dozen of them, if you included the company American Express card that he used when he was on his sales route. The lady looked through a booklet filled with numbers to check if Buster's card was cancelled. It wasn't, and we successfully checked in. There was always a breathless moment as a clerk flipped through the booklet.

The Ramada Inn surrounded a blue swimming pool with a sign stating "For Guests Only." The scent of chlorine wafted over invitingly. We were guests. We could take a dip. We had swimsuits and everything.

We lugged some of our luggage to our rooms. Sparky and I were to share a queen-sized bed and Sissy had her own bed in one room. The parents were in their own room adjacent to ours. There was a door in between the two rooms in case the parents needed to barge in.

Sparky immediately told me the ground rules for sharing the bed. He said I was not, under any circumstances, to venture toward his side of the bed. He told me that I needed to be silent during sleeping hours. "No excessive rolling over. Only when necessary." Considering our relative sizes, Sparky required two-thirds of the bed space.

I nodded as if I agreed.

Sissy told me to slug him. "Take your half of the bed," she demanded of me. "Don't compromise! Vive la France!" She waved her paperback copy of *Angélique in Revolt* at me.

I was already dressed in my board shorts. I took off my Ocean Pacific shirt and my Converse tennis shoes and announced that I would be going for a dip. "I need a towel, of course. I'm sure there are plenty in the bathroom."

"We're going to dinner in an hour," Sparky said. "Morrison's cafeteria. There's one downtown. I don't think you'll be taking that dip, little brother."

"If he's taking a dip, so am I," Sissy declared. "Last one in is a rotten egg."

"Neither one of you will be going for a dip," Sparky said. "I forbid it."

We considered what he said for a moment. Sissy went over to her suitcase and dug out her swimsuit, a pink one-piece number. She went into the bathroom with it. "I'll out be a minute. Don't go without me."

"I don't think you're hearing me," Sparky insisted though the door. "I said that I forbid you going into the pool."

"I heard you," Sissy said, emerging in her swimsuit. She had a towel in each hand and chucked one in my general direction. I caught it. "I don't care what you say, Mister Spock. I'm going in the pool. So's Buzz." She made a face at him and then stuck out her tongue.

"I will not allow you to defy me. I could spank you if I felt like it. I have authority over you. I'm in charge in this room. I'm the senior member of the family."

"Your authority means nothing to me. The revolution has begun. Come, little brother. We are going to the pool." We rushed over to the door and opened it before Sparky could stand in front of it, blocking our way. He was much bigger than us and could have physically prevented our escape. But he had short legs and wasn't as spry. We made good our escape, sprinting over to the pool with our towels jammed under our arms.

We tossed our towels onto a nearby lounge chair and leapt high into the air, grabbing our knees and shouting, "Cannonball!" We plunged into the pool and realized that it must have been 60 degrees. Probably colder. The shock took the air out of our lungs. We swam to the surface and over to the lip of the pool, hurriedly climbing out, our fragile bones shaking apart from all the shivering. We grabbed our towels and wrapped them around ourselves.

"That was horrible!" Sissy shouted. "Why did I let you talk me into it? You, the dumbest person alive!"

"How was I supposed to know it was that cold?" I asked, the cold having penetrated all the way through to my heart, which must have been frozen solid.

Sparky stood in the doorway to our room, his hands on his hips, a satisfied smile on his face, nodding his head in the affirmative. We'd gotten what we'd deserved for defying him.

We ran back to the room, but Sparky shut the door before we got there, and we were left outside with only the towels and each other to stay warm. I hugged my sister close as we double-wrapped the towels around us, attempting to get warm. "I'm sorry!" I whined.

"It's okay," she said. "We'll make it. Somehow. This is our retreat from Moscow."

Mom opened up the front door to her room. "What are you two weirdos doing now?"

"Sparky locked us out!" Sissy said. "We're going to die of frostbite."

"It's 80 degrees," Mom said. "You'll live." She walked outside and over to our door. She pounded on it. "Open up! We're going to dinner in ten minutes and these two need to put on real clothes."

The door opened up by about six inches and we crowded in the room. Sparky said, "Next time I tell you not to do something, don't do it. Do you see what happens? You think I don't have your best interests at heart? I expect an apology."

We did not apologize.

Instead, we took turns going into the bathroom to change and comb our hair. We both reeked of chlorine. I found another pair of board shorts to wear and an alternate Ocean Pacific t-shirt. Sissy put on her red shirt and white shorts. Our wet swimwear went on the floor. Sparky placed our swimsuits on the shower curtain rod after he spent time in the bathroom.

At Morrison's, we oohed and aahed at the brightly colored food that was shaped like food and tasted like food. I had a lemon meringue pie slice that was perfectly formed and bright yellow like the sun itself, the meringue white and fluffy like a cloud blowing past an Alpine maiden.

I had Salisbury steak and mashed potatoes. There were no lumps in the potatoes. And butter! There were little pats of butter in a dish on the table. I picked up a perfectly square dinner roll and spread the butter on it. I bit into it and closed my eyes. That roll tasted like bliss. The green beans weren't cooked into mush, nor were they barely steamed to the point of being raw.

We shoveled food into our mouths like it was going out of style. I burped. I untied the drawstrings to my board shorts. I swung my feet under my chair happily.

Sissy sat next to me doing the same. I watched Sparky as he chewed his food. He'd read in *Reader's Digest* that you needed to chew your food exactly twenty times in order for it to digest properly. I counted as he chewed each bite exactly twenty times.

Buster wiped down his plate with a dinner roll and belched contentedly.

Only Mom was dissatisfied with her meal. She poked at all the perfect food, finding it unsatisfactory. She finished it because not doing so would be a sin, and God might decide to strike her dead.

She told me once about how her father, if she didn't finish her mush in the morning, would make her go down into the basement and sit there alone on a stool until the mush was finished. She had to show him the empty bowl, otherwise she wasn't allowed out of the basement. She told me about all the shadows in the basement and the strange noises from the water heater. The ticking of the pipes. She tried not to eat the mush, but fear would overcome her and she'd choke it all down. "If I finished before he went to work, he'd give me a nickel. If not, if I managed to hold out, your grandmother would come down to the basement and tell me that it was okay, that I didn't need to eat it. That I could come upstairs. I didn't make it to that point most of the time. I collected a lot of nickels."

We went back to the Ramada Inn and retired for the evening. Eventually, it came time to go to bed and I found myself on the edge of the bed, not able to sleep, afraid of moving in case I woke up Sparky.

Sissy came over to me and patted me on the shoulder. "You awake?"

"Yeah."

"Come over to my bed. You can have half."

I got up and went over to her bed. We faced each other in the moonlit room, our heads on our respective pillows, our eyes open.

There is no one whose companionship I have ever treasured more before or since. She was my best friend.

The two of us silently shared each other's company, not falling asleep for an hour, maybe more.

What's Round on the Ends and High in the Middle?

Before we arrived at our final destination, a stop in Columbus was in order. We came to the massive stadium, called the Shoe, to pay homage to the greatest coach in the civilized world, Woody Hayes. Buster, who was not ordinarily reverent, stood outside the stadium having his own personal moment of silence. The rest of us stood with him, waiting for the moment of silence to end so we could get back on the road.

And then we were in the Ford family truckster on the final leg of the seemingly endless journey to Cleveland. There were relatives to mooch off.

We pulled into the driveway of the grandparents' house, road weary and slightly carsick since Mom had piloted the car up from Columbus, tapping the brakes while accelerating.

Our little grandmother came toddling out from the side door and greeted us with a wave. She was barely over five feet tall at the time but looked smaller. She was wearing a floral housecoat and slippers, and gigantic tortoise-shell rimmed glasses with a pink tint on the lenses.

We climbed out of the truckster, stretching exaggeratedly. Gretchen ran over to Grandmother, yapped a couple of times, and then made this ecstatic sound that we'd never heard come out of her. "Is this the new dog?" she asked us. "Come here puppy dolly and give me some lovings." I ran over so I could be first human to hug Grandmother. She gave up scratching the dog on the head. "My little dolly," she said. "Why aren't you growing?" She ran a thumb over my cowlick. "Grandmother's curl is still there." She radiated warmth, my grandmother. I basked in her love up until Sissy came over and elbowed me out of the way.

"My turn," she said, and then the two of them hugged for a while.

"You're getting shorter, Mom," Mom said.

"But my nose is getting bigger," Grandmother said in her scratchy voice, tapping the tip of her schnoz. "It'll happen to you. Just you wait. I hope I'm around to see it, too."

"To see me get shorter and for my nose to grow?" Mom asked skeptically.

"Of course!" Grandmother reached into her left housecoat pocket and produced a vial of pills. She popped one and put the pills away. She reached into the right pocket of her housecoat and produced a vial of pills. She popped one of those, too, and put them back where she'd found them. Cats had bells on their collars and my grandmother had the rattle of pills in her pockets. She leaned in and smiled at Sissy and me. "Would you like one of my pills, Buzz? I'll let you take one tonight before bed. Shhh." She placed a shaky finger over her lips.

"What are you telling my kids now?" Mom snapped. "What's the big secret, Mom?"

"You wouldn't understand, Lola dear. Not like this one." Grandmother tapped me on the chest.

Sparky made his way over and pretended to endure a hug from the little old lady. She was weird and depressive, but inside her was a vast ocean of love. Even the dog could tell.

In the 1940's, Grandmother tried to kill herself by drinking lye. All that she ended up doing was permanently damaging her vocal cords and her throat. Some important throat valves ended up being destroyed. She'd sip out of a bottle of Gaviscon and drink tonic water because she ruined those valves. Doctors in the 1940's weren't good at reconstructive surgery.

Buster nodded at Grandmother and made his way into the house to raid the beer fridge in the basement. My grandfather, who we called "Pop," was a fan of Michelob and Stroh's. He kept the beer fridge well stocked now that he was semi-retired. After retiring from the post office, he'd taken a part-time job in the mailroom of Halle's Department Store in downtown Cleveland. He was part of the union there and endlessly talked shop to us when we called up to say hello. When he got home from work, he was thirsty.

Mom insisted that this wasn't the same basement that had terrorized her as a child. The grandparents had owned a bigger home on the other side of the street when she and Ralph were children. But I was still afraid of somehow getting trapped down there, so I avoided going down if I could.

Sparky had gone to the back of the Ford family truckster and dropped the tailgate. He was removing all the luggage and preparing to tote it all in the house. I walked over and stood nearby. Sissy came up and tugged on my shirt. "Let him handle it. Let him be a martyr."

"I want to help." I desperately wanted to be a useful human being and I felt like I was failing at that every day.

"You can't even lift your own suitcase," Sparky said. "How are you supposed to help?" He grunted as he pulled out the oversized pieces of luggage. Sweat beaded up on his forehead.

"I could push," I offered helplessly. "I could grab one end."

"It's fine," Sparky said. "Go inside. Maybe you can help next year." He stopped and stared at me angrily. "Are you crying?"

"No," I said, wiping the tears away. "I just want to help, that's all."

"Take Mom's makeup case in then." He handed me the round piece of luggage. "Don't drop it."

"I won't," I said, holding it by the strap.

Sissy followed me up to the door and then held it open for me. I climbed up the three steps and walked into my grandparents' home. It smelled like El Productos with a hint of beer and a tinge of Canadian Club whiskey. I took the piece of luggage through the tiny kitchen, past the table that overwhelmed the tiny dining room and into the front room, where I found Pop and Buster sitting together silently watching the Indians on Pop's ancient black and white TV.

"This half inning of Cleveland Indians baseball is brought to you by Stroh's Bohemian Style beer!" Bob Brown said. "Nothing like a cold Stroh's, right Rocky?"

"You bet, Bob," Rocky Colavito agreed.

"Don't knock the Rock," Pop said.

I set the makeup case down and sat in front of the set. The dog trotted in, sniffed at the air, found nothing of value and headed toward the back of the house. It was hard to tell which group of blurry figures were the Indians and which were the California Angels.

"Your head's in the way, dummy." Buster slurped a Michelob from a glass bottle. He'd swiped the good stuff.

I got up and moved. I sat crosslegged on the rug near Pop's chair as he puffed his El Producto. If I was lucky, I'd get a slurp out of his Stroh's, which was on top of the metal TV tray next to him, next to the green glass ashtray that it would soon be my job to empty. I could live a useful life around the grandparents' house, doing all sorts of odd jobs for pocket change. Pop leaned down and said, "Man goes into a pizzeria. Orders a pizza. The cook asks the man, 'Would you like that cut into six pieces or eight pieces?' The man says, 'Six pieces… I could never eat the eight!'"

I laughed uproariously along with the old man. "Good stuff."

Something happened with the game and Buster argued with the TV set. "He was clearly out!"

I tried to watch the instant replay, but I couldn't make a thing out. I wondered if my eyes were beginning to go. Buster told me that all the reading and drawing I did would destroy my eyesight, and now I was wondering if he was right for once.

Sparky came trudging in, lugging a pair of oversized bags, huffing. He set them down next to where I'd left the makeup case. "I see that the bag you carried in almost made it to its destination."

"You can leave them there," Buster said, keeping his eyes focused on the blurry TV. "I'll put them up after the game is over."

"What's round on the ends and high in the middle?" Pop asked me.

"I don't know."

"O-HI-O," Pop said with a chuckle. "Get it?"

I laughed again. "Good one!"

Mom, Grandmother and Sissy disappeared into a back bedroom. I listened as the door closed. I used to be allowed in their all-girl convos, but I'd been banned recently. I was left with the males in the household, all of us shoving whatever feelings we may or may not have had deep inside, in a darkened interior cave, never to see the light of day. No amount of spelunking would ever extract those feelings.

I turned around to Pop. "What's red and green, and spins round and round?"

"I don't know," he admitted, puffing thoughtfully.

"A frog in a blender," I said, and laughed uproariously.

Buster actually cracked a smile at that one. After a beat, Pop decided that he'd laugh, too. "Not bad," he said. "Not bad at all." He stubbed out his cigar and asked, "You want to earn a nickel?"

I leapt up and grabbed the ashtray. It was unexpectedly warm. I set it back down. "Better wait for the ashes to cool," I said.

"Good lad," Pop said. "But you jumped to the wrong conclusion. How about getting me a beer to replace this one?" He handed me the empty Stroh's bottle.

Buster said, "I'm ready, too."

I took the two bottles over to the garbage can that was dedicated to empty bottles, lined with a paper bag from Giant Eagle, and then walked over to the dreaded door down to the basement.

Sparky came busting in with more suitcases, huffing mightily. "You could at least hold the door for me."

I held the door for him and watched as he lugged the suitcases into the area near the front room, piled up with the rest of the luggage.

"How are the Indians this year?" Sparky asked.

"They stink," Pop replied.

I opened the basement door and looked down into the darkness. I could end up being swallowed alive by such a basement. I propped the door open with a nearby wooden chair, dragged loudly across the wooden floor. I screwed up my nerve and dashed down quickly. Nothing to it. Nothing whatsoever. I grabbed two beers, both Stroh's, and started back up. Half way up the stairs, I saw Sparky remove the chair, saying, "How did this get here?" and the door slammed shut. I held onto the beers somehow, I had them gripped in each hand, and charged up the stairs.

I set the beers down on the top step and jiggled the handle. My hands were wet from the condensation. I couldn't open the door. I put my shoulder into it. The door wouldn't budge.

The ancient beer fridge took that moment to start up its motor. It kicked on and all the beer bottles stowed in there rattled in unison. I imagined that fridge coming alive. I imagined rodents waking up, sniffing the air, and catching my fear scent. Were rodents tool users? Didn't I see that on *Mutual of Omaha's Wild Kingdom* once? Rats with tools? Could they assemble little rat pitchforks and come after me? I was young and tender, like veal. It wasn't looking good. I beat on the door. "Help! Somebody help me!"

Sparky must have gone out for the last load of suitcases. Buster and Pop were enjoying the game in the front room. And rattling doom seemed to be making its way toward me. Could the ghost inside the ancient fridge—of course there was a ghost in the ancient fridge!—smell my fear? Would the fridge pop open upon coming to the top step and suck me inside, slamming the door shut? I knew from safety commercials that you weren't supposed to play inside old fridges, that they were death traps. Now, stuck in the basement, I was going to be swallowed whole by one of those death traps, with the ghost of an old steelworker trapped inside. That steelworker was embittered by the closing of most of the steel plants along the Cuyahoga River, and now wanted his revenge on someone who'd abandoned our dying town for Florida... me!

I beat on the door louder, with more urgency. "Let me out! Don't let Frank the dead angry steelworker trap me in the beer fridge!"

The door swung open. "What the hell did you do, dummy? Get lost?" Buster asked me. "Where's my beer?"

I handed him the Stroh's. "Here it is, Dad." I picked up the other Stroh's.

"Stroh's? Couldn't you see I was drinking Michelob? Go run back down and get me a Michelob. Put this one back."

I looked down the stairs in terror, then looked up at my father with equal terror. "I don't want to get stuck down here again."

"What did I do to deserve a wimp for a son?" he asked no one in particular. "Get out of my way, dummy." He stomped down the stairs with the Stroh's and came stomping back up a moment later with a Michelob. "Crap, I forgot to open it with the church key. Gimme that Stroh's, too. Might as well open it for your grandfather." He stomped back down the stairs and pulled the magnetized bottle opener off the fridge door, opened each bottle up, and then came back upstairs, out of breath. "Got my exercise in today, that's for sure. What are you doing just standing there? Get the hell out of my way."

I scrambled to get away from the basement.

"Wub-uh, wub-uh, wub-uh!" the beer fridge went, rattling the bottles. The basement door swung shut. I made a mental note to warn Sissy about Frank the dead angry steelworker trapped in the basement beer fridge for eternity. She needed to know to stay clear.

Sissy appeared in the kitchen a few moments later with Gretchen on a leash beside her. "Time to take the dog on a walk. What happened to you? Did you see a ghost in the basement?"

I told her about Frank the dead angry steelworker trapped in the basement beer fridge for eternity.

"I suspected as much," Sissy said, rubbing her chin thoughtfully. "Cleveland has to be full of dead angry steelworker ghosts. And since that fridge is ninety-nine and forty-four one-hundredths steel, of course he would choose it as a place to haunt. I say we get out the Ouija board before bed tonight and ask Frank some questions."

"Questions?"

"Pointed questions. Just like on *60 Minutes*. I'll be Mike Wallace. You can be Morley Safer."

"Won't that upset him?"

"He's trapped in the beer fridge, and that means he's stuck in the basement. So we have a distinct advantage over this guy. Plus, I'm sure that the afterlife is unionized, and unions have strict rules. We'll ask him who his shop steward is. That'll toss a scare into him. In the meantime, let's take the dog for a walk. She's sleeping with us tonight and I want her to be worn out by the time we get back."

"I'm not sharing a room with Sparky?"

"We decided that he is going to be in the attic. There's an old mattress up there. The parents are going to sleep on the hideaway bed in the front room. The women had a meeting to decide."

"Oh." I was pleased that I'd get to be with Sissy. "Good news then."

"We can have some privacy during the seance."

"Are we sure about this seance? I mean about having it?"

"You were attacked! No ghost is going to try to take a piece out of my little brother without getting a piece of my mind."

We walked around the neighborhood with the little dog pulling on her leash ahead of us. We took turns holding the leash. A couple of neighborhood kids rode up on their Schwinns and asked us who we were and why it looked like I was ready to star in an Elvis Presley flick in which he runs a helicopter operation in Hawaii.

"We're from Florida," Sissy announced ostentatiously. "We're here to see a few people. Relatives."

"Florida?" the boy asked breathlessly.

"Florida, for real?" the girl asked breathlessly.

"You've never been?" Sissy asked.

"We went to see an aunt in Baltimore last year," the girl said.

"They have the ocean out there," the boy said.

"Which is bigger than the lake," the girl said. "By a lot."

"That's what they said anyway," the boy said. "Not that I was buying it."

The two of them continued arguing about the relative sizes of Lake Erie and the Atlantic Ocean, ignoring us.

"We may have dodged a bullet, not growing up here," Sissy noted. "What a couple of idiots."

"What kind of dog is that?" the boy asked, interrupting Sissy.

"It's a doberman pincher. Deadly and spry," Sissy said.

"Nuh-uh. That's no dobie," the girl said.

"Bet you've never seen one this small," Sissy continued. "But the smaller they get, the fiercer they become. Her fangs are weapons registered with the state of Florida. If we stay more than 30 days, we'll have to register her fangs with the state of Ohio as well."

Gretchen trotted along merrily, oblivious to her own deadliness.

"Careful," I said, as the girl rode up onto the curb for a moment, "she can sense fear. And if you have recently been in contact with tasty sausage, she can sense that as well."

"I don't believe you," the boy said.

We stopped on the sidewalk, and the two of them halted their bicycles about six feet away from us. "Sit," Sissy said to Gretchen. She sat down expectantly. She thought she would get a treat out of this and when she didn't she'd become grumpy. "Lay down," Sissy said. Gretchen laid down. "Roll over." Gretchen rolled over and then got up and growled at us for her treat. Gretchen felt cheated.

In the meantime, the girl was making her way, slowly, over to Gretchen.

"Sit up!" Sissy shouted at Gretchen, and yanked on her leash.

The girl reached over toward her and Gretchen snapped at her hand.

The two kids screamed, mounted their bicycles and rode away at mach speed.

Sissy reached into her front pocket, retrieved a Liv-R-Snap and handed it to grumpy Gretchen, who nearly took her fingers off accepting the treat from her. She crunched it down too quickly, choked a bit, lapped up some crumbs from the sidewalk, turned and chewed on her own behind for a bit, making disgusting slurping and gasping noises.

"Might as well head back," Sissy said. "I think we've exhausted our outdoor entertainment options."

Back at the house, we got to watch Grandmother slowly create dinner. First, we witnessed the making of the cabbage rolls, each one carefully and individually crafted. Into the pot and then the oven they went. Then we watched her painstakingly make potato dumplings, shredding each potato so slowly that the end product turned out blue. The dumplings floated in a pot of boiling water. She roasted some pork in the oven and then made gravy from the drippings to pour over the top of the dumplings. Green beans went into another pot, each green bean cleaned and snapped lovingly. Then for dessert, she baked kolachkes, a sort of cookie with apricot filling. The whole process took hours and hours. By the time the food was ready to make its way to the table, one course at a time, we were all starving.

Each course was lugged heavily over to the table by the tiny old woman, who refused every offer of assistance. The kitchen was her domain and hers alone. Its sanctity was not to be violated.

Buster ate, but without his usual gusto. He considered this food to be foreign, and Buster had no use for foreigners and their foreign food and foreign ways.

We ate, and kept on eating. Every mouthful was fatty and delicious. She'd even managed to make the green beans taste fatty by adding some pork fat to the water they'd been steamed in. How could Mom grow up eating such wonderful food and end up becoming such a dreadful cook? I asked her years later. She said that she hated dinner when she was a kid. She hated that her mother would spend hours laboring over each meal, especially after having spent most of her day scrubbing down rich people's houses. She could never fully enjoy any of those meals due to all the guilt she felt about their construction.

But to me her cooking tasted like pure love. I appreciated those meals more because my grandmother had made them and had poured so much of herself into each morsel. She was an artist, and cooking was one of her finest art projects.

When she was a girl, she was a figure skater. She painted portraits of food as well, oil on canvas. She was an amateur photographer, using a Brownie camera to capture ecstatic shots of relatives and friends. When she was in a good mood, she elevated everyone around her. When she wasn't, she would disappear into her room, popping pill after pill.

When I was in college, I would ride my motorcycle from Gainesville to Nalcrest, the retirement home for postal workers near Lake Wales, to see my grandparents. On the way down one time, I stopped at an Eastern European food store I spotted near the road in Winterproof. I walked around inside, enraptured by familiar and lovely scents, and found a loaf labeled "Bohemian Rye." I bought it, placed it in my saddlebag, and when I arrived at their apartment in Nalcrest, I presented it to my grandmother. She was delighted.

The next time I came to visit, she pulled the loaf of bread out of the freezer and toasted a slice for me.

"I bought that for you," I said, feeling a bit hurt for no real reason.

"Oh, I couldn't eat your special bread," she said. "I want to watch you eat it."

I ate that loaf of Bohemian rye one slice at a time over the course of four years, eventually eating my last slice, a heel, when I was on leave from the Army.

I shoveled down my meal too quickly. I wasn't used to edible food and had the idea floating inside that it might disappear if I didn't slam it down my throat.

"You're not eating," Grandmother said to me.

"I'm full," I said.

"Just eat a little more," she said.

I'd hit capacity, but I tried. I gave up and stumbled off toward the bedroom I was to share with Sissy, untied my board shorts and lay groaning on top of the ornate comforter that our grandmother had made by hand. The bed swallowed up nearly the entire room.

Sissy came in and shut the door. She sat crosslegged atop the comforter laughing at me. "You should go throw up right now. You'll end up doing it anyway."

"But they'll hear and then Grandmother will be sad."

"I packed your transistor radio. Turn it on. When you're ready, turn it up and that'll give me the cue to bang on the door while you're puking and shout, 'I need to get in there.' That way they won't hear you puking."

"Okay."

"Pace yourself next time. Do I have to do all the thinking around here?"

Her plan worked to perfection. There was even a large, glass flask of Listerine that looked like it had been sitting in the medicine cabinet since the 1960's. I swooshed a chug of that around my mouth, spat it into the toilet and then wiped up around the bowl where I'd splattered. I felt much better physically after that, and tremendously guilty.

Sissy, the dog and I got up on the bed. Sissy closed the door and placed a red doily over the top of the little porcelain lamp on the nightstand. We sat crosslegged near each other. Sissy had been telling me about her psychic abilities since we were small, so I believed her. It wasn't until we were both in high school that she told me that her psychic abilities were "a load of horseshit" and that she found my reactions to the "spirits" so entertaining that she couldn't bring herself to tell me that it was horseshit. "I can't have everyone finding out exactly how dumb you are," she told me, "so I'm finally going to tell you exactly how dumb you have been so you can guard against your own stupidity in the future. In conclusion, I can't believe how dumb you've been."

The dog curled up near the headboard in between the two pillows. She was uninterested in spirits.

I had just made up Frank the dead angry steelworker trapped in the basement beer fridge for eternity, and yet I believed wholeheartedly in him already. That's how dumb I was.

Sissy placed the Ouija board on the bed between us. We placed our fingers on the planchette. Sissy said, "Spirit? Spirit, are you there?"

The planchette slid over to YES.

"Spirit, are you the dead steelworker known as 'Frank'?" Sissy rolled her eyes back convincingly. She blinked repeatedly as if possessed. Her mouth twitched.

The planchette slid over to YES.

"Frank, why do you haunt the basement? Is there someone here who has drawn you to this place?"

The planchette spelled out B-U-Z-Z.

I yanked my fingers off the planchette as if it was filled with ten-thousand volts of electricity.

Sissy snapped at me, "I hope you haven't broken the psychic link! We've got to get rid of Frank if he has it in for you."

I quickly placed my fingers lightly on the planchette again and Sissy immediately went back into her trance. "Frank, I would like to speak to your shop steward."

The planchette slid over to NO.

"I demand an audience with him. Bring him forth!"

The planchette slid over to YES.

"Is this the shop steward?"

The planchette slid over to YES.

We ascertained that the shop steward was named Bill and we initiated a formal complaint against Frank. The session ended with Bill assuring us that our complaint would be handled in seven to ten days and that in the meantime, Frank was to keep his distance from me if I had reason to go into the basement. No locking me up in the beer fridge, for starters.

The planchette slid over to GOODBYE.

"I don't know about you, but this calls for a couple of kolachkes. How's your tum-tum?" Sissy smiled at me.

"I can't believe that the afterlife is a bureaucracy run by union labor," I said. "Seems a little weird to me."

"The Ouija board cannot lie," Sissy said. "That's the law of the land."

"I guess so. But we'll be gone in seven to ten days."

"After all I've done for you, all you can do is whine. I give up." She folded up the Ouija board and put it back in its box along with the planchette, all of which went into her suitcase. "You'd better fall sleep tonight and not thrash around. That's all I've got to say."

Grandmother knocked and let herself in. She'd brought us each two kolachkes and a short glass of milk. She reached into her pocket and produced one of her amber vials of pills. "Would you like to sleep tonight, dolly?" she asked me. She didn't wait for a reply, tapping a tablet into my outstretched palm. I placed it under my tongue and felt it melting. "Better put on your pajamas quick. You'll be gone to sleepyland real soon."

I ate my two cookies, drank down the milk and went into the bathroom with my pajamas to change. I managed to get my pajamas on, opened up the bathroom door and fell face first onto the cold tile.

I heard my mother shout, "I told you not to give him your pills, Mom! He'd better wake up tomorrow, or you'll be charged with manslaughter…" Everything faded away.

I dreamt I was filled with feathers.

Family

After seven to ten days, we said goodbye to the grandparents while Sparky loaded all of the luggage into the car, hefting each piece with a loud grunt and then shoving them into the luggage compartment. No one seemed to mind or notice that he was doing all the hard work, least of all Sparky. It was expected of him. Or he'd assigned the work to himself because he hated sloppiness. Such were the wages of competence. I stood to one side watching him nervously as he stacked the luggage precisely, leaving the dog a perfectly dog-sized area to sleep. Why'd I have to be so small and weak? And sloppy?

The parents had done most of the visiting of boring, aged relatives on their own this trip, allowing us the opportunity to hang out with the grandparents, who were unboring aged relatives.

Pop told us stories about labor organization in the deep South in the 1920's, which often involved booze, loose women, guns, bribery, arson and the exploits of his union brother Harry O'Keefe, who may or may not have been in the Cleveland mob.

Grandmother taught us how to hide from the milkman when he came around to collect, and sat with me while I drew pictures and painted, telling me she thought it was all marvelous, but would I like to know a secret about how to make it a tiny bit better? Of course I did.

I wrote Brandy a letter, which was mostly drawings of bicycles, skateboards, tennis shoes and black squirrels. At the bottom of the letter was the Cleveland skyline as seen from the nearby beach. In the middle of this multicolored mess was: "Dear Brandy, How are you? I am fine. I am visiting my grandparents. My grandmother is an excellent painter. She helped me with my colors. Do you like my drawings? I hope so! Sissy says hi. She also wanted me to remind you that I am a 'stupid idiot' who spends too much time drawing. We'll be back after Independence Day. We're spending the day and night with our aunt and cousins in Lorain. Cousin Dougie says that he's going to shoot off fireworks that he found in a vacant lot. Who would leave fireworks in a vacant lot? I don't know. I hope to see you soon! Sincerely, Joseph 'Buzz' Pepper, Esq."

Pop took me to Cleveland Municipal Stadium for a game. I fetched him beer from vendors. I ate peanuts and dumped the shells on the concrete where Pop's cigar ashes were quickly accumulating. Pop told me everything wrong with the Indians, which took up until around the eighth inning, when Pop's voice gave out and he finally croaked out, "Listen, boy. They stink. That's the long and short of it."

Sparky and Pop didn't get along, so Sparky didn't come along.

Pop and I rode the Rapids back to Kamm's Corners, where Sparky stood at the train station waiting for us. "At last, you've arrived," he noted drily. "Grandmother's had one of her, um… episodes."

We walked back to the house down the sunny, tree-lined avenue. I rushed ahead, but neither Pop nor Sparky seemed all that concerned. When I got there, I ran in and called out, "Grandmother! Grandmother!"

"So dramatic." Sissy was seated at the oversized dining room table, one of her gothic horror paperbacks next to her, painting her fingernails strawberry pink. "How was the game?"

"The Indians stink," I said. "Where is she?"

"She fell down, so Sparky and I took her to bed. No big deal."

"How can you just sit there?"

"What do you want me to do? Dance a jig? Bawl my eyes out?"

I ground my teeth and went back to the grandparents bedroom. She was half-passed out in the darkened room, her eyes dewy and mostly closed. I hurried over to the bed and she said, "Come closer. Come closer, I want to tell you something." She took my hand and placed it over her heart. "These could be the last beats of my heart. These could be the last words to leave my mouth."

I wept openly. "Don't die!" I shouted out.

"Don't cry! I don't want the last thing I see on this earth to be you crying. Smile just once for me, dolly. Smile for your dying grandmother."

I heroically smiled for her and she pulled me in for a hug and a smeary kiss.

Pop walked into the room and said, "So no supper?"

"There's some leftovers in the fridge."

"Okay then. One of the kids can heat it up?" Pop had no idea about food and never even attempted to make a sandwich in my memory. I suppose he was the one whose culinary genes had been passed to my mother.

"Sparky can heat it up," Grandmother said. "I'm tired."

I left the bedroom and made my way out to the front room, where Sparky and Sissy were lounging around not paying attention to an episode of *Rawhide*. Sissy was blowing on her nails. "She tell you how she only wanted to see you smile once before she died?"

"Yes," I said, tears staining my cheeks.

"Oh quit crying, she'll be fine," Sparky snapped. "She took too many pills."

"'Where is Buzz?'" Sissy moaned mockingly. "'If only he were here, I could die happy.'"

"She said the same thing to me," Sparky said.

"Are you gonna heat up dinner or what?" Sissy asked him.

"We wouldn't want Grandmother's favorite to starve, would we?" Sparky asked her, and then both of them laughed at me.

"You're horrible!" I shouted at them. "She could be in there dying for all you know, and you're out here making fun of her!"

"Uh-huh," Sparky went. "Potato dumplings? I think I saw some leftover chicken paprikash."

"Anything so that sad little Buzz doesn't fade away to nothing," Sissy said. "That would be tragic."

"I hate you both!" I shouted and made my dramatic exit, going back to the room that Sissy and I shared and shutting the door behind me. I kicked my shoes off and crawled under the covers, placing a pillow over my eyes.

About an hour later, the scent of edible food pulled me from my bed and I tiptoed gingerly out to the dining room where a place had been set for me. Sissy decanted a bottle of ginger ale and placed it next to my plate. "She's fine," she said. "What's the matter with you?"

"I don't know," I said, as Sparky served up chicken on the bone. "Lots of stuff." The gravy was full of sour cream. I can eat sour cream directly out of the carton.

Eventually, Grandmother got up the next morning, and we were all laughing about it. She was happy, we were happy.

And now we were leaving, as soon as Sparky finished fussing over the placement of our luggage.

Grandmother called me over and ran her fingers over my cowlick again, Grandmother's curl. "You have to write me," she said, admonishingly. "You have to remember me."

I didn't have to work to remember her. She was the most essential part of me. She'd passed herself down to me through my mother.

Pop handed me a plastic cigar holder full of nickels. "Share it with the girl," he said with a wink. "Go out for some vitamins some time." Vitamins was his code for ice cream.

"Will do," I said. "Maybe the Indians will be better next year."

"I doubt it." He tapped some ashes that were picked up by a breeze and carried away.

He smoked cigars and drank whiskey and ate fatty foods. He would live to be 93 years old. He outlived Sissy. He outlived Grandmother by a year.

We had an overnight stop in Lorain before we headed back to Florida and our lives in the Sunshine State.

With Buster driving, we made it to Lorain in record time. Once we were off the highway, we drove to the part of town where poor white people lived, only hitting three potholes on the way thanks to more skillful driving by Buster, though the last teeth-jarring pothole made the dog fly up and hit the car ceiling. She yelped in frustration. We stopped the car and Sparky hopped out to chase down a hubcap that came loose and rolled away. He tossed it back with the dog.

We pulled up to the house and our cousins were standing there to greet us, all wearing what they thought were sly grins that hid their true predatory nature, but the grins hid nothing. In fact, they were all too revealing. I was always the last to get out of the car because of my position on the hump. I took my sweet time putting the leash on Gretchen. I picked her up and placed her on my lap. She saw the Peppers standing in wait for us and made a noise in the back of her throat that was somewhere between panic and sorrow. We both knew that we'd eventually be forced to get out of the car, but I tried to delay it for as long as possible by pretending to look for something. Gretchen got down on the car floor with me and sniffed around. She found some stale cheese balls and crunched them down.

"Oh my God!" Mom shouted through the open car door at me. "What are doing down there? What are you looking for?" Then she shouted at Sparky, "What's he doing? Did you ask him to clean under the seats or something?"

"He's delaying the inevitable," Sparky said. "But he's going to have to get out of the car at some point."

"You talk fancy," Cousin David said to him suspiciously.

"And you sound like a yokel from Lorain," Sparky replied icily. "If you'll excuse me, I need to get at least ten steps away from you."

"What? Why?" Cousin David asked.

"Purely a precautionary measure."

What Sparky meant was that Peppers were so calamity-prone that they rarely lived past the age of 50, and usually died much younger than that.

I'll use Cousin David himself as an example. About ten years after this particular 4th of July, David would get locked up in the Ohio State Penitentiary after robbing a convenience store. First, he tried to rob the till, but that only had $20 in it. So he led the clerk around the store making him fill up his cart with beef jerky and groceries. When he got to the beer section, he initially had him grab the Budweiser, and then corrected himself. "No! Let's gets the good shit!" So the clerk grabbed the Michelob instead. David, a three-time loser, was sent up for ten years and managed to survive the pen. When he got out, he decided to celebrate by procuring some heroin and shooting up while sitting on the toilet in his mother's house. His mother found him with his trousers around his ankles, astride the toilet, a spike in his arm and a dreamy smile on his dead face.

There are other examples. Cousin Dougie, the fireworks aficionado, died chasing a dropped dime out into traffic. He was hit by the crosstown bus. This was after he'd been released from the Ohio State Penitentiary for bigamy. He worked for the B&O railroad and had a wife on either end of the line—one in Cleveland, one in Baltimore. In case anything happened, he gave them each an "emergency number" to call. One day, one of his wives got curious and called the number. It was his other wife, of course.

Cousin Patty would see a life-changing movie, *The Amazing Dobermans*, starring Fred Astaire. She would decide to raise dobies as guard dogs. She did that, and then tried to make the dobies as vicious as possible by beating those poor dogs after putting on a homemade suit of armor made of old seat cushions, pillows, duct tape, hockey gloves, electrician's boots and a football helmet. She starved the dogs, too. I'll bet you can guess the end of this anecdote. That's right—she was mauled and eaten.

Peppers try to make it sound like it's a family curse, as if they have no control over the ends of their lives. Like life somehow has it out for us, when the opposite is true.

Those three doomed teenagers stood out in the sparse remains of their lawn waiting for me to emerge from the Ford family truckster.

Mom grabbed the dog's leash and walked her over to one of the only green patches of lawn. Gretchen peed on it, thus dooming it. Mom and the dog went inside.

I was all alone with the three Pepper siblings once I finally crept out of the car. My family had vamoosed, vanished, probably into the ramshackle house.

They were all impossibly tall, my cousins. The two boys were over six-foot-five. Patty was six-two. They had the same face as my father, which also freaked me out a bit.

"Look at him. He's shaking," Patty said sneeringly.

"No, I'm not," I said in a trembling falsetto.

"C'mere," Patty said, taking a knee.

I walked over to her, certain that whatever she had in store for me wasn't going to be good. I was right. I stood in front of her. She took my Ocean Pacific t-shirt into her fist. David got on one side and Dougie the other. They each slugged me hard on the upper arm. "Slug bug," Patty whispered, her breath smoky with whiskey and cigarettes. There was a VW across the street, I guess. Or maybe they didn't know the rules of slug bug. Patty's hard Pepper face leered at me, her eyes red, her nose lined with purple capillaries, her teeth stained brown, her lipstick unevenly applied and her rouge haphazardly slapped on. Her brown hair hung straight down. She may have been ironing it every morning, like some girls did back then. She let go after I didn't cry out, or even show that I was in pain. "Maybe you're a Pepper after all. We always thought your mother cheated on Uncle Buster for all three of you little shits."

I pushed away from her, as she and the two boys laughed brayingly. They were proud of what they were. They were proud of being coarse, violent and stupid. They thought it made them strong.

"Just wait til tonight. There's gonna be a show," Dougie said. "All them fireworks shot off at once. Ka-bang!" He made an explosion sound with his mouth. "New-cue-lure fucking war."

All three of them squinted at a man walking down the street. I turned and squinted at him, too. When I turned around, all three of them had vanished. I turned back to look at the man and saw that he was sprinting in my direction. I decided to stand there like an idiot waiting for him. He was wearing a brown plaid sports coat and brown polyester pants. I saw a revolver hanging from a holster under his armpit. I saw a badge hanging off his belt. He was a real live cop. I was excited to meet him, unlike my cousins.

"Hey son," the man said, puffing as he finished his short sprint. "How's it going?"

"Pretty good, officer," I said. "How are you? You okay?"

"I'm fine. Just fine." He took a minute to catch his breath. He pulled out a stained handkerchief and mopped his brow. "So what's your name?"

"Buzz," I said.

"That's a fine name. You got a last name to go along with that?"

"Pepper."

He smiled knowingly. "Well, aren't you well-mannered for a Pepper? You stonewalling me, son? Delaying so your brothers and sister can get away?"

"Them? I see them once a year and it's always horrible. Yet we keep on coming back because my father used to live here. Now his brother's ex-wife lives here with her new husband."

"You're Buster's son?"

"Yes, sir."

"Oh. Well. That's all right then. I went to high school with your father. I was a wide receiver on the football team."

"Neat," I said, remembering how Buster recalled all of his receivers as being incompetents who'd cost him a football scholarship to the Ohio State University.

"Your dad around?"

"Yes, he's inside. You want me to go get him?"

"Might as well. I'm not going to be making an arrest until your cousins manage to wander back here. You see any fireworks around here?"

"Not yet, sir. They promised me that I'd see them tonight, nuclear bomb style."

"That's what I'm trying to prevent. Also, the city of Lorain needs them back for the fireworks show tonight. You don't look very surprised."

"I'm not. I'll go get Dad." I extended my hand. "Nice to meet you, sir."

He shook my hand, doing a pretty good job of adding bruised fingers to my bruised upper arms. "Nice to meet you, too, son. A well-mannered Pepper. Never thought I'd see the day."

"You should meet my brother then. My sister, too."

I let myself in the front door of the house. The rich odor of pipe tobacco filled the air. It's the only tobacco smoke that I've ever enjoyed. In my teens and early 20's, I'd smoke Lucky Strikes and Camels, both filterless, as a restaurant worker, but I never cared for the smoking part, only the nicotine that resulted from it. The act of smoking was part of the enjoyment, too—lighting a cigarette, taking that first draw.

Late in my restaurant career, just before I left college and joined the Army, I woke up from a fitful nap. My dog Bear stood before me, a bright green tennis ball in his mouth. He dropped the ball on the worn rug of the cheap apartment that I shared with my brother, and then rolled the ball toward me with his nose. I tried to say something to him, probably, "Let me sleep," but instead I coughed and hacked up a tar blob into the palm of my hand that looked like caramel pudding. I studied it with horror, right up until Bear ate it and belched heartily. "Gross," I said, more about the dog eating it than this thing coming out of my lungs. That tar blob scared me. After that, I gave up smoking. I miss it from time to time, but I've never taken it up again.

A few weeks ago, I got it into my head that I was going to start dating again. I've never asked a girl on a date in my life. I don't like going to bars unless there's a band I like that's playing there and I'm too focused on the band to pay attention to anything or anyone else. I wouldn't have the nerve to approach a woman in a bar anyway, because women constantly complain to me that they hate it when a man approaches them in a bar. All of the women I'd gone out with were friends first. The pattern is this: I work with her, or go to school with her. At some point, she says, "I don't know why I'm telling you this, but..." and then she tells me her problems, usually having to do with a husband or boyfriend. So I listen. She tells me I'm a good listener. At some point, she invites me to lunch, and there is more talk. I find certain people endlessly fascinating. And, frankly, listening to people's problems makes me feel useful. At some point, she announces that she's left her boyfriend or husband. I tell her I'm sorry to hear that. Then she says something like,

"Listen. Would you like to go to a movie?" I say, "Sure." Sex may or may not occur. I do my best not to push, or to say how I feel. Then a few weeks or few months later, she stops calling and she stops coming by my apartment or my work station. I never get a fuck you, or anything like that. It just ends and I don't push it to continue. That's life, I suppose. People come. People go. The only woman I ever broke up with was my ex-wife. I left her after the two of us sat around watching our marriage die. What I'm saying is that I have no idea how to initiate a relationship, so I tried out computer dating. I fired up my modem and went online. I found a website that didn't charge a fee. Instead, they shoved pop-up ads all over my computer monitor and nearly crashed the overtaxed machine. I put in all of my information, and then forgot about it until I got an email (AOL chirping out happily, "You got mail!") from the service saying that I'd been matched up. Peggy and I wrote back and forth for a while. We wrote each other concerning our political opinions. We were both against impeaching the president over lying about a blowjob. We both liked punk and post-punk and the Beatles and country music. I sent her scans of my artwork. She said she liked it a lot. She worked in a boutique on Longboat Key. In short, we were two lonely people in our 30's who seemed to have a lot in common. She suggested that we meet. We decided on a place on Siesta Key that is near the beach and served chunks of fish deep-fried in beer batter. We'd seen each other in photographs, but that's not the same thing as meeting in person, is it? When I arrived at the place—after having driven up and down the street in my brother's old VW looking for a parking spot—I peered around and saw her. Peggy looked the same as her photo, a cute, curly-headed ginger with freckles dotting a pert little nose, wearing loose jeans and a Smiths t-shirt. She was puffing on a cigarette, blowing the smoke out of the corner of her mouth, reminding me of a gun mole in an old-timey gangster movie. She stood up and stubbed out the cigarette in a tin ashtray. I walked over to the table and saw the disappointment cascading across her features, from her face down to her shoulders, to her Doc Martens. To be polite, we sat down together for an hour, drinking a matching pair of Mai-Tais out of plastic, Tiki-themed giveaway cups and ordering a deep-fried platter of fish that slept in the Gulf of Mexico that morning, according to the menu that was covered over in Tiki-themed clip art that I had drawn for my company maybe a year before. Peggy did most of the talking, telling me about a friend who followed around Jimmy Buffett, "a goddamned parrothead. I don't even know why I hang around with her. I guess it's because Sarasota is goddamned Nowheresville." She told me that I was easy to talk to, but that I was "not what I expected." I told her I didn't mean to mislead her. "It's not you. Well, it is. You're not my type. I can tell." Her voice was gravelly, like Suzanne Plechette. Peggy grabbed a bar napkin and hacked into it. Before she crumpled up the napkin, she studied what was there: A

153

caramel-colored blob. Unlike me, she didn't find it frightening. It was of interest to her, certainly, but in a scientific sense. Neither one of us thought that we should mention it after the crumpled napkin ended up on her plate of half-eaten deep-fried fish and stubbed out cigarettes with mauve lipstick stains on the filters. We parted ways at the end of the meal and haven't spoken since. I went on two more dates through the service and both started the same way, with that look of disappointment. After date number three, I came home, fired up the modem and took down my profile.

I closed my eyes and enjoyed, for a moment, the aroma coming from Uncle Virgil's pipe. It was sweet like apple pie and spicy like cinnamon. Long story short, Uncle Virgil, Aunt Scotty's second husband, was not an actual relative. He would die of throat cancer eventually. He was the only person from my father's side of the family that I genuinely liked. Even though we carry the Pepper name, I rarely think of Sparky and Sissy and me as being part of Buster's family. We were our own hybrid. We were different from other Peppers.

I found my father drinking a Red, White and Blue beer in the kitchen. It was his brand, but he'd gotten used to high living at the grandparents' house. He took a sip and made a face. "I guess I should get used to this again," he groused.

"There's a cop out front looking for you," I said.

"You sure he's looking for me and not one of your cousins?"

"He's looking for them, too. Something about them stealing fireworks from the city. But he says he knows you from high school. Played football with you."

"Oh," Buster said, perking up. "That's all right then." He grabbed a fresh beer from the fridge to take out to the cop and left me alone in the kitchen.

A moment later, Virgil walked in. "Sorry. Didn't mean to interrupt."

Interrupt what? I was standing there wondering where Sissy was. "It's okay," I said. "I'm just a guest."

He snapped his fingers, like he was having a eureka moment. "You ever go with your folks out to Las Vegas?"

"No."

"So I guess you wouldn't know what *this* is." He reached up on the top of the fridge and picked up a green, metal machine. I could hear something rattling around inside it. He set it down on the kitchen table. He handed me a nickel and pointed out the nickel-sized slot in the top. There was a little arm on the side and three little windows showed a cherry, a lemon and an orange.

I placed the nickel into the slot and pulled the little arm. The pictures in the window spun. Eventually, three pictures of cherries appeared and several nickels ejected from the bottom. "Neat!" I went.

154

"Keep on playing if you want. When the nickels run out, you're done," Virgil said. "I'll be in my study."

Study? Why did he need a study? I don't know what he was studying. Putting nuts on cars? He worked on the assembly line at Ford and spent the rest of his time bailing his stepchildren out of juvie and promising the court that they'd behave themselves in the future. So maybe he was studying the law so he could represent them in court. Save himself a few bucks.

The kitchen window opened and I saw David slithering through it head first. He landed on his hands and eased himself to the linoleum floor. "That cop still out there?" he asked, hurrying to his feet.

"Yeah. My father is out talking to him. They played football together in high school."

"Are you shitting me? That's good news."

I slipped a nickel into the slot, pulled the arm and turned to say something to him, but was interrupted by a clanking noise coming out of the little machine. Suddenly, there was a cascade of nickels pouring out of the bottom, enough that I had to catch them with the bottom of my shirt. "I'm rich!" I shouted.

"My ass you're rich," David sneered. "Those are *my* nickels, you little shit. And you're going to put them back."

"Here, take them." I poured the nickels onto the kitchen table and tried to turn them into a neat pile. There were a lot more nickels in the machine than it looked like it should have.

"Nah-uh. You're gonna sit there and put them back in."

I looked at the pile of nickels and sighed. "Why can't you just take them?"

"Because I have to win. Me. Not you. I'm not taking your charity." This was someone who spent his life stealing other people's possessions, but he wasn't going to take charity. I suppose he thought of theft as hard work.

"Good news," Buster said, entering through the kitchen door. "If you take the fireworks back, no charges. I worked it out with the police. Doesn't hurt to have friends in high places."

"Thanks, Uncle Buster. You've been like a dad to me and that means a lot."

Buster melted. David was his idea of what his son should be like—tall, menacingly handsome and athletic. "Ah, well," he stammered. "It's nothing. I think of you the same. Nothing's too good for my brother Sonny's kids." They continued buttering each other up for a while, like I wasn't even there. "Well, you'd better get a move-on. They gotta have those fireworks before tonight."

"Dougie and Patty can take them back," David said. "I gotta watch this one put my nickels back in this one-armed bandit. They're *my* nickels, so he's not gonna walk away with them."

155

Buster looked at the machine and made a couple of appreciative noises in his throat. "So you've been working this machine for a while?"

"Every morning before school. And this one puts one nickel in and gets all my money. That's a bunch of bullshit."

"When you're right, you're right," Buster said, slapping my bruised shoulder unexpectedly. I cringed a bit, which instantly incensed him. "I barely touched you!" He crouched down and glared at me. "Damn right, you're gonna put all those nickels back. Keep an eye on him, David. I'll go find your brother and sister and tell them the plan."

While I spent an interminable hour or two shoving nickels into a slot machine under David's watchful eye, Buster and the two other kids acquired a flatbed truck and delivered the fireworks to a mysteriously unmanned city garage, and left them there. All but one, that is. Buster figured that he owed something to Dougie after he showed him his big sad eyes and pleaded with him, "Just one rocket, Uncle Buster."

Aunt Scotty came into the kitchen and shouted at David, "What the hell are you up to?"

"I'm watching him, Mom." David jammed his hands into the pockets of his cutoffs and sulked.

"He seems to be winning," Aunt Scotty said.

The machine paid off again, so I had to shove more change into it. It was unending. But it had one upside and that's that I have never since played a game of chance.

I once accompanied my wife to Las Vegas. She was there for the annual Visitors Bureaus and Chambers of Commerce convention. She gave me a quarter and pushed me at a slot machine. "Go nuts," she said.

"No thanks." I tried to hand her back the quarter.

"Is this about that stupid story you told me about your cousin forcing you to put nickels in some home slot machine? Because if it is, I don't want to hear it again."

"Sorry." By that time in our marriage, I was apologizing to her on a near-hourly basis. I was constantly trying to smooth things over, to make our married life as placid as possible. I did what I do best: I took all my feelings and shoved them deep inside. According to most experts, this is unhealthy.

She could tell I was placating her, and she hated it. She snatched the quarter out of my hand, walked over and shoved it into a machine. She pulled the handle and a few seconds later two dollars worth of quarters came out. She scooped them up and put them in her purse. "See? Easy. If you have any more stories about dead relatives, keep them to yourself."

My mother hated my wife. By the time I got married, Mom was in excruciating pain all the time from her cancer, so maybe that had something to do with it. The two of them had such a falling out that I rarely saw my mother up almost to the end. When our marriage was nearing its demise, I yelled at her about it. She shouted back, "Too bad Lola isn't here to say, 'I told you so!'"

Aunt Scotty told David to go fire up the grill and "try not to set yourself on fire."

"Why isn't Virgil doing it?" he asked, moping.

"Because *you* are, stupid," she snapped. "Go! Before I lose my patience."

He slammed his way out the kitchen door. Aunt Scotty watched him through the kitchen window. "Just put the nickels in your pocket and go find your sister. She's upstairs in Patty's room."

"Thank you."

"I should put that one-armed bandit out by the trash. It's been nothing but trouble since Virgil brought it home." She opened up the fridge and pulled out a jumbo-sized package of hot dogs, signaling that our conversation was at an end.

I climbed upstairs, past fading black and white photos of my Pepper relatives, who all, by the identical looks on their identical faces, were just about at the ends of their respective ropes. They'd all been cheated. None of them looked like he or she was over 50, a grim reminder of a Pepper's fate to die of inherent stupidity while young.

I peeped in each room. The boys' rooms had tool calendars with girls in bikinis licking wrenches. They had posters of The Who and Led Zeppelin.

Patty's room was painted entirely in pink. The walls and furniture were pink. The ceiling was pink. Leif Garrett was scotch-taped to the wall with pink hearts surrounding him.

Sissy was sitting on a pink rug on the floor. She had on her Oshkosh bib overalls with daisy appliqués, an orange shirt and Birkenstocks on her feet. She'd painted her toenails strawberry pink. Her hair was tied into ponytails with pink ribbons. "Look who the cat dragged in."

"This family is—"

"A bunch of idiots? Why, yes. I've noted that myself. This house is especially depressing. I said it once and I'll say it again: We dodged a bullet not growing up here."

"The parents could decide to move back."

"Only if we win the lottery so Dad can rub it in everyone's faces."

Judging by the wall portraiture, no Pepper had ever won the lottery. Not even close. "Sure."

"Enjoy your time with the Hee Haw gang?"

"The answer to that is—*no*. But at least Dad made them take back the fireworks. Dougie was planning on setting them all off at once."

"Of course he was. Bet you a pocket full of nickels that they conned him into not taking all the rockets back. And I'll bet you all the nickels in the cigar holder that the rocket hits a building and sets it on fire, because they're a bunch of morons."

That evening, Sissy won all her nickels. While Sissy and I ran around the sparse Pepper lawn waving around sparklers, we watched Dougie, drunk on Red, White and Blue beer, sprint into the lean-to shed in the backyard and come back out with a rocket the size of a man's arm. He snatched the sparkler out of Sissy's hand, laughing drunkenly, and made his drunken way over to the neighbor's back yard.

The city of Lorain's fireworks show was blasting over Lake Erie. I tried to watch it, but Sissy wouldn't stop poking me. "You're missing the real show."

The rocket lit and flew in a straight horizontal line, shattering the front window of an abandoned house across the next road over. It exploded and the house was quickly engulfed in flames.

"Oh shit!" Patty shouted, laughing. "You did it this time, Dougie! What a turd!"

We saw a couple of homeless men run out of the house. I think we called them "bums" back then. Or "tramps." The two bums/tramps were pulling on their singed clothes. They were coughing.

The Peppers were all laughing—my father, my three cousins.

Aunt Scotty said, "Christ almighty," and went inside. Virgil was nowhere to be seen.

My sister, my brother and I weren't laughing. Mom wasn't laughing. It wasn't funny. It was disgusting.

Buster took a breath from all the laughter and said, "We have to leave. Five minutes. We have to get out of state as quickly as possible. We don't want to have to testify."

"I want to testify," Sparky said.

"Well tough. I'm still in charge of this family and I say we're leaving. Now hurry up and get everything in the car. Where's the stupid dog?"

The dog was hiding in the weed-choked bushes alongside the house, scared to death. She was the smartest one of us all.

I did as I was told. We all did. We got the car packed and on the road in record time. The fire spread from one house to another. People were standing outside in their shorts and t-shirts, not watching the fireworks show, but the real life show. The one with all the tragedy in it. I was eleven. I looked out the car window at those people feeling sick to my stomach. I had no say in our departure, but I regret it to this day anyway.

I'm filled with regrets. Brimming with them.

Bastille Day

The Bondurants' dog, Bruce Lee, went missing. The neighborhood alligator, Old Charley, a 12-footer who prowled the fetid depths of the neighborhood pond, was to blame for many doggie deaths. He was a hungry critter and a danger to society. Steve meant to do something about it.

He told me his plan when I came by to find out if Brandy had received my letter. She wasn't there, but Steve was. I took a step back when he answered the door. The Ultimate El was nowhere to be seen, so I'd assumed the coast was clear. It was not.

But Steve was in a forgiving mood. "Tell me you didn't throw that rock at the Ultimate El, and I'll forget all about it," he said amiably.

I twitched uncomfortably, standing there on their front stoop, a slab of concrete adorned with coquina shells with a coat of resin on top of that. The welcome mat featured a gold fleur-de-lis, "Bienvenue" written in frilly script across the top. "I didn't do it?" I went, eyes darting, head on a swivel.

"Good enough, little man. You look bigger."

"My grandmother is a good cook."

"Come on inside and let me show you what I've procured to take on that alligator."

I can't explain how much relief I felt in that moment, and gratitude.

Steve was dressed in a tank-top and jean cut-offs, flip-flops slapping the bottoms of his feet. His blonde hair was luxuriantly shoulder-length, his mustache now trimmed into a fu-manchu, with a soul patch tickling his lower lip. I followed him back to his work-out room, which now featured the actual Bruce Lee in a poster on the wall shirtless and in full fighting stance.

Steve showed me his spear gun, scuba tank and diver's goggles, as he told me about the missing dog and his plan. "That motherfucker is gonna get what he deserves," Steve said. "Brandy cries herself to sleep every night. Bruce Lee and her are inseparable, but I let him out three nights ago when he was scratching at the sliding glass door, and that alligator done ate him up. I must right my wrong. I must take my vengeance. Excelsior, brother!"

I didn't like the thought of Brandy crying. My back went ramrod straight. Besides, I thought, that alligator could go after Gretchen next, though she wouldn't be much of a meal. I'd heard about the Perrys' dog, Fillmore, a French poodle, who was snatched by Old Charley when he was minding his own business, tied up in their backyard. Nothing was left behind but blood and bits of fur. Half the chain was gone. One night, I'd heard the baying of a beagle who lived down the street, following by his frightened shrieks, followed by silence. So, heck yeah, something had to be done. And Steve, the neighborhood legend, was precisely the man to do it. I was proud he'd let me in on his plan.

But he had more to say. "You're gonna help me, little man."

"How?" I couldn't imagine what I could do against such a formidable foe.

"You're gonna be my spotter. While I'm in the water, you'll be standing on the shore with a pair of binoculars. If you see him, fire off this starter's pistol." He handed me the fake gun. "I'll come up and you point him out. You and me, brother. We're gonna kill that fucker." Steve was swearing like a man now and had slapped on some Brut cologne. It was thrilling to be around him. It felt like a great adventure was about to be undertaken. "We gotta get out of here before my old man comes home and stops us. Brandy and Mom are at the airport waiting for him. By the time they get home, we should have an alligator for the old man to barbecue."

I had on my customary board shorts and a t-shirt with Clark Kent transforming in a phone booth into Superman and flying up, up and away. I had on my worn-out tennis shoes and no socks. I was dressed for this adventure. Steve hung the binoculars around my neck. They were the expensive ones and weighed, possibly, more than I did. There wasn't an ounce of plastic involved in their construction, just metal and glass.

Steve strapped the tank to his back and strapped some weights around his waist. He put the goggles on his forehead and shoved a pair of flippers under his arm. He handed me the spear gun. "Careful with that. You don't want it to accidentally go off."

"This is the greatest day of my life," I said aloud, not meaning to.

"It will be!" Steve enthused. "After we get us that gator."

We walked down to the neighborhood pond, trailed by neighborhood kids on bikes. They shouted, "Steve Bondurant! He's a bad man!"

"You know it, fellas!" Steve called back cheerily.

"You gonna kill that gator?" they asked.

"That gator is dead already. He just don't know it."

The binoculars weighed heavily on my neck. My shoulder muscles tensed. The starter pistol jiggled like a brick in my pocket, threatening to pull down my board shorts. The spear gun weighed approximately a ton.

All I could think about was Steve taking down the alligator, and then a victory parade for him, circling the block slowly in the Ultimate El as the neighbors threw confetti and popped streamers. At night, some sort of fireworks display, perhaps, as Old Charley spun slowly on a spit in front of all the dogs, who would eventually eat his roasted corpse in an act of defiance of all oversized reptiles who would threaten their happy domestic existence.

The mob of kids stopped at the waterline. Steve came to a halt and turned around. The mob dropped their bicycles in skewed formation around him and stepped forward. They expected a speech, and Steve Bondurant did not disappoint.

"I stand before you a man on a mission," he intoned. "And before I emerge from the waters of this pond, I will kill me a murdering alligator and will bring you his carcass. That, I pledge to you, fellas and gals. I see we have some of the fairer sex with us today. Girls, it's okay to turn away when I bring that bad old gator to shore. Maybe you won't want to see it. But men—and yes, I consider all of you squirts to be men—men! I am on a mission. Take note. Write down the date. Here on July 14th, in the year of our Lord, nineteen-seventy-five, yours truly will make a nefarious critter pay with his life for what he did to our dear dead dog, Bruce Lee, the truest companion that any girl—I'm talking about my sister Brandy here—ever had. Can I get a 'hell yeah' out of you?"

"Hell yeah!" all the boys shouted.

"Ew," one of the girls commented. Her name was Rosemary and she went to Catholic school with Sissy. Most of rest of the girls picked up their bikes and peddled away. Rosemary sneered at me. "I'm telling your sister!"

I jumped back maybe six inches. Maybe a foot. "Um."

She turned and shouted at the massed children,"She's gonna come down here and put a stop to this." They cringed in contemplation of my sister's rage. "Sissy Pepper's coming and if you don't want her to be mad at you, you'd better clear out!"

"We ain't scared of Sissy Pepper. Are we fellas?" Steve asked the boys.

"I gotta go home," one of them said.

"Me, too."

They all started picking up their bikes.

"Aw, come on. What's Sissy got on all you fellas?"

"It's not what she has on us," one of the boys said. He went to Catholic school, too. I think his last name was Reed. "It's what she's going to say."

"It's what she says," another boy agreed. "Sorry, dude. There's no way I want Sissy Pepper to be mad at me. No way. She's brutal." He slapped me on the shoulder. "Good luck, Buzz. Tell Sissy 'hey' for me. Wait, no. Don't tell her that. She'll know I was here." He looked nervously over his shoulder, like she might already be coming around the corner.

Rosemary got on her bike. "Last chance."

"We're doing this," Steve said. "Ain't that right, little man?"

"Yes," I said, happy to be on Steve's good side again. "That alligator must die."

"Attaboy," Steve said with a nod of his head. He put on the goggles and took the spear gun from my hands. "You go on now. You go tell that girl that we men are gonna take care of business." He kicked off his flip-flops and put on the flippers. He reached behind and turned on the valve on the tank and stuck the mouthpiece in. He waded out into the pond, turned once and held the spear gun over his head like it was a rifle and he was the last man standing at the Alamo, and then he was gone into the murky deep.

I pulled out the starter pistol and set it on the ground and then sat down next to it with the binoculars up, scanning the surface of the pond, on the lookout for Old Charley, ready to pick up the starter pistol and fire it on a moment's notice, even though Steve had failed to show me how it worked. I assumed that all that I would have to do is pull the trigger.

Several minutes went by. I was having a blast with the binoculars. It turned out I was exactly the wrong person to choose to be on the lookout, because I discovered that the *Donahue* show was on and it was some sort of episode that involved adult people who liked to wear diapers and suck milk out of oversized bottles. Ironically enough, I was peeping through the window of the Perrys' house watching the show, the people who'd lost the fancy poodle to Old Charley.

Sissy's voice interrupted my reverie. "Do I have to constantly supervise you? The answer to that is, obviously, yes."

I jumped a little bit. "Phil Donahue has a bunch of adults on who like to wear diapers."

"Where's Steve?" Sissy was wearing her Oshkosh overalls with the daisy appliqués and a pink t-shirt. Her shining blonde hair was tied into two ponytails. The flecks of gold in her hazel eyes twinkled in the bright sunlight. She had on her Birkenstocks, as usual, and her toenails were painted strawberry pink.

"Um."

"Yeah. That's what I thought. And the pistol? Where'd that come from?"

"Steve gave it to me."

"Uh huh." She picked it up and weighed it in her hand. "You're not gonna kill any creatures with this thing. The barrel is all plugged up."

"It's a starter pistol," I said, the expert for once. "It's to warn Steve in case that alligator is sneaking up on him."

"But here you sit, watching Phil Donahue through someone's window."

162

"Um."

"Good job, Buzz. Really, an amazing job. And why are we doing this today? You know it's Bastille Day in France, don't you? I like Bastille Day. It's mentioned in some of my favorite filthy books. And if you knew anything, you'd know that Brandy and I were going to celebrate it later on today because her family's French. Instead, you decide to sit here not watching Steve Bondurant kill an alligator. You know why he's not gonna kill an alligator? Want to take a guess?"

"I don't know."

"Of course you don't know. Allow me to show you." Sissy grabbed my shirt and we both stood up. "Aim your stupid spyglasses down the street."

I did so. I read on the back of a large, white truck: "Florida Fish and Wildlife." Two men were slamming the tailgate shut. "Um."

"They just captured your pal Old Charley after Captain Slidell's widow called them last week. I had to check in with her this morning after chatting with Brandy on the phone. The good widow is giving me lessons on dating older men. She said it might come in handy at some point."

"I… Uh… Crap."

"As always, little brother, you're deadly eloquent." And then, inexplicably, she gave me a hug and then pushed me to arm's distance. "Turn around, dum-dum. You're about to be a hero to your girlfriend."

I turned around and saw Bruce Lee tromping in our direction, snorting and coughing and spattered with mud. I sat down on the ground and held out my arms. He came up and collapsed in my lap, exhausted. I petted him for a while and then said, "Sissy! Fire off the starter's pistol and we'll wave Steve back to shore."

She already had the starter's pistol in her hand. She futzed around with it for a moment and then held it aloft over her head and fired it. It was louder than either of us thought it would be. Sissy dropped it to the ground like it had bit her. Bruce Lee stuck his head high in the air and howled. A flock of birds shot out of the Spanish moss-covered trees surrounding us and flapped loudly into the sky. Steve Bondurant came to the surface. He saw the dog and swam quickly to the shore, wading out looking like a World War II frogman who'd gone native on some tropic island. He quickly took out the mouthpiece and pulled off the goggles, dropping them next to the pistol. "Bruce Lee!" he shouted. "You found Bruce Lee!"

"Yes he did," Sissy said. "You'd better remember that."

"I'll remember it, Sissy. But I still want to get that gator."

"Too late," I said. "Florida Fish and Wildlife got him."

"Bummer." Steve sat down and took off the flippers, stinky water dripping from his drenched body. Bruce Lee waddled over to him.

"You're a sight for sore eyes, Bruce Lee. Don't go running off again. Brandy freaked out." He petted the dog happily.

"It's Bastille Day," I said.

"Yes it is, little man. Look at you, knowing your French history and shit."

"My work here is done," Sissy said, placing her hand over her heart solemnly. "I have to go home and watch Phil Donahue. He's got some adults on dressed as babies."

"Man, that's just weird," Steve said, standing up.

"And you smell like a sewer, Steve. Just saying. Who knows where all the water in that retention pond comes from?" Sissy shrugged. "Just thinking aloud. Sometimes I do that. You know: *Think*. It comes in handy sometimes, *thinking*."

Steve rolled his eyes. "I get it. Thanks."

"Don't forget your pistol that can't shoot anybody. Or your spear gun. Wouldn't want that to fall into the wrong hands, would we? It would be tragic for a non-thinking person to wander off with one of those. Who knows what stupid trouble they could get in?"

"Got it. Got it."

"Come along, Buzz. We have adults pretending to be babies to mock on the old TV."

I looked over at Steve. "Do you need any—?"

"No, no! Please take your sister and go home. Please. See you later, all right? Come on over for the annual wingding. We'll be waving the tricolor and having a good old time."

"Yes, I'll see *you* later," Sissy said, smirking evilly. "Oh, the stories we'll have to tell. Tales around the campfire. Nothing like it."

"Wait. You're not going to tell my old man about this, are you?"

"I don't know. I feel that as one of the few responsible people on this block, that I owe it to your father to tell him about his son's heroic exploits." Sissy turned to me. "What do you think, little brother? Doesn't this strike you as a great campfire tale? A ripping yarn for the ages?"

"Um," I went, looking back and forth between the two of them.

Steve looked absolutely panicked now. "What do you want?"

"Me?" Sissy said, her hand up to her throat as if she was shocked. "Why, I want nothing for myself. Not a thing." Then her eyes narrowed and she glared at him while pointing at me. "What I want is for you to leave my brother out of your idiotic adventures. You can talk to him. That's fine. But no more of these... *adventures*. I don't want to have to hear about him getting sucked into some sort of alligator killing scheme from someone I barely know from school ever again. You got it?"

Steve swallowed and blinked. "Got it."

Sissy immediately dropped her hand and smiled sweetly, showing off her white teeth and the dimple on her cheek. "Nice doing business with you. Come along, Buzz."

We turned and started along. I heard him say the word: "*Cunt.*"

Sissy turned around, enraged. "You got that right, pal. Remember!" She pointed at him. "No more adventures." She pulled in the hand and crushed it into a fist in front of her daisy-appliqué-covered chest. Steve's eyes were wide and he swallowed hard. No one on earth was more iron-willed than my sister. She spun on her heel and we walked away from him, and he didn't dare say another word. "Some hero you got there," Sissy snarled. "He folded like a cheap suit."

We made it home in time to watch the last 15 minutes of the adult babies. "Do you have someone else change your diaper?" Phil asked one of the men, identified in the lower third of the screen as a tax attorney.

"That's the whole point of it," Sissy and the man said at the same time. "That big baby owes me a Coke."

Mom and Buster were back at work, so the two of us had the house mostly to ourselves. Sparky might or might not be around. He'd learned some techniques from Grandmother and put himself in charge of the family dinner for that night, a roasted chicken. Buster would be on the road that evening, but Mom would be home from work early. She'd been transferred to the shiny new mall a mile from our house. Sissy and I had designs on going there. I had some lawn mowing money and wanted to buy a record. There was supposed to be a record store there—Camelot Music. I wanted to buy a Beatles album because I liked Paul McCartney and Wings. I wanted to hear songs that were new to me, not ones that I'd heard over and over on the top ten radio station, WKXY. *Charlie Lawrence on the giant 93! All hits all the time!* My spongy little brain was thirsty for something new.

"New from K-Tel Records! Twenty-two explosive hits! Gallery! The great Sammy Davis Junior! Olivia Newton-John! Hot Butter's 'Popcorn'! And many more! Only $3.99!" the TV shouted.

"Do you want to go to the mall?" I asked Sissy. "Maybe we can surprise Mom?"

"Let's not surprise Mom," Sissy said with a sigh. "Who knows how she'll react? How much money do you have? I heard there's a Chick-Fil-A."

"I heard there's an Arthur Treacher's."

"Gross! Who wants deep-fried frozen fish? We're eating at Chick-Fil-A. I have spoken. Also, you need to change. Bruce Lee got you all dirty."

I tried to beat the dirt off myself and failed. "Fine. I'll go change." I changed into my best Ocean Pacific t-shirt and another pair of board shorts. I decided to put on my newer tennis shoes, the ones that weren't worn out yet. I dug the money out of the bottom of my sock drawer. I kept a certain amount of cash at home. I had $14 saved up, in ones and fives. I rolled up my moola and shoved it deep inside my front pocket. I'd seen a movie called *Harry In Your Pocket* with Buster one time and had become paranoid about being targeted by pickpockets. I went into the bathroom and tinkled standing up with the board shorts around my ankles. When I finished, I chanted "U-S-A! U-S-A!" and then said in my best Sammy Davis, Jr. impression, "I don't care what anyone says! America is the swingingest country of them all, man!" I pulled up my shorts, washed my hands and then stole some of Sparky's Right Guard, spritzing each hairless pit under my shirt.

Sissy knocked. "You just about done in there? Some of the rest of us have to pee, too."

I swung the door open. "All yours." I boogied my way out of the bathroom past her, twirling my hands in front of myself, swiveling my hips, singing, "Woman! Take me in your arms! Rock your baby!"

"You're not going to get any women doing that," Sissy advised me, closing the door.

I turned off the TV set and then practiced some Kung Fu moves I'd seen David Carradine performing on the show. I did both sets of voices. "We gonna kill you, Chinaman!" I shouted in an angry Western patois. "I apologize for having to kick your ass," I said softly. Then I did several leg kicks. Gretchen emerged from her nap behind the couch, watched me for a moment, grunted discontentedly, and then went back behind the couch to continue her nap.

Sissy walked out and crouched down, peering at Gretchen behind the couch. "Someone may get some cute new baby clothes today. You never know!" Gretchen absolutely hated wearing human clothes and then having a Polaroid taken, but it had become one of Sissy's side hobbies.

"I got fourteen bucks."

"Maybe not. Or maybe we can con Mom into giving us some money." She leaned over toward the couch. "There's hope yet, Gretchen. Don't despair!"

"I thought we weren't gonna see Mom."

"I don't know. It depends, doesn't it?"

"On what?"

"On if the mood strikes."

I shrugged. "You're the boss."

"Don't you forget it."

The mall was a mile away, but there was about a half mile where we were on a two-lane blacktop that had cars going at highway speeds. It was mildly dangerous. People honked angrily at us a couple of times.

We parked our bikes in a rack in front of Sears. Throughout my life, whenever I go to the mall, I always park at Sears. As an adult, most of my clothes that aren't concert-related have come from Sears. We walked in through the car section and that took us through the ladies section and then we emerged into the mall proper.

It was so modern in there! It wasn't brown and covered over in wood. It was glass and white ceiling and shiny terrazzo floors. It reminded me of a space station in a science fiction movie. To our right was the Chick-

Fil-A. The scent of deep fried chicken called out to us. To our left, a little further down the mall, was the Camelot Music. I was torn, so Sissy made up my mind for me. "Food first."

We tore through the sandwiches like hungry wolves, slurped lemonade out of styrofoam cups and gobbled down waffle fries dunked in ketchup. We were done in minutes and ready to move out. My tiny stomach, stretched out during our sojourn at the grandparents', had reshrunk down to its normal walnut size during the weekend. Mom made her famous mushy spaghetti with watery sauce on Saturday and burnt a roast the following day. Sparky, quietly enraged by the poor quality of food, offered to cook a Monday dinner. This was another reason we weren't at home. We weren't sure how the dinner would turn out. Would it be Grandmother level, or Mom level?

We went into Camelot Music with $12. I flipped through records. There were so many of them. Some of them had pictures of dragons on the covers. I dug the paintings, especially of the guy who illustrated a band called "Yes." I almost bought one of their albums for the cover art.

"You don't want that, kid," a man in a short-sleeved dress shirt advised me. "Twenty-minute organ solos. What kind of music do you listen to?"

"Whatever's on WKXY," I said apologetically. "But I want to listen to something better. Do you have any Beatles albums?"

"Is this your first time buying an album?"

"Yes!"

"You want something good? Something really good? Something you'll be proud to say, 'This is the first album I ever bought?'"

"You read my mind."

Sissy pulled out a copy of a Paul Simon album and hugged it to her chest.

"Girls," the man said to me, nodding at my sister. "Am I right?"

"She's my sister."

"Paul Simon is, admittedly, a genius. But if I hear 'Still Crazy After All These Years' one more time, I may have to run outside and scream."

"Gotcha," I said.

We arrived at the R's and he pulled out a copy of *Exile on Main Street*. I looked at the weird photos on the cover and the seemingly scrawled in lipstick band name and album title. I flipped it over and read the names of the songs. "Soul Survivor" jumped out at me, as did "Turd on the Run."

I am holding that album in my hands right now, the same one I held back then. I still love this album. He was a good clerk. I went back to that store again and again. That man, whose name I never caught, led me on a musical journey. A few years later, he sold me *More Songs About Buildings and Food*, another album that I have never stopped loving.

"Ah, *there* you are," he'd say when I came back into the store, like we were long, lost friends. He never steered me wrong. I came home on leave from the Army. I think this was in 1989. I was dressed in a pair of faded black trousers, Doc Martens covering my feet, a baggy Clash t-shirt on. Camelot Music was somehow still in business at that point. I walked into the empty store expecting to find my clerk. I described him to the indifferent clerk sitting behind the cash register, who was reading an old copy of *Spin* with Morrissey on the cover. CD's filled most of the racks. The few records left were in a bargain bin. The indifferent clerk looked up at me. "Oh. *Him.* Um. Sorry, dude. AIDS." He went back to his magazine.

I went out to my mother's car, she'd lent it to me for the day, and I wept. I wish I'd thought to ask him his name. He changed my life and I didn't even bother to learn his name.

People come. People go.

Sissy and I left that shop with five dollars left to our collective names, toting our records in oversized bags. We walked past the Hammond organ shop and stopped for a moment while a man wearing a multicolored blazer played his heart out for no one. People were walking past this guy who could play the electric organ like no one's business. We clapped for him when he was done with his song. He was playing Ray Charles, I think, but without any singing. We picked up our bags and moved along.

We decided to go see if Mom was around and then go home and fight over who got to play their album first. I was not looking forward to Paul Simon after the clerk's panning of the one song.

We entered Maas Brothers and navigated our way over to the escalator, following signs that pointed toward FINE CHINA. At the top of the escalator, we saw what was, for us, an unusual sight. It was a woman in a dayglo pantsuit holding onto a leash that held a small child, who was straining against the leash.

Sissy, incensed, shouted, "That kid's on a leash!" and pointed.

There was a good size crowd. We were in front of the china department. Mom was behind the cash register, ringing someone up. Her hair was sprayed up high and she had on a lime green pantsuit. Everyone turned and looked at the girl who'd shouted, and then looked at the kid on the leash because Sissy was pointing.

"Oh my God!" Mom shouted back at Sissy. "What are you two doing here?" Then she said to the woman, "Have a nice day," and handed her back her credit card and the receipt. Mom walked over to us. "Well? I see you've been out spending Buzz's lawn cutting money. Let's see it! Let's see what kind of music you think is appropriate for our home."

Sissy pulled out the Paul Simon album.

"That's nice, honey. What about you? What did you get?"

I showed her the album.

"Oh my God! That's it! You're going to have to confess to Father John on Sunday. That's right—Father John! He'll know what kind of penance you'll need after you listen to that filth! Why can't you listen to some good music for once? Don't answer that! I'm not on my break and won't be for another half-hour. I hope your brother doesn't ruin that chicken tonight because food is expensive. Ask your brother if he's ever heard of inflation. I'm sure he has. I'm not on my break! Someone's paying for me to stand here and talk to you two when I should be working. Fine. Go home and ruin your hearing before I get there. The Rolling Stones! They do drugs!" She went back to her register and pretended we weren't there. She sang nonsensically under her breath. *Dut-duh-dut-duh-dah.* "Are they still there?" she asked a co-worker. "They'd better not be."

We found the down escalator around the corner and left the store.

"She's in a mood," Sissy said.

"I don't know why. Dad's on the road tonight."

"Can you believe that someone was walking their kid around on a leash? Who does that?"

"I don't know. Sure was weird."

"Do you want a Coke before we go?"

"My stomach feels funny from that chicken."

"Real food'll do that to you."

We shared a Coke out of a vending machine near the public restrooms, sitting on a bench next to some fake palm trees. We people-watched, with Sissy performing a running commentary.

It was an easy ride home. There was no traffic.

We sat on the kitchen counter together, watching Sparky prepare the chicken.

"He's not doing it like Mom," Sissy said.

"Yes, I'm following the directions in the *Good Housekeeping Cookbook* that Mom consistently ignores," Sparky said. He put the bird in a roasting pan on top of a row of celery. He slid it into the oven and then used a slide rule to calculate how long it should remain in there. He set the timer. "I'll be in my room," he said after washing his hands thoroughly and drying them with a paper towel.

We listened to the Paul Simon album on our sad Emerson hi-fi, bought with Green Stamps at the redemption center. The album was nice.

We listened to the Rolling Stones. You couldn't say it was nice, but it was different and my spongy little brain soaked up all the music. I sighed at the end, as "Soul Survivor" played.

The chicken was perfect. The only one who didn't like it was Mom, of course. For dinner, she'd changed over to her housecoat and slippers. "It's tough. Too chewy," Mom commented, while she ate the most tender and juicy piece of breast meat ever made in that house. I devoured one drumstick while Sissy devoured the other. Sparky made his mashed potatoes, which would have been much better if they had butter and milk in them instead of margarine and skim milk. He'd steamed fresh green beans perfectly. Mom groused that they weren't cooked right, but it was nice that Sparky made an effort, unlike some people who didn't even bother to pull the weeds out front like she asked them to, instead choosing to buy obscene records at the mall and embarrass their very own mother while she was trying to make a decent living and support everyone, unlike their father who was off galavanting around Southwest Florida in his fancy Ford charging expensive hotel rooms on his company credit card. Mom finished off her wine and shook the glass at Sparky. "You could get me a little more wine to chase down this nice try for a supper."

Sparky went into the kitchen and returned with the jug of Carlo Rossi and poured Mom a full glass. She emptied it and shook the glass again.

"Can we go down to the Bondurants' house tonight?" Sissy asked. "They're celebrating Bastille Day."

"No! I don't want you hanging around with those people. Who celebrates French holidays anyway? A bunch of weirdos, that's who! And that Irish mother? She's a lush! You should have seen how much wine she put away the other day! I don't want you around that Steve character. He's a bad influence. And speaking of bad influences, that girl who wears all the black clothes. What's that all about? Is she in permanent mourning or something? I don't get it." She polished off the wine and Sparky refilled her glass.

"So that's no, right?" Sissy commented. "I couldn't tell with all the babbling."

"Oh, you think you're so smart, don't you, Miss Tish? You and your smart mouth! That's it! I'm done with you. When your father gets home, whenever that is, he's going to hear all about your behavior."

"So are we done here?" Sissy snapped. "Or do we get to listen to you rant a little more?"

"I'll rant all I want. I'm the one paying the bills around here."

Sissy crossed her arms and stared at Mom. "Whenever you're done, I'll clear the table."

"Fine," Mom said. "Clear the table."

Sissy stood up and started stacking dishes. She turned to me. "You just gonna sit there?"

I stood up and helped her out.

Sparky wrapped up the remainder of the chicken in foil and placed it in the fridge. Sissy and I scrubbed the dishes down and put them in the dishwasher.

Mom sat at the table silently stewing. Finally, she said, "And after your brother tried to make a nice dinner. It was a nice dinner for a first try!"

Sissy shouted at her, "It's Bastille Day!" She ran out of the kitchen and we heard her door slam. A moment later, I heard "Rip This Joint" blasting out of her room. She'd taken my Rolling Stones record.

Bright Lights at the Roller Disco

Mom woke me up by yelling, "Oh my God! Look at this room! It's a disaster area. Someone call the National Guard. We need troops in here. What are all these drawings of? Is this that girl who wears all black from down the street? You got her nose wrong! I can't believe that one person made all this mess. Tell the National Guard to bring dump trucks and bulldozers. And where are your shoes? The good ones, not the crap ones you insist on wearing because you want to embarrass your mother. Everyone will think we're poor!" She walked around picking up various items—a sock, a watercolor (I was experimenting with watercolors), a t-shirt, a wrapper from a Little Debbie cake, an empty bottle of Fresca—and dropping them where they'd been. "I hope you don't expect me to pick up after you. Haven't I suffered long enough? This will make your allergies worse! We should burn down the house and start all over again. You'd like that, wouldn't you, you little weirdo? Of course you would." She tilted her head heavenward. "Why's he still in bed? That's the real question? If only he'd get out of bed and clean his room and maybe, on occasion, eat something? Would that be too much to ask? Anybody up there? I need a sign."

I was propped up on my elbows, blinking the sleep out of my eyes. "I'm sorry."

"Oh. Well. He's sorry," Mom said, still addressing God, I think. "Oh. Well. That makes up for the mess." She turned back to me. "Are you a test? Is that what you are? A test from on high? I'm failing the test. Look around this room." She waved her arms dramatically. "I raised you to be a slob. Sparky isn't messy like this. How did I fail you? It's clear that your mother has failed you. Will you at least eat a bowl of cereal? Will you do that for me? You're skin and bones. When you go back to school, the teacher is going to take one look at you and call the child welfare people and they'll cart you away to live in an orphanage. Who knows what you might catch in there? Lice! Fleas! Some dread disease that causes your teeth to fall out. Take it from me, you want to take care of your teeth. Your grandfather had all of his pulled in his thirties. That's how long he's been wearing dentures. You're not going to catch *me* wearing dentures. When was the last time you brushed your teeth?" She crouched down next to my bed. "Open your mouth." I did so. She sniffed my breath. "Oh my God! Go brush your teeth right now. Then eat something. Then brush your teeth again. Then you'd better clean your room before the National Guard shows up to do it for you."

I got up and stumbled into the living room, where I found my father Buster on his back in the middle of the room like a carcass waiting to be picked over by turkey buzzards.

The day before, Brandy, Sissy and I tried out luring turkey buzzards to the Bondurants' front lawn by playing dead. I was the one who lost his nerve when they were about a hundred feet above us, slowly circling. I leapt up and flailed my arms. Brandy and Sissy got up and Sissy said, "I told you."

Brandy pulled a tube of lipstick out of her pocket and handed it to Sissy. "A bet's a bet."

Both of them giggled at me as I stood there flustered and then I shouted dramatically, "I'm going home!" which made them both burst into laughter. "I'm not kidding!"

"Bock, bock," Sissy went. "Poor little chicken Buzz. There's not enough meat on those bones for a vulture."

I ran home and was angry at her for about an hour, and then she and Brandy walked in thick as thieves while I sat in front of the TV watching Ernest Angley, the tin-voiced preacher from Akron, Ohio. "Hey," I said hopefully to them. I was sorry I'd gotten angry, had shown that side of myself.

"Hey," Brandy said, and she sat down on the floor next to me.

I looked up at Sissy, and she'd already applied the lipstick. Her lips were much thinner than Brandy's, but Brandy (or Sissy) had done a fine job of applying the red lipstick. Then I noticed that Brandy had given Sissy the full treatment. Sissy would have looked like a fashion model if she wasn't wearing denim bell-bottoms, platform shoes and a t-shirt with a giant yellow smily face on it. "What's on the tube?" Sissy asked, sitting down on the other side of Brandy.

I was relieved that they weren't angry at me for throwing a tantrum. "The good reverend Angley. We're almost to the part where he heals people."

"Nice," Sissy said. "My favorite part."

We watched the show, mostly. But mostly I was aware of Brandy sitting next to me. Without taking her eyes off the TV, she said, "I'm sorry that I laughed at you."

I blushed and said, "It's okay."

"You're kinda cute. You know?"

"Don't start," Sissy said. "He doesn't need to hear that."

Ernest Angley called up a man on crutches. "Heal!" he commanded. "Demon, leave this poor soul!" And the guy threw away the crutches.

"I can do that," Sissy said. "I can do that, no problem." She turned her head toward the couch and sang out, "Oh, Gretchen!"

"You're gonna heal the dog?" I asked her.

"Clearly, that dog needs healing. She spends her days behind the couch. There's a demon in her."

"I don't believe in demons," Brandy said.

"You will after you see this exorcism," Sissy said. "Hold on. Gotta go get my robe for this." Sissy left us alone in the room.

Brandy said, "You're kinda cute."

I stammered out, "Th-thank you. You, too."

"You think so? I don't know."

I was tempted to hop up and go retrieve my drawings and paintings of her—as I mentioned before, I was experimenting with watercolors—but I didn't. I was frozen sitting there next to her, wanting this moment not to end. My mother always advised me to never get my hopes up, but my hopes did what they wanted and they were up. "You are," I said, blushing uncontrollably. "You're cute." I was overwhelmed with dizzying emotion at that moment, and then pushed it back down, deep inside, back where that sort of thing belonged. I was ashamed of how emotional I was. I remained ashamed of it. Love was not something we talked about in our family, but shame was. We were meant to be ashamed of any kind of feelings, but especially the positive ones.

Sissy emerged wearing a white terrycloth bathrobe. "Sinner!" she shouted in Ernest Angley's voice. "Come forward. I sense you out there. The name! The name is at the tip of my tongue. Is your name Gretchen? It *is* Gretchen. Step forward, sinner, and I shall heal you!"

Gretchen did not step forward. Gretchen remained behind the couch. She made a dissatisfied and slightly angry noise in the back of her throat.

"Brother Buzz, go forth and fetch the cookies to tempt the sinner!" Sissy commanded.

"Amen, Sister!" I said, and hopped to my feet to get the box of Liv-R-Snaps. I found them on the shelf in the pantry next to the dog food that was composed of the same thing as Fritos. I pulled one of the hard squares out and shook the box.

On TV, Ernest Angley was dunking a man in a giant bathtub.

Gretchen's love of treats overcame her common sense and she darted out from behind the couch. I tossed the Liv-R-Snap to Reverend Sissy and she snatched it out of the air.

Reverend Sissy held it about a foot above Gretchen's head. "Your sinfulness is showing, demon dog. Greed! Gluttony! Some sort of skin condition!"

Gretchen's rear end was covered in pink bumps where she'd nervously stripped the fur off chewing on herself. "The devil is strong in you! Step forward to be healed!" Gretchen sat down expectantly, hoping that it wouldn't be too long before Sissy's game was over and she'd get the treat. I suppose the dog was thinking, "At least she doesn't have baby clothes in her hand right now."

Sissy put the Liv-R-Snap in her robe pocket and knelt before the dog. She placed her hands on either side of Gretchen's head, closed her eyes and tilted her head, and shouted, "In the name of the Lord Almighty, I say, 'Demon...out!'"

Brandy laughed uncontrollably.

"Can you say, 'bay-bee'?" Sissy asked the dog. "Speak!"

Gretchen shrieked out in frustration and then emitted a sharp bark.

Sissy pulled out the cookie and gave it to her and she ran with it behind the couch. We listened to her crunch down the cookie.

"See?" Sissy said to Brandy. "What more proof do you need? Demons exist."

In that same spot, a day later, I was about to step over the beached carcass of my father, who was clearly not at work. "You okay, Dad?" I asked him.

"No, I'm not," he said sullenly. "Clean your room like your mother asked you to."

"She wanted me to eat something—"

"Don't make me say it twice!"

I turned back around and went to my room, where my mother was already cleaning it. "Do you have to be so sloppy?" she asked. "Why do you have to be so sloppy?"

"Why's Dad home?" I asked her.

"He's in between jobs now," Mom said. "Don't worry. Something will turn up soon. In the meantime, I need you to be on your best behavior."

"Is he going to be here all the time?" I asked, horrified at the thought.

"No. He's going to hit the pavement tomorrow. It's fine. Everything will be fine. Come here." I walked over to her and she did something uncharacteristic—she hugged me. I wasn't used to being hugged, the middle-aged women had given up on me lately, so I stiffened up for a moment. Then I closed my eyes and allowed her to hold me. My awful father was in the other room, but I was here with my mother and everything was okay for a moment or two.

"Lola!" I heard my father shout. "Lola, get out here. I got an idea."

I followed Mom out into the den, where Gretchen was dragging her ass on the carpet and making weird noises.

"I think the dog is ready to get knocked up. Call the breeder." Buster staggered to his feet. "How much did they say we could get per puppy again?"

Gretchen had no idea Buster was about to try to turn her into a cash register. She dragged and dragged and dragged her ass.

Mom made the call. The breeder said to bring her in. So Mom, Sissy and I ended up in the Ford family truckster, with Gretchen in the back of the truckster, dragging her ass on a stiff white towel stolen from a Holiday Inn.

The breeders were way out in the country, living in a stinking ramshackle house that looked like it had been built out of plywood that fell off the back of random trucks. The stench was from all the dogs, who were yapping like they were trapped in a doggie ring of hell. It looked like a doggie ring of hell.

Gretchen stopped dragging her ass as we pulled up to the shack. Her eyes went wide with panic. Somewhere deep inside her brain, she remembered this place, and the memory wasn't pleasant.

A woman in a stained dress wearing filthy slippers with an unlit cigarette poking out of her mouth came out of a door on the side of the house. A thousand puppies screamed out in anguish. The woman reached inside a pocket in her dress and produced a red Bic Clic. She lit the cigarette and smiled toothlessly at us. I remembered my mother's lecture about taking care of my teeth and took it more to heart.

"Where's my little darlin'?" the woman asked. "Where is she?"

Gretchen clawed at the back of the seat while I pulled her away from the Holiday Inn towel and into my lap. I carried her out of the car and her nails dug into my shoulder painfully. "Here she is," I said.

"Set her down and let me take a look at her," the woman said.

I did so and Gretchen shook uncontrollably.

"Ah, nothing to be scared of," the woman said, and then Gretchen tried to take a piece out of her, which didn't phase the woman one bit. "Hold her for a second."

I held Gretchen still and Sissy cooed in her face.

Mom said, "Well?"

"She's ready. I got something for you to sign, Mrs. Pepper. Then we'll take her on out back."

"And it's okay that she's having puppies with her own grandfather?" Mom asked.

"They ain't people. They don't know."

"But, I mean… inbreeding."

"I don't know nothing about that. I just know that my dog has papers, and your Gretchen has papers, so they're pedigreed and like that, so that makes it okay."

Mom and the woman went inside the shack while Sissy and I stood outside with the dog. Gretchen got right up against my leg and shook horribly. I crouched down and petted her, but she was inconsolable.

"This doesn't feel right," I said.

"You think?" Sissy snapped. "This is the worst idea Dad's ever had. And he's full of bad ideas. Those puppies are going to be mutated and stuff."

Mom and the woman emerged from the shack. The woman held her hand out for the leash, so like an idiot, I handed it to her without a word.

We followed her to a little pen set up in the backyard. It was filled with dirt and dog poop. There was a Miniature Schnauzer standing there. He was shaking, too. His penis appeared like a pale pink lipstick underneath him. The woman picked up Gretchen, took off the leash and set her down inside the pen with her grandfather.

Mom came over and stood between us.

The grandfather and Gretchen kind of circled around each other, and then the grandfather mounted Gretchen and shoved his lipstick penis in her back end. He pumped rhythmically.

"This is sex?" Sissy asked.

"This is sex," Mom said. "Feast your eyes."

"But it's different for humans, right?" I asked.

"Not really," Mom said. "This is about the long and short of it." Mom turned to Sissy. "Remember this when some boy pressures you for sex."

Sissy stood there with this expression on her face that I hadn't seen before. It was somewhere between disgust and despair.

Mom watched Sissy for a moment and then put her arm around her shoulders. Sissy didn't shrug it off.

The two dogs went at it for a while, and then the grandfather got off of Gretchen.

We loaded the dog in the car and got back on the road.

"Tell you what," Mom said. "How about I take you over to that roller rink and give you some money?"

"Roller rink?" I asked.

"The roller disco," Sissy said. "The one they opened up on Sawyer Road."

"You give me a call whenever you're done," Mom said. "Take the rest of the day. I'll give you enough money for some food, too."

"What about Dad being in between jobs?" I asked.

"Don't worry about that," Mom said. "You're children. You shouldn't have to worry about such things." She gripped the wheel a bit tighter. Her driving was more fluid, less herky-jerky. "You know why I took you to see that, right?"

"Yeah," Sissy said. "Got it."

"What about you?" Mom asked, looking at me through the rearview mirror. "You get the point?"

"I think so," I said.

"I don't want you getting some girl pregnant because you think you're in love with her. You're not going to fall in love with anyone for a long time, Buzz. Look at me when I'm talking to you." I looked up into the mirror. "Don't let some girl trap you into marriage. Sex isn't some mysterious thing. It isn't romance. It's just sex." I couldn't believe my Catholic mother was speaking this way. "Girls are going to try to take advantage of you. Don't let them. You should have a harder heart." She looked back to the road. "Don't look so sad all the time." Mom cheered up. "Some day, you'll each make some beautiful grandbabies for me. They'll have big heads! All of you kids had such big heads when you were babies."

Sissy eventually would have three babies and Mom would dote on them.

I'll never get to have kids. Mom's gone now, so she wouldn't get to see them anyway. I used to think about a romantic marriage to someone cool and punk rock, and we'd have a pair of children—one boy, one girl. I'd imagine doting on them, taking them for ice cream. I had fantasies about walking them to the bus stop for their first day of school and telling them not to be nervous. Or tucking them in at night. I craved the thrill of watching them grow into adults, and then having those adult children come by to see me and tell me about their lives. But it'll never happen. My ex-wife talked me into getting the old snip-snip—a vasectomy. She told me we'd make terrible parents, and I believed her. When someone tells me that I'll be bad at something, I generally believe them, because I think that I'm not much of a human being. My wife and I got divorced and now I'm floating through life aimlessly. I'm living in this tiny apartment without any friends, with only my drafting table and my memories to keep me company, so maybe not having children was for the best. But sometimes, in the middle of the night, I miss the son and the daughter that I never had the opportunity to meet. They're new ghosts to add to the ones I already have.

One thing's for sure: If I'd had a daughter, she would have been named, "Marie." That's Sissy's real name, the one she rarely used. I would have told little Marie stories about the aunt she never got to meet —the best friend anyone has ever had.

"What do big heads have to do with anything?" Sissy asked, irritated.

"We're almost there," Mom said, stomping on the brake and the accelerator at the same time and peeling into the dirt lot outside the Roll-A-Rama. We came to some sort of halt and Mom cranked the Ford family truckster into park. Mom opened up her purse and gave Sissy a twenty-dollar bill. "Try not to spend it all." She looked in the rearview mirror at me. "What? You would have given her the money anyway. I'm only cutting out a step."

I shrugged and got out of the car, but not before peeking back at Gretchen, asleep in the luggage area.

"Just us mothers left here!" Mom shouted at the dog as she drove away in a cloud of blue fumes.

We stood in the dirt parking lot, waving the dust out of our faces and then turned around and looked at the place. It didn't look like much from the outside. We could smell the Scotty's Lumberyard next door. It reeked of pine sap and the chemicals in treated yellow wood.

Across the road was one of the two drive-in theaters in town. I remember falling asleep in the back of the Ford family truckster in that theater during a showing of *W.W. and the Dixie Dance Kings*, the voice of Burt Reynolds arguing with the voice of Jerry Reed coming out of the galvanized tin box attached to the driver's side window, and then waking up in my own bed the next morning. I remember being able to sleep like that.

"Come on," Sissy said. "It can't be as bad as it looks."

We went inside and it was dim in there, like when you turn the lights out on Christmas Eve and only the tree illuminates the room. We saw teenagers rolling around in circles under a disco ball, with more lights moving and flashing in reds, greens and blues. A man stood behind a record player on a platform on the far side of the place, wearing a pair of headphones, shouting unintelligibly into a microphone. The music lowered and he shouted MERT MERT MERT. MERT MERT. YEAH. And then he dropped the stylus down and the record implored us to "Do the hustle!"

"Hey!" a fat dude behind a counter shouted at us. "Get over here!"

We walked over to him. "What?" Sissy shouted above the record.

"What's your shoe size?"

"That seems like a personal question," Sissy shouted.

"You have to rent skates to be in here, otherwise get out!"

We each rented a pair of skates. Then we rented a locker for a quarter and put our shoes and Sissy's purse inside. I stuck the locker key deep in my pocket.

"Please, mister, please!" Olivia Newton-John implored.

Sissy shouted above the crowd noise, "You're terrible at skating. This is a bad idea. We should call Mom."

"She won't even be home yet. It's okay. Give me some money and I'll buy a Coke and nurse it at one of the tables."

She handed me a buck. I fumbled my way over to the drink stand, got a waxpaper cup of flat Coke with a few chips of ice floating in it, and then somehow managed to make it back to a table without spilling it or tumbling over. The place wasn't crowded, so there were plenty of tables alongside the roller rink. Sissy waved at me as she glided past.

The sound system blasted out: "We got a kung fu bumpin' 'til it's time to go! Get on the floor and let the good times roll!"

I didn't notice, but Brandy was sitting across from me. I turned my head and there she was. She smiled sweetly. She looked exactly out of place, but somehow she was there. "Hi!" she shouted. "What's going *on*? What are you *doing* here?"

"Our mother dropped us off. I don't know why."

"Why are you *sitting* here? You should be *skating*."

"I'm no good at it."

"I can show you."

I blushed. "No. That's okay. You go out and have a good time."

"Come on. Let me help you."

"I'll make you fall down."

"Don't be silly. Let's go."

I managed to make it upright without falling over. Sissy skated up to the little opening and hopped out of the rink. "Hi, Brandy!" she said brightly. "Are you going to skate with Buzz?"

"Absolutely."

"Don't let him kill you both."

Brandy laughed. "We'll be okay."

We got out onto the rink and I stiffly rolled along. Brandy gave me a bit of instruction while she held my hand. Could she feel my heart hammering through that hand? I don't know. She was so good at skating that it seemed to make up for my lack of competence. We swayed as we skated. She was a good teacher, too. She lent me her confidence. I discovered one of my turn-ons in that moment: Competence. To this day, if a woman demonstrates some sort of competence, I find her attractive. I find confidence attractive, too, but only if it rides along with competence.

Brandy was dressed in a black sweater and black blouse with glitter sparkling on it. She wore dark jeans that went past her knees. Her skates were black with pink laces. They were clearly her own skates and not rentals. I asked her about it and she told me that she would never put her feet in skates that dozens of other feet had sweated into. "Gross," she said. I didn't realize it for a moment, but she was skating backwards. She was holding both my hands and looking me in the eyes. I can close my eyes now and see her in all those flashing lights, her dark hair fluttering around her head, her green eyes joyful. She winked at me and I tripped over my own feet and tumbled to the hard wooden flooring, sliding on my face and knees for about five feet.

Brandy had let go at the last second and stopped herself from going down with me. I rolled over onto my back and she was kneeling down next to me. She fingered her hair behind her ears. "Are you okay?"

"She'll be calling wildfire!" the sound system sang out.

"I think so."

"But your head is bleeding."

"Skate at your own risk," I said. "You're pretty."

"Stop it."

"You're very pretty."

"Now I *know* you've hurt your head."

"No one's told you you're pretty before? Then everyone's been lying to you."

"My daddy's says I'm pretty. He says I won't have to work a day in my life. Do you want me to help you up?"

"I'm going to try to get up myself. I'll never learn otherwise." I crawled on my hands and knees over to the side of the rink and pulled myself up to standing via some railing. Naturally, all this had happened in front of where Sissy was still seated, finishing off the last of my Coke.

"Good job," she said. "No, I mean it. You were actually skating for a while."

"Thanks. I should probably sit down."

"You should definitely sit down, lover boy. Did you tell her?"

"Tell her what?"

"'I wuv you, my widdle Brandy-wandy.'"

"I told her she was pretty."

"That's more like it." Sissy got up. "Think you can manage to make it five feet? This chair has your name on it."

I staggered over and plopped down, as Sissy shot out into the now-crowded floor, leaned over and placed her hands behind her back and sped away smoothly. Where had I seen that before? Then I remembered. We used to watch women's professional roller derby in the mornings back in Nebraska. Or was it in Missouri? She must have figured out how to skate like that at some point. Sissy had a pair of roller skates that strapped to her regular shoes. She must have been practicing. When did she have time to practice? We spent most of our waking hours together unless we were at school. Maybe she did it when I was in my room drawing. About once a month, Sissy managed to surprise me with something new.

I picked up a napkin and held it to the spot on my head that was bleeding. It wasn't much of a wound. The blood seemed to stop, so I wadded up the napkin and put it in the empty Coke cup. I was hurt so often that sometimes I became detached from my own body.

"Why can't we be friends? Why can't we be friends?" the sound system asked.

Brandy rolled up and came to a stop. She walked over to my chair. "Let me see your skates."

I turned in my chair and she took a knee next to me. "You didn't tie them right," she said. She retied them. This is the moment, right here, when I discovered the main thing that turns me on—an act of kindness. It was a nice, unselfish thing for Brandy to do. I was nearly breathless afterward.

She stood up and beamed at me. "Do you still think I'm pretty?" She was silhouetted in all those flashing lights. Her face glowed like she'd come down from heaven. I was dizzy.

"You're beautiful. You're the most beautiful girl alive," I said, my voice trembling with emotion. "And I'll fight anyone who says you aren't!"

The Price of Living in Paradise

On the last day of summer, before we had to go back to school, Buster decided that we, as a family, would go to the beach.

This wasn't the big news, however. Buster announced that he had a new job, working for one of his old paper company's rivals. "They're really gonna regret firing me," Buster said. "I'm looking forward to grabbing every one of my old clients back for myself. I was sick of Bert anyway." That was his old boss. "How could he say I was charging too much on the company credit card? This new place doesn't have a company credit card, just mileage, so I guess I won't be spending as much time in hotels. I'll get paid for driving home almost every night instead."

The question lingered, unasked, why he didn't drive home every night if he always could.

While he talked, potato shrapnel ejected from his mouth, along with meatloaf shrapnel. Since I was seated closest to him, I was the one who did most of the ducking.

Mom's meatloaf was a mixture of things she found in the pantry and vegetation that hadn't survived the crisper drawer in the fridge. I poked through my meatloaf slice like an archeologist trying to discern how some ancient civilization collapsed.

"Rye melba toast," I said aloud.

"That's right, Buzz," Mom said proudly. "Good eye!"

"Scallions, I think."

"Will you quit picking at that meatloaf and eat it?" Buster asked me, and I got a blob of store-brand barbecue sauce in my eye that had been used as the glaze. "Anyway, I don't know how the company could fire me over what was done with their credit card after it was stolen from my room."

"Someone broke into your room?" I asked. "Scary."

"I was asleep," Buster said.

"That makes it scarier, Dad," I said, shuddering at the thought. Thanks to Buster, I lived in horror of people walking in on me while I was asleep. "Who knows what they could do to you while you're asleep? They could stick things up your nose. Spit in your mouth."

"No one stuck things in my nose. I'd know about it."

"I'm not so sure about that, Buster," Mom said. "You're pretty out of it when you're asleep. Buzz might be onto something there."

"No one stuck anything up my nose! Okay? Jesus H. Christ! You're missing the point. Someone stole the company credit card and charged up a bunch of stuff before I could tell them it was missing."

"What did the cops say?" I asked.

"What do you mean 'what did the cops say?'" Buster eyed me angrily.

"Yes," Sparky said. "What *did* the cops say? You did report this to the police, didn't you?"

"I didn't notice the card was missing until late the next day, so what was I supposed to do? What were they gonna do? Dust for prints in a hotel room that was already rented out again?"

"Wait a minute," Sparky said. "Let's back up here. How did you know that it was stolen in that hotel room then? Was anything else missing? Was a window broken? The door ajar?"

"No, smart guy. The door wasn't ajar. Yeesh."

"And was anything else missing?"

"No. Just the credit card."

Sparky set down his fork and stared at Buster, who shifted uncomfortably in his chair. "So who is this mystery thief who broke into a hotel room, went through someone's wallet and stole only a company credit card?"

"Someone who knew what he was doing! Why are we talking about this?"

Mom said, "You brought it up."

"Okay. If I had to guess..." We all could see the strain of lying on our father. You would think a man who made his living in sales would be better at it. "Um, there are, uh, thieves who, um, specialize in certain, um, stolen stuff. Like company credit cards. Yeah. And they go to hotels, find out from the clerks who checked in with a company credit card and, uh, they get the room keys and go up there and just take the card."

"But nothing else out of the wallet," Sparky said. "Couldn't you have merely dropped the card at some point? Doesn't that make more narrative sense instead of deciding that it was stolen from your wallet in your hotel room at night by a mysterious band of highly specialized thieves with unusual access to the hotel's records and key system?"

"What are you saying, son?"

Sparky picked up his fork and smiled. "I think I see part of a radish in this meatloaf, Buzz. What do you see?"

"Ah hah!" I went. "That's what that is!"

I glanced across the table and saw Sissy nodding her head appreciatively at Sparky, a sly smile on her face.

Buster looked confused, angry and relieved all at the same time. That's when he said, "We're going to the beach tomorrow. What do you think?"

"Fine," Mom said tartly. She cut her slab of meatloaf with her fork and shoved a large cube of it in her mouth, masticated with great effort and eventually swallowed.

So we loaded into the Ford family truckster, minus pregnant Gretchen, who now lived in a large cardboard box lined with newspaper most of the time. Gretchen was more miserable than ever now, her skin diseases having migrated across most of her back. Mom's treatments involved feeding her brewer's yeast tablets and dabbing her back with Noxzema out of a blue jar, and shouting in her face, "You'll feel better when those puppies are out of you, believe me!" And then she'd jerk a thumb at whichever kid happened to be standing around and shout about the immense amount of pain she endured, and continued to endure, because of the kid standing there, and then she ended it by shouting in the dog's face, "At least we get to *sell* yours! I had to *keep* mine."

At the corner of the Tamiami Trail and Stickney Point Road, a massive billboard touted Siesta Key Beach as being the "third best beach in the world!" We drove across the bridge to Siesta Key, took a right and headed past private cabanas with names like Polynesian Gardens and Peppertree Bay, wending our way down Midnight Pass Road to the public beach, where there weren't that many parking spots and they all seemed to be taken. Buster drove around in circles and finally someone decided to vacate his spot. The Ford family truckster lacked maneuverability, so a happy couple in a Pinto swiped our spot. Buster rolled down his window and bellowed, "Goddamnit! Couldn't you see my blinker was on?"

"You're letting all the air conditioning out, Buster!" Mom shouted at him.

The couple in the Pinto got out of their car and pretended like we weren't there, like they hadn't just swiped our spot. They were a picture postcard couple, an advertisement for the good life in Florida, with sun-kissed skin, feathered blonde hair and winning smiles. Anita Bryant might, at any moment, emerge from behind a palm tree to sing their praises. They only lacked a carton of pure Florida orange juice to complete the scene.

Buster gave up honking and yelling and stomped on the gas, chirping the Ford family truckster's radials on the melty blacktop. We eventually parked alongside Midnight Pass Road near a sign that said that parking was prohibited alongside Midnight Pass Road. About a dozen cars were already parked there, "So what's one more?" Buster asked.

"We can't afford a ticket right now!" Mom shouted. "Sparky, run out and go find someone who's about to leave and then stand in their parking space until we can get there."

"Mom…" Sparky said, and then he sighed deeply, and got out of the car.

I slid over to his space from the hump. "So this is how the other half lives. Sparky's got a nice groove here, too." I wiggled my butt.

"Oh, how you've suffered," Sissy said. "My heart breaks thinking about it."

"Why can't *we* get out and go look for parking spots?" I asked. "I can stand in a parking spot as well as Sparky."

Mom turned her head and said, "No one would see you, honey. You're too short. They'd run you over."

"And then no one would be around to ride on the hump," Sissy added. "Because I'm sure not gonna ride on the hump."

Mom said, "Like it's such a big deal to ride on the hump!"

"It's a big deal to me," I said.

"That's it!" Buster shouted. "I'm getting out of the car and I'm taking the blanket. I'll be enjoying the beach while you sit here talking about some damn hump." He opened his door and got out without taking the key. He slammed the door shut. The engine continued idling, slurping down precious gasoline. The air conditioner blowed. The tailgate popped down and Buster reached in and grabbed his blue Air Force blanket. He'd gotten it when he dodged the draft by joining the Ohio Air National Guard instead of going off to fight in Korea. He grabbed the wooden picnic basket that contained some bologna sandwiches on white (with yellow mustard) and a big bag of Fritos. "Who's coming with me?"

Sissy and I looked at each other. We liked air conditioning. The car had a radio, too. I'd forgotten to bring along my transistor radio. On the other hand, Buster was taking the blanket with him, so that made him the leader of the beach expedition. Maybe the beach wouldn't be so bad this time. The last time, I'd forgotten to bring along my flip-flops and had burnt my feet on the sugar white sand. This time I had my flip-flops. This time, I'd also put on an ungodly amount of tanning butter because I'd burnt last time, with massive blisters followed by the skin on my shoulders and back peeling off in little curls, like mini potato chips. Mom shouted at me that I was going to end up with skin cancer and wouldn't that be a horrible way to die, but at least it would break her heart seeing me die like that and that would make it worthwhile for me, to die out of spite like that in order to break the heart of my long-suffering mother. "Typical of you," Mom concluded, like I was constantly dying in front of her out of spite.

"Let's go," Sissy said. "Sorry Mom."

"Fine," Mom said. She reached over and turned off the car. "Your father always gets his way. It's okay by me if we get a ticket and the car is towed and we end up in the poorhouse. As long as your father gets his way, that makes it all okay."

We got out of the car, made sure it was locked, pulled a few more towels out of the back, shut the tailgate and headed for the beach.

Along the way, we saw Sparky standing in a parking spot, several cars vying for the spot honked at him and each other. He sighed heavily and stepped away, and two cars darting for the spot had a fender bender. The drivers leapt out and berated one another.

Sissy turned to me and said, "That's the price of living in paradise."

We each had a stolen Holiday Inn towel hanging over a shoulder. They were scratchy towels, not suitable for human skin, but they were fine for sitting on while at the beach.

We were both wearing red bathing suits. Sissy's was a one-piece and mine were board shorts. Mom declared us "the Bobbsey twins!" when we emerged from our respective rooms. She decided that she'd take a photo of us in our suits in the living room. "Why in the living room?" Sissy asked. "Why not at the beach?"

"I'm not taking the camera to the beach! It'll get ruined!" Mom explained. Then she futzed around with the camera while we stood next to the couch getting more and more irritated. When she finally took the photo, neither of us smiled. Mom eventually collected hundreds of photos in dozens of photo albums in which none of her kids smiled because she took forever to take a photo. "I don't know what's wrong with them!" Mom would shout while some random visitor pawed through our childhood memories. "None of them ever smiled for the camera! Like it would kill them to smile every once in a while when I'm taking a picture."

"I'm so glad we've all decided to have a family day out together," Sparky said, catching up with us. "I suppose none of you thought to bring my towel."

"Do you want the keys to the car?" Mom asked him. "You can go back for your towel. That is, if the car hasn't been towed by now. Maybe you can beg the tow truck driver not to drag it away. I need that car to go to work!"

"You can walk to work," Sissy said. "Or ride one of our bicycles."

"You'd like that, wouldn't you!" Mom said. "Me, trying to sell china while I'm sweating through my work clothes. You'd love that. You'd get a big chuckle out of your poor old mother dripping with sweat while trying to sell overpriced china to people with too much money. Where's your father? Where did he run off to? Oh, there he is, talking to some floozy."

Buster set down the picnic basket and snapped the blanket out, laying it neatly on the burning white sand next to a statuesque lady wearing a string bikini that didn't have enough material in it to make a tea cozy. She had on a wide-brimmed white hat and oversized sunglasses. We got closer and we heard Buster say, "And here they come now. This is my wife, Lola, my sons Sparky and Buzz, and the apple of my eye, Sissy."

"Who are you supposed to be?" Sissy asked the lady.

"I'm one of your father's clients," she said. "You can call me Gloria."

"*You* work in a print shop?" Sparky asked her skeptically.

"Uh. Yes," she said, lowering her sunglasses for a moment to make eye contact with him. "I own one, as a matter of fact."

"Where is this print shop?" Sparky asked her.

"Why's your kid giving me the third degree?"

"He thinks he's smarter than everyone else," Buster said.

"He doesn't just think that," I blurted out. "He is. He goes to Pine View."

"Oh," Gloria said. "One of those." She touched my father in a way that made me nervous, running an index finger from his elbow to his wrist. She did this right in front of my mother, who pretended that it didn't happen. She stood there not saying a word. We all stood there not saying anything. "Buster, be a dear and put some lotion on my back. I'm here all alone." She took off the hat and the sunglasses and laid down on her beach towel face down. She reached behind herself and untied the two strings holding on her bikini bra. She was practically naked, her skin bronzed by a life spent in the sun. In the 1970's, it was considered a sign of good health to be that tan.

I stood watching this open mouthed. I looked around. Wasn't anyone going to put a stop to this?

Buster picked up a bottle of tanning oil from her blanket and poured a palmful, and then tipped his palm and let it drizzle on down to her back before placing his hand there. Gloria giggled and cooed a bit while he did this.

Mom sat on the blanket facing away the two of them. Sparky stood fuming next to me. Sissy grabbed my wrist. "Let's get out of here before I die of boredom," she said, yanking me along behind her toward the pavilion.

"Dad just rubbed oil on a naked lady's back," I said.

"She had on a swimsuit," Sissy said. "Don't be so dramatic."

"But—?" I couldn't figure out what to say, but it seemed wrong. All of it. "I mean, what's she doing here?"

"She's at the beach, like anyone else. What are *we* doing here? People go to the beach, Buzz. No need to make a thing out of it."

"Mom's pretending it's not happening."

"Nothing's happening," Sissy said. "What's the matter with you? Are you going to talk about that Gloria all day? She's only someone Dad knows from work. Big deal. Did you bring along some of your mowing money like I asked?"

Sissy had been working as my agent during the summer, selling my services as a lawn mowing professional to our neighbors. Most of them only had front yards, due to their backyards being filled with swimming pools, so it only took seven to ten passes to cut their entire lawn, a quick twenty minutes of work for seven dollars, which was my going rate. In late summer, during the rainiest of the rainy season, I could cut lawns twice a week sometimes. Captain Slidell's widow was particular about her lawn, so it took a little extra time. A couple of the retirees would stand out in their driveways to supervise, pointing and yelling at missed spots. With all the work, I was becoming more proficient. Some of them asked me do the edging as well. We had a manual edger with little blades that needed to be sharpened. It was much harder work than pushing the mower around, so I charged exorbitant fees for edging. Only Captain Slidell's widow took me up on it. She and Sissy would sit in aluminum folding chairs watching me from the shade of the widow's garage, Sissy sipping a lemonade from a glass etched with pictures of festive lemons and Captain Slidell's widow sipping brightly colored drinks out of tropical-themed glasses. Using the widow's wages, I bought, at the Camelot Music clerk's suggestion, a copy of the English version of *Rubber Soul* as my second-ever album purchase when I insisted to him that I need to buy a Beatles record. We had to walk over to a section labeled IMPORTS and it cost twice as much as the American version. It was wonderful. I listened to "Michelle" over and over, trying to memorize it so I could sing it outside Brandy's window some evening if I ever worked up the nerve. I imagined myself dressed up like a vintage mid-1960's Paul McCartney, Beatle boots and all, while doing so.

I pulled a couple of fives out of my pocket and handed both of them to Sissy. "This is too much. Put the other five away before someone sees it," Sissy said.

We went to the concession stand in the Pavilion and ordered two hot dogs, an order of fries, and a Coke that we'd share. Most of the time when it was the two of us, we only ordered one drink. We drank out of the same straw all the time. It ensured that we'd get sick at the same time and then we'd get to spend a day away from school together, though I don't think that either one of us had thought that through. Maybe Sissy did.

We made sure that we got one of the cement seats underneath an overhang. The last time we'd been at the beach, in addition to me burning my feet on the hot sand and getting my skin scorched off, I'd also had my hot dog stolen by a seagull who'd swooped in and snatched it out of my hands. A nearby older gent manning a metal detector snickered and commented, "Flying rats."

We sat down and the seagulls landed nearby anyway. Since they couldn't attack from above, they decided to mill about in front of us hoping that we'd toss whatever we didn't eat to them. I tossed them my mustard packet and after snapping at it, and then snapping at each other fighting over it, decided that the packet wasn't worth their time and gave up, leaving it mangled on the concrete. That gave us time to finish our hot dogs and fries. We gave those seagulls nothing. They flapped around angrily and then flew off toward their next victim.

"I hear you can kill seagulls by feeding them Alka Seltzer tablets," I said.

"Why would that kill a seagull?" Sissy asked.

"They can't burp, so they end up exploding."

"Who told you that?"

"I will not reveal my source."

"Then I have no choice but to make annoying sounds until you do." Sissy did her impression of Gretchen's angry whine when Sissy dresses her up in baby clothes.

It took all of ten seconds for me to say, "Steve Bondurant."

"Oh, well. Let's consider the source. It's my observation that Steve Bondurant is an idiot and a blowhard. You know, I have no idea how Steve and Brandy are in the same family. She must have gotten all of the smarts."

"And all of the beauty," I added.

"Widdle Buzz wuvs her!" Sissy said, pinching my cheeks.

"Cut it out!" I said, pushing her hands away.

"Widdle Buzz has a crushy-poo." Sissy went on for maybe another minute, but quickly got sick of teasing me. It was too easy. "My stomach is full, so I say let's go in the water and see if we cramp up and drown. Purely for science."

"I say we find a pharmacy and toss some Alka Seltzer at those seagulls. See what happens."

"Let's compromise and do exactly what I want to do," Sissy said.

So we went into the soupy warm waters of the Gulf of Mexico. We waded out to a sand bar, never going in water above our waists, and then sat down on the sand bar in ankle-deep green water watching the parade of Sarasotans wandering up and down the beach. No self-respecting tourist stepped foot in Florida in late August. We still had a couple more months until the snowbirds would arrive to gum up traffic, jam restaurants, fill the mall, and so on.

Sissy and I each made up a story about random people walking past.

Sissy's story was about how a man with a protruding belly wearing speedos was on the run from Interpol after a shady business deal had gone awry in Switzerland, and now he was selling stolen cuckoo clocks out of the back of his Pontiac. The law was closing in, but he didn't know it. Would he make a getaway before they caught up with him? Only time would tell.

I picked out a thin lady in a green swimsuit and said that she was actually from Venus, here on vacation because the weather was nicer than Venus, where it always rained according to my dated science fiction books. Also, she enjoyed eating the heads of human males after she mated with them. She particularly enjoyed crunching on their skulls.

"That took a gross turn," Sissy said.

"Thanks. I'll have to draw it later."

"Please don't."

We waded ashore and found the family blanket, which Sparky was folding up. Buster wasn't there. Neither was the lady from work... Gloria. Her blanket was gone.

"We're leaving," Mom announced.

"Where's Dad?" I asked.

"We're leaving without him. He can find his own way home."

"What's going on?" I asked Sparky. "What's happening?"

"Quiet," Mom said. "I don't want to hear it. I don't want to talk about it. We're going home and that's final. No questions, no talking. I hope the car hasn't been towed."

"It hasn't been towed," Sparky said. "I can see it. It's right over there." He pointed and we all looked. Our car hadn't moved.

We gathered everything up. I opened up the basket, and it smelled like cooked bologna in there. As we walked, I pushed the bag of Fritos out of the way and pulled out the sandwiches one-by-one and tossed them high into the sky, attracting seagulls, who snatched each sandwich, all five of them, right out of the air.

"You're wasting food," Mom said. "Don't you know that's a sin?"

"I can name other sins," Sparky said.

"I don't to hear it!" Mom shouted. "Why are you kids always testing me? Why? I don't want to hear it! I have a headache!"

We were silent after that. We all trailed behind her, not saying a word.

Class is in Session

My new classroom in the fall was in one of the trailers behind the school. Mrs. Simmons, our new teacher, referred to it as a "temporary building." Mrs. Simmons had a look in her eye that I recognized and appreciated. She was clearly out of her mind. I was looking forward to learning from her.

I also appreciated that Brandy was in my class this year. Mrs. Simmons had us sitting alphabetically, so I wasn't anywhere near her. Brandy sat close to the front, near the chalkboard, while I sat in the middle, near my friends Billy and Reginald.

Billy had spent the entire summer getting acquainted with a weight set. He'd developed actual man muscles and had grown several inches, but otherwise was unchanged.

Reginald had become a more serious person. He'd grown, too.

They both told me that I'd grown, but I was still the shortest boy in the class, and was still painfully skinny. My ribs stuck out. Mom had decided that I could let my hair grow, so my hair stuck out, too.

While we were waiting for the bus to school, both of us in our stiff new school clothes, Brandy asked me if she could touch my hair. "Not in a weird way," she said. "It looks *so* soft." She ran her hand through my wavy locks and I nearly passed out from the pleasure that brought. "It *is* soft," she decided. She wasn't dressed in all black, but she might as well have been. She had an aura about her. She was wearing nautical-themed clothes. Her mother, she explained, wanted her father to buy a boat, maybe in the spring, so they were preparing for the eventuality of being seafaring people by donning appropriate attire. "I have a captain's hat," she said. "I didn't wear it today."

I told her I'd like to see her with the captain's hat on.

"No you wouldn't. I look silly."

I told her that she could never look silly to me.

"Shut up!"

The bus arrived and we got on, but she sat with another girl and I made my way back to the bigger and brawnier Billy.

"You were talking to Brandy?" Billy asked.

"I was."

"Did she say anything about me?"

"We talked about how her family is going to buy a boat."

"Rich people call it a yacht. When are they buying their yacht?"

"In the spring, she said."

"Rich people always wait to do things until the spring. They take trips to Europe in the spring, too. They buy furs and stuff like that in the spring, even though they need them in the winter."

"I had no idea."

"Did Brandy tell you that we spent a lot of time together this summer? She played her weird records for me."

I froze. Did she like Billy? I looked at the improved Billy. Of course she liked Billy. Why wouldn't she? What was I thinking when I thought she liked me? Who could possibly like me? "Cool," I said, my voice shaking a bit. "That's cool."

"I'm gonna ask her to be my girlfriend this year."

My heart sank. Billy was clearly superior to me in every way. He was full of muscles and nice. I was skinny and weird. Who'd choose skinny and weird? "Cool," I said, my voice weakening. "Cool, cool, cool." I wanted to crawl under the green bench seat and curl up down where the dirt and chewed up gum was.

"Don't worry," Billy said, slapping me on the shoulder with one of his giant meathooks, "we'll still hang out together. You'll find a girl, too. You'll see."

"I won't find anybody," I said darkly.

"My mom says that all you have to do to find a girl is 'put yourself out there.' So if you put yourself out there, you'll be fine," Billy said, giving me a little shake. "And you can hang out with us! Unless we're kissing. Then you'll have to leave."

I felt sick. Cocoa Puffs were gurgling in the back of my throat, threatening to eject. I wouldn't get to sing "Michelle" outside Brandy's window, and I'd been practicing, too. If I did, it would only serve as accompaniment to a Billy/Brandy make-out session. A little noise came out of my voice box that was a bit like an unoiled hinge, "Eeeee."

"Cheer up!" Billy exhorted. "We'll find you somebody."

People have been threatening to find somebody for me and have been giving me that same sterling advice—*put yourself out there*—my whole life. But what if the self you have to put out there isn't all that great?

Once seated in class, roll call became easy. Seated directly behind Reginald was Carol Jones, a conventionally pretty girl who looked like a pre-teen Dorothy Hamill, helmet haircut and all.

At recess, Carol walked up to me while I was trying to find Brandy, and cornered me near the four-square court, against the chain-link fence. "Who are you?" she demanded. "Where do you come from?"

193

I tried to climb over the fence, but Carol was quick and stood between me and the fence. "Do you like me?" she demanded. "I think you're kinda cute."

She knew my name from class. I'd said "present" when it was called. "I'm Buzz."

"But the teacher said your name was 'Joseph.' Where do you come from? I've never seen you before! I have a hamster named 'Rasputin.' Do you want to come to my house and see him? We have a Habitrail!" She was bigger than me, half a head taller with broad shoulders. She was wearing a rainbow-striped shirt and rainbow suspenders with white painter's pants. Her breath was scented with cherry Sucrets. She was nimble for a big girl. And strong. She grabbed me by the shoulders and wouldn't let go.

"I go by Buzz," I said, attempting to jerk free and failing. "I'm from Cleveland."

She laughed and squeezed my shoulders harder. "That's funny! Cleveland! No one's really from Cleveland. You're funny. I like you. Do you want to come over to my house after school? Cleveland! You're silly!" Her hands were like vice grips. There was no getting away. Where was Billy? Where was Reginald? How was this happening?

"Cleveland is a real place!" I shouted. "We have sports teams!"

"But they're not very good," Carol said. "Are you going to come over to my house after school? I live three blocks from here. My daddy can give you a ride home. You can see my hamster Rasputin run through all the mazes I've built with the Habitrail."

"I don't know. I have to go home after school. I'm expected there."

"Then tomorrow you'll come to my house after you talk it over with your mother. You look like a celebrity. Do you know who you look like?"

"No," I said.

"Neither do I! But you look like somebody and I'm going to figure it out. You're kinda twitchy, too. You know that?" She threw her head back and laughed again. "Cleveland! You're funny." She let me go and I sidestepped away and then ran. "Bye-bye, Buzz!"

At lunch, I discussed the Carol problem with Reginald, while keeping an eye on Brandy and Billy. Brandy smiled talking with Billy. Somewhere in my tiny brain, I said, "Billy will make her happy. That's what's important."

"What are you complaining about, my man," Reginald said. "Carol is fine."

"I guess."

"You guess? You got a hot, Dorothy Hamill-looking girl who wants some Buzz-loving and you guess? Come on, man. I'd take that action."

Back in class, I received a note passed back to me from Carol... "I like you, do you like me?" The two check boxes were "Yes" and "YES." Carol was, literally, not going to take no for an answer.

I put the note into my book bag, now heavy with grammar and math textbooks and, at the end of the day, sprinted for the bus at the sound of the bell, arriving as the bus pulled to the curb and slapping my hands on the door. "Please!" I shouted through the window at the indifferent driver, a blue-haired elderly lady who took the job to "stay busy and get out of the house." She didn't say that then. But she would later on during our semi-frequent chats over the next several weeks as I attempted to run and hide from Carol. The bus driver peered through the glass admonishingly at me, and then slowly pulled the lever to open the door. I quickly made my way three-quarters of the way through the bus and ducked down in a seat.

"Who are you hiding from?" the bus driver asked.

"A girl!" I shouted back. "Don't tell her I'm here."

"What's she look like?"

"Dorothy Hamill."

"Gotcha." A moment later: "Here she comes. Get lower." I got lower. A moment or two later: "Are you supposed to be on this bus, sweetheart?"

"I'm looking for someone," Carol said.

"There's no one here."

I heard Carol climb out of the bus.

"She's cute," the driver commented, peering at me via the large rearview mirror. "You sure you don't want her to catch you?"

"She caught me once already. I don't think I'll survive a second capture."

"Suit yourself, sweetie."

I sat up, turned my head to look outside, and there was Carol outside my window. The window had already been lowered to let in air. Before I could put it back up, Carol hopped up and dropped in another note, this one vaguely more threatening: "YOU WILL BE MINE," with a large heart drawn in blood red crayon. She winked at me and shouted, "Rasputin!" and jogged athletically away.

"This is a disturbing development," I said, staring at the note. I stuffed it in my bag in time to watch Billy and Brandy arrive at the bus together and sit down in the same seat near the front. They seemed comfortable together. Relaxed.

"Oh," the bus driver said, looking at me in the big rearview mirror. "I get it now." I shrugged at her. "I'd go with Dorothy Hamill, sweetie. Bird in the hand and all that. Just my two cents."

A few weeks went by, and I finally took the bus driver's advice and allowed Carol to capture me. She caught up with me as I neared the bus. Once she learned the route I took, it was easy for her to catch up with me and make the tackle, grabbing me around the knees with a mighty leap and bringing me down into the St. Augustine grass outside the second graders' grotto. She helped me to my feet, dusting me off. "Caught you!

195

At last!" She'd been catching me at recess for a while, pushing me up against any solid or semi-solid surface that happened to be handy—the sides of buildings and temporary buildings, fences, a flagpole, a wall, a row of bushes. She demanded to know whether or not I liked her. I said in no uncertain terms that I did not like her, not a bit, and she laughed and told me I was funny. "And that whole Cleveland thing, too. That's funny!"

"It's not funny to me! I *am* from Cleveland. People can be from Cleveland. It's a real place!"

She found that hilarious enough that she doubled over and I escaped.

Carol frogmarched me home with her like I was a hobo she'd caught sleeping on a park bench with an empty bottle of MD 20/20 and she was taking me to jail to sleep it off. It felt like I was going to jail. I was going to meet her hamster Rasputin and see him crawl around in the prison she'd built for him out of yellow plastic tubing.

The house was one of the older ones in Gulf Gate, but it was well-appointed. Her parents were older when they'd had her. Her father was a World War II veteran and her mother was from one of the countries in Britain that wasn't England. Wales, maybe. Or Scotland. There were pictures of her elderly parents on the walls alongside pictures of her grown-up siblings. "I'm the baby of the family!" she told me. "Do you like peanut butter toast? I do. I hate jam! No jam on my peanut butter toast. You'll eat what I eat, because that's what good guests do."

I looked at a window longingly, wondering how quickly I'd be able to crank it open and pop out the screen so I could make my getaway. "Yes. Peanut butter toast. But what of the hamster?"

"Rasputin!" she bellowed. "I'm glad you mentioned him. See, you remembered something about me and that means that you like me. I knew you liked me. Do you like my haircut? I think I could be a figure skater just like Dorothy Hamill. I'm great on roller skates. Have you ever been to the Roll-A-Rama? We should go on couples' day and then we'll find out what our song is. I hope it's 'Love Will Keep Us Together' because nothing could be truer than that."

"I hate the Captain and Tennille."

She laughed and slapped her knees. "You're so funny! How did you get so funny? Did you study comedy albums? Do you like Steve Martin? I don't understand him." She brought me over peanut butter toast on a paper plate and a glass of tap water. We sat at the kitchen table and she kicked my shin while we ate.

"Are you kicking my shin on purpose?" I asked her.

"Why? Don't you like it?"

"No! Who'd like having their shin kicked?"

"My mother kicked my father in the shin back during the war and that's how they got together! Then after the war he married her and brought her home to America and it's the greatest love story ever." She kicked me in the shin. "And now you'll get a kick in the shin. Circle of life."

"I don't think that's how the circle of life works."

She laughed some more. "You are funny. You're not eating your peanut butter toast like a good guest."

I took a bite. It was so dry. I drank some of the tepid tap water. How did I end up here? Why am I such a pushover? "Can we go see the hamster at some point?"

"Finish up." She watched me choke down the toast and drink the tap water. "What do we say?"

"Thank you."

"It's okay if you don't tell me that you like me right away, but you'll have to say it at some point."

"But I don't like you." She laughed. "I'm not kidding. I don't like you."

"Can I touch your hair?"

"No!"

She reached over and ran her hand through my hair. "It's just as soft as I imagined. Can I cut off some of it? I'll wrap it in a rubber band and put it under my pillow."

"Oh my God."

"I'll go get my scissors." She got up and left the room. I ran to the front door and jerked it open. I found her elderly mother on the other side of it.

"Who are you?" she asked in an inscrutable accent.

"Let me out!" I shouted, panicked.

"Are you one of Carol's little friends?"

"Please, for God's sake, let me out."

She stepped out of the way and I ran past her. I sprinted down the road, took a turn and soon realized that I was lost. I didn't care. An hour later, maybe two, I was home. I didn't even have my schoolbooks. Brandy had found my bag and brought it to our house.

Sissy sat in the den watching *Hope Hospital*. The mad scientist had built a space station and was aiming a giant laser at Washington, D.C. The couple with the alliterating names along with the Australian spy were cruising up to it in an Apollo space capsule suspended by fishing line and held together by Testor's plastic cement. The good guys had lasers, too, but not the giant kind.

Pregnant Gretchen was sitting next to Sissy. They were sharing a box of Quisp. One for Sissy. One for Gretchen.

"Where have you been?" Sissy asked. "That psycho Dorothy Hamill girl finally abduct you? Brandy is worried."

"She made me eat peanut butter toast. It was so dry. And then she wanted to cut off my hair and put it under her pillow."

"I don't know why you're allowing this to go on. Brandy says that everyone at school thinks you're a couple."

"We're not a couple! She won't leave me alone!"

"Tell her you don't like her." Crunch, crunch.

"I've told her that a million times! She thinks I'm joking!"

"Do I need to get involved?"

"No," I said.

"I need to get involved, don't I?"

"No, you don't. You'll make it worse."

"I never make anything worse. When have I ever let you down?" Sissy sighed and shook her head. "I've put a lot of work into you." She patted the spot next to Gretchen. I sat down. "Why are you doing this? Why aren't you spending more time with Brandy?"

"She's happy with Billy."

"Sure she is. Wow. You're as dense as lead. And now she thinks that you're into this psycho Dorothy Hamill girl."

"Carol."

"Listen to you saying her name. Never say her actual name again. Her name is 'psycho Dorothy Hamill girl' from now on. Got it?"

"Okay."

"Now reach in and get your reward." I grabbed a handful of Quisp. I crunched a couple down. Gretchen turned toward me and indicated that she was a good girl via her expert sitting technique.

The next day in class, while Mrs. Simmons was telling us about how the ancient aliens—who were our ancestors because humans clearly did not evolve on this planet—built the pyramids by levitating blocks using anti-gravity rays from their flying saucers, a note from Carol was passed back to me that was covered over in crayon hearts. I opened it and it said, "Mrs. Carol Pepper." I craned my head around Billy and she was turned completely around in her seat, grinning ear-to-ear. She scribbled another note while I watched, which was quickly passed back to me: "See you at recess, lover boy!" I felt like I'd done everything I could to put an end to this travesty. I saw a future in which she had me in a full nelson at the altar, twisting me around painfully until I said, "I do."

The bell rang, signaling our release into the wilds of the playground. My heart sank watching Billy get up and lumber deftly over to Brandy, who accepted his outstretched arm.

Carol quickly dodged past Reginald and cornered me near where our dioramas were on display.

"Why don't you ever offer your arm like that? Like a gentleman?" she asked me.

"Because I don't like you, psycho Dorothy Hamill girl!" I shouted. "I don't like you! Why won't you leave me alone?"

"You think I look like Dorothy Hamill?" she said, and primped her hair a bit.

What could you say to a girl who constantly missed the point of what you were saying? "I give up," I said.

"Come on then," she said with glee, a twinkle in her blue eyes. "We'll go to the swing set and you can hold my hand while we swing together." She grabbed me by the collar and we headed outside.

We tromped down the wooden stairs away from the temporary building and walked to where the sidewalk ended. We traversed the dead grass pathway toward the swing sets, me with my head down like I was a prisoner on death row. As we passed by Brandy, I gave her a forlorn glance, but she and Billy had made their way to a spot under a spindly slash pine, finding a short stripe of shade on an otherwise shadeless playground, packed with screaming children, who were suddenly parting like the Red Sea.

A lone figure dressed in a green plaid jumper was pedaling through them on a bicycle, a red, white and blue purse cross-slung on her torso. It was Sissy, of course, who'd come to put an end to this nonsense. When she got within ten feet of us, she hopped off the bicycle and allowed it to drop to the ground with a clatter.

"You!" she shouted, pointing at Carol. "Psycho Dorothy Hamill girl! Hands off my brother. You get one warning."

"Are you his sister?"

"Are you an idiot? Yes, dummy, I'm his sister." Sissy unslung the vinyl handbag and held it by the strap. "You'd better run."

"You're gonna hit me with a purse? Big deal," Carol said, crossing her arms. I stepped away from her.

"I'm gonna hit you with a purse full of rocks," Sissy said, and then she grabbed the strap with both hands and spun it around her head, like David getting ready to fell Goliath. She leapt forward and spun the rock-laden purse in a horizontal arc toward Carol's mid-section, making solid contact, knocking cocky Carol to the ground. Carol quickly climbed to her feet. I could see that the full gravity of the situation had finally manifested inside her head. She turned and sprinted away, but Sissy was quick, even with a rock-filled purse, and successfully caught up with her near the swing sets, where Carol went to the ground a second time, tumbling through the ruts underneath the two swings. She rolled to her back in time for Sissy to stride up and place a saddle shoe on her torso. "You're gonna leave my brother alone. Say it!"

"But we're in love!" Carol said.

A crowd of children formed a circle around the two of them.

"You're not in love. But you are in pain. And you'll be in more pain if you don't say it. Say it!" Sissy roared.

Brandy was standing next to me. "Legend," she whispered to herself aloud.

"I'm not in love," Carol said, tears streaming down her cheeks.

A boy in a plaid shirt and dusty trousers whistled at Sissy. "Nice legs!" he shouted.

"You're next!" Sissy shouted, pointing at him, and he ran off. She turned her attention back to Carol Jones. "Now I want you to say, 'ham comes from a mallard duck.'"

"But ham doesn't come from a mallard duck!"

"You think I don't know that? Say it!" Sissy roared, getting the purse back in motion.

"Oh, my God! Oh, my God! Ham comes from a mallard duck, okay! And I'm not in love with Buzz. Please let me go!" Sissy took her foot off of her and she stumbled to her feet. "You're crazy! And I'm never gonna talk to you again!" She shouted that last part at me. She ran off.

Sissy turned her attention to me. "You like Brandy." Then she turned to Brandy. "And you like Buzz. Figure it out!" She dumped all the rocks out of the purse onto the ground underneath the swing set. There were a lot more rocks in the purse than you'd think would be able to fit. She slung the empty purse across her torso, waded through the kids, who parted quickly for her, and mounted the bicycle that she'd ridden in. It was an unfamiliar bike.

"Where'd you get the bike?" I asked.

"That's what you have to say?" Sissy asked, peddling past me. "I'm never doing this for you again!" She rode off the way she came, across the field filled with screaming kids.

Reginald walked over and slapped me on the back. "I'd heard of your sister," he said appreciatively. "Man!"

Billy lumbered over to Brandy and said, "Do you really like Buzz?"

She looked over her shoulder at me. "I'm sorry." She ran off, leaving me and Billy staring at each other woefully.

Billy said, "Rich people."

The bell rang, and we went back inside, where Mrs. Simmons told us about the connection between flying saucers, Bigfoot and the Trilateral Commission, which was run by the Rockefellers, who were from outer space. She told us that someday we'd all voluntarily carry around boxes with us that had all of our personal information in them, and those boxes would be the only way we could spend money. Also, the boxes would send information back to rich people, who would track us using them. There was a secret plan.

Brandy wouldn't turn around for either of us.

The final bell ran at the end of the day. Carol Jones got up and left, not saying a thing. True to her word, she never spoke to me again. Brandy gathered her books. Billy said, "Go to her."

"But you always walk her to the bus."

"I know. But she likes you. I can tell. I may be big, but I'm not stupid. Go to her."

I felt so tenderly toward Billy in that moment. He was bigger than me in so many ways. "I don't... but... your heart," I said.

"Don't worry. Old Billy will bounce back." He thumped himself on the chest. "Maybe I'll jog home and drink some Tiger Milk."

I quickly picked up my books and shoved them in the bag. Brandy was already outside. "Hey," I shouted. "Wait up."

"Hey yourself," she said, and then looked away from me for a moment. "Where's Billy? Why isn't *he* here?"

"He sent me," I said.

"Oh. Is that the *only* reason why you're here?"

"No," I said. I felt my heart racing uncontrollably. It might explode. "I... uh. I like you." I said it!

"I like *you*," she said. "Do you want to, I don't know, hold my hand?"

I reached over and took her right hand in my left. "I'm scared."

"It's okay. So am I."

That's when we started walking home from the bus stop together, hand-in-hand. I would stand and watch her go into her house, and then run home to my house, flush with joy. Every morning, I would stand outside her house on the sidewalk waiting for her to come out and the two of us would walk to the bus stop, hand-in-hand. We sat together at lunch. We sat together at recess. Her face was the first thing I thought of when I woke up in the morning and the last thing I thought of before I drifted off to sleep.

Miracle of Life

On occasion, my father would pick up the newspaper and cipher his way through it. He read an article in the Sports section about how the Boys & Girls Club of Sarasota was offering judo lessons, and that the club's judo students were eligible to go to a junior olympics competition in Orlando in the spring. He decided to scrape up some cash and sign up Sparky and me for lessons. "You like that kung fu crap," he told me, referring to the TV show starring David Carradine, the son of *Channel 44's Creature Feature's* greatest actor. Dr. Paul Bearer often drolly mocked Grasshopper's real-life dad, it didn't matter whether he wore a cape or a lab coat. "And your brother can keep an eye on you so you don't get killed."

"When you snatch the pebble from my hand, you can leave this place," I told Sparky.

Sparky acquiesced despite my remark. He went to Gulf Gate library and brought home a photo-illustrated book of judo techniques, made a study of it, and took me into the backyard next to the pitch back machine for a quick primer on the sport of judo. "In judo, you use your opponent's strength against him," Sparky said before he muscled me to the unevenly cut grass. He helped me up and then thumped me back to the ground, over and over.

"I'm not sure I'm learning anything here," I said, getting dizzy from all the trips over Sparky's shoulders and hips.

Sissy and Brandy played cards on the lanai, sipping on lemonade.

"Are you sure that you don't want to learn?" Sparky asked Sissy.

"Positive," she said, not looking over.

Brandy said, "I don't understand the rules to this game."

"No one does," Sissy said. "That's what makes it such a great card game." She laid out three cards and shouted, "Hacksaw!"

Brandy smiled sweetly at me and I felt a rush of happiness overtake me, as Sparky hefted me over his hip and flipped me onto the ground.

"You're not paying attention," Sparky said. "I'm wasting my time with you."

"What?" I went. "Are we done?" I waved over to Sissy. "Can you deal me in?"

"No boys," Sissy said. "We're not playing with boys today. It's girl time."

"Jim Jam!" Brandy said, laying out a half-dozen cards. "I win!"

"Let Sparky throw you around for a little while longer while we play. Don't be so needy. It's not attractive." Sissy checked the cards and then pushed the checkers we used as poker chips from the pot over to Brandy's stack. "You are now wealthy beyond human comprehension. Don't let it go to your head."

"I won't." Brandy was dressed head-to-toe in black. Her hair was black, her t-shirt was black, she wore a black skirt with black tights underneath and black shoes with black rubber soles. She wore silver rings on her fingers, and her mother had taken her to the mall to get her ears pierced.

Mom opened the sliding glass door and came out with a full pitcher to water all the dying plants. "Why are you standing around? Why are you covered with grass?" she shouted at me. She watered a potted plant on the corner of the porch. "They grow if you talk to them," Mom commented aloud, and then shouted at the plant, "Why aren't you growing? What's the matter with you?"

Our heavily pregnant dog came stumbling out, urinated on the concrete and then complained angrily at our mother about something or other.

"Oh, good!" Mom shouted. "The dog's giving birth! Miracle of life. You're all watching."

Sparky said, "I'll be in my room," and he slipped in through the open sliding glass door.

"You're not going anywhere!" Mom shouted in his face. "You're hanging around for this! She's *your* dog!"

"I didn't ask for her."

"Yeah, well that's life, kid! None of us ask for the things we get, do we? And we end up with them anyway! You're gonna watch the miracle of life and that's final!"

We took Gretchen over to her cardboard box and helped her in. Within a few minutes, a black blob slid out from her and Gretchen licked it. Mom had a dull pair of scissors that she'd doused in rubbing alcohol. She snipped the umbilical cord.

"Is this what it's like giving birth?" Sissy asked, as Gretchen licked and licked the new puppy, which was moving its tiny paws as if trying to swim away.

"I suppose so," Mom said. "The doctors knocked me out both times."

"*Both* times?" Brandy asked, not taking her eyes off the dog and her puppy.

"We adopted Sparky from Catholic Charities," Mom said. "I had a tipped uterus and their father has an undescended testicle. I couldn't get pregnant until we got Sparky. Then I got pregnant with Buzz. And then Sissy. How much did you cost, Sparky?"

"One hundred dollars," Sparky said glumly.

"That's right! It was a hundred bucks for the fee! We couldn't afford it at the time, but we paid it anyway because we wanted you. Unlike Gretchen here, who clearly didn't want any of this, having her grandfather's great-grandchildren right in front of us." Mom squinted at a second puppy following the first out. "It's a miracle, okay? A miracle of life."

A few years later, Sparky—sick of hearing about the $100, and flush with cash from his job—tried to pay Mom back, and she wouldn't take it.

"I'll be happy to take it," Sissy said, holding her hand out.

Sparky shoved the money in his front pocket and rolled his eyes.

"You mean to tell me that you've been torturing me my whole life about how much pain I'd put you through and you were knocked out the whole time?" Sissy asked peevishly.

"Hey, someone has to keep you on your toes, Miss Tish." Mom leaned down and shouted at Gretchen: "That's a tip, just between us mothers, Gretchen! Keep'm on their toes!"

Gretchen recoiled and the puppies mewled.

Mom cut another umbilical cord. The final puppy emerged and plopped down wetly on the newspaper. Gretchen had enough and leapt out of the box before Mom had the chance to cut the cord. The final puppy flew out of the box behind her and slammed headfirst onto the thin den carpeting. I grabbed Gretchen and Mom cut the cord. She placed the gooey puppy back in the box with its siblings. All four of them cried out. "I bet you're all hungry!" Mom shouted at the box full of pups.

"Try offering them your meatloaf," Sparky said. "That'll shut them up."

"If you think you can do a better job with supper, then you go ahead and try," Mom told him.

"Challenge accepted," Sparky said.

Sissy and I slapped each other five.

"You're *happy* that your brother is going to cook?" Brandy whispered to us.

"You have no idea what we've endured. We've taken Catholic suffering to new levels," Sissy said.

"I heard that!" Mom shouted. "Who wants to take the dog out and who wants to make me a Manhattan?"

"I'll make the Manhattan," I said.

"You're a good bartender," Mom said. "That leaves Sissy and her little friend to take out the dog. You may see things come out of the dog that you'll regret seeing later. But they're educational things. I need a stiff drink. Put the ice on the side this time, Buzz."

Sparky and I shared space in the kitchen. Sparky pulled out the *Good Housekeeping Cookbook*, which was a red plaid three-ring binder filled with traditional recipes. He made a quick inventory of the freezer and pantry and started pulling out items to manufacture an edible dinner. I opened the liquor cabinet and pulled out vermouth, Canadian Club whiskey, bitters, and I found the maraschino cherries in the fridge door. I pulled out two tumblers and filled one with ice, which I ground up by bashing cubes in a plastic bag with a tenderizing hammer. I eyeballed the amounts of vermouth and whiskey and then dashed it with a generous amount of bitters. In went four cherries dug out out of the jar with my fingers, and a little cherry juice. I licked the cherry essence off my fingertips. I brought my little masterpiece over to appreciative Mom, who'd clicked on the tube and was watching Paul Lynde quip his way through an answer on *Hollywood Squares*.

"What's Sparky doing in there?" Mom shouted toward the kitchen. "I hear something sizzling."

"Don't get up," Sparky said. "Do not try to assist me. Don't touch anything in this kitchen."

"He's getting mighty bossy now that he's a teenager."

"I've been a teenager for a while."

"I know that!" Mom said. "Your brother makes a great Manhattan. I hope you don't screw up dinner!"

The puppies mewled from their box. They wanted their mother.

Gretchen trotted in and hopped into the box. She made herself at home and the puppies all migrated toward her.

"Thanks for warning us, Mom," Sissy said.

"Educational," Brandy said. "That creepy creepster next door to you? He wants us to go swimming in his pool."

"You should ask your mother first," Mom said. "If you go, Sissy, you're bringing Buzz with you. Remember that your older brother is slaving over a hot stove, so you'd better be back in time for dinner."

"Well?" Sissy asked me. "You coming?"

"I guess," I said.

"I don't care that he's creepy as long as the water isn't too cold. Remember that motel in Tennessee?"

"That was the worst. We could have died from frostbite. Not that Mom would have cared," I said.

"I heard that! Put on your swimsuits and go over there. I want you out of the house." Mom took a long pull from her drink after tossing a few shards of ice into it. "You'll need to make me another one of these before you go. And maybe one for the dog." Mom shouted over at the box. "Can

205

you believe the ingratitude of children, Gretchen? Don't worry, you'll get used to it!"

"I guess I'll go if you go," Brandy said. "I'll go home and ask my mother. I'll meet you here?"

"We'll wait for you," I said.

"I'll wait for you," Sissy said. "He'll count the minutes that you're away. Oh, he's so sad when you're gone. It's tragic! Boo hoo hoo."

"And don't do anything over there to embarrass me in front of that old weirdo," Mom said. "'Creepy creepster' is right. I like that one. I'll have to remember it."

Sissy and I put on our suits and wrapped Holiday Inn towels around ourselves. We didn't bother with flip-flops since we were walking next door. We stood in our driveway waiting for Brandy. She came back wearing a black one-piece bathing suit, some sort of black open-toed sandals with a beach towel draped over her shoulders. She wore oversized sunglasses with plastic frames. She'd pinned her hair high on her head. I thought she looked like Audrey Hepburn.

Whenever I'm flipping around the channels, and I happen upon an Audrey Hepburn movie, I stop and watch it for a few minutes, because it reminds me of Brandy.

I carry all of the women I have ever loved deep in my heart. I've never stopped caring for any of them. If any of them ever showed up at my apartment and asked me to do them a favor, I would immediately agree to it, no matter what it was. Do you want a kidney? Have mine.

The three of us knocked on the front door. I rang the doorbell.

Mr. Gray opened the door. He was standing in front of us shirtless, wearing floral patterned trunks. "At long last, you've taken me up on my offer," he said. We followed him through his house, a much smaller house than the ones that we and the Bondurants had decided upon, and we exited through his sliding glass door, ending up on the white pool apron, which was rough upon my feet.

Brandy was fragrant with the scent of coconut oil. I hadn't bothered to put any tanning oil on because I didn't think we'd be there for long and I figured the chlorinated water would probably dissolve it anyway.

Sissy and I dropped our towels where we stood. "Is it cold?" she asked Mr. Gray.

He had an odd expression on his face. It took him a moment, but he finally replied, "Oh, no. It's quite warm."

None of us bothered to ask him where his wife was. She was a professional volunteer, her hair always having to be redone stiff and blue for her events, always gone somewhere.

Brandy got on the other side of me, like she was using me for a human shield. I stood watching Mr. Gray warily, while the two girls slipped into the pool behind me. His face worried me. The expressions on it. Adults were confusing to me. I didn't understand their drives. The problem with me is that I still don't understand a lot of things about other people. I don't understand sadism, for instance. I saw a lot of sadism while I was in the Army. It was upsetting and confusing, like the voracious look on Mr. Gray's face.

"I think we should leave," I said.

"Don't be silly," Mr. Gray said. "Hop in the pool. Maybe you'd like me to take some photos? I have an Instamatic."

"No," I said. "I don't want photos."

"Girls? Would you like some photos?"

"No," Brandy said.

The two of them were in the deep end, bobbing around with their heads above water.

I got in and the pool was tepid, like a bath near the end. I waded over to Sissy and Brandy. Brandy's skin was alabaster white, in contrast with Sissy's skin and mine, which were both deeply tanned. The deep end wasn't deep at all. I could touch my toes on the bottom and still keep my head above water.

Mr. Gray had gone missing, so we relaxed a bit and floated around. There was a beach ball striped in the same colors as a Wonder Bread bag, and we batted that around a bit.

Brandy waded over to me. We were the same height and she was close enough that the tips of our noses touched for a moment. I tasted her breath and felt thrilled to have air in my lungs that had just been in hers. She reached over and ran her fingers across my ribs. "You're so *skinny*. I need to make you some macaroons. You'll like my macaroons. They're so tasty." I gazed into her beautiful green eyes and was transported beyond the confines of the pool. I was outside of my body for a moment, one with the universe and strangely, unbelievably, happy.

Now, in my 30's, I don't do happy. I tell myself that happiness is overrated and that happy people are stupid. I think back to this moment sometimes, and know that I am lying to myself.

Out of the corner of my eye, I saw the flashbulb pop.

Sissy said, "I thought we agreed. No pictures."

"Oh, but you'll want to remember this, won't you?" Mr. Gray pulled the flash cube off the camera and replaced it with a fresh one. How many photos had he taken? "I have some cookies here for you. And some iced tea with lemon. Come on out of the pool and sit with me. I'm so lonely. My wife is never around and I'd appreciate your company. I'll take the film to the lab and get it processed tomorrow. You can come by next week to pick up the prints." There was nothing wrong with what he was saying. But I didn't like it.

Brandy slipped around behind me in the pool. "I don't like him. Can we go?"

"We're going," I said.

"Speak for yourself," Sissy said. "I'm staying."

"You're not staying," I said. "You're coming with us. And no more pictures."

"Don't be such a spoilsport," Mr. Gray said. "Stick around. Eat some cookies. Drink some tea. Have another dip. I have some money here for each of you. Seven dollars apiece. Stay and make a little bit of money."

"We're going," I said. "So is Sissy. We're all going and you'd better not try to stop us or we'll scream bloody murder and the neighbors will hear. Do you understand? I'm not cutting your lawn anymore. Do you understand?"

"Oh, now that's not fair, young man. What have I done other than offer you my friendship and a little spare cash? I've done nothing. Ladies, are you going to listen to this hysterical young man?"

"Yes," Brandy said. "I'm listening to him and I'm going. I will *scream* if you try to stop us."

"Jesus," Sissy said. "Fine. I'm going, too."

We waded out of the pool. Mr. Gray snapped a photo of us as we emerged. We warily picked up our towels and wrapped them tightly about us.

"Creepy creepster!" Brandy shouted at him. She shrieked.

"Okay, okay!" Mr. Gray said. He opened the screen door and we were out on his lawn.

Brandy forgot her sunglasses and Mr. Gray picked them up and waved them at her. "Come here! You forgot something!" He held some money in his other hand.

We ran away from him into our yard. "Stay away from us!" I shouted at him. "Stay away from my sister! Stay away from my girlfriend!"

We ran to the lanai and stood there shaking and wet. We dried ourselves with our rough towels and sat down at the table where Sissy and Brandy had been playing their card game.

"What did he want?" Sissy asked.

"You don't want to *know*," Brandy said darkly. She shivered and her eyes went wide for a moment.

I reached over and took her hand. "Do you want me to burn down his house?" I asked.

"What?" she said, startled. "No!"

"We are Peppers," Sissy said. "We're familiar with explosives."

"Fourth of July. Lorain, Ohio. We were there," I said.

"What are you *talking* about?" Brandy asked.

"Nothing." Sissy touched her nose and nodded and winked and I did the same.

"We'll never testify in a court of law."

"I'm your girlfriend?" Brandy asked. "I don't remember agreeing to that."

"It was said in the heat of the moment," I said.

"You have to *ask* if I want to be your girlfriend."

"Ask her, stupid," Sissy said.

"Do you want to be my girlfriend?"

"Walk me home," Brandy cooed coquettishly. "Maybe I'll say *yes*."

"Well?" Sissy went to me. She clapped her hands. "Let's get this show on the road, you two. I'll run interference with our delightful mother."

Brandy and I walked past Mr. Gray's house. We could sense that he was in there, possibly peering through a crack in the drapes, monitoring us as we walked past.

I was barefoot and Brandy wore her sandals, so she was taller than I was by an inch or two. We held hands and didn't say a word until we reached her house. We stood on the driveway. Without saying anything, Brandy leaned over and gently kissed me on the cheek and then ran over to her front door. She opened the door, turned around and said, "Yes!"

I reached up to my cheek where she'd kissed me. The world spun around me. I dropped to my knees without taking my hand away from my face. I stood back up, woozy.

I somehow made it home.

"Where have you been?" Mom asked me when I stumbled in the front door, love drunk. "Your father's been in an accident! We have to go to the hospital. Go get changed. Is that lipstick on your face? It is! Oh, my God! You're too young to have lipstick on your face! Am I going to have to lock you in your room until you're 18? Go wash your face and then change into something more appropriate for the hospital."

I went into my bedroom and flopped onto my bed. I needed a minute.

Sissy crashed in, already dressed for the hospital in her bib overalls with the daisy appliqués, pink shirt and Birkenstocks. She still smelled like chlorine from next door. "Well?"

"She said yes. She kissed my cheek."

"She did. I'd recognize her shade of lipstick anywhere." Sissy put her hands on her hips and sighed with satisfaction. "All the years of hard work are finally paying off. I feel that I might be able to release you into the wild at some point. Ten, maybe fifteen years in the future. Depending on continued good behavior."

"Thanks. What happened to Dad?"

"His car got hit from behind by another car. Sparky talked to the doctor. He'll live."

"We should eat dinner then. Who knows when Sparky will get another chance to make edible food?"

"I know! Did you know that if you roast Brussels' sprouts, they taste like food? He roasted them in a pan in the oven with some of that shake-on Parmesan cheese. Incredible. Totally different than when Mom boils them into mush."

"I want food that tastes like food," I said. "I want to eat those Brussels' sprouts. Why do these things always happen? Wait. Shouldn't someone stay behind with the puppies?"

"Sparky's going to do that."

"Which gives him the opportunity to get to eat food that tastes like food."

"He did make it."

"Right." I shrugged. "I guess I should get dressed."

"You gonna wash that lipstick off your face?"

"No way. Should I get rings for me and Brandy?"

"I'll look into that," Sissy said. "Let me do a little research."

She closed the door behind her and I put on a fresh pair of shorts, an Ocean Pacific t-shirt and my best tennis shoes, sans socks.

I went into the bathroom and, even though my bladder was full, I couldn't pee. My penis felt unusual, too. Bigger. I got panicky and then my penis returned to normal and I could pee. I had no idea what had just happened.

I washed my hands and then studied the smooch on my cheek in the mirror. Then I noticed my own face, which I didn't spend a lot of time looking at. I felt like there was no reason why someone as beautiful as Brandy would be interested in me. I was ordinary—a garden variety kid. No identifying marks. It was clear to me that Brandy, given some time for reflection, would eventually change her mind. And who could blame her?

I washed my face.

I found my comb and ran it through the tangle of hair sprouting erratically from my head. The comb didn't make a marked improvement. In fact, I looked even more ordinary with slightly more orderly hair. Deck chair rearrangement on the *Titanic*. I mussed it back up.

I wasn't old enough to be a failure yet. I'd have to work up to that.

I heard a rap on the door, opened it, and it was my brother. "I heard you talking in here."

"What? Was I saying all that stuff out loud?"

"Buzz, you can't talk that way to yourself. There are enough people in life willing to run you down. You shouldn't help them do it."

"Thanks. I wish I could eat your food."

He patted me on the shoulder. "I'll save some for you. We'll heat it up tomorrow. Be nicer to yourself, okay?"

"Okay," I said, not really meaning it.

"Sissy told me how you stood up to that pervert next door. You're a good kid. Any girl would be lucky to have you."

"Thanks, big brother."

"Okay. That's enough. I need you to get out of here. I have some business to transact in here that's going to take some time."

We stepped around each other and Sparky locked himself in the bathroom. I heard the ceiling fan turn on.

Sissy met me out in the den. We knelt peering into the box of puppies. Gretchen was passed out amongst them. "Miracle of life," Sissy said.

"They'll all be dead of old age in 12, 15 years, and we'll still be relatively young," I said.

"Speak for yourself. I plan on living hard and fast," Sissy said. "I'll die a rocker's death, choking on my own vomit in a hotel room in some far-off city."

"Who was it that got decapitated in a car accident? Was that James Dean?"

"It was Jayne Mansfield," Mom said behind us. "And aren't you two cheery? Get in the car. We're going to the hospital. I hope your brother doesn't let these poor animals die. We're going to need the money when we sell those puppies."

The Thrill of Victory

The first time coming back from Sarasota Memorial Hospital, I burst into tears sitting in the front seat next to my mother, who shook her head at me. "What are you crying about?"

Buster was all goofy on morphine and was nice to me, which I misinterpreted as him being on death's door. I was, as usual, the only one who was upset.

"Will you tell him what's going on?" Mom shouted at Sissy.

Sissy leaned over the front seat and said, "We don't even think he was hurt. We think he faked an injury for the insurance money."

"But the Torino's bumper is all smashed in!"

"They were on gravel," Sissy said. "It was like bumper cars."

"Your father saw the gravel, saw an opportunity to get rear-ended, slammed on his brakes and let the car behind him slide forward and knock into his bumper," Mom said. "Stop crying."

"But he was nice to me! That means he must be dying!"

"He was nice to you because he thinks there's a big payday coming up," Mom said. "Also, he was on morphine. Your father loves his morphine."

"Maybe we'll get our own pool out of this," Sissy said. "Depending on how convincing we all are in court. I plan on crying big old crocodile tears. 'My sweet daddy is a cripple!'"

"No one's going to testify in court," Mom said. "No one but your father. This is his scheme and you're staying out of it."

"Pain and suffering has to be proven!" Sissy declared. "I'm too cute to be ignored. I say, 'Use me.'"

"Did your brother make pork chops?" Mom asked. "I'm so hungry, I'm going to eat one cold."

"Yes, there are pork chops and Brussels' sprouts," Sissy said. "He said he was going to make a cheesecake, too."

"Out of my cream cheese?" Mom shouted. "I need that cream cheese for my melba toast!"

"He ground up the melba toast to make the coating for the pork chops," Sissy said. "He made some sort of egg batter. My mouth is watering just talking about it."

"Well, isn't *he* fancy? I'm sure it'll all be undercooked and we'll be going right into the hospital with your father, having our stomachs pumped." Mom glared over at me. "Will you get this kid a Kleenex? His face is sopping wet." Mom got a little angrier and shouted, "You'd better eat when we get home, mister! You look like a boat person who just escaped Vietnam! Quit acting like you're fleeing communist oppression!"

It was sunset when we pulled up to the house. I hopped out of the car and opened the garage door, and Mom pulled the Ford family truckster into the hole in the garage wall. I pulled down the door and we went inside.

The puppies heard all the ruckus and woke up. Gretchen grumbled as she awoke next to them, blinking her eyes.

Sparky was sitting on the couch reading, and looked up at us as we intruded on his solitude. "So?"

"It's a scam," Sissy said. "I fake-cried to the cop and he told me the whole story."

"I thought as much. I can reheat dinner if you like."

"I'm starving!" Mom shouted. "The only thing I've eaten today is four cherries. I hope you don't kill us all with undercooked pork chops."

"You'll live," Sissy said.

Sparky turned on the oven and reheated the pork chops and Brussels's sprouts while we all changed into our pajamas.

Even reheated, my pork chop was a revelation. I had no idea that pork chops could be tender and juicy. It was also the first time I ate Brussels's sprouts without gagging dramatically through the whole experience.

"Why, in heaven's name, did you burn these vegetables under the broiler?" Mom demanded. "And my pork chop is undercooked! If I wake up dead, you'll know who to blame!"

For dessert, Sparky brought out a baked cheesecake. I'd never eaten anything like it before. All of the cheesecakes I'd ever eaten were reconstituted from powder out of a box.

"Where did you learn how to do this?" I asked Sparky.

"I blew the dust off of Mom's cookbook," Sparky said. "I followed directions."

"That cookbook was a gift from your father," Mom said, picking at the cheesecake. "I think I had something like this when I went to Birdland in New York. We stopped at a New York deli. They served dill pickles on the table in a dish. I had a pastrami sandwich. That night, me and my best friend Patty saw Charlie Parker and Harry Belafonte. You know, I married your father—"

"Because he looked like Harry Belafonte," I said.

"Funny how you never say it in front of Dad," Sissy said.

"Quiet you!" Mom said. "Thanks for ruining a nice memory."

"Then you rode the train back to Cleveland," I said. "And then Patty died in a car accident a week later."

"Yeah," Mom muttered. "People come. People go. That's life. Don't get too attached to anybody. Any of us could go at any moment."

I swung my feet under my chair, my toes barely scraping against the rug. I stared at my mother and could see the sadness deep inside her. I wanted to hold her and tell her I would always be there for her, that she didn't have to be sad. But I didn't say a word because we weren't allowed to be sentimental. Mom hated sentimentality.

Mom glanced over at me, suddenly aware that she was being watched. "Are you crying again? What the hell's the matter with you? You're either smiling and making jokes or you're crying. There's no in between with you. You'd better straighten up, kid, or life's going to eat you alive!" She pushed away the cheesecake. "I'm done eating. Somebody else is going to have to clean up. Do you think you can make me a drink without bursting into tears? I need another Manhattan to make this day go away. And someone needs to take the dog out! And we'd better get on a schedule with those puppies, otherwise we'll have a bunch of dead puppies that we'll have to bury in the backyard, and then this one will cry some more."

Sissy was already on her feet, stacking the dishes. Sparky's dish was so clean that we could have put it back in the cupboard and no one would have been the wiser.

I went into the kitchen.

Mom turned on the TV. *The ABC Sunday Night Movie* was just about to start. It was a rerun of a sleazy classic, *Bad Ronald*. "You have to go to school tomorrow!" Mom shouted. "You'd better get everything into that dishwasher, run it, brush your teeth and get into bed. No complaining! Is my drink finished yet? You can throw the ice in it this time."

We rushed around, driven by the mania in our mother's voice.

I fell into a deep sleep that night and woke up from a dream in which I was much older, in my thirties, and I was alone and knew that I'd be alone for the rest of my life. I stood in an apartment with condensation dripping off the bare walls all around me, a 12-inch TV set atop a TV tray playing static, a baby screaming through the walls from next door, and a burn hole in the middle of the carpet from God knows what. It was a strange premonition.

Mrs. Bondurant volunteered to drive Sparky and me to our judo lessons. Brandy was in a cheerleader camp most weekdays nearby. Steve was supposed to be driving her, but he was unreliable, according to Mrs. Bondurant. "That boy, I don't know what I'm going to do with him," she said in her lilting accent, that both Sissy and I had mastered in our spare time.

At Sarasota Square Mall, the two of us would pretend to be Irish for the clerks at various stores and they found us enchanting, even as we told them that they were "auld tubes who were talking utter bollocks out of their holes."

Mrs. Bondurant, like a lot of people back then, was drunk driving. Being drunk behind the wheel had none of the stigma that it would later pick up. She weaved along, taking occasional swigs out of a chrome-plated flask. She was always fashionably dressed and had an expensive car, so no sheriff's deputy would dare pull her over.

She would give Brandy, seated next to her in their cream-colored Mercedes sedan, man-catching advice. "Don't eat and put on makeup! How are ya going to get a real boyfriend if you're not thin and pretty?" She glanced in the rearview mirror at me. "Sorry, lad, I know ya have a crush on her, but do ya really think you'll have me daughter? I mean, look at ya! She needs a real man, someone who can take care of her, not a sad wee fellow like yourself. Stop acting the maggot! And what are your plans, ya half eedjit? To be an artist? Well I'll not allow some starving artist to pair off with me daughter. I'm not slagging ya, I'm telling ya the truth." I knew she was right. I knew by saying it out loud, she'd planted the idea in Brandy's head that she could do better, and eventually she would.

Mrs. Bondurant would pull up to the curb—half the time over the curb—and we'd pile out of the car, Sparky and I in our judo gi's and Brandy in a generic cheerleading costume. We were both supposed to go to Brookside Junior High the following year where Brandy planned on trying out for their cheerleading squad.

Our workouts were on the same basketball court. Sparky and I would go over to the wrestling mats that were plopped onto a corner of the gym, and Brandy would go over to center court with a large group of pre-teen girls in similar costumes.

As Sensei Bob taught us how to tug on each others' sleeves to knock each other off balance, we were serenaded by endless chants about S-U-C-C-E-S-S.

Buster went through another round of surgery and this time he was completely incapacitated by it. His lawyer, who advertised himself on Channel 44 as "Mean Wayne Bean the Lawsuit Machine!" found a surgeon of questionable ethics to remove one of Buster's back discs. It was cracked, not ruptured, and Buster's initial surgeon had told him to take it easy and it would heal on its own. Taking it easy doesn't pay the bills, though. Having surgery apparently would sound better in court, so Mean Wayne Bean the Lawsuit Machine made sure that my father would spend the next six months laid out in bed. Buster came home in the back of the Ford family truckster. Along with the help of Mr. Bondurant and

Mr. Jorgenson, both of whom were on one of their rare visits home, we managed to haul Buster into the house and drop him into the master bed. He'd lost enough weight in the hospital that he was lean, possibly for the last time in his life. His face was ashen and his eyes dull from opiates. That's the way he would remain until the spring, when his court date would eventually come up. Buster remained in the darkened room, occasionally calling out for one of us to come in and empty his piss bottle or refill his water jug. His diet consisted mostly of pills, Gatorade and salty potato-based products.

Mom worked double shifts. She lost enough weight that she needed to pull out needle, scissors and thread and tailor her clothes. I found her doing that one night when I couldn't sleep. She called me over and I sat beside her as she expertly resewed the seams on her orange and lime-green pantsuit. "I never get to see you anymore," she said. "Still taking judo lessons?"

"Yes. Are you okay? Can I make you a drink?"

"Everything is fine. We're going to be fine."

Everything wasn't fine. One of my jobs was bringing in the mail, and I knew what "past due" meant. I'd also seen my father on one of the rare occasions when he left the master bedroom. He was rail thin and haggard, and clearly addicted to his pills.

We survived on Banquet frozen dinners in those months. They were cheap. I ate two meals a day at school courtesy of the Federal government.

"Hang in there," President Ford urged from our TV set. He also said that he found the word "detente" confusing. We weren't sure if he was all there.

A few months later, as we headed toward the Christmas season, Sparky was an orange belt and I was still a white belt. Sensei Bob, a barrel-shaped man with a ponytail, told me that I should stop apologizing on the few occasions when I managed to knock someone down. He said that everyone who wanted to go to the junior olympics in Orlando needed to achieve the rank of yellow belt first. One day, he handed me a yellow belt. "Your father paid for the trip in advance," he explained. "You've been here long enough, I guess. Congratulations."

On a Friday evening in December, Mom and Sissy drove Sparky and me to the Boys & Girls Club of Sarasota, where Sensei Bob sat behind the wheel of the Bluebird school bus, which a volunteer group of interested citizens had painted in feverish colors. There were so few of us that we each had a bench seat to ourselves, our overnight bags piled high in the center aisle by the back emergency exit.

Sparky sat behind me. He cracked open a mathematics textbook and set it down in the seat next to him. He opened up a ruled notebook and pulled out a mechanical pencil. I watched him take notes in his impossibly neat handwriting. He caught me watching him. "What now?"

"Are you gonna win a medal?"

"Maybe. I have a much better chance than you do, I think."

"True enough. After I lose, I'm going to try to draw some of the action. I've been thinking about the way people move lately."

"You should study an anatomy textbook. It'll help."

"Yes!" I didn't know why I hadn't thought of it. I spent a lot of time drawing people and thinking about the way their bones and muscles moved under their skin. I'd recently been holding out my hand and drawing it, paying attention to the knuckles and fingernails. I'd drawn Brandy's face too many times to count, working on the cheekbones and the dainty curve of her chin. Drawing and erasing and drawing and erasing.

Mom would occasionally run the vacuum through my room and wonder aloud why it made such a racket where I spent my time drawing. "You're not allowed to have food in here!" she shouted above the din of our ancient vacuum.

The drive up to Orlando took hours and hours. The interstate wasn't built out yet, so we made our way down state roads that were buckled by heat, bobbing up and down in our seats as the bus's suspension creaked and groaned beneath us.

We made it to the Boys & Girls Club of Orlando in the middle of the night. We slept on cots in the middle of the gym floor. In the morning, we ate sweet rolls pulled from cellophane wrappers and drank orange juice from waxpaper cups.

Sensei Bob had us dress up in our judo gi's. We tossed all of our gear into the bus again and made our way to the arena.

A dozen different areas were set up for competition. We were all put into weight classes. Because I was so thin, my weight class only had three people in it. I was immediately called to one of the mats for battle. The competition lasted less than fifteen seconds. We bowed to each other and then the other boy threw me to the floor and landed atop me. I was counted out. The boy got off of me, stood up and then gave me a hand up. We smiled at each other, each of us having gotten what we wanted. We shook hands. "Thank you," he said.

"You're welcome," I said. I went out to the bus and retrieved my notebook, pencil, red eraser (my favorite) and pencil sharpener. I sat crosslegged on the gym floor, sketching what I saw. Drawing was the purest time of my day. It was the only time when I was focused.

It still is. But now I get to paint, too. I think I may take up welding some day and do metal sculptures. I feel sorry for people who don't get to paint, draw, write books, or do something that takes them outside of themselves.

I bring my paintings to the monthly arts and crafts show at the Sarasota Art Center. I've taken to executing still life paintings of random objects from around my apartment, or things that I've found while I'm on my afternoon bicycle rides after work. In my head, I call it my "common objects" series. But saying that out loud makes it sound silly. A woman and a young girl came over to my booth and took their time looking at these paintings. "I like these," the girl said. "They make me feel less alone." I gave her the painting she was looking at. The woman, her mother, said, "We should pay you for it." I said, "Your daughter already did. Thank you for saying what you did." "You're welcome," the girl said smiling, holding the painting in her hands. I watched them walk away. I sold a few paintings that day and picked up a commission to paint a portrait of a man's boat—the *Rum-Tum-Tub*—but I consider giving the girl the painting that made her feel less alone to be the only real accomplishment of the day.

Sparky's weight class had over 20 kids in it, and they were all rough-and-tumble types. Sparky held his own most of the day, eventually finishing fourth in his weight class.

When it came time to hand out the medals, I wasn't even paying attention. I sat in the corner drawing happily when Sensei Bob ran up to me and shouted, "Get up there!"

"Get up where?" I asked him, puzzled.

"The medal stand! You've won a bronze medal!" Sensei Bob could finally claim that he'd mentored someone to a medal in the junior olympics. He need the photo for proof.

I ran up to the medal stand and climbed up on the one labeled "3."

A judge hung a bronze medal around my neck, and then hung the silver medal around the neck of the kid who'd beaten me, and then a gold medal around the neck of the kid who beaten him. We were three little squirts who'd never won anything in our lives, judging by the stunned looks on the other two kids' faces.

We hopped off our stands after the cameraman indicated he was done with us, and all three of us, united in victory, spontaneously hugged each other and then stepped back and ogled the medals hanging around our respective necks.

The closest I'd ever come to this kind of glory before was when Sparky built my wooden car for the YMCA Indian Guides Pinewood Derby. I (Sparky, actually) won sixth place for the state of Nebraska. I still have the trophy.

Eventually, we all loaded into the bus and headed back toward Sarasota. I turned around in my seat and said to Sparky, "Looks like one of us won a medal!"

"Uh-huh," he went, a tremolo of anger in his voice.

"Would you like to hold it for a moment, so you know what triumph feels like?"

"I watched your match. You went down in five seconds."

"I think it was closer to fifteen. The thrill of victory! I know what that means. Certainly, I will be watching the *Wide World of Sports* with more interest now that I am a medaled athlete."

"If you say one more word, I will kill you."

"I, too, was once a loser. But now—" I didn't get to finish the thought because Sparky reached over the seat and took me into a sleeper hold.

Sensei Bob stopped the bus and separated us before I had the opportunity to pass out. I was getting close. "Stop bragging about the medal," Sensei Bob advised me, as he placed me back with the luggage. "Or next time I'll pull the bus over and strangle you myself."

The next day, I wore the medal around my neck at mass. Father Grant, the hip young priest, was saying prayer three, the shortest prayer. It was a folk mass, so a lot of the singing parts were accompanied by the strumming of a guitar by a long-haired boy wearing a jean jacket and bell bottoms. He was very serious about the strumming.

Father Grant noticed the medal and asked me about it before inserting the body of Christ into my mouth. I told him that I'd medaled in judo at the state level. No big deal. In went Christ and the conversation was done.

Before we all left, Father Grant recognized me from the pulpit. "We have in our midst a bronze medalist..." Etc.

I stood up on my pew and raised my fists above my head like Ali knocking out Frazier. "I'm the greatest! I'm a bad man! And I'm pretty!" I shouted to general laughter and eventual applause.

"God give me patience," Sparky grumbled.

"Get down!" Mom shouted. "I've never been so embarrassed in all my life!"

Sissy doubled over laughing.

In the car, Sissy asked Sparky how many kids he'd beaten to finish fourth.

"Shut up," Sparky said.

"And how quickly did Buzz go down?"

"About fifteen seconds, I'd say," I said. "But you know, sometimes time slows down in these dire events and it can seem like hours when you recollect it."

"And does your match seem like hours?" Sissy wondered.

"No. It seems like fifteen seconds."

After the Ford family truckster was inserted into the garage successfully, Sparky went to his room, changed and then informed us that he had an important engagement and would be out for the rest of the day. He pedaled off on his bicycle.

Brandy came over after Sissy gave her a call. The two of them went off into Sissy's room. They shut the door in my face and I heard the lock click. I rapped on the door. "I'm a bronze medalist! I won't be treated this way!"

"Fifteen seconds!" Sissy shouted and both of them laughed.

My face flushed.

I went into the Florida room, where we kept all the furniture that we never sat on, moved the coffee table that never had coffee on it out of the way, and practiced judo rolls. In an ideal judo roll, you start on your feet, roll on your arms, slap the floor and stand up in the end. I rarely made it to the standing part. I was a medalist now, so I felt I had a responsibility to execute a judo roll properly.

Mom went to the bedroom to see if Dad needed anything. She watched me flopping around on the carpet for a moment. "Go clean out the box with the puppies in it," Mom said.

"It's not my turn," I whined. "It's Sissy's turn and she never does it. I always end up doing it."

"If you weren't such a pushover, your sister wouldn't take advantage of you all the time."

"Lola!" Buster moaned. "I'm out of water."

"Your father is out of water. Someone is going to clean up after those puppies. We've got plenty of newspaper. Either you do it, or you'll get your sister to do it. One or the other."

"Lola!"

"Anyway. Figure it out." She went into the bedroom and the door closed.

I performed a judo roll, and for once, I came to my feet at the end of it. I also slammed my head into the wall with a loud thud.

"Keep it down out there!" Mom yelled. "Your father is trying to sleep!"

I checked out the wall. It seemed fine. My head was kind of ringing, but there was nothing unusual about that. By the time I was 12, I'd taken countless blows to the head.

I went to Sissy's room and knocked on the door.

"What?" she went, and she and Brandy giggled.

"It's your turn to clean out the puppies' box." I felt a warm drizzle coming down the left side of my face. I touched my cheek and my index, middle and ring finger came away covered in blood. "Hmm. Must have hit my head harder than I thought. Hey, can you take a look at my head? I hit it on the wall."

Sissy opened the door. Her eyes went wide.

Brandy screamed.

Sissy said, "Go get Mom." She shut the door. "Go get Mom, you idiot! You're bleeding to death!"

"It can't be that bad." I went into the bathroom and turned on the light. The side of my face was covered over in blood and it was pouring out of the wound. Blood dripped from my chin. It was fascinating. "*The Masque of the Red Death*," I commented. "A Vincent Price classic! Boogity boo!" I wadded up some toilet paper and tried to stop it myself.

There was a flap of skin hanging, I noticed. I thought I could see my own skull underneath it. "I thought skulls were supposed to be white." After a while, I gave up trying to stop it. Plus, I felt a little lightheaded.

I went out in to the den and found Mom in there, cleaning up after the puppies. "I guess I have to do everything around this dump," she said. She turned around to continue snarking at me and dropped everything. "Bathroom. Now." She pulled me behind her into the bathroom and got me into the tub, making me raise my feet. She washed the wound with a washcloth and then had me hold a hand towel over the top of it. "Push hard. This is your life we're talking about." She went into my room and found a white undershirt and formed it into a cloth bandage. She taped the flap of skin with adhesive tape and then taped her bandage on top of that. "Do you think you can walk?"

"Yes."

She helped me to my feet. We stopped in the kitchen. She wrote a note: "Sparky, Took Buzz to the hospital. Heat up dinner. Take charge. Mom."

I laid down in the backseat, the small of my back on the hump. Mom piloted the Ford family truckster to the emergency room.

An orderly helped me into a wheelchair and wheeled me up to a registrar, who took down all my information. "Insurance?"

Mom arrived from parking the car and filled out the rest of the information. We sat in the emergency room for about an hour as my head throbbed. "I could ask you what you were thinking, but clearly you weren't thinking," Mom said.

"Judo roll."

"You're not a champion, honey. You shouldn't even be in that class. But your father insisted, so I insisted that Sparky keep you from getting killed. Your father is obsessed with making you into something you're not."

"I know."

"You don't have to do judo anymore. Okay?"

"Okay."

"You're my son. You're your grandmother's grandchild. Do you understand what I'm saying?"

"I think so."

"You draw your pictures. That's fine. Make art. But I'm going to tell you something: This is a hard life. You have to become harder. No one's waiting out there to take care of you. They're all out there ready to tear you down. I'm afraid you're not suited for this life. You have to be more like your brother. He's sensitive, too, but he hides it better."

"What about Sissy?"

"Are you kidding? She was born fighting. She's going to conquer life."

"You sound like you're proud of her."

"It's like God took the best parts of me and created a perfect little girl. Of course I'm proud of her! If you tell her I said that, I'll knock you in the head again and this time you won't have a doctor to sew you back together."

Eventually, my name was called and an orderly came over to wheel me into one of the rooms. Mom insisted on coming along and no one could stop her.

The doctor took off the bandage. "Nice job," he said to Mom. "Are you in medicine?"

"No," she said.

"You should be."

I found myself under a sheet. I felt little pinpricks from the novocaine needle and then the doctor sewed me up. I added a new scar to my collection.

Mom eventually did become a nurse when she was in her forties. Buster left her shortly after she took her first nursing job. She worked in a cardiac care ward at Venice Hospital. She and her fellow nurses would take cruises together. I remember driving her down to Venice to catch the bus with her fellow nurses down to Miami, where they'd booked a half-price cruise during hurricane season. When I pulled the car up into the strip mall parking lot, and the nurses saw who was sitting in the passenger seat, they all smiled knowingly and nodded their heads at each other like, "Now the fun starts." "They all need me to whip them into shape constantly," Mom said. "You should let me fix you up with one of the girls."

"I'm fine," I said.

"You're not fine," Mom said. "You haven't been fine since Sissy was murdered. Come to think of it, you weren't fine before Sissy was murdered."

"Mom, I'm fine."

"I'm not going to live forever, you know." She had cancer at that point, and she knew it, but she hadn't told anyone and hadn't gone to a doctor. She had a lump in her breast the size of a golf ball. She was committing suicide, but in the most Catholic way possible. God couldn't condemn her to hell for killing herself. The cancer was something He'd done to her.

"You'll outlive me. You'll outlive everyone," I said stupidly.

"No, I won't," she said. "You've got to harden your heart."

After Mom was diagnosed, I married the first woman who'd said yes. I loved her. I swear I loved my wife. But I married her because I was afraid of being alone. It was a selfish reason to marry someone. I never apologized to her for doing it. I am sorry.

When Sparky talks about the day I judo-rolled into a wall, he recalls coming home to a house drenched with blood. "It was like a crime scene," he says. "And then there was this cryptic note. I wondered if someone had shot you."

"No, it was me being me."

I'm not afraid of being alone anymore, by the way. I'm fine.

Man: The Most Dangerous Animal

It was the dry season—winter in Florida—so I rode my bicycle to school in the mornings instead of taking the bus. During the dry season, I wasn't drenched in sweat from merely being outside. That wasn't the only reason I rode my bike. I was avoiding Brandy at the bus stop. I'd decided, on my own, that I was spending too much time with her. I wanted to spend all my waking minutes with her, but I knew, in my heart, that if I did spend more time with her, she wouldn't like me anymore. After Sissy demanded to know why I was avoiding Brandy, I told her this and she declared me, "the dumbest kid alive."

"She cried because of you," Sissy informed me. "And I had to sit with her while she was crying. Do you know what that's like?" Sissy grabbed me by the shirt and shook me. "Huh? Do you know?" We were sitting on the floor in her room.

"It's better than Brandy getting sick of me," I countered lamely. "I'm sick of me. I'm going to be stuck with me until I'm 50 and die a stupid Pepper death."

We were playing Stratego-Monopoly, and she'd just had her troops kick in the doors of my hotel at Park Place, arrest the tenants and set the hotel on fire. I'd invested a lot in that hotel, but that's what I got for not defending it with my own troops, who'd somehow ended up going directly to jail without passing Go, without collecting two-hundred dollars.

"Did you know," Sissy asked in her Australian accent, "that man is the most dangerous animal?"

"I don't want to play 'Man: The Most Dangerous Animal' today," I said.

"That's too bad, mate," Sissy said. "Because you have ten seconds to run for your pitiful life." She reached into the drawer of her bureau, and pulled out the wrist rocket she'd made out of a bent-up wire hanger and rubberbands off of the morning paper. "I brought you to my private island for one purpose—to hunt you in my preserve." The speech was meant to give me time to attempt to run away. The rules of the hunt confined us to the house and the yard, which gave me couches and bushes to hide behind. "Don't plead for your life, mate. It's undignified."

"You lied to me!" I said, finally playing along. "You said you had a job for me tending to your leopards, monkeys and gazelles." I stood up and backed over to her doorway.

Sissy put on her straw hat. "I've grown bored shooting monkeys. Leopards, too! Now there is only one head left to add to my trophy wall, mate. Yours!" She picked up a clear plastic tube containing four ping-pong balls. If she shot me with one, I was dead. If she missed with all four, it would be assumed that I'd gotten away via a rubber raft and that I'd paddled out to sea, eventually being rescued by a pleasure craft filled with French tourists, who would ask me, "*Êtes-vous Américain?*" and I would reply, "I'm thirsty! I need water! Where's the American embassy?"

I dodged the first ball while weaving through the den. "Does this mean that I'm not getting my Christmas bonus?" The puppies jumped up and down in their box. They were almost big enough to sell now.

"That's right! And there's no health insurance plan, either, mate!"

The second ball clacked against the front door as I shut it behind me. I ran clockwise around the house and slapped myself up against the wall. I peered around the corner hoping that Sissy would go the other way, and then I could follow behind her. But she caught me peeking and pursued me. "This isn't happening! This isn't happening!" I shouted, as I sprinted across the backyard.

She was the same size as me, and better coordinated, so she quickly caught up and ponged me between the shoulder blades. I fell face-first into the grass, and she knelt beside me. "So this is what it feels like," Sissy said. "All right, lads. Cut off his head and mount it. The rest we'll feed to the monkeys." She switched back to being Sissy and sat down next to me. I rolled over onto my back. It was one of those gray winter days when there was almost a chill to the air. "You made her cry."

"Okay. Stop rubbing it in."

"You need to apologize."

"I'm sorry."

"Not to me, you dope."

"I'll ride the bus tomorrow."

"You need to apologize now."

"Right now?"

"Right now."

"This minute?"

"This minute."

225

I propped myself up on my elbows. "Can I wait til I get my stitches out?"

"No."

"Because the stitches make me feel like a jerk."

"You *are* a jerk. Do I have to march you down there?"

"She's not gonna want to see me and I don't blame her."

"Get up and follow me."

I had no choice. I got up and followed Sissy out of the backyard, to the sidewalk. She shoved the wrist rocket into the back pocket of her bib overalls. She stopped me and brushed all the grass off my front and back. I hadn't exactly dressed for the occasion. I was wearing my Superman t-shirt, board shorts and my well-broken-in tennis shoes. My hair was all over the place. It did what it wanted. I reached up and touched my stitches, which I wasn't supposed to do. It was mostly numb up there.

When we got to the Bondurants' door, Sissy knocked and then stepped behind me. Mrs. Bondurant opened it, a glass of wine in her hand. She'd just had her hair done. I could tell by the chemical scent. She wore a pantsuit and a kaleidoscopically colored scarf. "Look who it is. Himself. Come to apologize?"

"Yes, ma'am," I said.

"And this one is forcing you to do it."

Sissy said, "'Forcing' is a strong word. Let's say I 'urged' him to do it."

"Aren't you the politician? Come in!" We stepped into the foyer and stood there. "Brandy, your two wee friends from down the lane are standing here waiting on ya."

Brandy eventually emerged from the back of the house. She was a vision of loveliness, dressed mostly in cotton dyed black. She crossed her arms in front of herself. She was pretty even when she was angry with me. "What do *you* want?" she asked me.

"Say it," Sissy said, giving me a vicious poke.

"'Say it,' she urged," Mrs. Bondurant said.

"I'm sorry. I'm sorry that I've been avoiding you."

"You *have* been avoiding me. Even at school. Why? Why would you *do* that?"

"Because your mother's right. I'm not good enough for you."

"Go away, mother!" Brandy said. "Go somewhere else for five minutes."

Mrs. Bondurant took Sissy by the hand. "My friend and I are going to go discuss the disturbing developments that have transpired on *Hope Hospital*." They left together.

Brandy invited me over to the couch in their Florida room. I sat down and she sat close next to me.

"It's just that I'm afraid you're gonna get sick of me," I said. "A little of me goes a long way."

"Why do you *talk* like that?" She caressed the side of my face, from near my stitches to the jut of my chin. I gasped. I had to close my eyes for a moment. When I opened my eyes, she said, "Do you want to kiss me? On the lips?"

"I've never done that before," I said nervously, apologizing in advance. "Maybe I'll be no good at it."

"I haven't kissed a boy before," she said. "So neither one of us will know the difference."

We slowly leaned over toward each other until our lips met and we softly kissed. Did we kiss for ten seconds, or ten minutes? I do not know. I do know that every cell in my body vibrated and that my head filled with helium.

Afterward, we sat gazing into each other's eyes.

I'm in my thirties, and I can't recall a more perfect moment in my life. I'm lucky to have this moment. I pull it out of the scrapbook of my memories and hold it up. It remains perfect.

But like all moments, it quickly passed. Steve came slamming in through the front door. "What are you two up to?" he asked. "You're not trying anything with her, are you? Who am I kidding? Bet you can't even get it up yet!"

He was wrong about that. It was up.

Steve ambled through the foyer into the den. "Hey, Mom. Looks like Brandy is making up with little man out there. You better go keep an eye on 'em!"

Brandy sighed.

"You want to come over to our house and see the puppies? Last chance. My parents are selling them."

"I have Bruce Lee to keep me company here. He gets upset if he smells the puppies on me."

"Okay," I said, looking down at my hands, my shoes. "I'll ride the bus tomorrow. Will you sit with me?"

"Of *course* I'll sit with you. You ask the silliest questions."

Sissy and Mrs. Bondurant appeared on the foyer. Brandy and I stood up.

Luckily, my little boy erection had ebbed enough that my board shorts hid it.

"Look at you standing over there with your pretty face and me daughter's lipstick all over your wee mouth. If you weren't so harmless, I might be worried."

"We're going," Sissy said. "I'll do my best to keep him in line. He can be a handful at times."

"Surely you'll be coming back to watch *Hope Hospital* with me some afternoon. We'll have a proper visit, to be sure," Mrs. Bondurant said.

"Absolutely, Fiona. Be seeing you." Sissy and I left the house together. I turned around and saw Brandy blow me a kiss. "You're supposed to catch it."

"Oops." I pretended to catch it.

"Don't drop it," Sissy said. About halfway home, she said, "First kiss, eh? What was it like?"

"I nearly passed out," I said.

"You would nearly pass out, wouldn't you?" Sissy said, not cruelly. "Did she put her tongue in your mouth?"

"Ew! No!"

"Because that's called a French kiss. You'd expect a French girl to French kiss. I'll have to discuss this with her."

"Don't discuss this with her!"

"She's going to have to know how to take care of you while I'm not around. Maybe I should write it all down into a handbook. You'll do the illustrations since I can't draw."

"I'm not doing illustrations for some handbook on me."

"Fine. But you'll only have yourself to blame when you're drawn as a stick man."

We got home just as the breeder lady arrived in a stinking jalopy of a van. The wheel wells were eaten through with rust and gray and orange primer coated most of the outside. We couldn't tell whether it was a Ford or a GM. The breeder had come for her payment, which was the one male puppy of the litter. He was the only dog with a name that didn't come directly out of the 1930's—Harry. I'd named the puppy after Harry Crews, the great Florida writer whose book, *Feast of Snakes*, I'd found in the "What's New" section of the Gulf Gate Library. "You're a little young for this," the library lady told me. This was the same woman who'd recommended that Sissy read Stephen King's *Carrie*.

Mom had named the rest of the puppies—Mildred, Gertrude and Myrtle.

The breeder had on a stained dress and was wearing filthy Keds. She had an unlit cigarette jutting from the side of her mouth. Her hair was wilder than mine and dyed neon red with black and gray roots.

"Mom doesn't like smoking," I told her.

She plucked the cigarette out and put it in her pocket. "Y'all got the little sire ready?"

"Yes," Sissy said. "Mom's at work, but Dad is here. Let me go in and tell him you're here." Sissy went inside.

Buster was gaunt, ashen and thoroughly addicted to pills. But he was able to walk, slowly, around the block as part of his recovery. One or both of us would accompany him on these walks. My father on pills was a much different person. He was almost nice. He only wore threadbare boxer shorts and a v-neck t-shirt around the house. Sissy would make sure that he put on some pants and maybe some sort of button-down shirt. Shoes.

Looking at the breeder, I wondered why he would make any effort.

We stood uneasily outside together.

"You just get kissed, little boy?" she asked with a smirk in her voice.

"Yes. I kissed my girlfriend," I said defensively. "She's the most beautiful girl on earth. Someday we're going to get married and have two kids, a boy and a girl. No one will ever hit them or take them for granted. We'll live in New York City. She'll be a record producer and I'll be the guy who draws all the album covers." Sometimes, I had no idea what I was going to say before I said it. Words tumbled out of me out of their own volition. Before Christmas break, coming out of our classroom in the temporary building, I shouted over to Reginald Hightower, "I'm Marathon John and you're Quick Claude!" It was a line from a candy bar commercial that had somehow embedded itself in my psyche and then leapt out of my mouth for no real reason. Reginald gave me the oddest look and said, "You crazy."

"Guess you have your life all planned out," the breeder said, and she laughed for a moment, which caused her to cough spastically and then spit on our driveway.

Sissy called out to us from the front door to come in, that everything was ready.

I opened the door for the breeder and she went in ahead of me.

Buster was standing in the kitchen, dressed in a wide-collared paisley shirt and plaid sans-a-belt slacks. He had on his white dress loafers. He'd shaved today and had combed his wavy steel-gray hair. He looked less like Harry Belafonte and more like Rock Hudson in *McMillan and Wife*. His eyes betrayed his drug-addled state, along with his goofy, good-natured smile.

Three of the puppies were dashing around in circles in the den, yapping and playing with each other, while Gretchen and Myrtle sat glaring at them, like a pair of scolds.

Myrtle was the last puppy born—the one who'd hit her head on the floor while still attached by umbilical cord to Gretchen. She was the idiot of the bunch, the one that we wanted most to sell. We wanted to keep Gertrude, who was the runt of the litter, but clearly the smartest of all the puppies. She sprinted up and caught Harry, knocking him over. The two of them wrestled around on the carpet while Mildred leapt around the two of them yapping. Myrtle and Gretchen snorted out their contempt. Myrtle shivered and blinked. One of her eyes was a bit bulgy due to some sort of illness. The pregnancy and birth had only served to make Gretchen more neurotic. She spent most of her time behind the couch, only emerging for meals or baths with tar shampoo, which was meant to help with her skin problems. The skin problems kept getting worse and worse. The vet had no answers.

229

The breeder walked over to Gretchen, who growled and then trotted away. She went behind the couch and Myrtle followed. "I've seen that kind of skin problem before," the breeder said. "You should give her brewer's yeast. You can buy it at a health food store as tablets. It'll clear that bad skin right up."

"Good to know," Buster said woozily. He clucked his tongue.

"Anyhow, I'll take this little guy and be on my way," the breeder said. She was faster than I expected her to be. She snatched up Harry and he tried to take a piece out of her with his sharp puppy teeth. But she was used to dogs hating her and didn't seem to mind or care that Harry was trying to get away, squirming and snapping. "Why fight me?" she asked the dog, holding him up to her face as he growled and struggled. "You're gonna have a great life. Most men would give anything to have a life like yours. All you'll ever have to do is have sex and eat."

"That does sound pretty good," Buster said. "How does that sound to you, Buzz?"

"Okay, I guess," I said.

"It's better than okay," Buster said peevishly.

"I'll be on my way," the breeder said. She hugged poor Harry to her chest and walked toward the front door. Harry stopped struggling as I opened the front door for the breeder. He made the saddest sound I'd ever heard, howling like a tiny wolf. He realized what was happening. "Born to screw! I've lived my life in vain," the breeder sang, to the tune of the Ray Charles song, "Born to Lose."

I shut the door. We listened as the van door opened and closed. The van's engine revved and off it went. Harry was gone.

"It's okay," Buster said to me, when I came back into the den. "Stop crying. That's the luckiest dog in the world." He tried to be angry, but the drugs wouldn't let the rage come out. "I'm dressed, so we might as well take a walk."

I wiped the tears away with the heels of my hands and wiped my hands on my shorts. "Are you coming?" I asked Sissy.

"I'm going to play with the puppies for a while," Sissy said sadly. "Poor Harry. That place is dog hell on earth. We're still going to keep one, aren't we?"

"Unless I get an offer I can't refuse," Buster said. He toddled toward the front door. I followed behind him. Outside, Buster asked, "Left or right today?"

"Right," I said. If we went that way, when we passed by the Bondurants' house, I could see Brandy's back window, and maybe she'd be looking out the window and we'd get to see each other for a moment.

"Right it is then," Buster said, handing me the handkerchief out of his back pocket. "Wipe that lipstick off, kid."

I wiped my face and then stared at the red lipstick on display in the tattered white hanky. I tried to hand it back to Buster. "Here," I said.

"Keep it," he said. "I got plenty."

We walked past the house next door and then around our first corner, heading toward the next corner, which was Captain Slidell's widow's house.

"First kiss today? Or have you and whatshername been making out already and you haven't told your old man about it?"

"Brandy," I said. "First kiss. It was glorious."

"Attaboy." Buster mussed my hair proudly. "Don't go knocking her up or nothing."

"Knocking her up," I repeated. I wasn't sure how the process worked for that yet. We were supposed to get a lecture from a nurse at some point during sixth grade, and we did, but she skipped the part about actual sex. We were informed about the mechanisms in our own bodies—the girls in one classroom and the boys in another. I did finally learn what an erection was. I loudly went, "Oh! That's what that is!" when the nurse described it, smacking myself in the forehead with the palm of my hand. It got a huge laugh.

"First time I was with a girl, I couldn't complete the act," Buster said, dreamily recalling some girl from the 1940's. "She was a neighborhood girl who would do the dirty with you for food or money. I never had money, but I gave her a lard sandwich my mother made for me. You know what a lard sandwich is?"

"No."

"It's made with white bread, a scoop of lard and powdered sugar. Lard and powdered sugar taste just like the inside of a Hydrox cookie."

"What's a Hydrox?"

"It's like an Oreo, but better. Anyway, I had this lard sandwich and I gave it to her. She pulled up her dress and pulled down her panties and we did it in her old man's basement while he was upstairs listening to the Indians game. He kept cheering and I thought he was cheering me on while I was humping his daughter. Pretty funny. I can talk to you like this because you're getting older. You'll be a man soon. You like girls, right?"

"I like Brandy. She's beautiful."

"She's weird. Weird girls are okay, but, take it from me, you don't want to marry one." Was he talking about Mom? I didn't want to ask. "I'm a man of the world, Buzz. You can ask me anything about sex and I'll tell you about it. Ask anything."

"How do you knock a girl up?"

"Jesus! I thought you took that class already."

"The nurse told us about erections." I felt embarrassed now discussing this with my father. I wished he hadn't seen the lipstick on my face.

"Southerners. What do you expect? They lost the Civil War and haven't stopped bitching about it ever since. So now they won't tell you little Yankee kids how to have sex." We'd walked past the widow's house and were nearly to the far corner. We were halfway through the walk. We

231

came around the corner and I could see the Bondurants' house, but not Brandy's window yet. "So I guess it's up to me to tell you, huh? You get hard and you jam it into a slot in the front of her body. The whatchamacallit. The vagina. That's it. It feels great. Big mystery, right?"

So that's what Gretchen had done with her grandfather. I watched it, but didn't see. "Thanks," I said.

"Don't tell your mother that little story I told you," he advised me. "She thought I was a virgin before we got married." He chuckled.

We got close to the Bondurants' house and I stared at Brandy's window. The shade was pulled down. I sighed thinking about our kiss.

"That's their house, right?" Buster asked. "I've only met that Irish lady. The mother. She's a looker, that mother. Nice legs. Nice hooters, too." He licked his lips hungrily recalling Brandy's mother. "I haven't met the father. Is he home? Maybe we should stop and say 'hi.'" He'd met the father a number of times. They were on a first name basis with each other.

"No!" I said a little too loudly.

"You embarrassed to have your old man come over and say 'hi' to your girlfriend's family?"

I was exactly that. "No. I mean… Mrs. Bondurant and Brandy. And Steve. They were… getting ready. To go somewhere. Yes. They were getting ready to go somewhere."

"Oh," Buster said. "Okay. Never mind then."

I changed the subject, which Buster's drug-addled brain allowed me to do. "Are you gonna get your job back selling paper?"

"Nah. That ship has sailed. When we get the settlement, I'll figure out what to do. Maybe I can get my job at Goodyear back. We could move back to Ohio."

"No!" I shouted.

"Calm down. I didn't say we were gonna move. It's just a thought. Hey, I ever tell you about the time I saw my dad in a movie at work?"

"No," I said, my heart racing at the thought of leaving Florida and Brandy behind. "A movie at work?"

"It was when I was working for Goodyear. Late '50's, I think. It was right after me and your mother got married, when we thought we couldn't have kids. Anyways, I worked in the lab at Goodyear. I was an assistant to these engineers. They needed something mixed up, I'd go get the ingredients. Easy. But we had to take these courses that were boring. This one course was about making tires that wouldn't get waterlogged. I didn't know that was a problem. They're made out of rubber, right? So I'm sitting in this classroom and they're showing movies about cars being pulled out of the water. Lo and behold, one of the cars being pulled out of the water was the one my dad died in! You know how he died, right? He'd take a few days off work at Ford and would tie one on. My mother had died of a brain tumor the year before and my dad was having a hard time with it, so he was drinking more and more. He's driving his car on the road around Lake Erie. The cop said he was reaching for a beer and drove the car off the cliff. Bang! Right into the water. He gets knocked out and drowns. A couple years later, I'm seeing him again... in a movie! What a kick in the pants."

"Did you say anything?"

"I said, 'Hey, that's my dad!' Then one of the engineers pulls me out of the room and tells me that I can take the rest of the day off."

"You should have sued them," I said. We arrived at our house.

Buster stopped and stood there looking at me. "Sued them?"

"For pain and suffering," I said. I'd spent enough time watching TV to know that pain and suffering was a legal monetary thing.

"Do you think I could sue them now?"

"Probably not," I said authoritatively. "I'm not an attorney, but I watch them on TV."

"What?" he went.

"It's been too long since it happened. I mean, the '50's were a long time ago."

"I guess," Buster said. He put his hands on his hips and winced. "My back hurts. I think I'm going to take a pill and go to sleep. Your mother won't be home til late. You kids'll have to figure out dinner on your own."

"Got it."

"It's too bad you weren't around back then to tell me that. Damn it. I wonder what I could have gotten out of those jerks."

"I don't know."

Buster cheered up a bit. "Anyways, let's go inside. Don't play the stereo too loud while I'm sleeping."

"We won't."

My father and I haven't spoken in years. He's with his third wife somewhere in Florida—Lakeland, I think. When I was first married, he'd leave messages on my answering machine and my wife would delete them before I came home from work. She finally told me about it after it had been going on for months. "Don't delete the next one," I told her. "I want to hear it."

"I'm pretty sure you don't," she said, shaking her head. "But okay. I'll leave it for you next time."

I came home from work a few days after that and she was sitting in our dusty den waiting for me next to the answering machine. She pushed a button and my father's enraged voice came pouring out of it. He accused me of not being a man. He said that if my wife and I had kids, he would sue for the right to see them. He said that my mother had turned me against him and he railed against her, saying that he'd heard she had cancer. "Good! She deserves it!" And then he blamed her for the financial shape we were in back in the 1970's. "She was spending us out of house and home!" The phone eventually beeped, cutting him off in mid-sentence. I walked over to the answering machine and pushed the delete button.

"How many calls do we get like that?" I asked.

"Too many," my wife said. "I'm sorry that you had to hear that. I'm sorry that *I* had to hear that. I usually delete them once I recognize your father's voice."

"It's okay," I said numbly. "It's fine."

"It's not fine. You don't have to be so stoic all the time. You can cry if you want. You can yell. You can show some emotion."

"I'm fine. Everything's fine. If you can keep deleting those messages, I'd appreciate it."

"Okay," she said, warily. "I'm your wife. You can talk to me if you need to."

"What's there to talk about? I'm hungry. Let's go grab dinner. Where do you want to go?" She liked to eat out, and I liked to take her out. I liked watching her enjoy food that other people made for her. I wanted her to be happy, but we were both desperately unhappy people. It was never going to work out between us, but we pretended that it would. I thought that if we pretended long enough, ours would become real happiness.

Sparky came home too late that evening to make us dinner, so Sissy and I made each other sandwiches. Sissy made me a peanut butter, grape jelly and Fritos sandwich. I made her a radish, scallion and lettuce sandwich, held together with mayo. We each knew what the other liked and it was nice having someone make you something.

That evening, I leapt out the window of my room, dressed in my Sunday clothes. I'd shined my dress shoes and put on my clip-on bow tie. I walked through all the backyards, which were eerily lit by porch and pool lights. No one saw me. I picked flowers and made a bouquet of them.

Brandy's light was on, her shade drawn. Her window was cracked open to let fresh air in. In this dry season, the breeze was cool enough that we didn't need to air condition it.

"Michelle, my belle. *Sont des mot qui vont tres bien ensemble... tres bien ensemble!*" I sang. "I love you, I love you, I love you! That's all I want to say."

The shade went up halfway and she peeked out at me. She let me finish the song. She cranked the window open a little wider and I placed the flowers on the outside sill. "Don't look at me," she said. "I took off my makeup half an hour ago."

"You're beautiful," I said.

"Stop it. Oh, and you brought such *pretty* flowers. Where'd you get them?"

"Don't ask."

She popped the screen off the window and took the flowers inside. "I'll have to put them in water. Do you want to come in?"

"Yes, but I shouldn't. I don't want you to do anything you'd regret."

"I don't regret anything I do! Why should I?"

I heard their back sliding glass door open. "I have to run away now," I said, before sprinting off into the neighbor's yard and ducking behind a hydrangea bush.

"Goodbye!" I heard Brandy shout.

"Who was that?" her mother demanded, standing outside her window. "Was it that sneaky wee Pepper?"

"Mother!"

"Twas him," she concluded. "You can do so much better. You're so pretty and he's a dull thing. I won't tell ya to stay away from him. I'll not make this forbidden love. He'll show his true colors soon enough. They always do, his sort."

I waited until Mrs. Bondurant went inside and then peered through the bush at Brandy. She sat patiently waiting for me to come back. I wanted to go back, but her mother's words had cut deep into my heart. Eventually, Brandy pulled down her shade and turned off the light.

King Neptune's Frolic

Mrs. Simmons was telling us all about the plots being perpetrated by the Trilateral Commission when the intercom went off. "Joseph Pepper. Come to the principal's office."

"Oooh!" the class went all at once.

"You're in trouble!" Billy said. "What did you do?"

"I don't know." I hadn't ridden my bicycle that day, so I couldn't try to escape. The walk home was too long.

Mrs. Simmons smiled knowingly at me. "You're not in trouble," she said authoritatively. "You've been summoned for other reasons."

"Okay," I said, standing up.

Mrs. Simmons gave me a hall pass. I navigated my way via outdoor sidewalks to Miss May's office. I sat on an orange molded plastic chair with aluminum legs and flipped through a copy of *Highlights for Children*.

Eventually, Miss May's door opened. She and another woman emerged, laughing. The woman, who was dressed like a stewardess from one of those National Airlines "Fly Me" commercials, asked me to come with her to another room.

There was a box on the table, a notebook and some sort of form that she would fill out on a clipboard. She pulled puzzles out of the box and asked me to put them together while she timed me with the stop watch. She asked me questions about ordinary things: What's the average human body temperature? What's the capital of Texas? Who is the Secretary of State? I did a passable impression of Henry Kissinger for her. She had me read words off of a card. I saw "aborigine" at the bottom of the card. It's a fun word to say, so I said it three times. She had me do speed math while she timed me. That wasn't fun. I don't like math.

We got to the end and she asked me why I fell asleep in class so often. I told her it was because I had problems sleeping at night.

"So you're not bored?" she asked me.

"Bored by what?"

"School."

"Why would I be bored?"

"Because it's not challenging enough for you."

"It's fine," I said, squinting at her. "Are you going to send me back a grade? Is that what this is all about?" I'd seen this happen to other sleepy students. My grades were good enough. I was a B+ student.

"Lord, no," she said, crossing and then uncrossing her legs. Her pantyhose matched her bright red minidress, which matched her knee-high boots. Her blonde hair was clipped short, almost like a boy's cut. She told me my IQ.

"Does that mean that I'm dumb?"

"No, sweetheart. You're not dumb."

"Because I'm pretty dumb."

"You're not dumb. Good Lord! You have potential. Have you thought about what you want to be when you grow up?"

"I want to be a cartoonist. Or maybe draw album covers."

"But that would be a waste."

"A waste? Of what?"

"Your potential."

"I don't want potential. I want to draw."

"Your teacher, Mrs. Simmons, told me that you read *The Sound and the Fury*. And that you made a diorama of Quentin Compson drowning himself." The toothpick bridge was the hardest part of that diorama. I made the Charles River out of globs of indigo and titanium white acrylic paint.

"Sure, but I didn't like the book. My brother made me read it."

She flipped through the notebook and wrote in it with a ballpoint pen. "Why'd your brother make you read it?"

"He said I needed to stretch myself."

"Did you feel like you were stretching yourself?"

"Can I go now?"

"No. I want you to answer my questions."

"About some book I read with some sad people in it?"

"Why do you think they were sad?"

"Because I got to read their minds. So I knew they were sad."

"Are you sad like that? Like Quentin Compson?"

I immediately knew that something was up. Something dire. They *knew*. And if they knew, then my father would know and he would beat me within an inch my life.

How dare they.

I was enraged. I got up from my chair and swiped my arm across the table, flinging the puzzle pieces and stop watch around the room. I grabbed the notebook from her hands and tore the offending page out and ripped it in half. I flung the notebook across the table like a Frisbee. I ran to the door and tried to get out, but the door was locked. "Let me out!" I shouted, beating on it with my fists. "Let me out!" I was angry and

237

crying. I pulled on the doorknob, but I couldn't escape. My hands, or the doorknob, were slippery. I had to get away. I had to run off to somewhere far away. I didn't know where that would be.

The woman, a psychiatrist who worked part-time for the school board I later found out, came over to me and took me by the shoulders. She bent over and gave me a little shake and stared into my eyes, not unkindly. "Take a deep breath and hold it," she commanded, her face inches away from mine. I could see lipstick on her teeth. Her breath was scented with spearmint Tic Tacs.

I took a deep breath. A moment later, I gasped it out. "Let me go," I muttered, shaking my shoulders.

"Take another breath," she said.

I blinked the tears out of my eyes and took another breath. This one, I held a bit longer. It escaped from my chest raggedly. "Please let me go."

"What happened to you?" she asked me in a soft voice. "Did someone hurt you? Is someone beating you at home?"

"Please. I want to go."

"You can tell me about it. It's okay. You have potential. You can be so much more than someone who draws album covers."

I shrugged my way out of her grasp. "You can keep your potential. I don't want it."

"It's inside you. I didn't put it there. You could be an engineer or a scientist."

"Why would I want to do that?"

"To help humanity."

"I'm 12. I'm a dumb kid. I'm useless. Everyone tells me so. I can't help anyone."

She ran her fingers through my hair. "Anyone can see that you have potential. Your teacher was right to call us." She went over to her purse and found a package of Kleenex in it. She had me sit back down and she wiped my face. She held another Kleenex under my nose and had me blow. She cooed at me like you would to an upset puppy. "Are you feeling a bit better? Are you calm now?"

"Yes," I said. "Am I in trouble?"

"You're not in trouble." She got up and went over to the door and unlocked it. She opened it for me. "You can go back to class now. Don't forget your hall pass." She picked it up off the floor and handed it to me.

I walked back to class feeling numb and exposed. There was a secret that I was supposed to keep. I hadn't kept it. Why was I so transparent? I had the dread feeling that when I got home, Buster would be waiting for me with fists the size of hams.

"Potential." I didn't like the sound of it.

What did I end up doing with all my potential? I draw clip art in a tiny studio in downtown Sarasota. There are five of us in this studio, turning out drawings of golfers, doctors, nurses, clowns. What have you. I come home to an empty apartment and stare at the TV set. I drink. I'm not what I was cracked up to be.

I arrived back at the classroom in time to line up to go to lunch. I stood with the poor kids, all of us with red tickets clutched in our hands. The rich kids had blue tickets. Their lunch line was shorter. Their food was supposed to be the same as ours, but it was served from different trays.

I sat with Billy and Reginald. I poked at my pig in a a blanket. There was a serving of baked beans that was mostly brown sauce, a cube of pork fat resting in the corner.

"Are you okay?" Billy asked me.

"I was about to say," Reginald said.

"I'm fine," I said glumly. The scent of the food and the steam coming from the industrial dish machine was giving me a headache and a stomachache. "Where's Brandy?" I asked, looking up from my plate. I felt a bit of panic surging through me.

"Are you going to eat that?" Billy asked.

"What did they do to you at the principal's office?" Reginald asked.

"Tests," I said. "They did tests." And then I lied. "They wanted to send me back a grade because I'm so dumb. But I think the tests kept me with you guys."

"That's good." Billy picked up my pig in a blanket and ate it in two bites.

Reginald scooped up my beans and ate those. They both knew me well enough that they could tell when I couldn't eat that day. Wasting food is a sin.

I took my empty tray over to the dish machine operator and he took it from me.

I sat down next to Brandy. "There you are," she said. "What happened to you in there?"

"There was this lady." I shook my head, becoming upset with myself. I shouldn't have acted out. There would be repercussions.

"Wait. Did she wear clothes that were all the same color?"

"Yes."

"That's the school psychiatrist. What did she want with you? Was it about your diorama? The one with the boy committing suicide on it?" Brandy was good at guessing things. She was tons smarter than me.

"Yes."

"Did she tell you about how you could talk to her?"

"How did you know?"

"Because I've been talking to her."

"You have?"

"Yes. It makes me feel better."

239

"Talking?"

"Yes. Plus, they're giving me some medication so I don't feel as sad."

"Why did they call you in?"

"It was the black clothes, I think. They gave me an IQ test. You're sad, too. You can't deny it to me, because I know you."

"Yes. You know me."

"You can talk to me if you want to."

"I always want to."

She whispered in my ear, "And you can kiss me again, if you want to." We sat looking into each others' eyes. "You've been crying again."

"She tricked me into crying. She tricked me into being angry."

"Doctor Evelyn is nice. I'm sorry she tricked you."

"It's okay, I guess. I'm fine now."

"Every time you say you're fine, you're not."

"Are you going to King Neptune's Frolic on Saturday?"

"You changed the subject. That means you're not fine."

"Will you go with me?"

"I'll go with you, but only if you'll talk to me. We'll go sit by the neighborhood pond today and talk. Okay?" She whispered, "I'll give you a kiss."

"Okay."

"And, yes, I'm going to King Neptune's Frolic with my family. I'll ditch them. Where do you want to meet?"

"The Sarasota Opera House. Front door. Around noon?"

"It's a date."

Back in class, Mrs. Simmons explained how the mafia got together with Fidel Castro and the CIA to assassinate President Kennedy. She also said that Bob Dylan didn't write "Blowin' in the Wind," that it was actually a high school student in New Jersey. Also, Paul McCartney died in a car crash in 1966 and was replaced by a double. She held up the album *Abbey Road* for us to see that Paul was dead, John was the preacher, Ringo was the mourner and George was the gravedigger. It was all as plain as the noses on our faces. At some point, we got around to math, so she could explain to us that "New Math" was a conspiracy led by the Rockefeller Foundation. Also, the Rockefellers were going to force us, within the next ten years, to have our identities placed on a chip implanted in a box that we'd have to carry wherever we went, and then the Rockefellers would be able to track us and charge us money. "Sheep to the slaughter," Mrs. Simmons said, as the bell rang. "All of us."

Brandy and I got on the bus together and sat near the back. The bus driver caught my eye and winked at me. I couldn't suppress a smile.

I walked her home from the bus stop. "Meet me back here in fifteen minutes," Brandy said. "I'll be outside waiting for you."

I put on my casual clothes and hurried out of the house, past a smiling Sissy. "It's about time you learned how to be a boyfriend," she said.

"Brandy told me about the flowers last week. And you sang to her, yet somehow her mirror is still intact."

I'd also gotten my stitches taken out, which lent me a bit more confidence. "We're going to go talk by the pond. I'll see you later." I ran out the door and down the street as quickly as I could.

She was standing out front wearing a gray houndstooth-patterned dress with a large white collar and shiny pearl buttons down the front, black knee-high stockings and shiny black shoes. She'd put on more lipstick and a pair of large sunglasses that obscured her eyes, eyebrows and cheekbones. She took my hand and we walked silently down to the neighborhood pond. We sat on a bench under a holly tree. Red berries littered the ground around us.

She took off the sunglasses and blinked at all the sunshine. "You can kiss me, if you want. I want to kiss you."

"Okay." I leaned in and closed my eyes.

Her lips alit upon mine softly. Her fingers caressed my ears. And then, for a moment, I felt the tip of her tongue poke between my lips and touch the tip of my tongue. I jerked away.

"Did I do that wrong?" Brandy asked.

"I'm sorry I pulled away," I said. "It was… too much."

"So I did it right," she concluded.

"You did it right."

She took both of my hands into hers. "Tell me what happened with Doctor Evelyn. You have to tell me."

"She made me angry. I threw all of her stupid puzzles on the floor and her dumb notebook."

"Why did you do that?"

"I don't know."

"She's nice. She's been very nice to me. I've been seeing her twice a week. I've talked about you to her."

"You have?"

"Nothing bad. Did you say 'puzzles' before? What else?"

"She asked me a bunch of questions like what you'd hear on a game show."

"She gave you an IQ test. Did she tell you your IQ afterward?"

"I don't remember what it was." I was afraid that my IQ would be too low and Brandy would know, with certainty, that I was a dope.

"Was it above 130?"

"Maybe," I said defensively. "You're going to know how stupid I am now. Can we not talk about it?"

"Just tell me. I'm dying to know. I'll tell you mine."

I told her.

"We have the same IQ. We're the same. I knew it."

"But you're smart. And I'm a dope."

241

"I'm sorry to inform you that a boy who reads James Joyce and William Faulkner in the sixth grade is *not* a dope."

"How did you know that I was reading *Dubliners*?"

"Guess."

"Darn it, Sissy." I shrugged. "I was just trying to understand your mother."

"Yes. She told me that, too." Brandy squeezed my hands. "I'm telling my mother how smart you are. Then she'll *have* to let you take me to the junior cotillion."

"Junior cotillion?"

"It's a dance that you're going to take me to. I've saved up my allowance. I'm going to dress you up like Paul McCartney and you're going to sing 'Michelle' to me again. You have the prettiest eyes of any boy in the world. You're smart and you're sad. I can't stop thinking about you all the time. Do you want to kiss me again?"

We sat kissing under the holly tree until it was time to go home.

I collapsed on my bed, dizzy and love drunk. Sissy came in my room and sat on the edge of the bed. "Your face is covered in red lipstick, monsieur. I believe you've been French kissing with a French girl."

"*Oui, oui,*" I replied.

"Your school called today. Dad talked to them."

I sat up in bed. "Is he in a bad mood?"

"No. He's mostly in a drugged-up mood. You know."

"So he's not mad?"

"Is there some reason why he should be mad?"

I told her about the psychiatrist and about throwing her things on the floor. "I didn't say that Dad beats me. I didn't say it."

"I don't think she told him anything like that. It's more like you should be going to Sparky's school and not Gulf Gate Elementary."

"I don't want to go to Sparky's school."

"Yeesh. No kidding. One of Sparky's classmates called up the other day. Some boy genius kid who's graduating from high school at 12 or something. He told me that I sounded like a swell 'carbon-based unit.' No thanks on Pine View."

"They give you an IQ test at Incarnation?"

"You mean with the little crap puzzles that are too easy to solve, the silly math problems and the lists of long words? Yeah. They tried to suggest to Mom that I should go to Pine View, but Mom said that I need to be in Catholic school so the nuns can keep a close eye on me. 'She's trouble!' she shouted at the nuns. Me? Little old me? Trouble? You're darn right I am. With a capital T!"

"How can I be smart if I dumb?"

"That's an easy one. You can read and write and do a little math. But you have as much sense as one of those puppies out there."

"Thanks."

"You asked."

Saturday rolled around. Mom was working downtown at Maas Brothers due to King Neptune's Frolic, an annual Sarasota festival, much of which is a parade of pleasure craft down Main Street and Bayshore Drive. Boaters put their boats up on their little trailers and dressed them up. Some old dude amongst them would be elected King Neptune. His wife or girlfriend would become Athena. Neptune, god of the sea, would be aboard his boat, which was decorated with shells and flowers. Athena was on another boat. Eventually, the two of them would get married while cheered on by Neptune's "mystic crew." Girls would be dressed up as sea nymphs, a detail that I was just beginning to appreciate.

Mom had to work at her old store because it was in the midst of all this celebratory hogwash. We rode along to work with her, promising that we wouldn't do anything to embarrass her and that we'd meet her at work after she got off.

"I mean it!" she shouted at Sissy. "No nonsense. I know you! I know what you're capable of! You're not fooling anybody."

"What's that supposed to mean?" Sissy asked as we got out of the Ford family truckster in the employee parking lot.

"You know exactly what I mean! If Buzz gets in trouble, I know who to blame."

I felt around in the pockets of my board shorts and found the roll of lawn-cutting money. It was nearly $20. Plenty of moola to get into trouble.

"Are we done here?" Sissy asked. "Because I have to make sure that Buzz pulls down his pants in front of Queen Athena on Bayshore Drive."

"I'm pulling down my—?"

"Shut up!" they both shouted at me.

Mom said, "No one's pulling down anyone's pants around here unless it's me blistering your rear end."

"It was a joke, clearly," Sissy said. "Let's get out of here."

"I swear to God!" Mom shouted after us. "If you embarrass me…"

We ran down Main Street, past revelers in various states of undress. A girl selling hot dogs wore only a string bikini, which left not much to the imagination. "Should we get a hot dog?"

"Aren't you supposed to be meeting somebody?" Sissy asked me.

We synchronized our Timex watches and wound them up. We agreed to meet at that spot in two hours. She held out her hand and I put ten dollars into it. "Where are you going?" I asked her.

"Wouldn't you like to know?" she said, and wandered off into the crowd. My sister was a girl of mystery.

I stopped and bought two ice cream sundaes from a cart. They came with two wooden spoons attached.

I made it to the Sarasota Opera House with a minute to spare. Brandy was waiting for me there. I handed her a sundae and a tiny wooden spoon. "Aw," she went.

We sat down on a bench and polished off the little sundaes quickly. We walked around downtown aimlessly, our hands intertwined.

She led me over to a men's and boys' clothing store. In the window was a narrow-lapeled suit that was not in fashion in the U.S. at the time. "This is what I want you to wear to the junior cotillion. You'll look rad in it."

"I like it," I said. Then I looked at the price. It was over $150. "I can't afford that."

"Don't worry. I'm going to buy it for you."

"That's a lot of money. That's too much money to waste on me."

"I have enough money. Don't worry about it."

"But it's a lot of money."

"I know you don't have any money. It's okay. Please let me buy this for you. I want the night to be perfect. I want us to have a perfect night."

"But I'm not perfect."

"You are to me. Come inside with me. They need to measure you."

"What? Wait. Why?"

"Because I already bought it."

I began to hyperventilate, standing there on Main Street as boats on trailers went past. I coughed. She reached over and took my ear lobe between her finger and thumb and gently rubbed it. I calmed down almost immediately. "How did you know to do that?" I asked her.

"Sissy's owner's manual," Brandy said, and laughed. "Come inside and get measured. It's already done."

So I went inside the little men's store with her. The tailor and salesman were waiting for us. "Is this the young gentleman in question?" the large man wearing a tiny vest asked.

They had me stand on a platform and measured me with a tape. They had me stand up straight, which I'm not good at. Eventually, I put on the suit, which was a size larger than I was. Brandy sat watching this all. "Oh, he looks perfect," she enthused.

After it was all over, we walked outside into the bright Florida sunshine. Brandy said that we'd be the most looked-at couple at the junior cotillion. She offered to cut my hair so that I would look like Paul McCartney circa 1965. "I'm good at cutting hair. I cut Steve's hair last week. He's going to bring me down here to pick up your suit next week."

"I don't know what to say. This is the nicest thing anyone's ever done for me. I don't know what I can do to make it up to you."

"Be my date at the junior cotillion, silly." She kissed me on the cheek and I blushed uncontrollably.

"Thank you so much. Thank you for the kiss on the cheek. Thank you for being so cool." I gushed on and on for a while.

"Stop crying," she said, taking a tissue out of her pocketbook. She wiped down my face, including the lipstick she'd left behind. "Aren't you supposed to be meeting Sissy? I have to go find my parents before they send out a search party."

"I don't know why you're being so nice to me. But thank you."

"Go find Sissy. I'll see you later." Brandy smiled and my heart... oh, my heart.

I found Sissy back where I'd left her. She had on a dozen necklaces made out of coquina shells and a gold plastic tiara that said, "Little Goddess Athena." "I'm very popular," Sissy said by way of an explanation.

"I see that."

"Did Brandy buy you that Beatle suit?"

"Did you know about it?"

"Of course I knew about it. Nothing gets past me."

"It was too expensive."

"Her family's loaded. She'll be fine. I can't wait to see you in that suit, Paul McCartney, Junior."

"Mom's going to be upset."

"About the suit, or about my royal appointment? Either way, I don't care." Sissy waved to the boats as they were towed past. "Hello, my subjects! Please, don't bow! Or scrape! Groveling is fine!"

Stomach Flu

"Do you have a real illness, or are you still complaining about dinner last night? Because if you are still complaining about dinner last night, you're going to school! Wouldn't you rather be in school anyway? Isn't your depressing little girlfriend there?" Mom rattled on for a while but I lost track of what she was saying.

"My stomach hurts," I said.

"You didn't eat your cereal. It's a sin to waste food."

Sissy reached over and felt my forehead. "He isn't faking it."

Mom placed her hand on my forehead. "You're burning up," she concluded. Then she put her hand on Sissy's forehead. "You're sick, too! You're both sick! Where's Sparky? Where's your brother?"

"He went to school already."

Mom had thickened the gravy with baking soda the night before, but that wasn't the problem. We'd contracted some sort of gastrointestinal problem from food we'd shared at King Neptune's Frolic. More than likely, it was the bikini girl's hot dog. We'd taken turns taking bites out of one, and now we were both in lousy shape.

"Your father is going to be in court today so he can't watch you. I guess I'll call in and we'll all have a relaxing day," Mom said.

"We're supposed to testify tomorrow." Sissy knuckled her eyes and faked up some tears. "Oh the pain! Oh the suffering!"

"Your father assured me that they'll settle out of court today."

"We'll be rich!" Sissy declared. "I'll finally get the life I deserve. Furs. Diamonds. Exotic pets."

"We'll be lucky to get back the money your father didn't make while he was lolling around in his bed." Mom clapped her hands. "All right. Go put your pajamas back on."

I made it most of the way to my bedroom when I felt the world slip out from under me. I awoke in a bathtub filled with ice water. I saw Mom cracking open a tray of ice cubes and dumping them down into the water around me. I shivered.

I closed my eyes and I was trudging through a mountain pass, high in the west. I'd never been to the west, but I'd see several movies that involved bearded trappers living lonely lives and being attacked by bears. I arrived at a cabin, swung open the door, and Brandy was there, stirring something in a black pot hung over a flame in a massive fireplace. But why did everything smell like oranges? She was wearing a girl's outfit from *Little House on the Prairie*. Her hair was done up in pigtails. She picked up a massive shotgun and shouted, "Duck!" I dropped to the ground and the shotgun exploded. I turned and saw the inevitable bear groaning and roaring, standing on his back feet with his paws raised high. I realized it was a man in a bear suit. "She shot me!" my father's muffled voice cried out. "Why did she shoot me?" He collapsed on top of me, his warm blood oozing through the pellet holes in the suit. I was trapped beneath him. I could smell his breath.

I awoke for real and my father was standing over my bed next to my mother. He was dressed in a powder blue polyester suit with a white belt and white shoes. The pattern on his tie was making me feel sicker.

"He's awake," Buster said.

"I can see that, but it doesn't mean he needs to go to court," Mom said. "He's too sick. Take Sissy. She's fine. She's been practicing."

"Bring them both tomorrow. A sick kid is gold." Buster licked his lips.

Mom's hair was bright orange, like Lucille Ball's. She was wearing her housecoat.

"Where am I?" I asked.

Buster knelt next to the bed. I was in my bed. Buster's eyes were wild. "So help me God, if you can't make it to court tomorrow…"

"Now you're threatening a sick child?" Mom asked.

"Shut up, Lola. This is our livelihood we're talking about."

"Livelihood? You could have gone back to Goodyear, you know. A real job. That's a livelihood."

"And be a wage slave all my life? No, thanks." Someone had promised Buster a million dollars a long time ago and hadn't delivered on the promise. Buster found that upsetting. He grabbed the front of my pajama top and pulled me over so that our noses were almost touching. "Tomorrow morning, you're gonna get up, put on some clothes and get in the car with your mother. You'll be in that courtroom at nine a.m. on the dot. You got that?"

"I'm fine," I said.

"I don't give a shit if you're on your deathbed. You'll be there."

"No problem."

"Because if you're not, I'm gonna blast ya so hard your mother's gonna feel it."

"Okay." I could feel my energy giving out and I drifted off into another fever dream.

247

I was in a helicopter over Vietnam. I was a soldier. I heard rifle rounds pinging off the sides and undercarriage of the helicopter. It was as cramped as a New York taxi. I'd never been to New York. I'd never been in a taxi. I'd seen movies and read books. I'd never been in Vietnam, but I watched the war on TV with everyone else in the country—Dan Rather and Morley Safer tromping around in safari jackets behind American soldiers. Vietnam was hot and humid, just like Florida. A round pierced through the helicopter and into my back between my shoulder blades. I was completely paralyzed now and couldn't even speak. I could only make groaning noises. I tasted blood in my mouth, salty and metallic.

I awoke in another ice bath, my mother saying, "I'm sorry, I'm sorry. Your father needs us in court. He took your sister with him this morning. Where's your brother? Where is he? It doesn't matter, because your father doesn't want him to testify. I'm sorry. I'm sorry." She dried me off with a rough towel stolen from a Holiday Inn. She wrapped me in a larger, softer bath towel and carried me to my room. "I can't believe that I can still carry you. My God, there's nothing to you, is there? I've failed as a mother. I've failed you. I'm sorry. I'm sorry."

"It's okay. I'm fine."

"How much do you weigh?"

"Sixty-two. I think."

"Doctor Spock says you should weigh 90 pounds by now. You have to eat. Why won't you eat?"

"My stomach hurts."

"I mean why won't you eat when you're not sick?"

"My stomach always hurts." I was afraid all the time, but I couldn't say that. I couldn't say that I lived in fear. That would be wrong, I thought. That would be admitting something.

Mom dressed me like I was a department store mannequin. She put on my underwear and socks. She put on a pair of plaid pants and a yellow mock turtleneck. She laced my dress shoes on my feet. "We should take you to the doctor when we're done with these court shenanigans. We should find out what's wrong with you."

"I don't want to go to the doctor."

"I wish your brother was around. He'd know what to do."

"I want to sleep."

"I know, honey. But we have to get you to court or your father will be upset."

"Can I sleep in the car?" I blinked and I was in the front seat of the car, my face mashed against the passenger side door. I blinked again and I was sitting on a hard wooden bench in a corridor, surrounded by adults.

A woman dressed all in yellow knelt next to me. "Do you remember me?" she asked.

"The doctor," I muttered. "Are you here to take me to an orphanage?"

248

She laughed. "No! Orphanages don't exist anymore." She felt my forehead. "You're burning up. Where are your parents?"

"They're here. Somewhere." I closed my eyes and discovered that I was in the car again. "Did I testify?"

"No," Mom said tersely. "No, your father settled out of court."

"Are we rich?"

"No, honey. We'll never be rich."

Sissy was leaning over the front seat. "Fifty grand," she said. "Fifty-thousand smackeroonies."

"It's not as much as you think it is," Mom said. "Plus, the TV lawyer, the suing machine guy, took a lot of it."

"How much does Dad make in a year?" Sissy asked.

"About nine-thousand dollars," Mom said. "Give or take."

"So that's five years' wages," Sissy said. "Not bad. Dad said he could have got more if we'd testified, but that doctor lady told on you."

"I didn't imagine her?"

"She really does look like a stewardess on a fancy airline," Sissy said. "I'm Doctor Evelyn. Fly me. She happened to be there to testify on another case. She got pretty angry with Dad. Dad told her that she should mind her own beeswax and shut her pie hole. Or something like that."

"Your father swore in a courtroom," Mom said dismally. "He almost got thrown in jail. Now we're going to have to put up with him tonight. I hope you're happy."

"I'm sorry," I said.

"I wasn't talking to you. I was talking to your sister. You didn't do anything wrong. I did. I shouldn't have brought you downtown. I should have stayed home with my sick child. I'm the one who should be sorry."

"Always the victim," Sissy said.

"Me or Mom?"

"You. Poor, sad Buzz. Always stepping in it."

Mom glared at her in the rearview mirror. "Shut it, Miss Tish. No one wants to hear your commentary."

"I present it free of charge," Sissy said. "Many would gladly pay to hear me speak. Fifty thousand dollars."

"Twenty-five thousand once it comes back from the attorney. And then there's Uncle Sam to pay," Mom said. "So it isn't as much as you think. Once we pay off all our overdue bills, there won't be all that much left."

"I'm sorry," I said.

Mom reached over and felt my forehead. "I think your fever finally broke. That's one good thing that happened today. Will you promise to eat something when we get home?"

"Okay." My stomach felt queasy, but it wasn't from stomach flu at that point. It was the same queasiness that dogged me throughout my childhood. It dogs me sporadically to this day.

I was riding my bicycle through downtown Sarasota a few days ago and thought I saw my father sitting in one of the outdoor bistros. It wasn't him, of course. Buster wouldn't be caught dead at any place that served out-of-the-ordinary food. I went back to my sad apartment, turned the knob on my window unit a/c all the way over to MAX, got into bed and put my pillow over my eyes. My heart raced. I didn't sleep or eat. The next morning, I called in sick to my little job, which I probably do far too often. I ended up drinking all day and woke up at three a.m. the following morning to find that I'd snapped several of my graphite sticks in half and threw them against the wall. My hands were black. When I went into the bathroom, I found that I'd painted my face with acrylics in the same manor that I'd been taught in basic training. I'd written on the bathroom mirror in loopy cursive with a permanent marker:

Late at night when you're sleeping
Buster comes a-creeping all around
Comes a-creeping all around.

It took a while to clean everything up, including my face. I ended up peeling the paint off my face, which had the effect of removing my facial hair, including my eyebrows. No one bothered to mention it to me at work. Instead, I had the usual conversations with my co-workers. They'd missed me, they told me. They told me their problems. I gave them advice. The sick feeling passed. Everything was fine again.

Buster arrived home in the middle of the night after we'd all gone to bed. He yanked the door to my bedroom open and hoisted me up over his shoulder like I was a sack of potatoes. He carried me outside and chucked me into our dewy, weed-choked lawn. "You know how much you cost this family?" he asked me in a loud voice. "But you couldn't help yourself, could you? You couldn't stop yourself from whining to some social worker, could you? You can sleep in the lawn tonight with the dog shit. I don't want you in my house. You ruin everything." He stomped over to the front door, threw it open and then slammed it shut behind himself. I heard the bolt clunk.

"You ruin everything." I took those words to heart. I understood them to be true. It was why I was never allowed to help, especially when I wanted to help.

I was afraid to move. The wet grass seeped through my threadbare pajamas. I didn't know what time it was, but it was late. It was hot and humid. Stars and planets sparkled in the sky. I heard the Florida fauna cycling through their chirps, croaks and bleats. We didn't have a neighborhood alligator anymore, but that didn't mean that other creatures weren't prowling around outside. I stayed there for maybe a minute, or maybe an hour. It was probably closer to five minutes.

Sparky emerged from the house and walked over to me. He helped me to my feet and brushed the grass from my back. He walked me back inside. I shook uncontrollably as we walked through the house. The dogs gurgled and snorted behind the couch. I went into my bedroom and shut the door.

I hid under my bed that night. I did not sleep.

In the morning, Mom came into my room and found me there. She coaxed me out. "Your father is in a better mood this morning. The attorney said that we can come down and get the check this afternoon. It's for a lot more money than we thought we'd get. Everything's fine now."

Mom really did have orange hair. Sissy walked in and said in a Cuban accent, "Lucy, you got some splainin' to do."

"Will you give it a rest?"

"You're supposed to say 'Wah! I want to sing with the band!'"

"I thought I'd dreamt your hair," I said.

"More like nightmared it," Sissy said.

"Look, we didn't have the money for me to go get my hair done, so I did it myself while you two were laid up. It didn't work out as well as it should have."

"I'll say," Sissy said.

"Your father seems to like it," Mom said.

"He would," Sparky said. He was taking the day off from school at our mother's invitation.

Now all of us but Buster were in the same room. We were essentially hiding from him, which he didn't like. He always interpreted moments like this as being a conspiracy against him. "Dad will get angry if he finds us all together like this," I said.

Mom immediately got up and left.

I crept out into the den and was relieved to find that Buster had vacated the premises. Sissy poured two bowls of Buc-Wheats and brought one to me. We sat on the floor watching TV and crunching down the maple-coated cereal. "I guess this is another sick day," I said.

"I guess," Sissy said. "What happened last night?"

"I don't want to talk about it."

"I heard—"

"*I don't want to talk about it.*"

"Calm down. We won't talk about it. Jeez."

I took a bath after Sparky was done in the shower. There was hardly any hot water left, so it ended up being a short and shallow bath. I shampooed my hair with Prell and rinsed it under the spigot. I looked at myself naked in the huge mirror. Mom was right. There was nothing to me.

Standing in front of the mirror now, I have the same experience. As an adult, my weight has rollercoastered between 140 and 200 pounds. I'm

251

either cramming as much food as possible into my belly or my stomach hurts so much that I can't eat. I'm always worried that something bad will happen. Or that I'll screw something up. On the rare occasions when those feelings go away, I eat.

I wrapped myself in a big towel and went to my room. I got dressed. There was a knock on the window, which startled me momentarily. I pulled up the shade and there was Brandy's face peering in at me. "Are you okay?" she asked through the glass. She stepped back as I cranked open the window.

"I'm better," I said. "How are you?"

"I'm better, too," she said. "How's your tummy?"

"It's okay." It gurgled as I said that. "I ate just now."

"I missed you," she said. "I wanted to see you."

"Shouldn't you be in school?"

"I asked my mother to call in sick for me so I could visit you."

"She did that?"

"Yes. She knows that I'm here."

"Why didn't you come to the front door?"

"I saw your father coming out of the house. I'm sorry, but I don't like him."

"That's okay."

"What are you doing today?"

"I don't know. I think we'll probably go out to supper tonight. Dad is going to go get a settlement check, so we'll have money again."

"That's good." She smiled and tilted her head to the side. "I like you. Do you like me?"

"I like you a lot."

"Anyway, I thought I'd walk down here and see you today because I miss you." Brandy backed away from the window. She was wearing an oversized bright red New York Dolls concert t-shirt as if it were a dress. She'd put on a thin black belt across the middle. Her hair was piled up prettily atop her head. "Bye." She ran away through the backyards.

I cranked the window shut.

My father was standing behind me. I froze. "That girlfriend of yours is a hot little number," he said, patting me on the shoulder. I said nothing. "Cat got your tongue? Never mind. I went out and bought some wood today. Your brother is working on putting together a bookcase for you, because you like books, don't you? I don't know why you buy so many books. Seems like a waste of all that lawn mowing money to me. You should go help your brother out. He's in the garage."

I walked around my father like you would an alligator you came upon sunning itself in the driveway. I went out to the garage and found my brother marking up pieces of wood with a number two pencil, preparing to saw them. "Please let me help."

He sighed. "Fine. When I tell you to hold onto a piece of wood while I'm sawing it or nailing it into place, you hold on."

I watched my brother bang together a solid bookcase out of seemingly random pieces of wood. He designed and built the bookcase himself. It was sturdy and heavy. We stood it up on sheets of newspaper and Sparky painted it with some old enamel paint he'd found.

We went inside for lunch and heard Buster and our mother having sexual relations in their bedroom. It was a set of sounds that we hadn't heard in a long time.

Sissy made us sandwiches and the three of us sat watching the midday news. Roy Leep and the Pulse Weather Team told us about a tropical depression that was making its way toward the Suncoast. "We're all gonna die!" Sissy said.

"Puh," Sparky went.

We turned off the TV and each retired to our own rooms. I fell into a dark, fitful sleep. I awoke with Buster shaking my foot. "Don't give me that look. Like I'm so scary. Your brother needs your help getting your bookcase to your room." I looked at the clock. It was three in the afternoon. I got up and followed Buster to the garage, where Sparky was attempting to lift the thing by himself. "I got you some help."

"I don't need his help," Sparky said. "I'll figure out how to get it there myself."

"Nah. He's gonna help you. Aren't you?"

"Yes," I said. "I want to help."

"He always wants to help," Buster said, chuckling a bit. He put on a whiny, lispy voice, "I wanna help! I wanna help!" He chuckled some more.

Buster stood to the side and watched as Sparky instructed me on where to hold the bookcase. The thing was heavy, more so for a 12-year-old who barely weighed over 60 pounds. I got on one end and Sparky got on the other. My hands were sweating from nerves over what would happen if I dropped it. The paint had made the wood slick, too. We lifted the bookcase and I immediately lost my grip, dropped it and it landed on Sparky's thumb. He grunted and shook the pain out. "You better make sure you don't drop it again," Buster said, leaning in to me. "I went to all the trouble to bring that wood home, so you'd better not ruin it."

We managed to make it all the way into the den before I felt myself losing my grip. My muscles were being taxed well beyond what they could reasonably do. My hands were sweating. "Can we set it down?" I asked.

"Yes." Sparky counted to three and we set it down.

Buster was right there with us, supervising. "You two gonna take all day?"

I shook my arms out and flexed my shaking hands. I knew that the moment that we picked it up again that I'd drop it and then the consequences would be dire.

We picked up the bookcase on three and I immediately dropped it. It wasn't on purpose. I sprinted to my room. "Dad's gonna hit me!" I shouted to Sissy, and she backed into her own room again. Buster followed me in and closed the door behind him. I saw the look in his eyes. He was enjoying himself. He was enjoying this. He cocked his fist, reared back and punched me in the guts. The wind shot out of my lungs. I doubled over in excruciating pain. "Go ahead and cry." He licked his lips. "Go ahead and cry like a baby."

I gasped for breath. I dropped to my knees holding my stomach. But I did not cry. My eyes did not fill with tears. Instead, I went ice cold inside. I gritted my teeth and glared up at him. I wouldn't give him the satisfaction. I wouldn't give him my tears. I wouldn't give him my fear. He would get nothing from me, no matter what he did.

In the years to come, I would give him something new. I would give him my rage. I would give him my hatred.

I still hate him. Mostly, I hate him for turning me into the sort of person who would hate him this much.

I climbed to my feet and stood before him, ready to take another punch, but the fun was over for him now. He left the room wordlessly.

I pulled up my shirt and saw the fist-sized bruise growing on my abdomen. So did Sissy, who stood looking at me from the doorway. So did Sparky, who'd placed the bookcase on the upside-down bathroom rug and was sliding it toward my room. I let the t-shirt drop and said, "I'm sorry, Sparky. I'm sorry I dropped it."

Sparky said, "*Fuck him.*" It was like a thunderclap hearing that word come out of his mouth. We didn't swear. We were good Catholics. "Where do you want this set up?" He didn't wait for me to tell him. He set it up in the spot where it was meant to go, and then he immediately started filling it with the books that were sprinkled around my room in piles, arranging the books on the shelves in alphabetical order. When it was full, he said, "Looks like you need about five more of these." He gave me a rare smile. "You're a good kid. Okay? Don't let him change you. I'm going to my room." He walked down the hall to his room and shut the door.

Sissy pulled up my t-shirt and whistled at the bruise, which was already turning black. She let the shirt down and gingerly hugged me. We stood hugging each other in my room for a while. Sissy cried this time and I did not.

That evening, flush with cash, we went to Demetrio's Pizza. Mom drank most of a bottle of red wine by herself. We all sat around pretending like nothing had happened. Buster flirted with the waitress and acted like a big wheel. I got salty black olives on one of the pizzas and ate the olives out of Sissy's side salad. Sissy made fun of Sparky chewing each bite of pizza 20 times before swallowing by counting out each chew and then intentionally counting some of them twice or skipping a number.

We were a happy and normal family out for a happy and normal family dinner and nothing whatsoever was wrong.

Junior Cotillion

Sissy and I took the dogs on a walk. Myrtle was nearly grown up, but something was wrong with her brain. Gretchen, post-pregnancy, had become grumpy. We didn't get Myrtle's ears clipped. It seemed cruel, though the breeder thought we were cruel for allowing her to keep her ears. Both dogs had horrible skin problems and each constantly chewed on her own ass. It didn't help that it was always muggy outside. We'd entered the rainy season again.

The Bicentennial was coming up. The country was ready to celebrate something instead of thinking about inflation all the time, or kicking ourselves for what we'd done or hadn't done in Vietnam. I saw a fake campaign button at the mall that said: NIXON... HE'S TANNED, RESTED AND READY! It was on a table with real campaign buttons for Governor Reagan, President Ford and "The Man of Tomorrow! Jerry Brown."

There was no draft anymore, so the Army had enticing TV commercials concerning the wonders of Army service. The ads burrowed deep into my soft, little brain. "Join the People Who've Joined the Army!" It looked like a fun summer camp. Some blonde-haired kid joined the Army and then his mother sent him brownies, which he shared with all his buddies.

When it looked like I was flunking out of college, I joined the Army, remembering those commercials and the Bill Murray flick *Stripes*.

Sparky was my college roommate, and he couldn't believe it when I got back from the Military Entrance Processing Station in Jacksonville, after riding the Greyhound bus back from an overnight stay there. "You? Joined the Army?"

Mom had the same reaction. "I didn't raise you to be a soldier."

The only one who didn't have that reaction was Sissy. "At least it gets you out of Florida." Then she sang the Bo Donaldson and the Heywoods song to me, "*Billy, keep your head low-oh-oh.*" She also added, "Hey, at least someone is going to pay you to draw."

The first thing our drill sergeant said to us after we arrived at our barracks was, "Only an idiot volunteers. And since this is an all-volunteer Army…" We all drew our own conclusion.

I was walking Myrtle and Sissy was walking Gretchen. Gretchen was the easy one. She had two goals during a walk. The first one was to get the walk over with as quickly and efficiently as possible. The second was to someday kill a duck. The neighborhood was lousy was muscovy ducks, possibly the ugliest and meanest ducks in existence. Gretchen wanted them dead. One of the few ways to excite Gretchen was to lean over and whisper, "Ducks!" and watch her lose her mind.

Myrtle followed Gretchen's lead, but I got the feeling that Myrtle didn't share Gretchen's animus toward the ugly ducks. She merely liked getting excited about something. Myrtle often barked at oversized mushrooms that would grow in our yard overnight, or palmetto bugs that invaded our house and buzzed and clunked up against the sliding glass door.

We passed by the Bondurant house, which was still and quiet, the cars all missing. It had been like that for a while. Brandy had assured me that her family was only going to be gone for a short while. They were taking a trip to Los Angeles. It had something to do with her father's job. She'd made an arrangement with Mrs. Simmons to take all of her exams early, so she was essentially finished with the sixth grade.

Mrs. Simmons had been giving me extra assignments. She asked me to stop erecting dioramas of the books I'd read and actually write out essays. I'm a visual person, so it took a lot of extra effort for me to write something versus drawing it out, or making some sort of art. My grandmother had given me her manual Olivetti typewriter, so I turned writing the essay into an artistic assignment, writing out my essay first on a page in a spiral notebook with *The Six Million Dollar Man* on the cover. Most of my notes inside were drawings that surrounded maybe a paragraph or two of actual text. I found a blank page and wrote out my thoughts about the book, a gothic thriller called, *The Cottage: A novel of terror!* that Sissy insisted that I read. Then I painstakingly typed out the essay onto some cream-colored stationery that I'd found in a paper sample case that Buster had left in the garage. I would learn how to touch-type in high school, but at that point, I was hunting and pecking. I found a manila envelope in that same sample case and drew a cottage with a dark spirit seeping eerily out of a chimney on it. I slipped the typed essay into the envelope and I handed it in.

Mrs. Simmons gave me a B+, my usual grade. "While I appreciate the creativity," she wrote on the third and final page of the essay, "you, once again, turned an essay into an art project." She placed an eagle-themed Bicentennial sticker next to her comments. I drew a cigar in the eagle's mouth. A wisp of smoke came from the cigar and down below, at the bottom of the page, I drew a pile of accumulated ashes.

We arrived at the neighborhood pond. Gretchen growled deep down in her throat. Sissy made her sit down. A group of muscovy ducks grumbled and snapped at each other near the little park bench underneath the holly tree. There were more and more of them now that we didn't have a neighborhood alligator.

I made Myrtle sit down, but she wasn't bright enough to remain seated. She kept forgetting that she was supposed to be sitting. I pushed her tender backside until her pink, rashy butt hit the grass. She growled along with Gretchen, peering around for what she was supposed to be growling at.

We took off their leashes and Sissy shouted. "Ducks!"

Gretchen tore off toward the ducks in a sprint. Myrtle watched her for a moment. Sissy poked her backside with the tip of her Birkenstock, and Myrtle flew off after her mother, barking crazily.

The ducks flew off seconds before Gretchen arrived. Myrtle slammed into Gretchen's backside and the two of them tumbled around. Gretchen gave Myrtle a nip to get her attention, and then the two of them barked at the ducks, who'd flown all the way to the other side of the neighborhood pond.

Captain Slidell's widow clapped from the shade of her garage. "Bravo!" she shouted. "Good dogs!" Then she said, "Don't forget to pick up after them."

We'd brought along plastic bags. We made our way over to Gretchen and Myrtle, who were both defecating at the same time. When they finished, we poop-scooped and secured the warm little presents in their respective bags. We released the dogs and walked over to Captain Slidell's widow's house and stood in her garage. She was dressed in an orange bikini, a pair of high-heeled open-toed shoes with cork soles and a wide-brimmed straw hat. She let us toss the poops in her trash can and then invited us and the dogs into her "palace of iniquity" for cocktails and cookies.

"I don't eat cookies myself," the widow said. "I keep them around for visitors… gentleman callers and the like." She ruffled my hair and commented on its softness. "Why do some boys get great hair and I'm stuck going to my hairdresser's every other week?" She tossed her hat on the kitchen counter and invited us to sit down on barstools.

"I don't know," I said.

"It's a question for the ages," Sissy said.

"Speaking of questions for the ages, have you read '*Salem's Lot* yet? I have the paperback over here if you want to borrow it," the widow said. She slid the book over to Sissy.

Sissy snatched it up. "*Carrie* was so great."

The dogs sat down in the kitchen, staring up at the scantily clad widow. "Who wants a treat?"

Myrtle made a weird, anxious growl. Gretchen sat upright and wiggled a bit to show off her superior sitting skills.

The widow handed each dog a cookie and they snapped them right out of her hands, running under her dining room table, trailing their leashes behind them, greedily gobbling down the cookies. "I hope *you* don't try to take off my fingers," she said, handing each of us a cookie. "These are sugar cookies. They're all I know how to make."

Sissy and I each took a luxurious bite, savoring the cookies. Gretchen and Myrtle magically appeared below us, seated. "You had yours!" Sissy yelled at them.

The widow made us each a liquor-free cocktail and placed them in drink glasses. She added a maraschino cherry to each. "Bottoms up!" She poured herself the same cocktail and then added a few ounces of clear rum to hers. We clinked glasses. "Cheers!" She looked around her house. "I owe the Navy a debt of gratitude. They certainly know how to treat a sad old widow."

"How old?" I asked.

Sissy and the widow gasped. "You never ask a lady her age," Sissy said.

"It's okay, I guess," the widow said. "I'm 35. I'll be 36 in another month. The good captain was shot down over Hanoi. He didn't have to fly anymore, but he was a leader of men. His parachute didn't open. He was a gentleman. He treated me with respect. After he died, I had to move out of base housing in Pensacola. I didn't want to leave Florida, so I moved down here. Now I get his pension along with the life insurance settlement. If I play my cards right, I'll never have to work again."

"You worked?" Sissy asked.

"You could call it that." She smiled. "Maybe when you're older, I'll talk about it. You're such sweet-faced kids."

We finished our cookies and the good widow shooed us out of the house. She had a gentleman caller coming over, she told us, and the yapping, nervous dogs might spoil the mood.

We walked the dogs back home and found the house blessedly empty. Sissy unlocked the door with the key hanging around her neck. We were still in our school clothes, so we went and changed.

Sissy decided that we would play, "Dare You to Drink It!" She pulled the blender out and made me go to my room. She clicked on the stereo to WKXY for some background noise. The Doobie Brothers were "Takin' It to the Streets." Jesus was mentioned.

I heard the blender going. The only rule to "Dare You to Drink It!" was that everything in the drink had to be edible. No soap. No dirt. The drink was served in an Archie jelly jar glass. My glass was labeled, "Jughead wins a pie-eating contest!" Sissy's was labeled, "Betty and

Veronica give a party." They had both once contained Welch's grape jelly.

We had to write down what was in the drink that we each prepared. In the case of a tiebreaker, we would have to attempt to name what was in the drink we each swallowed. It rarely came to that. I had a horrible gag reflex and Sissy knew exactly what would trigger it.

The blender really seemed to be struggling with Sissy's concoction. "Frozen Brussels' sprouts," I muttered. "That's mean."

"Ready!" she shouted. She'd already poured me a glass. "It's a little chunky, so don't try to drink it all at once."

"Chunky," I went. I steeled myself and chugged it. I slammed my glass down like a cowboy who'd just finished some rot gut at the local saloon. I grinned toothily at her. "Man, that was awful."

She washed out the blender and said, "All yours. Oh, and your teeth are green."

"Thanks," I said, and sucked on my incisors.

Sissy retired to her bedroom. I got to work. I found an open can of chocolate frosting. After eating two tablespoons, I added most of it to the mix. I added apple cider vinegar, olives, cherries and some capers. I wrote down all the ingredients. I hit the frappe button. "Victory shall be mine."

I called Sissy back out, poured it in front of her so she could see the delightful texture. She slugged it down, gagged, ran over to the sink and threw it up. She stuck her mouth under the spigot and gargled with the tap water. "Oh my God," she said at last. "That was horrible!"

"Thank you!" I couldn't remember the last time I'd won one of these games with Sissy. "I want to thank the Academy and my agent. Mom, dad... if you're somewhere out there in the audience, we did it! We finally won!"

"Don't get a swelled head." She snatched up the list. "Definitely tasted the frosting and the vinegar. I'm betting it was the capers that finished me." We shook hands. "Well played."

"You went back to the Brussels' sprouts one too many times. I was ready for it."

"Ah hah. I'll remember that."

We cleaned up and sat down on opposite ends of the sofa. We hung out and talked for a while. Sissy told me stories about her classmates at the Catholic school. I told her about Mrs. Simmons' essay assignments and my workarounds. Finally, we ended up talking about Brandy.

"You love her," Sissy said. "I'm not making fun of you this time. Just admit it." Sissy was the only person in our family who talked about love.

"I like her a lot," I said.

"Just say it. You'll be happier if you do. Say the word. Love."

"I think I should say it directly to her if it needs to be said."

"Okay," Sissy said.

We heard the garage door go up and the rumble of the Ford family truckster. We walked out into the garage in case Mom had gone to the store. She hadn't. She didn't look like she was in a good mood.

"I suppose I have to make dinner," Mom said. "I suppose you two have been doing nothing but hanging around since you came home and you didn't even do any homework or take the dogs out."

"We took the dogs out," I said.

"Why are your teeth green?"

"He's trying out a new type of health shake," Sissy said. "For his health."

"Uh huh. Likely story. I'm too tired to argue with you. You two are going to have to handle your own supper. I'm going to take a shower and take a nap. I have a headache." The dogs emerged from behind the couch and followed Mom into her bedroom. We saw them leap up onto the bed before Mom shut the bedroom door behind her.

"I feel like I already ate," I said.

"Not me. I vomited."

"Where's Sparky? Is he here?"

"Who knows?" Sissy shrugged. She went into the kitchen and dug through the pantry. She pulled out a bag of egg noodles. "I'm thinking of an all-white dinner."

She boiled up the noodles and I dug a cartoon of sour cream out. I found a stick of margarine in there, too. We ate the entire bag of noodles with healthy dollops of sour cream, cottage cheese and melted margarine. We shook black pepper over the whole mess.

Buster arrived home. He'd gotten a job with Royal Typewriters as a salesman. It was another job that required him to go out on the road for days a week, hawking typewriters to government offices, businesses, schools and the like. He lugged in the sample typewriter, which was in an enclosure the size of a suitcase. "I can't believe I have to carry this thing around with me all the time," he said, setting it down in the foyer and walking to where we sat in the kitchen. "What are you two eating? Plain noodles? I'll never understand you two. Don't you have any other friends? Why are you two always together?"

Sissy hugged him, which temporarily shut him up. "Who else am I supposed to hang out with?" she asked him. "Buzz is my best friend. You made him for me."

"I was born first," I said. "I don't know why I have to keep pointing that out."

"I made him for you? I guess I did, sweetheart." He looked around. "Where's your mother?"

"She had a headache," Sissy said.

He gazed off toward the bedroom. "Can you boil up a hot dog for me?"

"Sure." Sissy rinsed out the pan we'd used for the noodles and put some more water into it, then took it over to the stove.

Buster tiptoed into the bedroom and emerged wearing a v-neck t-shirt and boxer shorts.

I dug through one of the refrigerator drawers and pulled out the hot dogs. I tossed three in the pan. Then I got out three pieces of white bread and laid them on a plate. Next came the Cheez Whiz, which I spread across the white bread in sticky globs. I gave each piece of bread a thump of ketchup out of the bottom of the bottle and tossed the bottle into the trash. By the time I was done, the hot dogs had exploded in the boiling water. I dug them each out with a pair of tongs and served it up with a can of Red, White and Blue beer.

Buster took it all into the den and turned on the TV. Walter Cronkite was on. He argued with the most trusted man on TV for about a half-hour until it was time for *The $10,000 Pyramid*. We cleaned up the kitchen and snuck out of the room.

The next day, I saw Brandy walking toward me as I stood at the bus stop. She was dressed all in black. She usually didn't do that for school. I waved to her. She smiled wanly. Something was wrong.

We sat together on the bus, but she wasn't in a mood to talk. She only brightened when I mentioned the junior cotillion. "I have your suit," she told me. "We're going to have a perfect night together." She cried a bit.

"What's wrong? What's going on?"

"I'll tell you after the junior cotillion."

"Is someone dying?"

"No. It's nothing like that." She sniffled. She wouldn't let me comfort her. "We have to have a perfect night."

I looked around the bus and it seemed like everyone in sixth grade had paired off. We were all couples now. Billy was with a girl named Tammy, who was the shortest girl in the sixth grade. Despite their size difference, they seemed to be well matched.

The school year ended on a Friday. I said goodbye to Reginald. We performed our special handshake. We looked around to make sure no one was paying attention, and hugged. "See you at Brookside," he said.

"I hope so," I told him.

"I'm pretty sure I'm going there, but who knows? Do me a solid, Pep. If we don't see each other again, you try and remember me. Okay, my man?"

"Okay."

"Aw, come on, man. Don't go crying on me. I gotta boogie." Reginald climbed on board the bus to Newtown, and he was gone. Just like that.

The Sarasota County telephone directory for 1998 arrived on my doorstep the other day. Each year it gets heavier. I carried it inside my tiny apartment and set it down next to the phone. I had a few beers. The sketching was going poorly, and I tossed aside my pad and pencil. I took a couple of shots of Jack Daniels, picked up the directory. I looked up Bondurant. There were several of them. I stared at the names. "Bondurant, B." was one of them. "Bondurant, Stephen" was another. My index finger slid over to each phone number. I dog-eared the page. I closed the phone book. I drank for a while longer, quietly. I stared at the wall. The Clash's *London Calling* poured out of my defective old stereo. I flipped over the record and almost dropped it. I went back to the telephone directory and tore out the page I'd dog-eared and set it on fire in my kitchen sink. The only way I'd call the numbers was if I was rip-roaring drunk. I wouldn't have the nerve otherwise. And anything I said to Steve or Brandy in a drunken state wouldn't be what I actually wanted to say. I flipped through the directory and found several Hightowers, but none of them were "Hightower, R." What would I say to Reginald after all these years anyway? I laughed at myself. My mother had raised me to be unsentimental. I looked up to the ceiling and spoke to my dead mother. "Did you see that? Did you see me getting sentimental?"

The junior cotillion was on the Saturday after school ended at the Old Heidelberg Castle on US 301 in downtown Sarasota. The Old Heidelberg Castle was a mock-up of a fest tent in Munich, complete with an oompah band most nights, acrobats and tumblers, and waitresses dressed in dirndls. For the junior cotillion, all of that was stripped out of the place. It was emptied of the fest tables and all the Teutonic touches were gone.

Brandy's mother Fiona was our chaperone that evening. She was one of the chaperones for the event, too. She dressed to the nines for the occasion, as did Brandy, who was stunning in a long, black dress, her shining black hair pinned high on her head and pearls around her slim neck. She and I were approximately the same height most of the time, but she was wearing heels, which elevated her above me.

After school that Friday, Brandy invited me over to get my hair cut. She had a pair of kitchen shears and a pink plastic comb. I sat on a barstool in her empty garage while she snipped away at my overly long hair. I blushed over and over. When someone does something nice for me, I become very emotional. Also, she was so close to me in that garage. Her fingers slid through my hair and across my ears and forehead. I trembled a bit. I managed to keep it together. When she held up a hand mirror at the end to show me, I couldn't even take it from her, my hands shook so much. I thanked her over and over.

My suit was hanging from a nail on the wall. "I should make you try it on for me. You didn't even go to your final fitting," she said. "I guess I should have faith that it will fit you perfectly. I want tomorrow to be perfect."

"I do, too," I assured her, my voice shaking as much as my hands.

"You should go home now and try on the suit there. I'll see you here tomorrow, okay? Please don't be late."

"I won't be late."

I wasn't late. Her tipsy mother jangled the keys to the Mercedes in her hand. Brandy and I exchanged flowers. Brandy placed the boutonniere on my lapel. I tied a corsage of a single red rose with a black ribbon around her wrist. "I love it," she whispered. "You look like Paul McCartney."

The suit fit perfectly. In a few months, I'd give it away to Goodwill, having outgrown it after a sudden growth spurt and finding that staring at it wouldn't make Brandy come back, no matter how much I wanted that.

Should I skip to the end and tell you the horrible news? Or should I make you wait for it? I'll make you wait, but not for much longer.

At the venue, each of the girls was announced upon arrival. The junior cotillion was a coming-out party for girls. They were all wealthy kids. Debutants. I was announced as her escort for the evening.

We sat at a round table with a fancy tablecloth and silverware that I had no idea how to use. I watched the other kids eating and emulated them. Brandy and I sat next to each other and she kept slipping her hand into mine under the table. The meal was mostly foreign to me. I picked at it. The chicken cordon bleu was confusing. The desert tasted weird.

Then it was time to dance. A DJ, hidden somewhere, announced each song. Brandy took my hand and led me out to the dance floor. We slowed danced to "Shannon," our heads each resting on the other's shoulder. Henry Gross sang in falsetto—

Shannon is gone I heard
She's drifting out to sea
She always loved to swim away
Maybe she'll find an island
With a shaded tree
Just like the one in our backyard

We made our way to a darkened area, somewhere on the periphery. Brandy slipped out of her heels and stood in her pantyhose feet on the bare floor. We kissed as "Sara Smile" poured out of an overhead speaker. It was an out-of-body experience, almost too much happiness to bear. I stumbled backward and ended up sitting in someone's abandoned chair.

"Are you okay?" Brandy asked me.

"I'm fine," I said.

That's when she decided to blurt out the news. "We're moving to LA."

"What?"

"I said, 'We're moving to LA.'"

"What. Um. What?" My brain refused the information. "No."

"I'm sorry I didn't tell you sooner. I'm sorry." Brandy ran away, shoeless, crying.

I was numb. I stood up. I leaned over and picked up her shoes from the floor. I wandered around the venue with her shoes held out in front of me in a daze. I bumped into one or two kids and excused myself. I found Fiona, Brandy's mother, drinking wine out of a goblet. "There he is. Himself! Aw, I see that she told ya the news. And your wee heart is broken. Tis the first time, too. But it won't be the last, I'll guarantee ya. You'll get your heart broken over and over."

She was right about that. "Um." I handed her the shoes.

"Brandy ran off without her shoes on! She'll get a talking to later, to be sure. Where is she?"

"I don't know."

"And look at the tears streaking down that wee face. You're a sweet lad. But you knew it was never going to work out, didn't you? You knew that?"

"I knew that."

"I'm not being cruel. I'm stating facts."

"I know."

"You have a good heart, but you don't come from quality. Your father is vulgar. Your mother is straight off a factory floor. There's nothing wrong with that, but I want something more for my only daughter. She'll marry a good provider. You and your soft artistic ways... you'll never be the type of man who can make a good living. Stop your crying! You know it's true!"

"It's true," I admitted. "I'm nobody. I come from nothing."

"Dry your face. Here's a napkin. Dry your face and be brave. Here she comes. You don't want her to remember you being this way, do you? Well? Do you?"

I dried my face with the napkin and steeled myself just like I'd been doing when my father beat me. I went cold inside and turned to face her.

"Where have you been?" Brandy asked me, the mascara having run down to her chin. "I've been looking all over for you."

"I'm fine," I said.

"You're fine? Did you say you were fine?"

"I'm fine. Everything is fine. I'm fine."

"Stop saying that!"

"Let's go home, children," Mrs. Bondurant said. "Bottom's up." She chugged down the rest of her wine and placed the goblet on a nearby table. She drove us home. The two of us sat on opposite sides of the backseat, each gripping the armrest on the door.

Mrs. Bondurant dropped me off in front of my house. I got out of the car. "Bye," I said to Brandy.

"Bye," she replied without looking at me.

I shut the car door and watched the taillights as Mrs. Bondurant drove the quarter mile down to their house. I stood out in the humid night air watching them get out of the car. I heard Brandy shout, "Mother!"

A few days later, without fanfare, movers came to take away all their stuff.

Sissy and I rode our bicycles down there and watched the movers. There were no Bondurants around. "Hey," Sissy shouted to one of the movers, a spindly man with a curved spine and long hairy arms. "Where are the Bondurants?"

"They left already," the man said, heaving a box into the van. "They're gone."

We looked at each other and then at the man, who continued going about his business. He left and was replaced by another man who was smaller and fatter.

We continued peddling our bicycles around the block, going over to the neighborhood pond. I rode my bicycle directly into the pond, feeling the warm fetid water engulfing my body.

"Buzz!" Sissy shrieked. "Buzz, no!" I swam out to the edge of the pond and Sissy furiously grabbed at my arm, pulling me out of the water through sheer force of will. Once I was safely ashore, she slapped at me angrily, but not hard. "Don't do things like that! You're not allowed to! I won't give you my permission!"

"I don't need your permission."

We sat together gasping for air. Finally, she said, "Did you tell her? Did you tell her that you love her?"

"No."

Sissy stood up, shaking her head sadly. "I'm going to ride home and get the Zebco." It was a cheap rod and reel. When we caught fish with it, they were too small to keep.

"Why?"

"Because Dad will kill you if he finds out that you lost your bike. So we're going to fish it out of there."

Long story short, it worked. Everything worked for Sissy, even fishing for a bicycle. The two of us pulled the bike up out of the muck and reeled it to shore. I rode it home wet, smelling like a dead squirrel.

For the next few days, I found that I couldn't get out of bed. Sissy came in and sat with me for a while each day. She brought me a sugar cookie from Captain Slidell's widow. She brought me a piece of toast with jam on it. She brought me an Oh Henry bar. I didn't finish these things, so she did. We didn't say anything. There was nothing to be said.

Mom came in on the final day. She stroked my hair and said, "Get out of bed, you lazy bum. You've been milking this for too long. So you lost a girlfriend. So what?" It was the way that she said it that made me sit up and smile. She hugged me and I hugged her back. "There are worse things than being alone," Mom commented darkly. We sat in my bed holding each other.

At the Pizza Hut

If you're looking for a villain in this story, I'm it. I'm the bad guy. I am my own nemesis. I am a self-defeating fool. When I look back on my life, I'm the one who thwarts my own ambitions, who stands in between me and all the things that I think that I want.

After her family moved to Los Angeles, I saw Brandy twice more in my life.

The last time was at my sister's funeral. I was sitting in the front pew, Sissy's casket before me. I was dazed with grief. The night before, I'd gotten rip-roaring drunk and staggered around my mother's house. At some point, I'd torn the towel rack off the wall in my mother's bathroom and vomited messily into and all over her toilet. I remember listening to "Bridge Over Troubled Water" over and over while drinking. I remember bargaining with God. "Please take me instead of her," I begged the deity. "Please let me swap places with her."

I woke up and was still alive for some reason.

Mom stood in the doorway of my room. This wasn't the Gulf Gate Woods house, by the way. It was our third house in Sarasota. It was out in the country on a five-acre lot that needed continual mowing. It was the last house that Buster had built in Sarasota before abandoning Mom and heading back to Ohio. "Look at you!" Mom shouted from the doorway. "You should be ashamed of yourself."

"I never stop being ashamed of myself," I told her.

"Good!" she shouted, and my head nearly exploded. She walked me over to her bathroom and showed me the destruction I'd caused. "Before you do anything this morning, you're cleaning that toilet."

A few months earlier, I'd been allowed to leave active duty early. The Army was "right-sizing." I did not fit. I was expected to go to reserve drills, but I'd neglected that part of my agreement with the Army. I allowed my hair to grow long. I shaved every few days or so. I was an incomplete mess.

The phone rang on the nightstand next to my mother's bed. I ran over to it, certain that Sissy would be on the other end and we'd have a good laugh about this whole mix-up. She'd be fine. Or she'd be recovering in the hospital from a minor gunshot wound. Everything would be fine. I would be fine.

Instead, it was the head of the art department at the University of Florida, Professor Alvin Geist, who said, "Hello, Mister Pepper. How are you doing today? I'm calling to confirm that you'll be attending the MFA program this fall. Can we count on you?"

"Yes," I said, confused that it wasn't Sissy. I needed to get this guy off the line in case she called. She hadn't died in that Pizza Hut. She was alive somewhere and we didn't have call-waiting, so if she was calling right that moment and couldn't get through, it would be Professor Geist's fault.

"That was a pretty morose 'yes,'" the Professor commented. "Who died? Heh-heh."

"My sister. She died," I said, and upon saying it, it became real again and I burst into tears that became gasping sobs.

"What?" he went.

"She was m-m-murdered," I stuttered. I dropped the receiver like it had bit me. I picked it back up. "I'm sorry. Are you still there?"

"Yes. Uh. Wait, was that your sister on the news? At the Pizza Hut?"

"Yes."

"I don't know what to say."

"Nobody does. I certainly don't."

Mom grabbed the receiver out of my hand. "This is his mother. We have a funeral to go to today. If you don't mind, I'm going to hang up now." Then she hung up. She turned to me. "Clean the toilet."

I did as I was told.

For some reason, I found myself getting into a limousine. I sat next to Sparky, who sat facing forward stoically. Mom, Uncle Ralph and Ralph's three daughters were there, too. A few years later, when I was married, Sparky called me up, drunk, and rambled his way through recounting a recurring dream in which Sissy was inside the Pizza Hut, her face pressed again the glass screaming, while Sparky was frozen in place outside, unable to save her. He said that he had dreamt that every night since she was murdered. On this day, he showed no emotion. He was always the man of the house, even when Buster was around.

I, on the other hand, was barely holding it together. Sparky led me into the church and sat me down. For some reason, I peered around the church and saw her. I saw Brandy. She sat in a pew in the back, dressed in her customary all-black. She wore black sunglasses indoors. She was just as stunned as I was. I could tell. I stared at her for a few moments. She pulled off the sunglasses and I saw the tears pouring across her cheeks. We looked into each other's eyes for a moment, and then she put the sunglasses back on. I turned around to face the casket.

"Was that the Bondurant girl?" Sparky asked.

"Yes."

"I always wondered what happened to her."

"Me, too."

That was the last time I saw her.

The other time that I saw her was when Sissy and I were in high school and working at the Bee Ridge Pizza Hut with our friends Dave and Albino. That wasn't Alan's real name. I gave him the nickname because he was so pale. I had a new girlfriend at that point—a 26-year-old woman named Cindy, a college graduate in English from the University of New Hampshire. I was 17-years-old and a full-on punk rocker, my wild hair dyed jet black, wearing a Black Flag t-shirt under the bright red Pizza Hut uniform smock, a pair of beaten-to-death Chuck Taylor's on my feet, stained and torn black pants, and a scornful sneer on my face.

It was a Wednesday night during the school year. Sissy was the sole waitress out in the dining room, serving up pizzas and pitchers of Mountain Dew to the few customers we had that evening. If any of them ordered beer, Cindy would bring it out to them. She was the night shift manager. She sat on the make table swinging her feet. She was blonde and apple-cheeked, her blue eyes dulled by all the drugs she took to maintain her sanity. Most of the drugs were illegal, and she sold them on the side.

Albino stood at the cash register, staring out at Sissy, pining for her. If the phone rang, he'd write down the carryout order and hand it to me.

Dave was in the back working the dishwasher and scrubbing out the rusty pans for the newfangled pan pizza that had just replaced the thick-and-chewy on the menu. No matter what we did, the pans were always orange with rust.

"You should sit down next to me," Cindy said. She patted the spot next to her. "Come keep me company."

"I'm busy," I lied.

"You're gonna hurt my feelings if you keep this up and then I won't be in the mood after work." I glanced over at her and my heart hurt. She was so beautiful. She had taken my virginity in the nicest way possible only a few weeks earlier. I knew it wouldn't last. Nothing good lasts.

The bell over the front door rang, announcing that a customer had entered. I turned my head, annoyed. I didn't feel like making pizzas. I felt like being held in Cindy's soft embrace, the both of us nude and relaxed. I glanced again at Cindy and she was smirking at me.

"Buzz! Buzz, is that you?"

I turned my head and saw her standing there, like a ghost from my past. She was almost grown up now. We stood looking into each other's eyes from 12 feet away. It had been five years since I'd last seen her, and yet I felt exactly the same about her at that moment as I did when we shared our first kiss. "Brandy," I said aloud.

Sissy came running over from where she was restocking the salad bar and the two of them hugged.

"Hey, stranger," Brandy said.

"Hey yourself," Sissy said. "I heard you were back in town."

"You heard right," Brandy said. "We've been back for about a year. I heard you were living in Lake Sarasota?"

"Yeah," Sissy said. "In a real dump that Dad and Buzz built. Can you imagine living a house that Dad and Buzz built? I'm afraid that if I sneeze, it'll all fall down."

I walked up to the front counter in a daze and stood staring at her. I realized that Albino was shaking my shoulder. "I said, 'Who's she?'" he said.

"Brandy," I said. "She's Brandy."

"Dude. You should introduce us. Don't be rude, motherfucker."

Dave emerged from the back, the front of his red Pizza Hut smock black with grease. "Hey, ladies. You mind redoing the whole hug thing? I missed most of it. You know that I'm a connoisseur of hot girl-on-girl action."

"Shut your trap," Sissy said. "This, everyone, is Brandy. She's an old friend of ours."

"Hey," Brandy said, her eyes skipping from Dave to Albino and then resting on me.

"Careful," Sissy said. "You could swallow flies if you leave your mouth open like that for too long."

I closed my mouth. I tried to be cool. "What's happening?"

"Are you almost done for the night?" Brandy asked.

"Wait, you've been back in town for a year?"

"Yes. I wasn't aware that I was supposed to check in with you."

"Fair enough," I said with a shrug.

I realized that Cindy had walked over. She was staring at my face, and then when I looked over at her, she glared at Brandy. She stomped away. I heard from the back of the house, "If you know what's good for you, you'll get back here!"

"I'll be right back," I said, excusing myself.

I found Cindy in the back of the restaurant leaning next to the cans of black olives stacked in an industrial shelving unit. "Don't lie to me," she said.

"What's that supposed to mean?"

"Tell me that you're not in love with that girl," Cindy demanded.

"I'm not in love with that girl."

"Liar!" She raised her fists over her head and then thumped my hollow chest with them. "Liar, liar, liar!"

"What do you want me to say?"

"Tell me you're in love with her. Go on! Tell the truth! You can't lie to me. I can tell when you lie!"

"I'm not in love with her," I said.

"Liars go to hell!" Cindy shouted. She pushed me away from her. "Get out of here! Go! I can't even look at you!"

I walked back to the front of the house feeling stricken, my heart hammering in my chest. I was in trouble in so many ways.

"Someone's in the doghouse," Dave commented with a snicker.

"So, if you're not in love with Brandy…" Albino said, making significant eyebrow movements and nodding toward Brandy.

Sissy walked around the counter and thumped him on the forehead with a middle finger propelled off her thumb. "Down, boy." She turned and pushed me around the corner so that I stood facing Brandy. She never approved of my relationship with Cindy. Sissy once threatened to show up at work with her vinyl handbag filled with rocks to pound the living shit out of Cindy. I talked her out of it.

"I need your help," Brandy said. "It's Steve."

"Help me, Buzzy-Wan Kenobi! You're my only hope!" Dave trilled.

"Shut the fuck up, man," I snapped at him.

"I hitched a ride out here hoping you'd be here," Brandy said. Her black hair cascaded over her shoulders. Her green eyes sparkled. She wore a black Misfits t-shirt and skintight black jeans, a pair of black Doc Martens on her feet with bright yellow stitching. Her full lips were painted blood red. Her arms and neck were pale from lack of sunlight. If she'd told me to jump off a mountain, I would have shouted "Geronimo!"

"Let's go," I said. "Sissy, can you punch me out?"

"Go," she said. "I'll handle your boss."

"She's *your* boss, too," Albino said.

"Theoretically," Sissy said.

The first car that I ever owned was a brown Chevy window van. It sat in the parking lot near a dumpster filled with moldering pizza dough, unclaimed pizzas, chewed up pizza bits, raccoons and flies. The odor was, to say the least, off-putting. I unlocked the passenger side door and Brandy climbed in to sit in the only other seat in the van. The back of the van was filled with old carpeting that I'd glued in and a couple of couch cushions. It had a three-on-the-tree manual transmission that was wonky at the best of times. I started up the van and asked, "Where are we going?"

"Riverview," she said.

"The high school?"

"Steve drove his car onto the football field, drunk. I heard about it at this party. I hope we can get there before the police."

"Is he still driving the Ultimate El?"

"No. He sold that when we moved to LA. He has a Camaro now. Can we hurry?"

I pulled the Chevy out onto Bee Ridge Road and stepped on it. We rolled down the windows. I popped a cassette into the player that I'd installed myself under the dash. A tinny speaker I'd glued to the dash blasted out Jello Biafra screaming—

Efficiency and progress is ours once more
Now that we have the neutron bomb

"I knew you'd become a punk," Brandy said.

"Yes," I said jokingly. "I hate nearly everything now." I turned my head and smiled at her, the old feelings welling up inside my chest. "I don't hate *you* though. I make exceptions. Flexible, that's me."

"I never stopped thinking about you," Brandy said. "I remember you bringing me flowers you picked out of other people's yards. You sang 'Michelle' to me. You were so sweet."

"Not anymore," I said, my heart turning cold suddenly. "Sweet doesn't cut it in this world."

We drove silently for a while, eventually turning in to the Riverview High School parking lot. If I'd stayed in public school, this is where I would have gone. Instead, I went to Sarasota Central Catholic, where I denounced the nuns as pawns of the fascist state when they demanded that I get a haircut, or chastised me for getting D's in "Moral Guidance." I told a nun during one of those classes that God was dead, killed by hippies and cops during the Democratic convention in '68.

I parked as closely as I could to the football field and killed the engine. I turned off my headlights and opened up the sliding door on the side of the van.

We hopped over the fence that Steve had destroyed on his way onto the field. A full moon glowed overhead, showing off all the destruction that Steve had created. He'd done several donuts on the field and had run over both goal posts—the Camaro wrapped around the east goal post. "That car's not going anywhere," I muttered.

We found Steve sitting on the sideline, swigging out of a bottle of Cuervo Gold. "Little man? Zat you?"

"It's me, Steve," I said.

"And you're back with Brandy? Shit, dude. That's awesome."

"We're not back together," I said. "We're here for you, man."

"Dude. You're all she talks about. Buzz, this. Buzz, that. Buzz is so sweet. I'm like, go find that little squirt if you want him so bad and stop talking about it."

"Hey, can I have a drink?" I asked him.

"Sure." He handed me the bottle. I chucked it as hard as I could at the aluminum stands and watched it explode.

"What'd you do that for?" He was more hurt than angry.

"You're drunk enough."

"I'm never drunk enough," Steve said.

"Let's get you up," Brandy said.

We each slipped under an arm and toted him toward the van. In the distance, we heard some sirens. We pushed him through the opening and shut the sliding door. We rushed to our seats and I got it started on the first turn of the ignition. I drove out of the parking lot with the lights off, motored a couple of blocks and turned the lights on just as a pair of sheriff's deputies blasted past with their flashers and sirens on.

"They're gonna find the car," I said.

"It was stolen," Brandy said. "We were at a party together and someone stole Steve's car. You gave us a ride home. Do you still know the way?"

"You're living in your old house?"

"We never sold it. We rented it out."

"I'm old enough to drink," Steve said.

"That's awesome, dude," I said. "Don't vomit all over my van, okay?"

"Gotcha covered, little man."

Brandy and I stole glances over at each other the whole ride home. It was weird driving into the old neighborhood. It was familiar and foreign at the same time. I parked on the driveway next to a new Volvo.

Brandy and I helped Steve out of the van. We each got under an arm and spirited him to the front door. Brandy unlocked it and we guided him back to his old bedroom. We dumped him on his bed under a black light poster of Jimi Hendrix. Brandy took his shoes off and told him he was on his own.

We found Fiona in the den with her arms crossed. "And who is this?" she demanded, nodding her head in my direction.

"You don't recognize him?" Brandy asked.

She glared at me and then her face softened. "Is this himself? Little Buzz? Oh, but didn't he turn into a darling teenager? You dyed your pretty hair black. Isn't that just about criminal?"

"We're going to talk for a few minutes, if that's okay with you, mother."

"Outside," I said.

"Go on ahead," Fiona said. "I'll be waiting for you right here, Brandy." She walked into the kitchen and poured herself a glass of chardonnay.

Brandy and I walked out the door, shutting it silently behind us. We sat on the curb facing away from her house, close enough to hold hands, but not holding hands. I sat staring at my hands, cracked and chapped from all my attempts to wash the pizza stink off them.

"I sent you a birthday card every year," Brandy said.

"I know. I read them," I heard come out of my mouth, petulantly.

"Why didn't you respond?"

"What was the point? What's the point of anything?"

"You knew I was back, but you didn't try to contact me."

"So what?"

"Buzz, I want to tell you something."

"Who's stopping you?"

"I love you," she said. "You're my one true love."

I was taken aback, not only by what she said, which sounded like an admission of guilt to my ears, but by the word itself. We never used that word, love, in our house. I never heard my father say it to my mother. I never heard my mother say it out loud to any of us. It was a cringe word.

I would hear a few more women say it out loud to me in my life, each one seemingly meaning it, too. When I hear, "I love you," I think: *This is it. The clock is now ticking. Things will be ending soon enough.*

"I love you." I said it back to my wife, but I was unconvincing. I ended up leaving her, if you can believe it. Me, the neediest person on earth.

I said it back to my high school girlfriend, a 26-year-old Pizza Hut shift manager, a college grad who found my idiocy enchanting. She ended up moving away.

My college girlfriend said it to me. I found out later that she was married.

It would become a familiar pattern in my life, and each time these women ended up leaving me behind, for good reason I will add, the pain was intense enough that I was physically ill, sometimes for months. Sometimes for years.

When I was younger, to make the excruciating pain of a broken heart seem less horrible, I would slug myself in the face so hard that it looked like I'd lost a prize fight.

Now, in my 30's, the thought of finding someone to love is nearly impossible to me. As I said, I'm my own nemesis. I will always thwart anyone who tells me that she loves me. I will defeat them, and in so doing, I will defeat my enemy—myself.

I stood up and dusted off my ass. "Nice to hear." I walked over to my van, got in, turned over the engine and drove away. I looked in the rearview mirror and saw her standing in the middle of the road and I burst into tears.

I yelled at myself for crying. I willed myself to stop crying.

I'm such an asshole. You can hate me. Feel free. It's okay. I hate myself.

Do you need me to spell out why I am the way I am? When a parent beats you and tells you that you're worthless and tells you that you ruin everything, after a while you believe him. After a while, it becomes part of who you are. If you love someone, you want her to have the best life, and that means that she needs to find someone else to love as quickly as possible. She doesn't need someone who is worthless and ruins everything.

And now there is no one left in my life save my brother Sparky, and he seems to be hellbent on drinking himself to death. Soon, I'll be all alone—my nemesis's plan will have come to full fruition.

I don't have the guts to kill myself, so I'm riding out life. It'll end eventually, I'm sure. Statistics tell me so.

I drove back to Pizza Hut. I found the place dark and abandoned. Sissy must have bummed a ride home off of Albino. I looked for Cindy's car and she was gone, too.

I drove over to the house that Cindy was sharing with an old high school classmate of mine and found her sitting on a papasan chair on the back porch torching up a roach. I sat down next to her on an aluminum-framed chair and we stared off into the hot, moist night for a while, sharing the joint.

"You need a shower," Cindy said. "You stink."

"I'm sorry about tonight."

"It's okay. We all have a past." She took me by the hand and led me inside.

About the Author

John L. Sheppard is the author of *Small Town Punk*. He lives near Chicago.

For more adventures of Sissy and Buzz, be sure to pick up a copy of *Small Town Punk*. Another follow-up to *Small Town Punk* will be released by Paragraph Line Books in 2021.

For more releases by Paragraph Line Books, visit paragraphline.com.

www.ingramcontent.com/pod-product-compliance
Lightning Source LLC
Chambersburg PA
CBHW071448170626
46811CB00007B/2504